# The

# Maelstrom

# Ascendant

## Books by Duncan Smith

The Vortex Winder

The Maelstrom Ascendant

Cultown

Conquest By Concept

The Tightarse Tuesday Book Club

The Vast and the Spurious

Hammer and Heat

## Music Albums

Vortex Winder

The Maelstrom Ascendant

Cultown

Waves Upon Waves

**Website – www.vortexwinder.com**

# The Maelstrom Ascendant

Duncan Smith

Alfadex Books

Second Edition, Published by Alfadex Books, Sydney, 2023.
Copyright © Duncan Smith 2023, 2015.

A CIP catalogue record for this book is available from the National
Library of Australia.
ISBN 978-0-6450372-4-1

1. Fiction  2. Drama  3. Music

Cover design by Ivan Hruszecky.

Duncan Smith is an Australian author and musician.

He is the guitarist and songwriter with Lighthouse XIII, a rock band whose albums include *Cultown, Vortex Winder, Waves Upon Waves,* and *The Maelstrom Ascendant.*

He is the author of the books *The Maelstrom Ascendant, Cultown, Conquest By Concept,* and *The Tightarse Tuesday Book Club.*

Website - www.vortexwinder.com

Part One

Part Two

Part Three

Part Four

# Introduction

*The Maelstrom Ascendant* came out in 2015. It is the sequel to *The Vortex Winder*. Nearly a decade later, both books have been revised for a second edition.

It is hard to classify these books by genre. Should they go under thriller? Fantasy? Psychological drama?

I prefer to simply call *The Vortex Winder* 'a modern fairytale' due to the mix of real and supernatural elements, and the theme of an innocent making his way in the world.

*The Maelstrom Ascendant* is darker, 'a Jekyll and Hyde story set in the corrupt world of showbiz.'

The books are also unusual because they come with music albums by my rock band, Lighthouse XIII. The album *Vortex Winder* goes with Book One. As for Book Two, it has two albums - *The Maelstrom Ascendant* and *Waves Upon Waves*.

You don't have to hear the music to appreciate the books. Each stands alone - but for those who are interested, the albums are available on iTunes, Amazon, Spotify, and YouTube.

Duncan Smith,
September, 2023.

# Part One

# 1

# The Unwild West

It felt so good to be a quitter.

There I was, having given up on my dreams and resigned myself to a quiet life. My guitars were in storage and the Vortex Winder lay dormant, as it had for the last three years.

Even Sandra was back on the scene, having forgiven me my madness of the years before. We'd left the glamour of Sydney's east to live in the unwild western suburbs. After all, that's what she wanted. It was in fact west of the west - in the Blue Mountains, out past the city limits. I retired from music, got a real job, and settled into a quiet domestic life.

Sandra? The Vortex Winder? Forgive me. I must remember that many readers have no knowledge of my past adventures.

And whose fault is that? Yes, this book is a sequel. Goddammit - if a few more of you guys had read the first one, we wouldn't be having this difficult conversation! As it is, not only am I forced to give a summary of that book, it has to come without spoilers. Otherwise none of you will ever go back and read it at all now, will you? Really, you are very thoughtless at times.

So here's the deal. I'll give you a spoiler-free summary of the first book. In return, you will agree to suspend your disbelief about the strangeness of the events described. There's no denying the story was rather bizarre. That's just the way it is. It will soon be obvious that we're 'not in Kansas anymore,' just somewhere that looks very like it on the surface.

It all began one night when I fished a drowning cockroach out of a hotel toilet. And granted, while that was probably the most appalling start to a book in recorded history, this random act of kindness changed my life. As if in a modern fairytale, the cockroach turned out to be a shape-shifting being named Iolango.

He rewarded me with the 'Vortex Winder' - a wish-granting device which awakened my old dream of being a famous writer and musician.

In pursuit of that dream I broke up with my girlfriend, Sandra, and began a wild ride. The Vortex Winder led me down a path that included a love affair in Germany, a period as a pro gambler, and a hellish stint in an Asian prison. After my escape from the prison, I did release a book and an album. Yet the only fame to result came from a ludicrous YouTube video that went viral. Finally I was drawn into a showdown with my nemesis, Elijinx. A shape-shifter like Iolango, Elijinx took me to within a breath of extinction before I escaped to fight another day.

Out of remorse for the trials he'd put me through, Iolango offered to return me to the point in time where the story began, erasing my memory so I could take a different path in life. I refused, choosing not only to preserve my memories but to relate them as 'fiction' in a novel.

The novel was itself called *The Vortex Winder*, and I had high hopes when it came out. I'd believed it could be a hit - but it never really took flight. Turned out the book industry was on its knees. It had been hard enough to sell books ten years before. Now, like many other traditional trades, the book world was being eaten alive by the internet. Bookshops were closing down, publishers were going broke, the whole system was falling apart.

The novel even came with a soundtrack album of songs by my band - but as the music business was as equally screwed as the book business, that didn't help much.

In my efforts to promote the book, there *had* been one flicker of interest from the publishing world, although it turned into a bit of a comedy scene in the end. I'd gotten through to a literary agent who'd taken a mild interest in my work. Let's call him Richard. He was willing to help republish it with a bigger company and more promo, but only if there were some major rewrites. I dropped into

Richard's office one day to find he'd made it through the first six chapters.

'I've got to tell you, Jimmy, you've got something here. This whole modern fairytale shtick is a new twist on an old genre. It's contemporary and you're keeping some kind of realist edge without going the full-Potter. I like that - and the soundtrack music certainly adds something new. But there'd have to be some big changes before I'd even *think* about taking it on.'

'Changes? Like what?'

'The cockroach for a start. Not a very charming animal, is it? Your Iolango's a shape-shifter, after all. Let's change him into something a whole lot cuter.'

'A kitten, perhaps?'

'That's more like it. I mean, a cockroach in a toilet? At a heavy metal show? Please! You can't expect me to sell that.'

'Why not - what's wrong with it?'

'What's the largest demographic for fiction? Women thirty to sixty years old. You'll have lost half of them by the end of chapter one. If you want to reach that market, then write for it. I mean chapter six, the love affair with Freya - that's more like it. But why make her German?'

'Why not?'

'Why not make her Italian? Or at least French.'

'Uh... because she was German.'

'If you want an exotic foreign location, you'll find Italy and France road-test better with our focus groups. Why not roll with that?'

'That's pretty offensive to the Germans.'

'That's the research. For the same reason, I'd get rid of all the heavy rock stuff. Take out all the irrelevant little comments about music. Frankly, I'd change the soundtrack too.'

'You said it added something.'

'Sure, but again you've got to write for your demographic. Don't take it personally, but you'd be better off with an album of R&B or show tunes. If you can't do that style yourself, hire some pro songwriters.'

'This is a joke, right?'

'It's common sense. Also, dump the gambling chapter.'

'But it ties in with the themes of the book and it's crucial to the plot. How do I - I mean how does he - get the money to go overseas if he doesn't master the Black Art?'

'Why not let him have a big win on lotto or the pokies? That way you can get rid of all the boring detail and cut it down to a couple of pages. Get to the point.'

'Did you even read what I said about lotto in that chapter?'

'If you really must talk about sports gambling, at least pick a sport with more global appeal. Rugby is only played in a few countries, isn't it? You'd be better off talking about real football. The round ball version. Why not make him a Manchester United fan? They're a global brand.'

'Because that's not the way it was. Everything you're suggesting has nothing to do with what really happened. I can't change the facts.'

'What facts? It's fiction, you can write whatever you want. As long as it's what readers want too. If you want to make a saleable product then think about your target audience. Look, how about this - would you be open to workshopping the story with a small focus group?'

'Creation by committee? Dumbing the whole thing down to the middle ground? Taking away the quirks that make it unique? I don't think so.'

'Then I really can't help you.'

'Let's wrap it up then, Richard. You want me to change Iolango from a cockroach to a kitten, dump the heavy rock for show tunes, and make Freya Italian. You want to change it from a creation with quirks and the ring of truth into a bland product with mass appeal. And you're only on chapter six. Forget it.'

I walked away from Richard's office and decided to pack it all in. The encounter was only the latest in a long line of obstacles in the quest to sell the book and album. It was clear that the countless hours of work it had taken to make them had been largely in vain. So I quit, got a job, got back with Sandra, and we took out a joint mortgage on a house in the Blue Mountains.

You remember Sandra, right? Well, you would if you'd read *Vortex Winder*. She was the yin to my yang. The teasing yet warmhearted pragmatist I lived with for a while, before going off to chase my dream. Unlike me, Sandra was secure in the corporate world, a manager with a salary several times my own. A sensible girl, she'd set herself up with superannuation, health insurance, and all those other practical perks I'd missed out on in my risky life as a muso.

Although Sandra respected my artistic side, she did not approve of me spending thousands of dollars making albums that wouldn't sell. When I'd followed that path instead of taking out the mortgage she aspired to, it put us under a terminal strain.

It was my own fault. Sandra really can't be blamed for turning her back on me and taking up with someone more suited to her station - a fellow executive from the corporate world. Yet the affair didn't work out as she'd hoped. I don't know the full story but it seems the guy was a self-centred workaholic who never had time to do with Sandra all the things she liked doing with me. So by the time I finished my Vortex Winder adventures, she'd returned to her status as a single woman and replaced both of us with a cat.

It was the cat who got me in the end. Some cats are aloof and unfriendly but Finzi was a grey-haired, green-eyed purring machine. I met him the first time I called on Sandra, a couple of years after our break up. After chatting with her for a while, I stood up to take my leave and Finzi literally jumped into my arms. As

Sandra later told me, she saw this as an omen and it swayed her to thoughts of reconciliation.

It seems that Finzi had a fine instinct for Sandra's best interests. She trusted this and made good use of it. After breaking with the exec, Sandra had a string of suitors. But whenever she had a prospective new boyfriend, the litmus test was always his first meeting with the cat.

Finzi, circling sternly like a disapproving father, would check the guy out using his impeccable feline radar - and woe betide him if he didn't measure up. As soon as a prospect walked in the door, Finzi sniffed and stared at him with the utmost suspicion. If Finzi turned his back on him, Sandra took it as a bad sign. If Finzi sat between her and the date on the sofa, the fella may as well have walked out the door then and there. On the other hand, if Finzi gave his approval with a purr and the consent to be stroked, the guy had passed the test and was allowed back for another meeting.

This sort of vetting procedure had been going on for some time when I decided to look Sandra up. It had been a while but she hadn't changed a bit. She still had those glamorous Italian-Australian looks, combined with the voluptuous curves I'd always found so appealing.

I entered her flat and gazed at her with fond remembrance, settling back easily into the domestic scene. As soon as I arrived, the cat's green-eyed scrutiny was upon me - yet instead of showing disapproval, he set his purring machine in motion and blessed me with a lap-sit. A light went on in Sandra's eyes, although I had no idea why. I was simply glad to be back in her company. The cat added that note of warmth to the scene. Towards the end of my visit, talk turned to my recent retirement from music.

'So you *did* end up making your album, Jimmy,' said Sandra. 'How'd it turn out, then?'

'Great - I'll send you a copy.'

'I'll buy one, of course. What did it cost you in the end?'

'About ten grand, all up.'

'Wow.'

'That's nothing. The big bands spend at least half a mill.'

'And you got it all back?'

'Not even close. It's tough selling music these days. Nearly all the record shops have closed down. Haven't you noticed?'

'Now you mention it, I suppose they have. I wonder why.'

'The internet, of course. People download their music now, or stream it on Spotify. Same with books. You can buy them cheaper on the net, so most of the bookshops have closed down too.'

'I see.'

'So here's me with impeccable timing putting out a book and a CD and nowhere to sell them.'

'You wrote a book too?'

'I was coming to that. It's mostly fiction, so don't get upset - but actually, you're in it.'

'Me?'

'Under another name, of course. Nothing bad - you're a likeable character. Apart from when you went to Melbourne and dumped me. That was in there - but I admitted it was my fault.'

'Really Jimmy, if you were going to put me in a book, you might have let me read it first.'

'Sure, I meant to. But who cares? No one read it anyhow. This cat's a champion. Where'd you find him?'

'He found me. So what are you up to now - still playing music?'

'Nah, forget it. All that work, thousands of hours - and for what? I've got a real job now. Holiday pay and all. Might be normal for you but it's a real novelty for me. I've turned to the dark side at last.'

'You've really settled down this time? I can't believe it.'

'Come on, I'm past forty. I haven't just thrown in the towel, I've thrown it out. You were right all along. A job, a mortgage? Bring it on.'

'Are you sure, Jimmy? It's weird seeing you like this. So if you've gone straight, I guess you're married too.'

'One of these days. Why not, if I meet the right girl? Well, great seeing you, Sandy.'

I stood up to take my leave and gently moved Finzi from my lap to the sofa - only for him to crouch and take a giant leap right back into my arms! I found myself clutching the cat and laughing in surprise. Sandra too was smiling, for her own reasons. You can guess the rest. It was only a matter of time before our romance was back on the table and we'd taken out a mortgage on a house in the Blue Mountains.

So, between the efforts of Richard the agent and Finzi the cat, Sandra and I were rejoined and I became a normal person at last, living a simple life in the unwild west forevermore.

Or so I supposed.

# 2

# The Unwelcome Guest

Hell, I'll say it again - it sure felt good to be a quitter.

The sense of liberation was immense. No more struggling for success. No more frustration at the uneven playing fields of the human world. Life was so simple once you gave up trying. All I had to do now was go to work, pay my bills, and hang out with Sandra and Finzi when I got home. It wasn't a bad life at all. A simple domestic life in a new breed of family - man, woman and cat.

Now, I don't want to go on about the damn cat too much but the fact is he does play a part in this story, as you will see. So allow me to channel my inner James Herriot and tell you how our little family group came to be.

By the way, just in case 'Richard the literary agent' wants me to pump up the story to hook in readers, sorry, it ain't gonna happen. Maybe some readers are wondering when the sex, drugs and rock n roll is going to kick in. Give me time, I'm just warming up! The evil, the corruption, the whole sordid tale of how I became the Black Phoenix - all that will be along in due course. If some people can't be bothered waiting, that's a sad reflection of the lazy, instant gratification nature of the modern world.

Finzi had come on the scene for Sandra a year or so earlier. One day while shopping, she happened to pass the vet where abandoned animals were window-displayed in the hope of rescue by kindly strangers. She glanced in to see a handsome feline face meowing soundlessly through the thick glass of the front window. Unable to resist going inside, she picked up the orphan cat, who placed a paw on each of her shoulders, buried his face in her neck and purred ferociously. After that, Sandra had little choice but to take him home.

As I said, some cats are aloof and standoffish. Not Finzi. He liked to be involved in whatever people were doing. When an electrician came to the house to set up the internet, Finzi crouched a few inches in front of him, staring in fierce concentration as the guy lay on the carpet wiring it up. According to Sandra, he'd done the same thing when she had her bathroom renovated the year before. Finzi had taken such an interest in the builder's work on repeat trips to the house that the builder dubbed him 'the supervisor.'

Finzi also took an uncanny interest in my guitar playing, which I still dabbled in from time to time. Most of my guitars were in storage, but I'd kept back one acoustic and one electric for basic needs. I'd be plucking away only to feel Finzi's furry head brushing up against my right hand as he tried to bite the strings. Of course, there's that classic photo of him with his paw raised to strum the guitar as it stands vertical on the floor. There's no doubt he was a musical cat. I even gave some guitar lessons to make a few extra bucks and he'd curl up in his cat-sized round bed half asleep, half listening as the student and I played.

At other times Finzi was happy to hang out with Sandra and I as we lounged around watching TV, either lying in his little bed or curled around Sandra's voluptuous, horizontal form like an expensive living mink.

Not that he was any kind of animal angel. When he was wearing what we called his 'bitey-face' we knew to approach him with caution. In such a mood, he was wont to lash out with his paw or give us a light, warning nip if he was displeased. Yet if ever we had to take him somewhere in the car, he turned to jelly, meowing pitifully in fear of being abandoned again.

Although I didn't know it at first, I later learned that Finzi had once been in 'showbiz.' In hindsight, it all makes sense. Now the old boy was retired and living in the unwild west with us like some washed up movie star gone to seed. Truth be told, Finzi was quite the role model to me. He liked nothing more than to fall asleep in a warm spot of sunlight. He might occasionally stand up to stretch, arch his back and yawn extravagantly, but it would not be long before he returned to a state of regal repose.

I tended to follow his example, for I too was just another old has-been lying on the couch. I did have a day job but that's another story, which will soon be told.

Being with Sandra and Finzi was a drug to me. In their presence, all my tensions melted away and my past struggles vanished. It all seemed not to matter anymore, as if I'd been slipped a powerful opiate upon arriving home each day.

To some degree, I was the beneficiary of Sandra's practical nature. As mentioned, she'd done all the sensible things - like having a steady job with super, health insurance and so on - that mature adults are supposed to do. Sandra was not very ambitious but her natural competence had seen her rise, almost in spite of herself, to a senior level in the corporate world.

With her hard work, Sandra had earned her downtime. She spent it indulging in the simple luxuries of 21st century life - shopping, gourmet food, and lying around watching cult television shows on her big screen TV.

I fully embraced this lifestyle. It was so much easier to be a consumer than a creator. There was a feast of cultural riches on offer and as a born again quitter, I was happy to partake.

If there was still darkness in my heart, I was prepared to see it played out onscreen rather than in my life. In *Dexter*, for example, the title character worked for Miami police by day, tracking down murderers. By night he was secretly catching and killing them himself. He channelled his inner darkness into his line of work - and for Dexter, there was never a lack of work to be done.

At other times, Sandra and I watched tales of New Jersey mobsters in *The Sopranos*, and drug lords in *Breaking Bad*. Or we'd shift back in time to the world of *The Tudors*, a stirring account of 16th century royalty. It was a brutal world where political and marital problems alike were solved on the executioner's block. But how far had we really come? The very day after seeing Anne Boleyn beheaded onscreen on trumped up adultery charges, there was a news report about a woman being stoned to death for adultery in some third world kingdom today.

Whether it involved your royal or street level psychopath, the darkness of the human heart was on ready display. There was no class distinction here. I wondered at the source of this darkness. 'The Maelstrom', Elijinx had called it. If the Maelstrom was real, it certainly seemed to have the world in its sway.

According to Iolango and Elijinx, there was a dire struggle going on in the world. Good and evil were at war, and the fate of humanity was at stake. Iolango and the Vortex Winder were aligned with good. Elijinx and the Maelstrom were joined with evil. Or so it would seem. Once before, Elijinx had convinced me this was too simple a view, that indeed it might be the other way round. Still, I now preferred to opt out of such questions. It was nothing to do with me.

No, nothing at all. If there was evil, let it happen in faraway lands. Or in these brilliant TV shows! I watched all this drama from the safe, passive position of a comfy lounge chair in a home theatre. As I had now shed any aspirations to greater involvement in life's affairs, this darkness was nothing but an abstract concept and a form of entertainment. Yet a part of me wondered how much, if anything, I had in common with Dexter. I wondered what circumstances it would take to make me kill a man myself. Did I have the capacity and if so, what extreme provocation could ever draw it forth?

This was all purely academic. I was no longer a player on life's stage, only a spectator. I honestly thought it was all over for me, that life would take a predictable path from now on. The first sign I was wrong came subtly and without warning. One morning, Sandra came inside grumpy after being unable to drive to work.

'What's up?' I asked her.

'Flat tyre. I'd better call the NRMA.'

'They'll be ages. Why don't I take a look at it?'

'You, Jimmy?' she said with raised eyebrows.

'It's only a tyre. How hard can it be?'

While I'd never changed a tyre before there seemed no reason not to try, so I strolled out to the car to have a go. It took less than five minutes. Surprised, Sandra sped off to work.

I felt rather ashamed of myself for never having changed a tyre. Perhaps it could be blamed on upbringing. My father wasn't the practical type, so I was never shown how. Still, there was no reason I shouldn't take the initiative from now on. I walked to where my battered fifteen year old Ford was parked and lifted the bonnet.

The engine was a revelation. What had been a mass of unexamined, poorly understood mechanical parts now had a clear and obvious structure. I tut-tutted at the poor state of the engine and decided to give it a tune up with some never-used tools lying around in the back shed. It wasn't that hard once you got started. When it was finished, I lay down under the car to complete a full inspection.

With a sense of achievement, I decided not to go to work that day, but stay home and fix a few little things around the house.

When Sandra and I decided to move in together again, there were a few ways our personalities clashed. For example, Sandra was a 21st century woman while I was still stuck in the 20th. All her music, books and movies had long since made the transition from physical to digital form. This allowed her to adopt the Japanese style minimalism she favoured in her choice of decor.

I, however, was still in the retro mode of owning physical books, CDs, and so on. All these took up space and led to the type of clutter that drove Sandra up her spartan, minimalist walls. Yet this conflict had a simple solution. With real estate so much cheaper in the Blue Mountains, we bought a two storey house of which Sandra took the upper floor and myself the lower. She rarely ventured into my cluttered domain, although Finzi liked to wander in and find new places to sleep. Not that I was all that untidy, but it was certainly harder to keep order with so many physical objects to house.

Inspired by the episode with the car, I began constructing a set of storage shelves for my abode. I spent the afternoon sawing, measuring and hammering. It was the most strenuous day's work I'd done for many a month, and by the time I downed tools just before 6pm the place was transformed. Books, CDs, and papers were neatly stacked in the new set of shelves and cupboards I'd knocked up.

To unwind after my labours, I tried to go online only to find that in the frenzy of the day's activities I'd tripped over and disconnected my internet wiring. Fired by frustration and the day's zeal, I couldn't stand to wait for an electrician to visit so decided to have a go at fixing the damn thing myself.

It was only the sight of those little wires that pulled me up short. Tyres, engines and shelves were one thing, but those wires were potentially lethal if you didn't know what you were doing. In the drive of the moment, I pressed on regardless.

In just a few minutes, I was hooked up once more and able to log on to the almighty net. As I sat there, however, a quizzical voice sounded in the back of my mind. Wait a minute. I'd changed a tyre, fixed a car engine, set up a stack of shelves, and rewired my broken internet. How could this be?

With sinking heart, I dove into the back of my wardrobe and fished out a small metal object. It couldn't be, could it? Surely not - it was the last thing I needed. Yet there it was, the Vortex Winder glowing slightly, emitting a low-pitched hum.

The Vortex Winder was the magic talisman which bestowed special powers upon me. According to Iolango, who'd given it to me, it could tap into my psyche and awaken latent powers which had never been used. Today, it had clearly brought forth my inner handyman.

The Vortex Winder was about the size of a phone. Its screen usually displayed an explanation of the type of power on offer at a given time. The explanations were direct if I was lucky, or rather cryptic if I was not. Today, the message simply said:

*A little practicality goes a long way.*

Unfortunately - or not - these powers rarely lasted longer than a week. Yet the Vortex Winder had lain dormant for years like some tiny extinct volcano. Why was it waking up now?

I realised with a sense of dread the implications. I was content with my simple life and had said a firm goodbye to the Vortex Winder and the adventures it entailed. Did its sudden awakening mean that the craziness was all going to start up again? Was my mentor, Iolango going to pop up, or - far worse - Elijinx?

As I pondered the disturbing development, Sandra's car pulled up in the drive.

# 3

# Hindsight

I said nothing to Sandra of my suspicions. She had by now read *The Vortex Winder*, yet naturally thought it merely the work of my fevered imagination. When she arrived home amazed at my handyman heroics, she did not for a moment put it down to magical powers.

I stayed home for a week. These powers don't last, so I hurried to fix and finetune as much as possible at the house - until it all came to a sorry end the next Tuesday. Halfway through repairing Sandra's laptop, I lay down for a nap and woke up with no idea how to finish the job. The parts which had combined with such ordered clarity were once more a mystery.

Although the end had been inevitable, it was hard not to sulk when it arrived. There was nothing for it now but to go back to my real job. The job I'd been avoiding for reasons that will soon become clear.

The next day, I sat at breakfast glum as mud while Sandra chirped away oblivious, praising my recent repairs and reminding me to install that set of blinds in her bedroom. She was far from impressed when told I was going back to my day job in the city.

'Why?' she said. 'Didn't you take a couple of weeks off?'

'I really should show my face, you know. Show 'em I'm not fazed. Stay away too long and they'll think I'm in hiding. I'm burned out, anyhow. This home handyman game's no picnic. I'm over it.'

'Don't say that, Jimmy. I've seen a different side to you this week and I like it.'

I laughed uneasily.

'We all go through fads and phases. Like you learning Spanish last year. Remember that? Dragging me off to the Spanish film festival, making me dust off my flamenco style and the rest of it. What happened to all that?'

'Oh, that was just a little craze.'

'Then you'll understand how I feel about home renovation.'

Sandra gave me a dismissive look.

'I'll pick it up again when there's time. There's too much going on at the office.'

'Same for me. I really should put in an appearance.'

'Before you go, can you at least fix the toaster? Look, it won't stay down.'

I went through the motions of examining this marvel of mass production. Summoning a studious frown, I gazed at the toaster as if it were an art forgery. Sure enough the bread just wouldn't stay in place, no matter how many times I pushed it down with clueless optimism.

'This is a job for an expert. I'm in over my head here.'

'It's a toaster! Last week you fixed the dishwasher, the vacuum cleaner, and the garage door.'

'Sorry Sandra, I've lost my mojo. Maybe I can pick up a new one from the hardware shop. Oh, and by the way - your laptop.'

'What about it?'

'Better take it to a specialist.'

Sandra picked up the laptop, an indignant expression forming as she perused my handiwork.

'Well, thank you very much, Jimmy. It won't even turn on now. That's just terrific!'

Finzi jumped up onto the kitchen table and meowed. The diversion worked. Sandra, transferred her annoyance from me to the cat.

'Ignoring you, were we? Can't stand not being the centre of attention for five minutes?'

Finzi paid her no heed and began grooming himself, licking his paws so he could wash his face. Still brooding on the day to come, I stared at him absently and was overcome by an odd impression.

The sharp contours of our kitchen blurred. The walls became misty and the kitchen seemed to exist inside a much larger room. To be more accurate, it was as if the two rooms were superimposed one upon the other. I could see both. It was only a question of which one came into focus at any moment. Finzi had not vanished. On the contrary, he seemed to act as a focal point linking the two rooms. It was his image upon which my double vision hinged.

The second, much larger room was an open space, mostly unfurnished. There were a series of cages round the walls, resting on tables. Each cage contained one or more cats, of various breeds and sizes. Some of them were adorned with coloured ribbons. I could dimly make out a number of people wandering about, looking into the cages. Despite seeing the larger room, I knew I was still in our kitchen with Sandra, who seemed unaware of my strange experience.

While Finzi was the link between the two rooms, his appearance was not constant. In the kitchen, Finzi was quite a big cat. When the other room came into focus, he seemed younger and more slender. His appearance ebbed and flowed from one to the other. My fascination with the double image was only broken by the sound of Sandra complaining about being ignored. This was somewhat hypocritical in light of her recent remark to Finzi himself. The larger room vanished and the kitchen came back into full focus.

'Jimmy! You're doing it again.'

'Doing what?'

'Pretending to listen. You know I hate that.'

'Tell me something - how old was Finzi when you got him?'

'About eight or nine.'

'And what sort of life did he have before you met?'

'He was a show cat.'

'A what?'

'You know, those cats that travel round to be exhibited in animal shows. They told me all about it when I adopted him. He was a real pro, had all these certificates and awards.'

'You don't say?'

'He was bred for it and raised in a cattery among other cats. Then he was on the show circuit for years.'

'How'd he end up at the vet's where you found him? Abandoned, wasn't he?'

'Pretty much, far as I can tell. It's hard and ruthless, the show-cat world. I've seen photos of him in his prime, and he must have let himself go. As soon as he got older and put on weight, my guess is they didn't want to show him anymore and dumped him.'

'That's harsh. I had no idea the cat showbiz world was so cutthroat!'

'I suppose 'dumped' is too strong a word, considering the vet had all his papers and awards. Still, the fact is his owners left him there. Finzi passed his use by date some time ago. He's a washed up old has-been.'

'Must be why we get on so well. We've a lot in common.'

I looked at the cat and sang a few bars of the *Rocky* soundtrack.

'Come on, Finzi, you can still make a comeback. Start lifting some weights and running a few laps of the garden. You know what they say - form is temporary, class is permanent. Fire up, son, we'll show 'em yet!'

As I left the house to go to work, I wondered if Sandra had ever told me about Finzi's showbiz past. If so, I could not recall it. How then to explain my odd experience at breakfast? I'd seen the other room vividly - the cats on display, people viewing them, and Finzi himself with a younger and slimmer physique. Had I somehow received a psychic impression of Finzi's past? Or was the more mundane explanation that Sandra had already told me the tale and

I'd conjured the scene from memory? I mused upon this question as I boarded the train to Sydney. It would be answered decisively before journey's end.

I took a seat near the front of the carriage, facing backwards so most of the other passengers' faces were visible. There was an Indian girl in her mid-twenties facing me about halfway down the carriage. Or so I thought, before I realised she was a Sri Lankan born in London and was pushing thirty-five. I knew this because as soon as I focused on the girl, her life flashed before my eyes like a highlights package.

She was a second-generation migrant born to conventional Sri Lankan parents in England. A steady average at school before some textbook rebellion involving alcohol, soft drugs, and an affair with an English man ten years her senior. A few years of job-hopping, then marriage to a Sri Lankan-born engineer as a strategy to both appease and escape her family. The award of a two year government contract in Sydney to her new husband, the move to Sydney's western suburbs. The contract was nearly up and they were arguing about returning to England. She wanted to go back but the husband wasn't keen. Now she'd just learned she was pregnant with their second child. I wondered where the first one was at the moment, then wondered how I knew any of this in the first place. I shook my head, and looked away from the woman.

My focus turned to a wizened old man a few seats in front to my right. He looked like an aged tortoise. The skin was pulled tight over the shrivelled head. Glancing up, he caught my gaze and, in what seemed a reflex action, gave me a textbook *what are you looking at?* stare. The ferocity of that stare seemed at odds with this withered relic of a man. It would have been fearsome had it not come from so feeble a source. I saw now that the head was not so much tortoise-like as that of a venomous snake. The skin was leathery enough to pull off the impression.

The man was an anachronism. His clothes were a ludicrous throwback to the past, out of step with the 21st century. Yet at that moment, the picture changed. The anachronistic rags were now smart, cutting edge fashion. The leathery snake head filled out and became that of a powerful male, still reptilian in nature yet ruthless and imposing, a force to contend with. Strong men on either side of the law had gazed at their boots rather than lock eyes with this predator.

I pulled out of the vision and drew the Vortex Winder from my bag. A new special power? It must be. According to the writing on the screen, I now possessed the power of hindsight. Indeed the old VW was in a poetic mood.

*From each moment, pathways wind*

*Sideways, front, above, behind*

*Some reveal what lies ahead*

*Foresight bound by hope and dread*

*Others show what came before*

*Hindsight now your open door*

So there it was. It seemed the pragmatic power of being a handyman had been replaced with something much more exotic - the ability to pick up vivid psychic impressions of people's past experiences.

Thrilled and certainly afraid, I returned my gaze to the man. Behind him, I no longer perceived the train carriage, but Sydney streets as I'd seen them in old photos from the 1950s and 60s. The dark side of the city was his habitat - rough backstreets, hotels and brothels, various dens of iniquity. This man had walked those bleak streets with the swagger of a T-Rex. I saw a parade of images, shocking in their brutality. Shopkeepers stood over, street fights between gangs of boys, boozy race meetings and their aftermath. Bashings of relentless force, recurring feuds - and surprisingly, a wife and kids at home.

We were in a backstreet. It could have been Darlinghurst, or maybe Redfern or Surry Hills. Unfamiliar smells hung in the air. The sound of a too loud TV stood out in the otherwise quiet street. The Australian accent from the TV was strangely antiquated. I turned towards the sound. Inside a house, a man in a white singlet sat watching an oversized black and white TV. There was a longneck of beer in his hand. Behind him, a wiry woman loitered near a stove.

I looked away from the house and back at the man from the train. His name was Carlisle. He was standing a few feet away from me, watching a hotel on the corner. From time to time, men went in or out of the pub, but not the man Carlisle was waiting for.

After a few minutes, the right man emerged. He was barely taller than a jockey, yet had the physique of a welterweight and an air of swagger. Billy 'Whitey' Rankin. In knowing his name, presumably I was in contact with Carlisle's mind, for Carlisle certainly knew him. He stepped out of the shadows to confront the fellow.

'Whitey,' he said softly.

The man's right hand went to his belt, just to the side of the buckle but not so near his pocket as to trigger Carlisle.

'Well, if that don't beat all. Speak of the devil, Craw. I was just asking after you.'

'You know where to find me.'

'And to think as I was only down the White Horse Tuesday and the Crown Thursday. Where you been hiding yourself, mate?'

'Never mind that. Time to settle up.'

'Why'd you think I was down the Crown for? There I was with a down payment.'

'Well?'

'So I done the right thing and went to the meeting today to find you. While I'm waiting, there's young Tulloch, a dead cert. Never lost at Randwick, said Johnson. That's a cove has a case to answer. Had two seconds as a two year old. O'Reilly set me straight in the bar after. I was only trying to do the right thing by you, Craw, but I was robbed and no mistake. It ain't my fault. So let's step inside and it's my shout til chuck out. Next week we'll square up and I'll give you me hand on that.'

With these words, Rankin pulled a cut throat razor from his pocket and held it in front of Carlisle like a crucifix before a vampire. Carlisle, who had been holding some kind of blunt instrument behind his back, struck out at Rankin's outstretched arm. The razor fell onto the street with a clatter and Carlisle proceeded to beat the fellow, presumably to death - although so sickened was I by the sudden violence that I pulled out of the vision. The last thing I saw was Rankin prone on the pavement, before the whole scene went misty. Back in the train carriage, I shook my head to clear it, then looked up in repulsion at the decrepit old man in front of me.

The aged Carlisle stared back with hateful intensity and, if he'd been able to walk, I may well have met the same fate as Rankin some fifty years before. I stood up to move to another carriage and in passing could not resist a shot at this once feared predator, humbled by time. I would have never dared do it in his prime. It was, therefore, a cheap shot, yet the vile images I'd seen needed some kind of exorcism.

I stopped in front of the old gangster, stared directly into those snake eyes, and spoke just loud enough for him to hear.

'Now then, Craw. I've a message from an old mate. Whitey Rankin. Says he's waiting and you won't blindside him next bout. Tulloch's a cert this time and he's ready to square up, with fifty years interest to boot.'

The old fellow went whiter than Billy Bones at the sound of a crutch on cobblestone, and I moved to the next carriage.

Seeking to clear my mind of Carlisle's disturbing slideshow, I focused on a group of teenagers but they had too little back story to satisfy me. A more substantial feast was required. I sought out once again the aged, settling at last on a woman so elderly it was surprising she had managed to board the train in the first place.

Betty had reached the point where the normal observer could no longer even imagine her youthful beauty, if such she had once possessed. Yet the gift of hindsight showed she had once been keenly courted.

This time, power of a different sort was on display. Quick wit, beauty and vivacity formed a deadly flame that drew many moths. A string of suitors paid her court, some boldly, others desperately. They bored or amused her with their declarations of love and the golden futures they promised.

It wasn't enough. This woman could have been a politician or entrepreneur to match any of her suitors. This was an unusual path for a women in those days, but a stronger will could have seen her rise above her times. Her surrender to social convention led to a certain bitterness, and scorn for those around her. Sooner or later, there were consequences.

It was a hot day for a funeral. No one spoke of the cause of death or questioned the closed casket. Neither did they doubt her second husband's reasons. It was well known his business had been faltering - but only she knew his discovery of the affair also played a part. Strangely enough, if he had allowed his wife to work with him in the business, as she'd wanted, neither problem would have occurred. The business would not have failed and the affair never happened. His overly traditional values led to his demise.

I retreated from this sorry tale and sought relief in the face of a woman who looked barely into her twenties. As with the teenagers, the girl's shorter lifespan should make her back story less taxing -

but this time it hit in more compressed form. It was a sad tale of a once bright, happy child in the grip of a charismatic and dangerous boyfriend. He was a charming tyrant, reigning over her.

Once the back-story was perceived, it did not require any magic powers of foresight to see how the tale might end. The girl was under his spell, one that only a shock and some divine intervention could break. I tore a page out of my work folder and scrawled a note in haste lest the girl should get out at the next stop.

'Sybil, this is a message from your future. Tony will never change, but he'll change you for the worse. There'll be no happy ending. Leave him and run as far and fast as you can, before it's too late!'

The train slowed up as it came into the station. I thrust the note into the girl's hand, then took my own counsel and rushed to the exit, eager to escape the exhaustion of all these humans with their desperate lives.

# 4

# Die Sonne

The power of hindsight was one of the strangest of my time with the Vortex Winder. Yet 'tis better to give than receive. Having feasted vampire-like on the back-stories of others, it is now time to relate my own. Here then is the tale of how I came to be travelling to my job at the University of Southern Sydney on this day, and the reasons for my sense of impending doom.

But where to begin - where does *any* event really begin? Should this story start with my first day on the job, or the award I won a few years before which made it possible? Does it begin with the arrival of my enemy, the evil Jacinta Lynton? Should I go back to my break up with apparent 'soul mate' Jane Mara? Or further still to my discovery of the Hartford Papers themselves some eighteen years ago? It is easy to say 'begin at the beginning' yet there is no clear genesis point to this protracted tale.

Let's begin then with the present drama and try to untangle the chain of events that led to it. In my job today, I did not know if I was going to be sacked or promoted. Judging by the look on my boss's face last week, my money was on sacked. There's no doubt I'd made mistakes and some enemies in my time here - and now my three year project on the Hartford Papers was in jeopardy.

Three years! That's how long I'd been working on this. After my escape from Elijinx's island, I gave up on music and decided to get a job. I ended up taking employment as a PhD student at the University of Southern Sydney. Yes, a student. One might say it's not really a job, but the fact is that they were paying me a weekly wage to do it. They called it a 'scholarship' rather than a wage, but the bottom line is they were paying me so in my book, that's a job.

There was also a hell of a lot of work involved, far more than in most other jobs I'd ever done. The brief was to come up with a three hundred page report - known in the trade as a 'thesis' - which had to be heavily researched and then written up. This involved endless hours reading books and articles, taking notes, sorting them into concepts, writing up chapters, revising, and so on until doomsday. By the time it was all done, it amounted to thousands of hours of work. The finished product, the thesis, was the tip of the iceberg, the visible end result of everything that had gone before.

I'd studied at the University of Southern Sydney - let's call it USS from now on - some years back. I'd earned the scholarship by winning an award but had not taken it up at the time. Now, having survived Elijinx and my year with the Vortex Winder, I accepted a three year contract. My brief was to come up with a PhD thesis on a topic of my choice.

To me, this was the chance to come up with something groundbreaking which might shake up the field a little. I later learned that this attitude was not shared by my peers, some of whom saw a PhD as a means to an end - getting an academic job - and tried to be as uncontroversial as possible. Yet to my mind, here was a chance to produce a work of great substance and innovation.

The department where I worked was called the 'School of Philosophy of Science.' Its task was to look at the world of science as an outsider and reflect upon what it all meant. This could include all manner of things - technology, the history of science, or the entire meaning of life and the universe itself. Its areas of study ranged from the microscopic to the galaxy-sized, from the trivial or obscure to the ultimate.

It was up to me to come up with a suitable research topic. I chose 'the Hartford Papers' which was a highly unsuitable one - at least, if I wanted an easy life. In some respects it was a foolhardy choice, doomed to failure. Discussing such a scandalous body of work might open up a world of problems for me at the department. Yet I had my reasons. As mentioned, I wanted to produce something faintly earth-shattering that people might actually read, rather than a dull report which would be filed away to gather dust, and never be touched by human hand or mind.

If I was being evasive, as was often the case in those early days, I would describe the Hartford Papers as an 'esoteric philosophy.' More dramatically, you could call it a book of the dead, for the Hartford Papers was a body of work written by an author who was no longer alive. So what, you might say? Most of the great authors from history are dead and people still study their works. That's true, but they all composed their books before they died. That was not the case with the Hartford Papers. The material was supposedly written by a person who had died and moved into the afterlife - and then composed the work. It was given through a medium. The Hartford Papers claimed to offer a view of the world as seen by a personality who had passed on and was seeing it from the outside.

Say what?

Yes, it sounds farfetched. That's what I thought too - until I actually read it. This is not the time to go into detail about the material itself. I will say only that it is a fascinating body of work. Here, it seemed, was a fresh view of the world unlike that given by any living writer. That its author was outside the world gave him a unique advantage over those still within it. Hartford was able to offer a fresh perspective on classic questions to do with human nature, life on Earth, life after death, and the nature of reality itself.

My first encounter with this material as a young man eighteen years before had led to a lifelong fascination. There were several reasons it appealed to me. Unlike many 'spiritual' views of life, it did not have an overly moralistic tone. It valued the physical world rather than putting it down. It was compassionate rather than authoritarian. Intellectually, it offered a fresh look at life's big questions. Fran Stuart, the medium who delivered the work, was herself a charming and intelligent woman. The Hartford Papers had a broad appeal for me.

It is one thing to have a discreet interest in such material, it is quite another to bring it out in the open as the subject of a PhD thesis. Let's be clear - the views expressed in the Hartford Papers were at odds with the views of those who worked at the School of Philosophy of Science at USS. Yet the Hartford Papers offered a new slant on many topics relevant to the School. I could not understand why such an intriguing body of work was not better known - except for the obvious reason that respected intellectuals who went to university did not believe in such things as mediums or manuscripts delivered from the afterlife.

That sort of prejudice was a red rag to me. Why *shouldn't* they take such work seriously? Weren't philosophers and scientists supposed to be open-minded? They seemed anything but that. Indeed smug certainty seemed far more on show than the humble self-doubt which both science and philosophy claimed as core values.

Having realised that such a conservative bunch would never take the Hartford Papers seriously, I abandoned any thought of a deferential approach. Instead, I set out to ruffle a few feathers. I named my thesis *Above and Beyond: a View From the Balcony*, adding the cheeky subtitle *Ghosts With Vigour and Men of Rigour*. The thesis itself made heavy use of satire in the early chapters to cast doubt on established beliefs. Then it went on to a detailed discussion of Hartford's views.

To some degree, I must admit to a note of zealotry in my approach. I decided to act as an advocate for this ignored work, the Hartford Papers, and shake up these smug academics who would dismiss it so readily. Yet there was a certain playfulness as well. Coming from a rock n roll background, I was used to a theatrical presentation and thought this might be a welcome change from the dull, dry style of most work in the field.

There was also a personal element fuelling my quest, for the Hartford Papers had played a part in costing me one of the loves of my life. Yes, one of them. The idea of soul mates - that each person has only one true love - is surely overrated. Is it not insulting to the rest of the human race to suppose only one of its members is good enough for your love? There are many people you could love, not just one. And for me, long before Sandra, before Freya, there was Jane Mara.

Jane was a strange character, which is probably one reason we got on. The girl had her quirks - a punk rock rejection of both femininity and feminism, an odd refusal to plan anything ahead of time or indeed ever to *turn up* on time - yet we clicked mentally and had a lot of laughs. Our rapport wasn't perfect, but in hindsight it should have been enough. Like a fool, I pushed for more and chased after the illusion of perfection.

The Hartford Papers themselves played a part in our downfall. Jane was a hardcore scientist and atheist and, characteristic of the type, felt entitled to see her views as the correct ones for all rational people to accept. She dismissed the Hartford Papers as wrong, unimportant, and probably fake. Indeed she saw me as mentally weak for reading them, as if I were the brainwashed member of a cult. All this despite never really reading the material herself with an open mind. Naturally, none of this went down too well with me and I tried to make her read Hartford's work so we could argue it out. This led to a feud which drove a wedge between us and contributed to our demise.

I see now it was a mistake to try to change Jane. I should have kept the Hartford Papers to myself and let her keep her own beliefs. To think that being honest about my own views would lead to a better relationship - well, frankly it was a mistake. A grave mistake. That sleeping Cerberus should have been left to lie.

I should have accepted what we had instead of grasping for more, an idea which was an illusion anyway. Instead, the Hartford Papers cost me - no, not a soul mate - but a good relationship. Writing a PhD on the topic now was partly an effort to salvage something from the loss and also, to be frank, a means of revenge. It was a continuation of my 'war' against the arrogance of the scientific worldview to which Jane subscribed. At least, that's how I saw it at the time. All this was part of the back-story which led to my present moment as a PhD student at USS.

The job went along smoothly for the first year. Every few months I'd write up a chapter or two for the thesis, then review it with my supervisor, who always approved of my progress. There was some other work to be done, such as tutoring student classes. At the start of the second year, I reunited with Sandra and bought the house with her. Everything was rolling along smoothly at home and at work - until the arrival at USS of my enemy, Jacinta Lynton.

Was ever evil masked by so lovely a facade? I was reading a book in the USS post-grad common room one morning when a milk-skinned, dark-haired beauty swept into the room. She must have been mid-twenties, and bore an uncanny resemblance to the girl playing Snow White in Rammstein's 'Sonne' video. If you call up the clip on YouTube you'll have a vivid sense of her appearance.

At that time in my early-forties, with the glasses I wore for reading giving me a distinguished look, the girl seemed to take me for an academic. I found myself pinned in the high beam of a radiant smile, which made a rapid exit when she learned I was just a post-grad student like herself. The facial eclipse lasted a moment before the smile returned just a tad diminished.

With her composure regained, Jacinta invited me to coffee at the downstairs cafe. Turned out she was at the same level as myself, a second year post-grad student, and had just transferred from another uni for reasons she did not disclose. Naively charmed, I responded freely to her questions about the department, taking them at face value as a sign of her interest in the place. In hindsight, it's clear I was being pumped for information so she could work her way inwards and upwards. She found out, for instance, that Steve Hutton tended to breeze into lecture rooms like a rock star in between flying off to conferences at every chance, and that atheist zealot, Oliver Dregg, had just taken over as head of department.

There were few early signs of Jacinta's true nature, other than a strange vibe and some minor incidents that were only significant in hindsight. For example, one day I found her alone in the common room in a minor rage, storming about the place, throwing drawers open with a vehemence that seemed at odds with her angelic facade.

'Something wrong?' I inquired, still at the charmed stage of overlooking any flaws in the girl's character.

'Car keys!'

'Your car keys? Lost them, have you?'

My powers of inference were running hot. Indeed my impersonation of Captain Obvious had Jacinta on the verge of a withering response, which she barely restrained.

'Yes. I have. Lost. My car keys.'

'Maybe you locked them in the car. I've done that a few times myself.'

Jacinta stormed out to the car park without answering and I trailed along in her wake. There were the keys alright, insolently stuck in the ignition. The car was just old enough to have predated remote electronic locking and there they were as useless as could be. Jacinta swore like a losing punter and I added an empathetic cry of 'fuck!' in solidarity with her distress. Meanwhile, the sweet girl looked like she was ready to exact vengeance on the car by punching out its side windows. I chimed in with another helpful suggestion.

'Call the NRMA roadside assistance. They'll soon unlock it for you.'

Jacinta's mood was unchanged after making the phone call.

'That's perfect, isn't it? They could be anytime in the next ninety minutes and I've got to tutor those idiot first-years in ten minutes.'

'Never mind. If they're not here in ten, I'll sub for you til they show up.'

'You'll wait by the car?'

'No, I'll take your class until they get here.'

'You'll do that for me?' she said, her furious expression switching rapidly to one of affection. 'Jimmy, you're an angel,' she said brushing my cheek with her fingertips.

'I wouldn't say that,' I said, well aware of the falseness of her statement in one sense, yet not aware enough in another.

I went inside to take Jacinta's class, expecting to be relieved of the job at any minute, but the hour passed. I strolled out of the building just as an NRMA vehicle pulled into the car park - yet there was no longer any sign of the damsel in distress or her car.

'Hey mate,' said the driver. 'You the one with the keys locked in the car?'

'No, that's Jacinta - but her car's gone. You didn't catch her then?'

'I just got here.'

That was odd. After waiting a couple of minutes, the guy shrugged and drove off. I forgot the incident until Jacinta walked into the common room a few days later.

'What happened with your car keys?' I asked. 'The NRMA rep said he missed you.'

But Jacinta seemed to have forgotten the whole thing.

'Oh that,' she said. 'Right after you left, Ian Laney saw me waiting with the car. He picked the lock then and there - took about a minute!'

Ian Laney was a department member specialising in the history of technology. It was good to see that his knowledge of the field was not purely academic. No doubt he had rushed to the fair lady's aid.

'Old Laney, eh. How chivalrous of him - and if he ever tires of lecturing, he can always fall back on a career as a car thief. But why didn't you come and take over your class?' I asked, genuinely puzzled.

'You'd already started. It didn't seem right to interrupt.'

'I was waiting for you. So was the NRMA guy. Didn't you ring them to cancel the service call?'

'Why would I do that?' It was Jacinta's turn to be perplexed.

'You could have saved them a trip. Looks like they were flat out if the guy took that long to show up.'

It's not normally my go to chastise a colleague over matters of trivial ethics but I felt she'd taken advantage of my help. Jacinta's face hardened.

'Listen Jimmy, those guys are driving round the city all day anyway. I've got more important things to think about than them.'

She left with no further word and I realised I had erred. There was something unnerving in her expression - a fleeting glimpse of malice and the capacity for harm. After a minute's reflection, I sought her out and apologised. Sure, it's weak to apologise when you're not at fault - but as it's unwise to make enemies at work, it seemed the right thing to do from a practical if not an ethical standpoint.

Then there was the 'seminar incident.' The custom was that every second Friday, a staff member or post-grad student gave a talk to the rest of the department. There'd be a Q&A afterwards, then activities wound up for the week.

I found these talks fairly dull most of the time - overly formal, too specialised, and usually drier than the Sahara. Unfortunately, they were on straight after lunch when I tend to nod off, as a rule. So one of the biggest challenges posed by these seminars was the struggle to stay awake, or at worst, to feign wakefulness and doze off discreetly. It was often a dire struggle and on a bad day I'd wear dark glasses and hope to doze upright in my chair without snoring. Once the main lecture was over, I only had to get through the

Q&A before escaping to another peaceful weekend at home with Sandra and Finzi.

One week some big shot from another uni showed up to give a talk about science education in schools. The guy was on a mission to raise the standard of thought in general, so there was a certain zeal to his work which brought it to life. Finding such semi-evangelical types interesting at the time, I had no trouble fighting off sleep on this occasion. Jacinta sat two chairs to my left. The visiting big shot finished his talk and called for questions. Right away Jacinta raised her hand and beamed that radiant smile. She fired off a sycophantic question that was right up the old boy's alley and would allow him to hold forth once more.

Big shot took the bait and was off and running. The whole time, he gazed at his questioner and was bewitched enough to ask her name at the end. This was unusual, to say the least, and certainly pushing the boundaries of seminar convention. I can't recall it happening any other time.

She was not at all daunted and replied with both names - 'Jacinta Lynton' - as if presenting a business card or announcing herself at a ball. I mean, surely 'Jacinta' alone would have sufficed. The attempt at networking was so shameless I'm surprised the girl didn't follow up with her website address, Facebook page and Twitter account. I found it cringe-worthy. It's one thing to schmooze someone in private but to brazenly do it in front of a roomful of academics was in really poor taste.

As with the car keys, it was a minor incident. For me, Jacinta's charm had begun to fade yet she did not seem to be any kind of threat. At this stage I saw her as just one of the many personalities you find in any work environment. Her behaviour was mildly irksome but as it didn't affect me, I didn't care. She was a faint irritant on the edge of my life. It wasn't long, however, before her toxic influence oozed in to contaminate my own affairs.

It happened early in my third and final year at USS. As fate would have it, I was ordered by the head of department himself, Oliver Dregg, to collaborate with Jacinta on one of the next seminar presentations. God knows what possessed him to do this but who was I to argue? The man was essentially my boss and had to sign off on my grant renewal each year. If that's what Dregg wanted, so it would be.

It's unlikely Jacinta was any more thrilled than me by the idea but she faked a smile in front of Dregg. With the seminar to be given three Fridays hence, we did the civilized thing and divided up the workload between us. After two weeks, I emailed her my part of the work but got nothing back and was met only with a series of evasions as the days passed. Finally, a few days before deadline and with the ominous phrase 'we have to talk,' Jacinta called me to a meeting in the post-grad room. I was there besieged with crocodile tears and a tragic tale about a stolen laptop, medical complaints, and other assorted calamities.

Still under the thrall of her physical beauty, I was a sucker for those tears and did not resist as this Rammstein Snow White pressed herself into my arms. The flesh was sweet even if the soul was corrupt. For a few moments I succumbed to the unsought embrace, knowing all the while I was being played for a fool. This awareness was heightened by the sudden entry of a young girl, Kate, whom I recognised as one of the students in Jacinta's second year tute group. I pulled away from the embrace, a movement which must have seemed awkward and incriminating.

Jacinta's tears dried up like magic and she asked if I would excuse them a moment. I idled outside the room waiting for them to conclude their business and was surprised to hear angry voices. Or rather, it was only one voice, the same one which had been overcome by tragedy just minutes before.

I edged forward to eavesdrop. It seemed Jacinta had somehow coerced the younger girl into taking on some of her workload - the marking of essays or exams - from students in Jacinta's first year class. Kate had failed to finish the job in time and Jacinta was standing over her like a high school bully. The words 'cheating' and 'plagiarism' were audible once or twice. Clearly Jacinta had some kind of hold over the girl and was lording it over her. Through the door crack, I saw that Kate's posture was cowed and tense. Whatever Jacinta had on the girl was more than enough to intimidate her.

I could barely believe my ears and in hindsight wish I hadn't listened. A moment later, Jacinta opened the door to catch me eavesdropping. There was no coming back from that. Jacinta's true colours were revealed and we were enemies from that point on.

When Kate left, we resumed discussion of the seminar as if nothing had happened, yet the mood was so awkward that I offered to finish the rest of the work myself, just so I could get away. Jacinta would only have to turn up to help give the presentation itself. I was used to being a lone wolf so working on my own would not faze me unduly.

By the time the two of us jointly presented the seminar to the department, I'd done a fine job to prepare it. Yet Jacinta did an even better job presenting. The highlight of our presentation was a witty dialogue I'd composed. But Jacinta was a polished actor and won over the room with ease. For once, the seminar was entertaining, and drew unprompted applause at the end. I looked up into the audience to receive my due plaudits and saw that not a single eye was upon me. Every face was magnetically drawn to the magnificent radiance of Jacinta Lynton.

A few days later I was summoned to a meeting in Oliver Dregg's office. After some cursory small talk, Dregg got to the point.

'You may not realise but we're quite understaffed at the moment. Jan Crooks is overseas and with Dave Kinsky on leave we need the post-grads to pick up some of the load. We've created a new position to be filled from next week.'

'Thank you, Professor Dregg. It's most flattering to be asked - but I'm a little behind with my research. It would be a stretch to take on anything else just now.'

'Then you'll be pleased to hear Jacinta Lynton has already accepted the position.'

'Jacinta?'

'Yes, you and the other post-grads are to answer to her from now on. Everyone else has been informed by email but I've called you in personally to make sure you understand what's required of you.'

'Why me?'

'To be frank, I've received some complaints about you. You're not really pulling your weight around here.'

'What do you mean?'

'The presentation last week that young Lynton came up with, for a start. It was nice of you to show up but you didn't exactly contribute much else, did you?'

'Sorry - I don't understand.'

'Jacinta told me she had to do all the research herself and when she asked you to help, you refused.'

'You must be joking.'

'It's not good enough, Brandt. No wonder you're behind with your thesis if you can't even be bothered to work on a seminar I personally asked you to prepare.'

'It was the other way round! I was the one who had to organise the whole seminar myself. Jacinta did absolutely nothing except show up at the end.'

'Please. Watching that presentation last week, it was quite obvious whose baby that was. You might at least be honest about it. I may as well warn you, Brandt, you're on pretty thin ice around here. What's your thesis topic again?'

'The Hartford Papers.'

'And what is that?'

'It's a sort of... esoteric philosophy. I'm researching how it relates to the big questions that interest this department.'

'Really? Yes, I do remember hearing something about that. Frankly, I don't know how that got green-lighted in the first place. You're lucky you got started before I took over here. Who's supervising you? Has your work been checked?'

'Joe Kingston's my supervisor and he's approved each of my chapters so far. Not only that, my end of year review was fine.'

'You may find it a little tougher next time around. We don't hand out research grants for any old rubbish, you know. You're expected to make a serious contribution to what we're doing here. Right now, part of that will involve working under Jacinta.'

I shook my head in bemusement.

'I don't understand how she got the job. I mean, what does she actually do around here? I take her classes for her, I do her research. Does she ever do any actual work in this joint?'

'Jacinta's a very impressive young woman. The department thinks highly of her. There's little doubt she has a bright future here. You on the other hand are another story, and I'm afraid you'll have to either work with her or resign your position. And there's a rather more serious matter to raise. Jacinta's made a complaint of sexual harassment against you.'

'That's insane. What's the substance of this complaint?'

'Jacinta reports that she's seen you looking at her.'

'Looking? So that's sexual harassment now, is it?'

'Then you admit it?'

'Of course I've seen Jacinta from time to time. It's hard not to when we work in the same building every day.'

'You've not only seen her but *looked* at her. That's highly inappropriate.'

'I may have occasionally looked at her. Who hasn't? The eye is drawn to aesthetic objects. It's natural.'

'Objects, indeed! A fine way to refer to a woman. This isn't the nineteenth century, Brandt.'

'The girl may be a bully and a liar but there's no denying she's very attractive. Of course I've looked at her from time to time. You lot were certainly going at it pretty hard at the seminar. I suppose you had a license for a good stare because she was up there presenting.'

'I beg your pardon?'

'Well, you certainly weren't looking at me!'

'I only wish that looking was the full extent of your harassment. Last week, you were seen attempting to embrace young Lynton, something she was most distressed about.'

'What! You mean that day she gave me the sob story about the stolen laptop? She laid that on as her excuse for doing no work, then collapsed into my arms without warning.'

'The incident was clearly witnessed by another student, who can verify it if required. Now be warned, sexual harassment is grounds for having your grant instantly suspended or cancelled. Jacinta has very kindly and reasonably agreed to overlook the incident and is happy to act as your boss in the new position. Very decent of her, I would say. Not many would be as forgiving. So, Brandt, I'm placing you under Jacinta's supervision and I expect you to give her your full and unreserved cooperation. Is that perfectly clear?'

'Oh yes. Everything is quite clear now.'

I left Dregg's office determined to keep my head down, get my research done, and have as little to do with anyone else as possible. Yet this would now be partly subject to the whims of the poisonous Jacinta Lynton. I had inadvertently made an enemy who was not only a colleague, but who was now effectively my boss. As if my struggles for credibility and survival in the department were not already at risk to begin with! Time would tell if I'd be able to see out my three year contract without further mishap, or whether Jacinta's malice would prove fatal to the whole enterprise.

I exited the department building just in time to see Jacinta behind the wheel of a much newer and more expensive car than the one in which she'd once locked her keys. No doubt this model had remote electronic locking. Catching sight of me for a moment, Jacinta smiled radiantly, revved her engine, and sped off into a bright future.

# 5
# The Black Sheep

It is said that power corrupts but that old line doesn't apply here. Jacinta Lynton was fully corrupt long before she became my boss at the University of Southern Sydney. I know this because I saw her back-story. Yes, we are almost back to the point reached in chapter three when the Vortex Winder gave me the power of vivid hindsight. Before we come to that disturbing vision, I will conclude the tale of Jacinta's reign of terror at USS.

It started in petty, predictable ways. She'd interrupt my work with requests for small but tiresome tasks like photocopying. I'd be given a few books and ordered to copy random sections for her class. With fifteen to twenty class members, this could amount to over three hundred pages. The request, trivial as it was, was meant to demean me. Here I was, a mature aged PhD researcher, being treated like an office boy by a woman ten years my junior. Yet due to Dregg's order to obey her, and with my research grant at stake, there was no choice but to comply. With less than a year to go on my three year contract, it would be silly to lose the job at this late stage.

Of course, on returning the pile of papers to her, it turned out Jacinta had changed her mind and half of these were no longer required. A fresh batch had to be made to replace them. This was the sort of trivial power play she thrived on.

Another move was the attempt to exclude me socially. Jacinta set up a lunch date for all the post-grad students one day. I got the email like everyone else and turned up at her office with the rest of them. She waited til everyone was assembled, then asked me to stay behind to finish an 'urgent' job she needed done. Unfortunately for Jacinta, this one was a misfire. Her lunch date was neither here nor there to me. I merely raised an eyebrow, shrugged and walked away.

Her next strategy, however, was a winner. As I later learned, psychopaths like Jacinta are skilled in being able to sum up the particular weakness of an intended victim. She eventually did this to me. Having failed to bruise me with her manoeuvres so far, Jacinta swapped the vinegar for honey. This allowed her to get close enough to detect a certain innocence in my nature and turn it against me.

Jacinta's ruthless new tactic was to be nice to me and pretend to take an interest in my work. After the sustained campaign of intimidation she'd waged, this came as a relief. Suddenly the girl was surprising me with cups of coffee, friendly small talk, and polite inquiries after my research. Suspecting some new trick, I stonewalled her at first. Yet finding no hidden 'buckets of water' landing on my head, I was fool enough to conclude that Jacinta had come to her senses and wasn't so bad after all. This was mere wishful thinking and also stemmed from my disbelief that people can devote so much energy to politics at the expense of actual work.

We even had the occasional lunch together. At one of these, she asked about the seminar I was due to give the department in a couple of weeks.

'Sorry Jimmy, I can't remember your research topic. What was it again?'

'It's the Hartford Papers,' I replied. 'That weird esoteric philosophy I mentioned when you first arrived. Can't say I'm looking forward to it. The department is so straight, my talk will go down about as well as a stripper in church.'

Jacinta pricked up her ears and leaned forward as I continued.

'In fact, if the seminar weren't compulsory I'd skip it altogether. Maybe I should just present some other topic instead.'

'You can't. You have to discuss your actual research.'

'I know, but at least I might tone it down a bit. Try to fit in, if possible.'

'What do you mean, fit in?'

'Most of these seminars aren't that exciting, are they? They're dull, to be frank. I'm not sure why. It's something I don't get about philosophy in general.'

'What about it?'

'A lot of the stuff you read is so dry, don't you think? Even the classics - the great philosophy texts everyone's supposed to read. To say nothing of what's in the journals. Most of it has this awful style - it's so dry and mannered, so rule-based and orderly. Where's the theatrics, the emotion? The humour? Sure, there's the occasional wild loon like Nietzsche, or that guy David Stove who was at Sydney Uni. He wrote *The Plato Cult*, you know. That was a welcome change from the ridiculous reverence we're supposed to show the 'great philosophers.' A lot of philosophy seems so uptight. Maybe it's the heavy metal guitarist in me, but I was expecting a bit more excitement.'

'So now you're a heavy metal guitarist, Jimmy? You don't look like one.'

'Appearances can be deceptive. Check out my album if you don't believe me.'

'I'd love to hear it!'

'I didn't know you were into heavy rock anyway.'

'Sure - big fan. I saw Metallica when they last came out.'

'Really - on the *Death Magnetic* tour? So, you think that record was a return to the form of their first four albums, or was it too little too late?'

Jacinta changed the subject. In hindsight, this was a red flag. In her attempt to feign an interest in heavy rock, she'd simply named the most well known metal band, yet without showing any real familiarity with their work. Failing to pick up on this, I blundered ahead.

'You know what I'd really like to do for my talk? Walk into that seminar room with some real heavy intro tape blasting out and give a speech to wake everyone up. Get away from this idea of philosophy as some kind of polite gentlemen's club. Put some real fire into it. At least no one would be falling asleep, would they?'

Jacinta eased forward until her exquisite face was uncomfortably close and clasped my hands between hers.

'That's a fantastic idea, Jimmy! You should do it.'

'I'd like to, sure, but Dregg and the rest of them would have heart attacks.'

'No, you're wrong. Once they see what you've done, they'll admire your originality and courage. You're right about philosophy. Those seminars can be pretty dull. The whole field needs shaking up. I say, go for it! I'll support you fully. All the post-grads will - I'll talk to them myself and round up a cheer squad. It'll be the coolest seminar ever!'

'You sure? It was only a fantasy. I never meant to actually do it.'

'You've *got* to! You can't get out of it now you've told me. Look, let's clear the air on that seminar we did together last session. I got the applause but it was all down to you really. You did all the creative work. We both know that.'

'According to Dregg, you said you wrote it and I only showed up on the day.'

'What? I never said that. Right, that does it. I'm going to tell you something in confidence, as long as you swear to keep it to yourself. Let me give you a heads up on old Dregg. He tried to hit on me a couple of times and when I threatened to file a sexual harassment complaint, he back pedalled and offered me a job. I wouldn't believe a word he says.'

'Is that right? Oliver Dregg! Who'd have thought? Thanks for your support, Jacinta - but are you sure? The Hartford Papers make for a controversial enough topic already. Shouldn't I be toning it down instead of pumping it up?'

'That's the wrong strategy. So your work's controversial. Don't hide it, flaunt it. Out and proud, that's the way to win them over. This is your moment. You never got the raps for that seminar we did. Here's your chance to make up for it. I say go for broke - you'll kill it.'

'Yeah, maybe you're right.'

'I mean, look at the last two seminars. Cath and Rob. Terrible, weren't they?'

These were two of our post-grad colleagues. Rob's talk was about medical advances in the nineteenth century. He gave a laboured analysis of an article which was already well known. Everyone in the room would have read it years ago. Not one new fact or opinion was offered that day. It was hackwork at its finest, if you'll forgive the paradox. In other words, if one was trying to achieve excellence in the art of sheer mediocrity, Rob had nailed it.

As for Cath, it was hard to know *what* she'd discussed as her talk had been almost inaudible. The poor girl clearly believed herself a tremulous gnat with no right to address the exalted congress of professors at USS. Both seminars had been highly forgettable, although one thing I did recall was Jacinta warmly congratulating both speakers. I'd put it down to tact and good manners at the time. Now she was expressing her real views.

'I hate to agree with you, Jacinta, but those talks were embarrassing. The post-grads are supposed to be the future of the department, and there's Cath letting us all down with her insipid performance. As for Rob, could he be any more boring if he tried? They both believe this rubbish about being 'apprenticed into academia' as if we're barely fit to be in the same room as the professors. They think they have to debase themselves in front of their 'superiors.' It's appalling.'

'You're so right - and it's up to you now, Jimmy. You've got to raise the bar for all of us.'

'At the very least, I'll walk in there and give them a show, and say something they haven't already heard a hundred times.'

'That's right. These academics are no better than us. Go in there, kick some ass, and get us some respect back!'

'Don't worry, I will.'

'We'll be right behind you.'

Oh my, how easily I was played. You've got to hand it to her. Jacinta homed in on my weaknesses alright - my ego and desire for recognition, my hatred of hierarchies, even my insecurity about the research topic and status as black sheep of the department. Instead of pretending to be a merely greyish sheep, as I'd planned to do for the seminar, Jacinta had talked me into dyeing out even the few flecks of grey in my fleece until I was the blackest sheep that ever worked there.

She was cleverer than me. She correctly divined a certain innocence in my nature - because to me the idea was all quite reasonable. It was just a bit of fun. *Why not* walk into a university seminar to the strains of a blazing heavy metal soundtrack? *Why not* discuss a controversial 'occult' philosophy in front of a bunch of strait laced academics? Why *not* should have been obvious. While there was indeed genius in the idea, there wasn't much common sense.

Come seminar time, I prepared the room in advance by blacking out all the windows and setting up my audio gear and a slide show. By the time all the academics were assembled, the lights were dimmed so that the room was almost dark. I turned on the projector and hit play on the music.

The intro to Slayer's song 'Hell Awaits' rose up in the darkness. That's the one with the weird sound effects and the backwards Satanic chanting. We're talking the genuinely evil version off the live album *Decade of Aggression*, not the cartoonish original studio recording. On the live track, the noise of the crowd is overlaid with the Satanic chanting, which enhances the whole effect.

While the audio chaos was unfolding, my slide show was flashing up a stream of occult symbols on the big screen at the front of the room. Then, at the moment Slayer hit the stage with that first mighty guitar chord, the title of my talk appeared onscreen. 'Non-Teleology: A Modern Fetish.'

As Hanneman and King fired out their monstrous guitar riffing, a series of academic quotes and definitions appeared in the slideshow. Never before had such terms been defined to the backing of extreme metal music. After three minutes, the music stopped and I began a confident reading of chapter four of my thesis. The experience as a whole could not have been any further removed from the timid and tedious talks given by Cath and Rob.

As for the content of my talk, it was always going to make more enemies than friends. I've said that the views in the Hartford Papers weren't in accord with the views of my colleagues in Philosophy of Science. My talk did nothing to play that down. On the contrary, I implied that some of my colleagues' cherished beliefs were delusional. I also directed a few caustic remarks at some world famous authors in the field. In my view, these remarks weren't personal, and as they were relevant to the matter at hand it was all in a good cause. But looking back, perhaps I may have gone a little too far.

From time to time, I looked up at the room full of academics to find most of them staring at me like I'd escaped from an asylum. The stunned silence in the room was broken only by suppressed sniggers at the odd witty remark from my talk. Dregg himself was sitting halfway down the room to my right with a face of thunder. I ploughed on regardless.

In truth, Dregg's expression was a little disturbing. I looked over to Jacinta for reassurance, glad that I could at least count on her support. To my surprise, she seemed to be in a state of distress and dismay. Indeed, fifteen minutes in, after I'd made a particularly cutting remark, Jacinta stood up and walked noisily from the room.

Some other students - her suck ups - followed her lead. Whether this was pre-arranged or a spontaneous attempt at sycophancy, the effect was the same - an embarrassing rejection of my talk from my so called supporters.

The next morning I was again summoned to Dregg's office. I took a seat in front of his desk but he ignored me for a couple of minutes as he worked at his computer, checking emails or some such urgent matter. This type of childish power play was unworthy of someone in his high position, but that's the kind of guy Dregg was. Finally, he looked up.

'So, Brandt, care to explain yourself?'

'With regard to what? You mean my talk? I thought it went quite well.'

'Are you trying to make fools of us? This is a university, not a nightclub. It's a place of learning.'

'You mean the music? Look, Professor Dregg, you don't know this but I used to be a rock guitarist. There are different cultural norms in that line of work. It's all about drama and putting on a show. I was just trying to mix genres and embrace some cultural exchange. Put a bit of the rock n roll into philosophy - know what I mean?'

'Did you discuss this with your supervisor?'

'No, but I did talk to Jacinta Lynton about it. She thought it was a great idea.'

'Brandt, please. We all saw her walk out yesterday. It was pretty clear what she thought of your efforts and I can't say I blame her. She's actually rung me this morning and apologised for your talk. Although why she should be apologising for something *you've* done is beyond me.'

'She was the one who encouraged me to do it!'

'Jacinta told me you did mention your seminar idea and she did her best to talk you out of it. But stubborn as you are, there was just no telling you. You had to be the trouble maker, didn't you?'

My jaw dropped, and it took me a moment to respond.

'Why can't you see through this woman? You've a Masters in astronomy, you've published more books than I could count. Yet one gorgeous Goth with blood red lips and your critical faculties take a sabbatical.'

'And there you go again. Judging by last night, this is exactly the tone of insolence which seems to be your *forte*. I've heard just about enough from you, Brandt. This is your final warning. I advise you to keep a very low profile around here and concentrate on finishing your thesis. You might think about some major revisions while you're at it. If you're expecting to get through with the kind of rubbish we witnessed last night, well, I wish you luck in finding easy examiners. That's about all I can say about that!'

I walked out of Dregg's office and as USS was about the last place I wanted to be, I made my way home to the Blue Mountains. The very next morning, Sandra had a flat tyre before work. I fixed it and spent the rest of the day as a home handyman, thanks to the Vortex Winder's reawakening.

I stayed home for a week. And all the while, as I fixed and finetuned everything at the house, my mind was turning over the troubles at USS with a special focus on the evil machinations of Jacinta Lynton. By the time I returned to the university, I was possessed of two things: the magical power of hindsight and the determination to confront my tormentor directly.

I walked into the department building and down the corridor, then entered Jacinta's office without knocking. She was sitting at her desk and greeted me with the same radiant smile I'd seen at our first meeting.

'Hi Jimmy. So sorry I missed the end of your talk.'

At the sight of that smile, an impulse rose up within me - the urge to upend that desk and fling its contents to the four corners of the room. Yet before I could even speak, I was besieged by an awful vision - the back-story of Jacinta Lynton.

The trail of devastation led from the infants playground to the present day. I saw a long line of victims - fellow schoolgirls bullied in high school, one to the brink of suicide; a trail of male admirers ground into the dust; work colleagues knifed or shoved out of the way on the career ladder. A parade of 'extras' used and discarded when they'd served their purpose.

Here was a young lifetime's worth of evil compressed into a minute of vision. With evil so raw and relentless, there could be no reason, no negotiation. It fed upon interaction of any kind. The only recourse was to run. I staggered from the room with one thought uppermost - the resolve to have nothing more to do with Jacinta Lynton in any shape or form, regardless of any Dreggian orders from above. I left that room vowing never to return - and that was a resolve I was to break only once in my remaining time at USS.

# 6

# At War With Oxford

At last I finished my PhD thesis on the Hartford Papers. It ran to three hundred pages and looked like an old style encyclopaedia. The weighty leather-bound book, with the title blazed in gold upon the spine, could not have pleased me more.

To finish the thesis was one thing, to get it through the system was another. It had to go before three examiners who would sign off on it. Or not, as it turned out. One passed it but two refused - and so began the next stage of my war with the university.

Although a whole book could be written about what happened next, I'll keep this part short. Many an editor would advise me to omit it altogether - yet I refuse to insult the reader by dumbing the story down too much. What matters here is the truth and a certain depth of context. While this *is* a slight divergence from the main narrative, it's all part of how I turned to the dark side and became the Black Phoenix.

Having said that, I concede that casual readers may not be interested in the finer points of my PhD struggles, so I'll give them a free pass to skip the next bit if they like. Sooner that than give up on the book. Hell, I'll even make it official, like it's a dispensation from the Vortex Winder itself.

*This is a free pass to move on to Chapter Eight.*

There you go. I gave the same pass for the Black Art chapter in Book One. While my mind is naturally prone to obsession, I realise that not everyone will share the particular obsessions that are mine. Many will be more interested in the time when my moral decline began, which was when I entered the evil and corrupt world of rock n roll. That tale will soon be told. But first, for those who remain, is the tale of the evil and corrupt world of university life.

As for the real Vortex Winder, by the way, I became so caught up in the whole PhD dispute that I more or less forgot about it. Unfortunately, it seemed to forget me too. I could have done with some magical powers at the time.

It was at *this* point, however, that I began keeping a journal of my experiences, making notes of conversations, meetings and so on. This was partly so I could back up my version of events if required. Indeed, I still have a copy of every report, letter, and email from that time. I also extended the journal to the events of my private life and all that came after. I had a hunch it might lead to a new book, the sequel to *The Vortex Winder* - and so it turned out.

The three examiners of my PhD thesis were Aaron Dyson, Jeff Marriot, and Martin Capette. Let's begin with the good examiner before moving on to his evil counterparts. Aaron Dyson passed the work. While noting its eccentricity, he mentioned 'the many virtues of the thesis: in particular its boldness / originality / open-mindedness towards unconventional ideas. I learned many interesting things from his pages... which is more than I can say of many a doctoral thesis that I've OK'd without qualms.' The other two examiners, Marriot and Capette, were both hostile in their rejection of the work - Marriot in his coldly supercilious way, and Capette as a head-kicking, bully boy. It was a case of bad cop, worse cop with those two.

What did they object to? It really only came down to two things - the style and the content!

It's true the thesis was written in an unusual style. It was breezy, almost conversational at times, with a penchant for humour and dramatic touches. This was quite deliberate. It was an attempt to get away from the awful constipated and deadly dull style afflicting so much of philosophy. There are many vices mistaken for virtues in this field, and that style is one of them.

Apart from the unusual style, my work was frank and opinionated, not at all the humble offering of an apprentice seeking to enter the academy. One way and another, my approach had antagonised the examiners, that much was clear. Yet to be awarded the PhD, the thesis had to get past all three of them. Marriot and Capette were prepared to make it hard for me.

What made it impossible, however, was their rejection of the basic premise of the thesis - that it was a discussion of the Hartford Papers. This was strange, to say the least, as that was the topic they agreed to read about when they accepted the job as examiners. Now they were more or less insisting I change the topic of the work. I would still be permitted to discuss the Hartford Papers but it would, in effect, be reduced to an appendix to the main work, or at best a minor section within it. They were basically demanding the writing of a brand new thesis.

That was never going to happen. I was exhausted after three years of hard work. The last thing I was going to do was start again. More to the point, I was entirely happy with what I'd written and saw no reason to change it. After all, it was *my* thesis. Who were Marriot and Capette to interfere? When I began three years before, they had played no part in the creation of the project - and as far as I was concerned nothing had changed. Their involvement was quite arbitrary. They were critics, not creators, and gravely overestimated their rights in the matter.

I was hardly of a mind to comply with the examiners' demands in the first place. Capette's critique was extremely hostile. It was also riddled with errors. Not just basic errors about the nature of the work, but many specific mistakes that, once pointed out, would have been obvious even to the casual observer. I was hardly going to cave in to such a hostile yet flawed assault.

The examiners criticised me for departing from some academic norms - but again this was deliberate. I suspected that even if I set out my reasons, they wouldn't have a bar of it. Apart from that, some of their suggested changes were impossible to make without drastically changing the thesis. I explained all this in the detailed report which I later wrote for the appeal. I won't repeat that material here.

To summarise my position - I was faced with impossible demands as well as the order to write a new thesis in which the Hartford Papers would hardly feature. If I refused, there would be no PhD, it would be the end of my career at USS, and this in turn would jeopardise the happy life I was enjoying with Sandra and Finzi out in the unwild west.

For that reason, I considered caving in to the examiners' demands. But no, it couldn't be done. It would mean capitulating to behaviour I could never condone. It was at best creative interference and at worst, sheer bullying. After all, it's not as if the examiners wanted to improve my thesis on the Hartford Papers. No, they wanted me to erase it altogether and write something else. Well, they could forget it. It was one thing to do a little fake photocopying for Jacinta, quite another to destroy my PhD thesis on the say so of a couple of random academics for whom I now had very little regard.

Of course, I had to have it out with Sandra. Not for the first time, our conflicting natures showed themselves under the stress of a difficult situation. She found it hard to get her head around the predicament I was in. As she gave me a friendly interrogation, her sculpted eyebrows were raised in anger and concern.

'So they want you to make a few changes. Isn't that fairly normal?'

'It's hardly a few changes, Sandra. These guys have rejected the basic premise of the thesis - that it's a discussion of the Hartford Papers.'

'Isn't that what they agreed to read about when they took on the job?'

'Well, yeah!'

'Can they do that?'

'Apparently they can do anything they want - and I have no right of reply. I'm to bow down and obey. Which I'm not going to do, in case you're wondering.'

'But what about your PhD? I was looking forward to calling you Dr Brandt.'

'It doesn't look good, I'm afraid. Still, my motivation was never to call myself Doctor. At least I've done the thesis of my choice and done it exactly the way I wanted.'

'So you're going to just give up - after all your hard work?'

'What do you want me to do? It's out of my hands.'

'Can't you just do what they say?'

'No, not really.'

'Why not?'

'Why not? How long have you got?'

'Oh God, here we go. He's started pacing.'

Sandra rolled her eyes. I was indeed going back and forth like a caged tiger, righteous rage adding to my velocity.

'You want to know why I can't just do what these guys say? For starters, I'm done in. This project nearly killed me. Thousands of hours I put in over the last three years.'

'I know.'

'And these bastards want me to start over! It's pretty much a new thesis entirely, that's what they want. Well, forget it. I mean, where's my motivation? I could cop all those hard yards on my own account. Buggered if I'll go through it all again dancing to someone else's tune. It's like Eddie Van Halen said when the record company tried to make him do a record of covers. I'd rather bomb with my own stuff than make it with someone else's. That's what he said - and I couldn't agree more.'

'Are you sure that's really the same thing?'

I ignored her as my clenched right fist sent a savage, involuntary punch into my left palm.

'Besides which, why would I destroy my own baby on their say so?'

'What baby?'

'My thesis, of course. It's my baby. By the powers, I'll do something drastic before I let some swab come in and make me abort it, you may lay to that!'

'Oh God, he's talking pirate. That's always a bad sign.'

I barely heard her. Sandra continued in her self-appointed role as the voice of reason and moderation.

'Do you ever think you might be a bit over-attached to your work? Surely your thesis is just a means to an end. You know, so you can get a job at uni.'

'There's plenty see it that way, Sandy. Not me. This project was never a means to an end. It was always an end in itself, and the best thing I ever did too. I stand by it one hundred percent. I see no reason to change it. None whatsoever.'

'Except that you might get your PhD.'

'If having a PhD means condoning this sort of bullying and interference, then I'll give it a miss. I'll make it on my own terms or not at all. I mean, who the hell are these guys?'

'Well, they're your examiners?'

'I don't give a damn who they are, Sandra. This is *my* PhD thesis. I don't care if it was Socrates and Aristotle themselves examining me, I'll not be told what to write about.'

'Calm down, please. You're upsetting Finzi.'

'Don't blame me.'

'What do they actually want you to do?'

'For starters, one of them wants me to justify my work with a high level critique of the latest theories in philosophies of mind. The other wants an in depth discussion of parapsychology. Then having run their ridiculous obstacle course, maybe I'll get to discuss Hartford in the last chapter.'

'Can't you just do it?'

'I've no interest in discussing parapsychology. Why should I? I want to discuss Hartford's views, not a bunch of boring lab experiments.'

'Oh, come on.'

'As for philosophy of mind, that's not my area and never was. These guys want me to spend the whole thesis justifying why I should be allowed to even *begin* the thesis I actually want to write. Except you only get to do one PhD in your life, Sandy, and I'm not going to waste it on this rubbish.'

'Oh dear. Looks like we're stuck then.'

'Besides, can't you see what the bastard's doing? Philosophy of mind! Marriot wants to draw me onto difficult foreign terrain so he can cut me down at his leisure. Only a fool would fall for that. And here's the thing - even if I *did* do what they say, who's to say they won't turn around and deny me anyway? They just want to take me down a peg for being a smartarse.'

'Oh God, it's typical you. Why'd you have to write on such a controversial topic? Why couldn't you just do something simple?'

'Yeah, why not be a hack like Rob and churn out drivel for the sake of a pay cheque? That's really going to advance the cause of knowledge, ain't it?'

'What were you thinking being so confrontational? Look where it's got you.'

'I know, but at the time, it seemed the right thing to do. Maybe I was wrong, but hindsight's always 20/20. Looks like I gambled and lost.'

'What's going to become of you now? What about me and Finzi and the mortgage?'

'I know, Sandra, but remember that when I started this project, you and Finzi weren't around. If you had been, I may have done this all quite differently.'

'We're here now though, aren't we? Without your PhD, you won't be able to get a job at uni. How will you earn a living? Can't you just rewrite your work, if not for yourself, at least for us?'

'If only I could, but like I said, these guys are basically asking for a brand new thesis. It would be at least another year of fulltime work, more likely two, and my funding's already come to an end.'

Sandra put her hands to her head.

'Besides, it's an ethical matter,' I continued. 'I don't approve of the way this has been done. Not in the slightest. See, it's not like the American system where you can stick up for yourself and argue with them. You can't do that here. They think they can order me around and I'm just going to buckle under. Well, it ain't honourable and I won't cop it! A man without honour is nothing, Sandy. It's better to die on your feet than live on your knees.'

Sandra raised her eyes heavenward.

'What I don't understand is this,' she said. 'Didn't your supervisor say your thesis was OK?'

'Yes, of course, or I wouldn't have put it in. He approved of every chapter. Apart from that, my work had an annual review the last three years and went through without a hitch. And don't forget the other examiner, Dyson. He gave it a pass.'

'Then how can these other guys knock it back?'

'Good question. This examination caper is a bit of a lucky dip. You do get a say in who does it, and you can try and pick someone you think will be sympathetic. But if you end up with someone difficult, you're screwed. Take Capette, for instance. He finds my thesis a failure as a study of parapsychology, but that's not surprising because it never tries to be one and doesn't even mention the topic. How do you deal with a criticism like that? Not only that, the guy reckons he can trash my work, but his own report is full of errors itself. They're not even specialist errors - *you* could understand them, and you've no knowledge of the field. But if I point any of them out, you can guess how well that'll go down.'

'Oh for God's sake, Jimmy, think of something. You've put three years of your life into this. Surely it can't all be in vain just because of *these* guys.'

'Apparently it can, Sandra. Apparently it can.'

There was still a glimmer of hope. I would take a middle path which would maintain the integrity of my work but allow the chance of a peaceful resolution. I made some minor yet genuine revisions. I toned down the confrontational style of my work. At least a little, just enough to acknowledge that it had gone too far the first time.

Two new chapters were also added. The first was some new material on the Hartford Papers in response to the examiners' comments. The second was a reasonably polite defence of my work in which I answered their criticisms.

I was, in effect, standing up for myself, arguing with the examiners, albeit in a civilized manner. The hope was that Marriot and Capette would be big enough men to take it and even respect it. After all, was not philosophy, of all fields, one in which the willingness to argue should be seen as a virtue, not a vice? Surely these two gentlemen would realise that at post-grad level, a writer must be prepared to stand up and defend his or her work against criticism, rather than crumbling meekly before it. As men of honour, they would respect this far more than a spineless capitulation. This was my hope, forlorn as it turned out to be.

The more likely outcome was that Marriot and Capette would behave in an authoritarian manner. If their orders were not obeyed, they would reject the work entirely. Sadly, that is exactly what happened. I sent in the revised thesis. When the news came back it had been rejected, it was no surprise at all.

My next action was to go to arbitration. I gave a written report to a board of three people from USS. This time, not a punch was pulled. I'd tried to be diplomatic and given the examiners the chance to act fairly. Now that had failed and the case was under appeal, I gave my honest opinion of them. My written report ran to fifty pages. It discussed what I thought of Marriot's efforts. It made a long list of Capette's errors and pointed out his impossible demands for change. If my report did not shred their entire case, it certainly went a fair way down that path.

This written report went to the appeal board, then a date for my hearing was set. The panel was led by one Stephen Peebles. It also consisted of another academic and a token student, this last presumably there to take my side.

Stephen Peebles was no tyrant in himself, but he struck me as the sort of middle manager who'll always defer to bureaucratic procedure and authority. He could have been working for the worst regime in the world but as long as his superiors wore smart suits and spoke in deep voices, he would have gone along with it all. To his credit, he did not reject my report outright, but handed it over to a 'higher power.' He called in what was meant to be an 'independent opinion' from a senior academic from the USS philosophy department. Note that this was a separate department to the one where I was employed, the School of Philosophy of Science.

Enter 'Dr Jones,' as I came to call him. Jones was handed the examiners' reports along with my detailed rebuttal. He then made his own judgment in a four page statement. As I read it through, it was clear that there was nothing impartial going on with Jones' handling of the case. He had sided with the examiners entirely. If Jones had handed down a scorecard, it would have read Examiners 100, Brandt 0.

This was a basic tactical error on Jones' part. If he'd been more intelligent, Jones would have at least made a show of pretending to see both sides. He'd have realised it was unwise to parade his bias so openly when he was meant to be impartial. He might have twigged that it was implausible the examiners had not got a single thing wrong and Brandt not a single thing right.

This basic point surprised me. It seems that certain people are so used to practicing an institutionalised form of bullying - and getting away with it - that it does not occur to them to protect themselves with even the pretence of fairness. Jones, in particular, should have known better than to expose himself so plainly.

That was not the only mistake in Jones' report. He made a few basic points which even Sandra could see were wrong - and Sandra never seemed to agree with me about anything these days, so that was saying something.

I was given one more right of reply to Jones' report. This was part of official procedure but the appeal board was just going through the motions by now.

By the way, I never knew who Jones actually was. He refused to give his identity, preferring to destroy my career from a safe hiding place. To this day, I do not know the fellow's name. For the sake of answering his report, I dubbed him 'Dr Jones,' a derisive tag that mocked his demand for anonymity. The fellow was no Indiana, that's for sure.

In my reply, which ran to a mere fifteen pages this time, I dissected Jones' obvious bias and blatant mistakes. If this had been a boxing match, the referee would have stopped the fight after page three. There's no doubt I won the argument, but if anyone is skeptical about this, the document is freely available. If required, I have no problem presenting this and other documents for the world to see, to back up my views on this whole dispute.

Now, I say again that a referee would have stopped this fight very early on and ruled in my favour. Unfortunately, there was no referee in this dispute. The whole thing was a sham with about as much credibility as Stalin's 20th century show trials. When the appeal board handed down its decision, my reply to Jones was swept aside as if it had never been written. The board was clearly going through the motions with never a thought of any other result. I was finished. There would be no PhD for me and my university career was dead and buried. As I walked down the corridors of USS once more, I knew it was for the last time. So with nothing left to lose, there were now some scores, not to settle, but at least to address.

I called in at Jacinta's office and inquired after her health.

# 7

# Temporary Kingdom

Jacinta answered with a dazzling smile.

'Never better! How lovely to see you, Jimmy. I suppose you've come to congratulate me on my promotion.'

'Another one?'

'My doctorate's been approved and I start here as a lecturer next session.'

'So it's Doctor Psychopath now, is it? How about that - you getting promoted and me sacked on the same day. There's a certain poetry in that, don't you think?'

'I'm sorry to hear your PhD bombed, Jimmy. At least Rob and Cath got through.'

'That figures. So you'll all be PhDs together. How inspiring to know the future of the university is in such good hands. Oh by the way, before I go, I want to pass on a message.'

I pulled a blank scrap of paper from my pocket and pretended to read it.

'This is from Debbie Mills, Jane Crowley and Brett Stebber. They want you to know they're on their way and you're finally going to get what's coming to you.'

At the mention of three of the victims I'd seen during her backstory, Jacinta's face blanched whiter than that of the Rammstein Snow White she so resembled. Of course, the message was entirely made up but if it gave Jacinta some sleepless nights, then let her believe it.

I smiled radiantly and she shot me a last look - this time one of naked, unbridled malice. For a moment I recognised something which jolted me into a sudden speculation. Had it been Elijinx himself blighting my path these last two years? His shape-shifting abilities made it possible. Yet in my experience, he had never sustained a role this long. No, it wasn't him. The legions of his foot soldiers are numberless. The girl was worthy of him but still only an apprentice, not the master himself.

There were a few more foot soldiers to address before I drew a veil on this sordid affair. Next was the USS appeal board, who received the following missive from me.

Dear Stephen and friends,

Last week, I received your judgment about my PhD. Since then, I sent a further two polite emails asking you to reconsider. They had no effect. Now that all hope is lost of justice in this affair, here is my own judgment of you and the job you did.

The appeal process was a sham. You ignored the many clear and vital points made in my report. You uncritically accepted what was said by Marriot, Capette and 'Dr Jones.' The final letter you sent me was nothing more than a list of bureaucratic processes, along with a dim and wilfully obtuse summary of the case. It did not respond to any of my grievances against Marriot, Capette or Jones.

By its decision, the appeal board condones a university system in which bullying runs free. It endorses policies whereby spineless yes-men and hacks are allowed into the system, while original thinkers or those with the backbone to stand up for their work are kept out.

The appeal board has no idea about the type of values that should be associated with university work, let alone at postgraduate level. Through its conduct in this affair, the board has brought shame upon the University of Southern Sydney.

Following the farce that has just been enacted, I have lost any remaining regard for the processes of justice at USS.

Disrespectfully,

Jimmy Brandt

Next were Marriot and Capette. I mailed each of them a copy of my fifty page evaluation of their efforts, asking for a reply, which of course never arrived. Indeed it was only when I received a cease-and-desist letter from Alan Duckworth, a big shot at USS, that I learned they had received it at all. Turns out Marriot and Capette had complained to my university about me having the nerve to send them a critique of their work as examiners. I sent a reply back to Duckworth.

Dear Alan,

I received your letter about my attempt to contact the PhD examiners. I was pleased to learn that my messages had gone through, as they have not given me the courtesy of a reply.

As for whether I will contact them again, I have just sent them my final message and now consider the matter closed. Don't forget that before I took that step I went through the full processes of arbitration at USS. It was a complete waste of time. The detailed case I made in writing was swept aside, with not a single point answered in the appeal board's final report.

Once the case was closed and I'd given up hope of a fair hearing, I wrote to the examiners to let them know what I thought of their performance. In so doing, I was exercising my democratic right to voice my opinion. In turn, Marriot and Capette had the right to reply. Clearly, they lacked the courage to do so and chose instead to complain to you. I'm not sure why. It is not for USS to deny me the right to express my views. But if you do have a problem with it, Alan, then I suggest you unleash the full majesty of your powers and disqualify me from receiving the PhD. Oh that's right, you already have.

It is indeed the case, as you say, that the processes of arbitration do not permit me to contact the examiners. Yet those processes are over. It is laughable that you still expect me to abide by them. Those processes were ineffective at the time and they are meaningless now.

Alan, I suggest that you return to your duties. Instead of looking to censure me, your first task should be to lead an inquiry into the scandalous conduct of the appeal board. I have finished my communication with the examiners, but that has nothing to do with you. Do not make the mistake of thinking I have any respect left for anyone at USS.

Jimmy Brandt

Now for Dr Jones. Nothing could be done to reverse his decision but I *could* let him know what I thought of his efforts. I would send him my reply, the one I'd written for the appeal panel. Yet how to reach him? He'd hidden behind anonymity and I knew only that he taught philosophy at USS. There was nothing else for it but to flush him out. I wrote the following letter and put a copy under every office door in the Department of Philosophy. The first part was addressed to the staff as a whole, the second was to Jones himself.

To the Philosophy Dept,

My name is Jimmy Brandt. I've just been involved in a dispute over my PhD thesis. The case went to arbitration and was heard by Dr Stephen Peebles and two others.

Dr Peebles sought an independent opinion from 'a senior academic from the school of philosophy' at USS. This academic gave his opinion anonymously. From now on, I will call this academic 'Dr Jones' and address the rest of this letter to him directly. A copy of this letter is being given to each member of the school of philosophy. The real Dr Jones can then stand up.

Dear Dr Jones,

You were asked to adjudicate on my PhD dispute. Your report contained some inaccuracies which should be set straight. I would like you to read my reply and respond to it by mail. Once you have done that, I will consider the matter closed.

The problem is that your decision to remain anonymous means I do not know where to send my reply. All I know is that you are a member of the philosophy department. Yet I insist upon a reply, and ask that you reveal your identity so I can send it to you.

Of course, you may prefer to stay anonymous and not receive my letter at all, let alone answer it. So you will decline to disclose your identity. If that is the case, I will simply place an unsealed copy of my reply under the door of each staff member from the school of philosophy so that everyone can read it. This will be a less than ideal solution for you, given some of the matters that will be aired in what I have to say. If you wish to avoid the voyeurism of your professional colleagues, you had better reveal yourself. Of course, your colleagues would still not know who you are, but it would certainly make for some interesting rumours and speculation.

Dr Jones, I will offer you a compromise on the matter of your identity. As a concession to your diffident nature, I will allow you to remain anonymous as long as you read and answer my reply. To enable this, you will have to offer a non-residential postal address, such as a PO box, so I can mail it to you. I'll even send it c / - of the department if you like - but only on the condition that you read my letter and send your response to me.

I will give you four weeks to either reveal your identity or provide the anonymous postal address. You can send these details to me at the following address.

PO Box 424,
Cartwell Point, 1968.

When you have given me the information, I will send you my reply. If you do not do so, I will simply send a copy to each staff member from your department. The choice is yours.

Jimmy Brandt.

That was all I wrote. I agree that my message is a little hostile in tone. Yet please remember the sequence of events I had been through. Jones' brief was to give me a fair hearing in arbitration, which he completely failed to do. He had basically destroyed my career, when he could have saved it. I did not threaten him with any kind of physical contact, nor did I intend any. I merely wanted to tell him in a letter what I thought of his conduct.

My message must have put Jones in a quandary as to how to respond. However, he seemed to decide that the best strategy was to ignore it in the hope I was bluffing. If so, Jones had again underestimated me. I printed twenty copies of my 'Reply to Jones,' went to the university at 7am one day, and put a copy under each office door in the department. It was not easy to do that but I was simply not going to let these people get away with what they'd done without staging some kind of protest.

I heard nothing back afterwards so that's where the story ends - but there's an amusing postscript. A couple of months later, I happened to be passing by the uni and decided to walk through the grounds for old times' sake. In the course of my stroll, I wandered past my old department and was surprised to find it fitted with security doors.

Now, I am not so self centred as to assume this was the result of my actions - yet the timing is certainly interesting. Never before had I seen security doors at any department of the university - yet suddenly there they were.

It was easy to speculate on the reason. To these timid fellows a chap who would write a thesis on the Hartford Papers, play Slayer music at a seminar, and stand up to bullying academics was clearly some kind of dangerous lunatic. Who knew what such a man was capable of?

Yet the irony is that I was the *victim*, not the villain, in this whole affair. It was the *university* which was guilty of unethical conduct. I had merely sought to stand up for myself. Yet here I was cast as the bad guy, the 'dangerous lunatic.' I was the one who had to be locked out with security doors.

All I'd sought to do was let Dr Jones know what I thought of his conduct as an 'independent judge.' It was a matter of honour and the determination to hold the bastard accountable. He had let me down badly. Indeed, he was prepared to destroy my career from a position of anonymity, and never took responsibility for his words or actions. In a university, of course, words *are* actions.

So that was it - it was over. As I left the University of Southern Sydney for the last time and mused on the travesty that had just played out, the true state of the world was clear. If there was some kind of battle between good and evil, there was no doubt which side was winning.

In the battle between good and evil, my PhD dispute might seem trivial compared, say, to horrendous acts of war or entrenched poverty in some third world nation - and so it was. But the university was not a third world regime. It was one place where you would expect real values and ideals to be at work. Reason, justice, and decency should prevail here, if nowhere else. Yet the whole affair had been a shambles. Acts of injustice had been committed and all of the perpetrators had gotten away with it.

Marriot had given a shoddy and inaccurate report on my thesis, and refused to let me answer any of his criticisms. Capette had been allowed to give an error-riddled trashing of my work, demand impossible reforms, and generally carry on like some kind of academic thug. Jones had been derelict in his duty as 'independent' arbiter. Meanwhile, Jacinta Lynton, a villain as yet lower down the food chain, had been able to lie, scheme, and manipulate her way up the academic ladder like the ruthless psychopath that she was.

And they got away with it. Each and every one of them.

Jacinta had won. Jones had won. Marriot and Capette had won. The processes of 'justice' had proven to be a ludicrous facade.

I saw with clarity that evil ruled this world. A university was one place you'd expect to find noble ideals and ethical practices. I certainly hadn't seen them during my PhD dispute.

Evil ruled. There could be no question of that now. In the terms given me by Iolango and Elijinx, if there was a battle between the Vortex Winder and the Maelstrom, there was no doubt which side was winning. From the lowest to the highest, in every realm of human affairs, one power ruled, and one image prevailed above all.

The Maelstrom Ascendant.

# 8
# Nowstalgia

You can revisit the site of an old love but if the source of that love is no longer there, it's a graveyard. Those times live on only in the heart, cherished and mortal as they were. You learnt the truth of it too late, when the end crept up like a hired assassin. My beloved home in the Blue Mountains with Sandra and Finzi is one such graveyard, and I am a restless ghost forever trying to escape.

Wait - what possesses me? There's no call for such morbid thoughts. Everything is alive and intact, just as it will be until the end of our days. Here we all are in the garden, bathing in the midday sun. I'm dozing in a chair. Sandra is sitting beside me reading a book. Finzi's asleep, curled into a ball, his little cat face tilted upwards.

What's come over me? If my beloved family is here safe, why this sudden melancholy? Nothing has been lost. Everything is just as it should be, and will always be. Still, a cloud hangs over this idyllic scene. I hear the toll of the old death knell - 'this too will pass.' Finzi is no longer a kitten. How long does a cat live? A few more years at most. There will be other cats but never another Finzi.

Neither will Sandra be spared. Our time together is finite. At best, we will grow old together. Perhaps I will even survive her and as an old man look back with sweet sadness at days like today. Still, that is far in the future - why feel the emotion now?

I resumed brooding on the PhD affair and contemplating my next move. There must be some way I could avenge myself. Closing my eyes, I turned my attention to that problem. There must be a path to follow. Surely it couldn't end like this.

Perhaps I could go to a higher court of appeal. Or enrol in a different university and resubmit my thesis under another title.

After all, one of the three examiners had passed it. If I could only find some allies in the academic world, or at least someone neutral who had no axe to grind.

When I opened my eyes again Finzi was gone. He must have wandered off to one of his garden haunts. Yet there was something amiss. A change in the atmosphere, a sense of dislocation. Turning to my right, I saw that Sandra too had vanished. The sun had retreated behind a cloud and a chill mountain wind ruffled the trees.

A wave of dread rose up, forcing me out of my comfortable chair. My surroundings had lost all familiarity. The garden, no longer shaped by human care, had grown wild to the tune of nature's unruly dance. It was as if I had dozed for twenty years, waking to find all those I loved had aged and died. The sense of surrealism was surpassed only by a rising panic. Yet there must be a meaning to this nightmare. The answers might be within reach, if I could only push the boundaries of this dream a little further. I forced myself into the house.

Entering, I recalled a dark moment from childhood. Once as a young boy, I'd gone to my grandparents' house and, not knowing they were away, rushed inside expecting the usual welcome. To find their house deserted had been oddly unnerving, for their absence stripped the house of warmth and meaning. The same sense of desolation seized me now. The house where Sandra and Finzi had once lived was ghostly, an empty seashell washed up on a shore in a world long abandoned by the human race.

I woke in my garden chair to find Sandra beside me once more. With tenderness, I gazed at her face, so familiar yet so doomed. My relief was tainted by a sense that the nightmare had not quite gone. It lingered, peering over the fence from the nether world into my waking life. Sandra's return was but a stay of execution. I searched her familiar face and saw that she had already passed from summer to autumn. Her soul beauty would sustain her into winter, then once that season had played itself out, Sandra's day would be done. Gone forevermore. So let me hold her 'til doomsday.

I went inside to see if the Vortex Winder if could shed any light on this strange experience and discovered that 'nowstalgia - nostalgia for the present'- was the new reigning power. There was a brief explanation.

*In the flower, the seed and the husk.*

*Wait not for the morrow to cherish the day.*

Nostalgia for the present? There was a certain symmetry in it. The power of hindsight had let me see pasts spiralling backwards. Now it was the future that shone a light on my own present moment.

Yet if that was the magic power, surely I was a little short changed. Nostalgia, after all, is a sweet emotion. There was only grief in what I had just gone through. Perhaps the gift was poisoned by my bitterness over the PhD affair and fears for the future.

I returned with urgency to the garden and held Sandra's hand as if she were on her deathbed. Our clasped hands gave small, futile comfort in the face of overwhelming forces.

Sandra frowned.

'Are you OK, Jimmy? You look weird.'

'You know, Sandra, even though we argue at times, there's nowhere I'd rather be than here with you. You are my home. The PhD, my music... it's all meaningless compared to you.'

'Well, it's nice to have the odd random declaration of love, I suppose.'

'You are my world. Being here with you and Finzi is all that matters.'

'That's very sweet of you, Jimmy, but we won't be able to stay here if the mortgage doesn't get paid. How are we going to live now you've chucked in your job?'

Oh Sandra. Practical as ever, even when I was so anguished myself. Still, she was not under the thrall of nowstalgia and the experience I had just suffered. The vivid hallucination had gone but the sense of dread remained. I remembered afresh what a crippling force love could be. All that mattered now was to make sure our love was secure and take away these awful fears.

There was no longer any anger or impatience in me as I sat with my beloved. Any fire, any strength or fight had been quite drained. Indeed, the thought of conflict or controversy of any kind was anathema. Nothing mattered except quiet domestic contentment with my beloved, and all other activities would now be dedicated to that end. The petty struggles of the recent past were as if in a dream. It was unfathomable I had ever courted such disasters, or raised a voice or a pen in anger. Well, no more. I would never again jeopardise our love. I replied quietly and without any hint of argument to Sandra's remark.

'I didn't chuck in the job, Sandra, I was fired. I lost the appeal, remember? But that's all over now. I'm not angry anymore - the whole episode is quite meaningless to me.'

'Are you sure? Last week I thought you were going to head into the uni with a bomb strapped to your chest. I was quite worried about you.'

'Please, Sandra, even the *thought* of conflict makes me nauseous. I can't bear it.'

'Oh good. How about some lunch then?'

'Impossible. I feel sick. I couldn't keep down so much as a lettuce leaf, or a single grape for dessert.'

'What's wrong with you? You're acting very strangely.'

'I've changed, Sandra. I'm not the man I was. Last week feels like a lifetime ago. Nothing matters now but a quiet life.'

'So, you're going to become a librarian or something?'

'A librarian? A librarian! That's a wonderful idea - I very well might. There's nothing I'd like more than to be surrounded by books in a peaceful hall of learning and quiet adventure. I'll look into it first thing in the morning.'

'OK Jimmy, whatever you think best. As long as this isn't another of your fads.'

'A fad? Please, Sandra. Give me some credit. All I want is a quiet job, a steady wage, and a simple life with you here. That'll do me. I'm going to study librarianship and apply for a job.'

'You're not going to tell them about your thesis on the occult or play heavy metal music at the interview, are you?'

'Sandra, please. That was another me. How could I ever have done that? It was asking for trouble. What on Earth was I thinking? It's clear now I brought it all on myself. The Hartford Papers! Whatever possessed me to write a PhD thesis about that? I tell you what, Sandy, if only we'd been together three years ago when I started, it would have all been very different. I would have picked some simple, respectable topic and done the most boring thesis possible. Goddammit, I might be an academic with a salary by now.'

'Have you been drinking or something, Jimmy? You really don't sound like yourself.'

'Myself? Who am I anyway? I'd rather be someone else.'

'You look like you've seen a ghost.'

'Maybe I have.'

'You've gone all... limp, or something. If this is the new you, I'm not sure I like him.'

'Time, Sandra, give me time. Everything's catching up with me. I'm evolving into someone quite new. The old me has gone, perhaps never to return. Maybe when the dust has settled, some parts of who I once was can rise up again.'

'Sounds a bit over-dramatic. So you lost your job - it's not the end of the world, you know.'

'I've seen the end of my world, Sandra. It's teaching me how to live.'

'And does that include lunch?'

'Not for me, Sandra. Not on this dark midday of the soul.'

Sandra shook her head.

'Get a grip, Jim! Who do you think you are - Hamlet or somebody? Stop being such a wanker! It's a beautiful summer day in Australia, not some Danish winter night.'

'Forgive me. I can't expect you to understand what I've just been through. You go and have lunch, I'll stay here and rest a while.'

Sandra left me to my inner torments. In my current state as an emotional cripple, every sentence she uttered was unbearably rich and painful. Why did love hurt so? I was questioning everything now. Changing, undoubtedly. Growing old. Perhaps I would indeed get a day job, become a librarian, or even move into the corporate world. In short, try to become more like Sandra. Assuming that would be a good idea. In some ways, Sandra had always been the yin to my yang and it had worked so far. A yin-yin pairing might be a disaster.

I had often wondered what drew us together. We were no pod-peas. Sandra was so straight. Conservative by nature, she'd never been one to take chances or tarry with the dark side of life. She didn't listen to metal, she'd rarely taken drugs or drink even in her youth. She'd always had the 9-5 job, insurance and all the other hallmarks of good common sense.

Her qualities were along the lines of order, solidity, and hearty warmth rather than dynamism or wild individuality - and how I yearned for it. After the drama, stress and loneliness of my affair with Freya, Sandra's simplicity was a great source of comfort.

Even so, there were times Sandra and I both wondered if we were really best suited. Yet here we were, still together. We weren't ideal partners but we were too old to hold on to fairytale notions of perfection. Having once foolishly thrown away my love with Jane Mara, I wasn't going to repeat the mistake just because Sandra wasn't perfect. Who the hell was I to ask for perfection?

Whatever our differences, ultimately it was that powerful opiate that kept me there. The warmth of companionship, the comfort of loving care and a home, the purring pussycat in his little round bed - all this the antidote to grim loneliness and the harshness of life.

And I just could not leave Finzi. The cat loved me. He'd hold onto to me like a grey koala, his little paws around my neck, purring so hard I could feel the vibrations. At times when Sandra and I argued, he loitered anxiously, even hiding under the bed if one of us raised a voice.

Finzi was not the only one afraid, for at such times I feared that the end was near. This immediately conjured a bleak, imagined future. The cat would be a sad footnote in the affair. As powerless as a child, he'd be the hidden victim, completely at the mercy of his adult guardians.

I imagined myself parting amicably with Sandra, perhaps moving on with someone else, staying in touch with Sandra from time to time. And always our conversations would end with my inevitable anxious query, '... and how is Finzi?'

Sandra would reply that he was fine, if perhaps missing me a little, or - as I would hear with a stab - getting on well with her new boyfriend. Yet inevitably the day would come when my query would be met with a stifled sob and the words, 'I'm sorry, Jimmy, Finzi died. He was very old and you knew it was always going to happen one day.' The thought of this scene filled me with an awful dread - and this, long before the Vortex Winder ever stirred up the power of nostalgia for the present.

Of course, I also thought of Sandra growing old, whether we broke up or not. Even if we stayed together, I feared my reckless past would one day catch up with me and exact its price. Letting Sandra down with my early death was my secret fear. She deserved better. Why should she, a healthy and responsible woman, be left to grow old alone because my youthful indulgence in booze, drugs, and rock n roll had taken its toll? What right had I to her love and loyalty now, if I was to leave her bereft in her twilight years?

Such was my pre-emptive sense of guilt towards her, stemming from the knowledge that she deserved care into her old age. At its most perverse, the guilt manifested in the 'consoling' thought of Sandra being struck down by illness, dying first, and absolving me of having let her down. The human mind works in strange ways.

As I swam fitfully around this morbid emotional soup, the only straw to clutch onto was that my path was now clear. I was on the straight and narrow, for good and for keeps. No more heavy rock or bizarre PhD theses or the other ridiculous nonsense of my youth. I would live a quiet and dignified life as a librarian and devote myself to the role of sober and loving husband for the rest of my days, content that I would do my best to never again let Sandra down or leave her to grow old alone.

# 9

# SMS: Save My Sanity

Under the grip of nowstalgia - nostalgia for the present - I spent much of the week gazing longingly at my loved ones. Yet Sandra soon tired of the attention. Even Finzi got sick of being picked up, and gave me a little warning nip. It was fortunate that after a few days I woke to a definite change in the atmosphere. The urge to moon around in a daze of hapless gratitude was replaced by a call to action. The Vortex Winder granted me 'the power of miniature reform' and gave an admonishment.

> *Don't try to save the world, only your own small part of it. Emotions without actions are empty.*

I could take a hint. Maybe it was time to get a job. The mortgage wouldn't pay itself.

Sandra's quip about becoming a librarian had struck a chord. The idea had a certain quiet dignity. Marshall stacks would be replaced by library stacks. I would spend my days in service as a custodian of learning and wholesome recreation.

Some training would be required, perhaps an actual degree. Surely that could be fast tracked. There'd be credit for prior study and I could knock off the rest at night after working during the day. Inspired, I decided to visit some local libraries to soak up the atmosphere and ask the staff what was needed to enter this noble profession.

I was no stranger to libraries after the three years at uni, but it had been a while since I entered a suburban one. It was a fond memory from childhood and as I settled into a soft chair, the old sense of peace came flooding back. I found a copy of Paul Gallico's *Love Let Me Not Hunger*, an extraordinary yet little-known book, and was soon absorbed in this dark fable of the human heart. Yet after a few minutes, my immersion in Gallico's world was shattered by a fearful anomaly - the discussion, in booming female tones, of house prices in 21st century Mosman.

The source of the intrusion was a middle-aged woman bellowing into a mobile phone. I'd come to expect this sort of thing in shops or on the street - but in a library? The barbarians were storming the citadel now.

I returned to the book and tried to ignore the woman's voice, hoping she'd wind up the call - but in the quiet of the library it was impossible to filter out the intrusion. There were two librarians at the main desk not fifteen metres from us. Why didn't they say something? If I'd been in charge, the woman would have been out on her ear. Yet there they stood, staring down at their desks like two little mice, too timid to step in and do their duty. Oh my, how standards had slipped since the days of the stern, strict librarians of my youth.

I directed a disapproving glare at the woman on the phone, to no avail. The 'monologue' as it effectively was, continued unchecked. It was time to step in.

'Excuse me,' I said, hoping no further words would be needed.

The woman seemed put out at the interruption. 'Do you mind? I'm on the phone.' She turned her back on me and resumed talking. I was for a while struck dumb. After a few seconds of pure astonishment, breath and strength returned.

'Excuse me. Can you take your phone call outside? This is a *library.*'

To my further surprise, this provoked a torrent of language such as one would not expect to hear in the leafy suburbs of Mosman. There would be no voice of reason here today. Shaking my head, I put Gallico back on the shelf and left the building.

Well, libraries had certainly changed since my day. If this was acceptable now, maybe the idea of becoming a librarian wasn't so great after all. Pristine halls of silence? Hallowed cloisters of learning? More like a goddamn cafe at Sydney airport. Perhaps this event was a warning. How would it be if I went through all that training at night only to get the job and find that libraries were no better than shopping malls? This called for a Plan B. So, if not a job in a library, perhaps some quiet sector of the business world, or a sleepy shop without much human traffic. Anything but this.

I stopped at the bank. The queue was long and the service short. Some management big shot must have earned himself a bonus by laying off half the staff. The guy in front of me in the queue, as bored as me, pulled out his phone and made a call. His voice filled the room until there was no space left in it for me. For the second time in an hour, I beat a retreat.

The third phone incident happened the next day. I'd caught the bus into town for a job interview. The job was nothing special, just a short term filler to tide me over.

To make the bus trip pass more quickly, I'd taken a list of German phrases to study. Not that I was planning a return to Germany or Freya - that was years in the past - but it's nice to keep your hand in. Generally, the Vortex Winder's powers are here one week, gone the next. If their value is to endure, it's a matter of trying to retain some of what's been learned. Last week's power of nowstalgia had made a mark. The lesson stayed with me and affected my present actions. In the same way, I remembered some of the other past powers. For a brief time, the Vortex Winder had given me perfect command of the German language. While that had passed, the memory inspired me to try to reach those heights on my own - so I made occasional efforts to learn the language in spare moments.

The bus was nearly empty and I sat near the back, memorising the words. Before long my concentration was broken by a strange voice. A young man had boarded the bus, sat behind me, and begun a conversation on his phone. I moved to the front of the bus but his voice was still audible. Naturally I had no interest in this guy's affairs and only wanted to sit in peace and study my German phrases, but his phone call went on and on. Finally, he got off in the city. As he left the bus, he put the phone in his pocket and pulled out a packet of cigarettes. Taking a cigarette from the pack, he lit up and walked away.

At that moment, I realised why we have laws. Why had the guy not smoked on the bus? It was nothing to do with regard for other people. The only thing which stopped him smoking was the law against it. Without this law, he would have chain smoked for the entire trip and been just as indifferent to the effects on others as he was to the effects of his phone call. The only thing stopping him was that smoking on the bus is illegal.

Not everyone needs laws. There are some people who are not oblivious to the rights of others. They realise that there are other human beings around and we should consider them, treat them well, and try not to annoy them. These people are a minority but they exist. They would behave the same even under a state of anarchy.

For everyone else, we have laws. The laws step in where nature and nurture have failed so miserably. Truly it would be a good world if we could count on people to always be polite and considerate of others. But that is not the world we are living in, so we need laws to do the job of compelling people to act as if they were polite and considerate of others, even though they are not.

In the past, people were allowed to smoke on buses. Eventually, it became illegal, mainly for health reasons and also because non-smokers did not want to be engulfed in smoke in a confined space. So all we have to do now is wait for the law to catch up with the far worse habit of people making phone calls on the bus. Speaking for myself, I would far sooner be engulfed in smoke than forced to listen to random phone calls.

While some readers may nod in agreement at this point, others will wonder what I'm on about and think me a dreadful old whiner. *But why?* they may ask. *What is your problem?* Of course, they are entitled to their views - but if I can respectfully make my case, perhaps my reasons will become clear.

It's like this. A bus is a public place and unless you can afford both a car and a parking space in the city, it's a necessary evil. The idea is to make it less rather than more evil. The fact is we have to share the bus with others for a short time each day, crammed in together against our will. We're already invading each other's personal space and shouldn't make it any worse. We should let each other travel in peace.

So what's wrong with a phone call? Well, remember that during my bus trip, I'd brought along a list of German words to learn. Does anyone care about this? No, not at all. As it happens, I'm learning the German language - but this is irrelevant to most other people in the entire world. Knowing this, I confine myself to memorising the words silently.

If I were a thoughtless person, I might read the words out loud. Can you imagine? I'm sitting there on the bus reciting a list of German words and phrases. My voice is loud enough for the whole busload of passengers to hear. Would they appreciate hearing me loudly and clumsily reciting a list of German words? No. Not unless, by some amazing coincidence, they were also learning German and were at the same level as myself. In that case, they might be thrilled to hear my halting, schoolboy recitation. But it is far more likely none of my fellow passengers are learning German. While they might respect my personal quest to master the German language, they have no wish to share it while innocently taking a bus trip into town.

After all, it's likely that some of the other passengers will be reading books. If so, I should let them read in peace. It would in no way enhance their reading experience to superimpose an aural stream of badly pronounced German.

To put it another way, imagine one of those reading passengers decided to read her book aloud. In fact, loud enough for the whole bus to hear. Perhaps, if she read from the start of the book, people might be interested enough to listen and then buy the book themselves. Yet the chances are our reader would not be reading from the start. On that bus trip she might, for example, be reading from page 81 to page 89. Unless, by a huge coincidence, her fellow passengers were reading the same book and were also up to page 81, it's unlikely anyone would want to hear her reading it aloud.

It's safe to say most people on the bus aren't interested in hearing me recite German words any more than they are in hearing some girl read aloud page 81 to 89 of a random book. That's why we do our reading silently, because we know other passengers only want a peaceful bus ride into the city, have no interest in us, and it is not OK for us to inflict our affairs on them. We know that our own interests are fascinating to us but boring to others.

Why then is it alright for someone to bellow his or her equally boring affairs into a mobile phone?

The habit seems to be normal now, and taken for granted. You can't even blame the younger generation, because many older people are just as bad. Young people would have no memory of the time when you could travel on a bus quietly, (just as they have no memory of vinyl records, cassettes, or even CDs). So future generations will have no experience of being able to travel on the bus or train without a bunch of phone calls polluting the air.

Anyhow, back to the job interview. It was a waste of time. The interviewer seemed to have already picked someone and was just going through the motions. As compensation, I bought myself a cheap twelve string guitar from a pawnshop. At least I'd have something to show for the trip into town. I boarded the bus for the journey home, placed the guitar in the seat beside me, and took out my book once again.

No sooner had I settled down in my seat than there was a disturbance behind me. A loud male voice started up as enticingly as a lawnmower on Sunday morning.

At this point, the thought occurred that not only was I becoming obsessed with this phone issue, but the obsession was *itself* attracting such incidents! Either that, or else phones were just everywhere now and there was no escaping them.

The 'conversation' went something like this, although of course we only got his half of it. There was a gap of several seconds while the other half, unheard by us in the bus, was spoken.

'Hi honey. Just finished. I'm on the bus... I missed you too... How was your day? Uh huh... huh... You don't say? Well, how about pizza? Anything, as long as they deliver. I'm not going out again.'

The guy was interrupted by another high pitched ring tone, apparently from his second phone.

'Sorry honey, got another call. Ring you back... Pete? How ya doing? No, still no word. Fucking Melbourne, what do they do all day down there?... About as much use as an ashtray on a motorbike... Have you tried Webby? I'll give him a bell and find out... Mate, it's not a problem... Yeah, I know. I've had better service at King's Court... Leave it with me, big fella. I'll call him now, then give my wife a quick buzz and get back to ya.'

So, now there were three phone calls queued up. Melbourne, the wife, and Webby - and still another forty-five minutes til my bus stop.

'Babe? Sorry, that was work... No there's no prob, I'll tell you later... What?... Awww, I missed you too, honey.'

Missed her? They were only on the line two minutes ago. What are they, newly-weds?

'How's Jayden, honey? Did he do OK in kindy today?'

Kindergarten? So they've been together at least five years and they're still on the honeymoon. Oh well, good for them - but why do I have to hear about it?

'Hi buddy. How was school? Awww, that's nice Jaydee... I'll be home soon and you can tell me all about it... Really? You did, did you... I can't wait to see it... OK, put Mummy back on... Hi honey... You what? The smaller kitchen? Sure, it makes sense if it gives us pantry options. Or we could leave it alone and have that more spacey feel, know what I mean? But the other option would be...'

Let's leave it there. Now, tell me - *do you really want to know?* Do you want to know what Daddy, Honey, and Jaydee's other kitchen renovation options were? I sure didn't. I turned around to face the guy and called on inner reserves of politeness.

'Excuse me, my good sir.'

He ignored me.

'Excuse me, sir,' I said louder. He heard this time but seemed confused at my archaic mode of speech, so I modernised it.

'Hey champ, can you please get off the phone? I'm trying to read my book.'

The guy looked a little put out.

'Honey, hold on a mo. There's some kind of weirdo on the bus. Call you back in a minute. What's up, mate?'

'Listen, mate, can you save your phone call for later? I'm trying to read here.'

'I'm just talking to my wife.'

'You're gonna see her in a few minutes anyhow. Why not talk to her then?'

'Because I want to talk to her now. What's it got to do with you anyway? It's none of your business.'

'Exactly my point. Your marriage is none of my business. Let's keep it that way?'

'Huh?'

'Like you said, mate, what you do with your wife's got nothing to do with me. So why do I have to hear about it? I don't care what you're having for dinner, big fella.'

The dude was getting angry now. He puffed up his chest and glared.

'I was *talking to my son!*'

'Good for you, but you see him every day at home, right? You don't have to call him from the bus too. Look, I wish your family all the best, but I don't need to hear about your business deals or your personal life. I just want to read my book in peace.'

'There's no law against making phone calls on the bus.'

'And don't I know it.'

'This is a public place. It's not a private vehicle for your own personal use. Stop being so selfish.'

That one took me by surprise. Strangely enough, from his own perspective he was right, and I had no business telling him what to do. But I didn't see it like that. It took me a moment to reply.

'Why don't you think about what you just said?'

'There's no law against phone calls and I have every right to make them.'

'Yes, but it would be public spirited not to.'

'If you've got a problem, buddy, then take a taxi.'

'I should spend fifty bucks on a taxi because you can't wait fifteen minutes to talk to your wife?'

'Look, get over yourself, you moron. It's not my problem if you don't have a life. Some of us have jobs, you know, and if a client calls me I'm gonna talk to him. Some of us have friends and wives and kids. Maybe if you got some yourself, you'd be able to make some phone calls on the bus too instead of sitting there like a knob reading a book.'

'Thanks for the tip, champion. Now here's one for you. Instead of talking 24/7, why not spend a few minutes a day in quiet contemplation? Try reading a book yourself sometime. Learn a musical instrument. Anything!'

The dude glanced down at the guitar case I'd picked up in the city. He snorted.

'What for? So I can be like you with your little guitar there? You don't like my phone calls? OK Bob Dylan, why don't you write a protest song about it.'

So that's exactly what I did - and it came out so well that the next logical step was to go into the studio and record it.

# 10
# Waves Upon Waves

On hearing the news that I was recording new songs, Sandra performed a handstand, cracked a bottle of champagne, and fell to her knees before me in lustful homage. Or at least the Sandra in some other universe did. In my universe she just lay on the couch watching *The Office* on TV.

'You hear me, Sandra? I'm going to lay down some new songs.'

'Making another comeback, Jimmy?'

'Who said anything about a comeback? It's just a few guitar riffs that have been around for a while and the lyrics finally caught up with them.'

'What happened to your big dream of becoming a librarian?'

'Yeah, maybe. First we've got to make it the kind of world where it's *worth* becoming a librarian.'

'Huh?'

'Maybe the power of miniature reform is still operating - through my songs.'

'What on earth are you talking about?'

'I'll explain later. And before you ask, of course I'm still job hunting. The music's just something to do in my spare time.'

I meant it too. This was never a comeback. There was no thought of fame and glory this time. I was too old for that and all the crap that went with it. But music as self-expression, sure, why not? With the price of recording studios, you can't say it was 'cheaper than therapy' but it was much more effective. The new song 'Temporary Kingdom' was the best example of that - six verses of pure hate against those involved in the PhD dispute. A vow to my enemies that they would be held accountable for their crimes, if not in this world, then in the next. Whether or not this would actually happen, it was a relief to articulate the idea.

By comparison, 'SMS: Save My Sanity,' the mobile phone song, was almost a comedy piece. "Everywhere I go, there's dickheads on the phone" - straight to the point from the first line. Another one was called 'Leuchtturm,' the German word for lighthouse, which dated back to the Freya era.

As the songs came together, I felt a sense of surprised excitement. It wasn't a bad batch of songs at all - and before long, the old megalomania stirred from dormancy once more. Maybe these songs would be the ones to do it for me, to finally take me somewhere in this world. These thoughts were not spoken out loud but they were implied in some of the lyrics. There was a renewed sense of purpose and possibility. 'Waves Upon Waves' was 100% fighting talk - a statement of intent against all the enemies who thought I was dead and cold in my grave. Meanwhile 'LHXIII' was an invocation of divine energy from above and beyond. I had named the band 'Lighthouse XIII' when the *Vortex Winder* album came out, now here was the song to match it. It was like when Zeppelin had an album called *Houses of the Holy* but the actual song of that name didn't appear until the next record.

I'm condensing this story to avoid boring the reader. Who, after all, wants to hear about the long, complicated process of songwriting, rehearsal and recording? It holds little interest for people whose only concern is the final product. Yet in turn, please do me the honour of realising it didn't all happen in a puff of magic fairy dust. I will omit the boring details if you'll at least acknowledge that those boring details existed. The songs did not somehow emerge fully formed on a CD or on Spotify!

So let's move the story along. The five new songs were recorded with my old mates Dave on drums and Steve as producer. The songs made up a new EP called *Waves Upon Waves*. I did all the guitar and vocals. Results exceeded expectations. Even Sandra, no heavy rocker by any stretch, was impressed - although still hopeful the project's end would signal my return to gainful employment.

It would probably have happened too if not for the 'SMS' video going viral on YouTube. The video was little more than a low budget comedy skit. I hired a few young actors and paid them to be annoying in public places. Hell, I doubt there was much acting involved! One of them played me trying to read on the bus, getting pissed off by people talking on the phone. There were several other good scenes. My favourite is when he throws that paperback Frisbee style and knocks the phone out of the woman's hands in the library. Although the one where he lobs the businessman's phone into the restaurant fish tank runs a close second.

The final video was quite the laugh when we watched it back on YouTube. Even Sandra chuckled along, although she stopped short of sending it to her friends. When it became a hit, they started sending it to her. The clip's popularity was nowhere near that of my appalling 'Chica Boom' sensation of a few years before. That embarrassing clip had long since faded into the murk of YouTube obscurity, thank God, but 'SMS: Save My Sanity' ended up something of a hit in its own right.

It must have been those bloody wannabe actors I hired. They probably sent it on to all and sundry, and watched the thing on a loop to get the view count ticking over. The subject matter of the song also struck some kind of discord with the public. Seems I wasn't the only one over the mobile phone fad, although in truth the video did also draw a lot of counter aggression like I'd copped from the guy on the bus. I considered disabling comments on the video. But no, if I was to make a complaint, others were entitled to answer back - and it was all good publicity.

There were consequences to the song's success. When I became semi-recognisable from the clip, some people made a point of making calls if they spotted me nearby. Apart from that, an ironic side effect was that the riff from 'SMS' became a popular ringtone.

Yet the biggest consequence was the rebirth of my music career. Before long there were a few inquiries about 'coming gigs' by

Lighthouse XIII. A little light went on at that point. Not just in my head but on the screen of the Vortex Winder. There were only two words on there.

*Why not?*

Why not?

Coming gigs, eh? Hmm, why not indeed? Maybe there was a tiny window of opportunity here. I could sling Dave a few bucks to play drums, then as long as I could force myself to front up on vocals, all we needed was a bass player.

Sure enough, by the time the video was up to 100,000 views on YouTube, Dave, myself, and a newly found bass player named Viv had a set's worth of material ready to go live. The set was made up of the new tracks, along with some of the easier songs off *Vortex Winder* - 'Black Art,' 'Trade Winds' and 'Z Club' for example. 'Elijinx' was too hard to play and sing so it never got a run back then. 'Temporary Kingdom' with its hyperactive riffing and vocals was in the same category.

It all sounds very easy, doesn't it? Yes - when the tale is condensed into a couple of pages. Don't forget I'm omitting all the finer details - the hours of preparation and rehearsal, the hassle of moving heavy equipment around, my own grave anxiety about whether I'd have the balls to get up and sing in front of a crowd.

Having said that, I'll admit the YouTube smash gave us a turbo boost through several of the steps a band normally has to face on the hard slog upwards. We didn't have to scrap like stray dogs for gigs just to get a foot on the ladder. We rarely faced the blank, indifferent stares of crowds who had no idea who we were. We didn't have to slog and pimp for every crumb of publicity.

No, there's no denying that without 'SMS' becoming a YouTube hit, we would never have made it past square one so quickly - or at all, to be honest. Yet all of a sudden, here we were playing gigs in pubs to decent sized, appreciative crowds. It was a fast ride from oblivion to some kind of basic success.

Although still daunted by singing in public, I'd learned to live with the idea. Having appeared in the 'SMS' video, I'd gotten through the barrier of being unknown and was less worried what people would think of a forty year old guy up on the stage. A singer - me? Why not? Why shouldn't I be?

In time, I even got comfortable enough to get a bit of a comedy routine going. 'SMS' was the one song everyone knew, so me and the drummer, Dave, had this shtick where we'd play the first two verses then I'd stop and start fumbling round in my pocket. The audience would quit moshing and wonder what was going on. I'd take a phone out of my pocket and say 'sorry, I've got a call.' There'd be boos, a few blank looks, and some titters. Then I'd say, 'wrong number' and toss the phone to Dave. He'd smash it on the floor of the stage and we'd go straight into the guitar solo. It was cool once people caught on to the joke. We had a bagful of second hand phones backstage and smashed a different one every night.

One Saturday after a good show the night before, I was hanging out at home with Sandra.

'You surprise me, Jim. Who'd have thought of all this? But where do you see it heading from here?'

'South.'

'I thought you'd be a bit more optimistic after what's happened.'

'I mean, we've been offered a three week tour of Victoria and South Australia.'

'Really? That's great, I suppose - but Finzi and I will miss you.'

'It's only three weeks. At least it'll help me catch up on my share of the mortgage.'

Events were indeed moving fast. To help me make sense of it, I continued my practice of keeping a journal about my experiences. First the PhD dispute and now this. Perhaps it would all end up in a new book, a sequel to *The Vortex Winder*.

At this stage, Lighthouse XIII did not have a record deal but both the new EP and the *Vortex Winder* album were selling a few copies online and at our gigs. After so long in the wilderness, it was a novelty to have a taste of success. I was so caught up in the euphoria of the moment it was easy to downplay the less agreeable aspects of life in a band, especially once the three week tour started. The tedious travel, the poor sleep, the general weirdness of being away from home and cooped up with a bunch of guys in a van. In those heady early days, none of this fazed me much. That we were going over well with the crowds and selling a few CDs made the whole thing a lot more palatable.

Suddenly, there were even a few business proposals on the table. A number of managers took an interest. However, they either promised too much or too little. I was not so naive as to think this business would be easy, so a couple of guys who seemed to offer the world were viewed with suspicion. I also resisted those who offered contracts binding me for years, or that were conditional on making basic changes to the band.

The one I ended up going with was a guy named Ted Hoffman. In his sales pitch, he seemed to strike a balance between realism and hope. He took a personal interest in me and showed no sign of wanting to take away my creative control. Ted showed up one night after a gig in Adelaide. I was sitting up the back of some club in Hindley street, having an after-show beer when he approached me and sat down at my table.

I saw a man of about fifty who, despite having made no effort to dress or act like any of the club's much younger patrons, somehow seemed to be the coolest person in the room. His greying hair lent him gravitas, yet his eyes hinted at jocularity. Although he spoke simply, his accent was that of an educated Englishman. I was drawn to him at once. We shook hands and he gave me his card.

'Ted Hoffman, Solar Eclipse Management - and my first question is, what's a band as good as this doing without a manager?'

'Touring, making records.'

'You mean this?' Hoffman said, holding up the purple *Vortex Winder* CD. 'Fair play to you, old boy. You've had the chutzpah to put out your own album. Yet you don't have a record deal or any kind of plan. How far are you going to get then?'

'I thought record deals died out a few years ago for small bands, didn't they?'

'Good Lord, no - not at all. Still, if you're happy flogging a few CDs at little club gigs like this, then by all means stay as you are - an indie muso. See how long you'll do that before the thrill wears off. I'm afraid it's only a matter of time before you limp off into the sunset.'

'Of course I'd like a proper deal. You got something? Maybe we can talk next week when the tour's over.'

'I'm back in London by then, so let's get to the point. You're a talented artist who deserves a chance. I'm a manager who can give you a shot at the UK and Europe. I'll get you a contract and distribution deal with Momentum Records in England and a spot on a three month package tour of Europe.'

'What - playing supports?'

'It's a four band package. You'll be third or fourth on the bill to start but we'll bump you up a notch if it's going well. You'll also have the chance to open for a couple of major league acts, perhaps even some festival spots.'

'Festivals? Which ones?'

'There's Wacken in Germany. The UK Download Festival. That's two for a start.'

'I can't play in front of that many people. We've only been gigging a couple of months.'

'Don't get ahead of yourself, old boy. We're only talking the second stage at Download and next year, not now. You'll build up to that. Three months in Europe will harden you up. You need a lot more exposure. A novelty hit on YouTube is a start but long term it won't have much legs - and you need proper distribution or it's all just wasted energy. Momentum Records will give you that. We'll get you onto iTunes and the rest of the digital stores. Sure, you've got talent and some good songs - but how are people ever going to hear them without proper promo and distribution? And how are they going to know to look for your stuff in the first place if you're not out there touring? This deal covers both sides.'

My head was spinning. Record deals, festivals, touring? Still, everything this Hoffman guy said made sense. He seemed like a real straight shooter too, neither buttering me up nor trying to intimidate me, just telling it like it is. I also liked the way he didn't try to pose as some kind of hard-ass by filling every sentence with swear words. No gratuitous fucks, motherfuckers, or the rest of the standard rock patter. I had to hear more of what he had to offer.

'This is all very interesting, uh, Ted,' I said, squinting at his business card, 'but are there any conditions attached to this deal?'

'Conditions?'

'Would I have to change the style of the music, get another singer in, that sort of thing?'

'Here at Solar Eclipse Management we have a strict policy of non-interference. The artist takes care of the art and we take care of the business. It's not for us to tell you how to play. That's your domain. If we didn't believe in you, we wouldn't be here in the first place.'

'We're on the same page then - but what do you think of the vocals? I never meant to be a singer, you know.'

'Neither did James Hetfield or Dave Mustaine, did they? You'll find a lot of guys ended up doing it by default and it worked out in the long run. Let's play it by ear for now. I do know a couple of singers who might be available if you want to go down that path. There's Damien from Rat Finger, for one. He's just walked out on them.'

'Walked out, did he? What is he - some kind of diva? There's a strict no-dickheads policy in this band.'

Hoffman raised his eyebrows.

'Let's hope that policy isn't applied too widely or this would shrink to a very small industry indeed. Although in reality a lot of those ones fall by the wayside. It's the decent, easy-to-work-with types who go the distance.'

'How's it work, this European tour? Who's going to organise all the shows and hotels and the rest of it?'

'As a Solar Eclipse artist, you'll be given a tour manager who'll take care of all that for you. Your job is simply to play, stay healthy, and make sure you put on a killer show every night.'

'I'd love to say yes, Ted, but it's not like I can just pick up and go. How am I supposed to put my life on hold for three months?'

'You married, Jimmy?'

'No, but I live with someone. Sandra.'

'Been together long?'

'A few years on and off.'

'Any kids?'

'Just a cat.'

'So Sandra, doesn't she support your dreams?'

'Uh sure, more or less. I mean she does in a way, up to a point. One thing for sure, she won't be too thrilled about me going to Europe for three months.'

Hoffman slapped his open hand on the table-top and gave me a stern look.

'Jimmy, my boy, you've got talent. Are you going to use it or let it go to waste? There's a clear choice here. You can get a proper record deal and tour your music through Europe and the rest of the world, or you can stay here playing tiny clubs in Australia then go home and massage your wife's feet? Wait, she's your girlfriend, right? You're not even married, are you?'

'No.'

'Then what are you waiting for? Are you going to let your girlfriend hold you back? It's positively criminal.'

'Of course I want to go, Ted, but I can't just drop everything.'

'Then let me say this. At Solar Eclipse, we believe in keeping the artist happy. We don't believe the rubbish about great art coming out of suffering. Or to be fair, even if does start out like that, you're not going to stick it out on tour if you're not enjoying yourself. So, because I like you and believe in you, I'll make you a special offer. We'll fly Sonia out for the last four weeks of the tour.'

'Sandra.'

'Indeed, Sandra. We'll pay the airfare but you'll take care of expenses. Just between you and me though, if Sandra doesn't make it, there's plenty of Sonias out on the road, know what I mean? Plenty of beautiful girls in Europe, right?'

'I'm not doing this to pick up girls, Ted, I'm too old for that.'

'You're only as young as you feel - and there are plenty of ways to feel young on the road. You may lay to that.'

'Let me think it over and talk to Sandra.'

'Very well, Jimmy, I'll leave you with one final question. When you're lying on your death bed, what are you going to regret - the things you did or didn't do?'

Back in Sydney, I spent the weekend in a state of content at the tour's end and my family's obvious delight in my return. Finzi constantly asked to be picked up and purred his little head off when I obliged. Sandra was equally pleased to have me home. Yet Hoffman's offer nagged away and by Sunday night, there was no more delaying the talk we had to have.

'Sandra, the band's been offered a record deal and a three month tour of Europe.'

'Three months? You've just been away three weeks.'

'You might have at least said congratulations.'

'I suppose it's what you've always wanted, isn't it - but three months?'

'Not much point going all that way for three days.'

'What's this deal anyway?'

'It's with Momentum Records in England. I'll be signed to Solar Eclipse Management - some guy named Ted Hoffman I met in Adelaide.'

'Is there any money in it?'

'There'd better be, surely. I've not had a chance to look at the numbers yet.'

Sandra said nothing and seemed to be undergoing an internal struggle. Finzi, sensing a change in the atmosphere, had stopped purring and was sitting on the floor looking anxiously from one of us to the other. Finally Sandra broke the silence.

'I've got to be honest, Jimmy. It's amazing what you've done. You proved me wrong. But it's not what I want - someone who's away half the year on tour.'

'Half the year? It's only three months.'

'What about the next tour, then the one after that? I'd much prefer it if you had a normal job, like that librarian job you were going to train for.'

'You're always on about paying off the mortgage. What if I make it big over in Europe? We can pay it off super quick and retire.'

'How long's that going to take - two years? Five years? You going to slog it out that long?'

'Maybe in five years I'll make enough money to never have to work again.'

'And what if you don't? What happens if you slog it out for five years and there's nothing to show for it at the end? You'll be pushing fifty. What then? You'll be too old to train for a new job.'

'I'm getting a real glass-half-empty vibe here.'

'I worry about you all the time, Jimmy. What going to happen to you? If you blow all your money on this, I guess it's going to be me and my savings supporting us both down the line. You'll end up as some annoying old man, half deaf, a washed up rocker without two coins to rub together. Ozzy without the money! Then it'll be up to Super-Sandra to step in and save the day.'

'Wow, that bad! Look on the bright side. If I do turn into an annoying old man, you can always have me put down.'

I was trying to lighten the mood partly for the sake of poor Finzi, who was alarmed by the tension in our voices. Sandra didn't laugh.

'You can joke about it, but how much fun will retirement be with no money saved?'

'Not much, I agree. So it's probably best to hang up my guitars and get back on the straight and narrow for good. Question is, would I ever forgive myself? On my death bed, would I forgive myself for passing up the chance of a record deal and a tour of Europe? I'd never know what might have been.'

'I know. That's why I can't stand in your way. It's a terrible thing to say, but sometimes I wish we'd never met.'

'You're right. It *is* a terrible thing to say. Look Sandra, I know it's a risk and you're no risk-taker. That's your nature. Squeaky clean, straight down the line. That's just you. But the fact is, no matter how safe you play it, there are no guarantees. There's plenty who did everything by the book and never put one foot out of line - only to get struck down by cancer or something and found out the whole thing was a lie. Life's a risk no matter what course you take. I have to give this a shot. How about a middle way? I'll do this one tour and if we don't see some real progress, I'll throw in the towel for good.'

'Can you do that? What will your manager say?'

'If he says no I won't sign. The record deal and one tour, no promises after that.'

'OK Jimmy, I can see this is something you have to do. You've explained it to me. Now, explain it to him.'

She pointed at Finzi, sitting in a chair looking at us with anxious green eyes. With a pang of genuine sorrow, I picked him up. He put his sweet little cat face against my cheek and his paws around my neck. The purring machine went into effect, but I fancied I could feel a stutter within it, a terminal uncertainty.

'Don't worry, Finzi. It's all going to work out for the best. I'll take photos of your European cousins and send them to you. Then before you know it, we'll all be back together again just like always.'

# Part Two

# 11
# The Dream

So, there I was out on a rock tour at last. It was a dream come true. A glorious rock n roll nirvana to die for. Right?

Not quite.

Some people have the idea that the rock star life is a never ending parade of limos, five star hotels, drugs, groupies, wealth, and adoring crowds at sold out shows. It may be like that if you're U2, Metallica, or that sort of league - but for an up and comer it's nothing like that at all.

Don't get me wrong, it was fun at first. The tour was a blast for a few weeks - part overseas holiday, part booze-fuelled rock party. The exact point it morphed into hellish grinding slog isn't clear, but it probably started with a hangover and went from there.

The tour began in the UK in the last month of summer. There was us, Acador, Bioscream and Crank Hammer. As Ted Hoffman had promised, our album was out now through Momentum Records and on iTunes. We'd done another video, for the song 'Life Line' this time, and we were generating some buzz and a few sales. Nothing seismic, nothing to email home about - but it was a start. We were the second act on the four band bill, and going down well most nights. A typical setlist from that time was like this:

1. Vortex Winder
2. SMS
3. Z Club
4. Black Art
5. Mountain Gods
6. Waves Upon Waves
7. Trade Winds

By the time we moved on to the Netherlands, Belgium and France we were doing a little business and tightening up as a live act. It was a buzz being in a different city every day or two, playing the show, partying while the last two bands played, then waking up and doing it all again the next day.

I tried not to let the partying get out of hand, although in that sort of environment it can be hard to escape. At the very least, it could be balanced out by getting up early enough to see some of the town we were playing that night. It would be a hell of a waste visiting those old European cities if we did nothing more than go from the tour bus to the gig and back.

And what of the Vortex Winder? It seemed to have gone to sleep. I pulled it out of my luggage every two or three days but the little screen remained blank. Perhaps it figured that now my rock n roll dreams were coming true, its work was done.

The four bands were spread out over three tour buses. Acador, the headliners, had their own bus, as did Bioscream. The lowest ranked bands, Lighthouse XIII and Crank Hammer, had to share the third bus. The crew guys bunked in as well, while a couple of trucks followed with the equipment.

There was no single point at which this whole escapade changed from dream-come-true to hellish grind. It was a gradual process which began to set in from about the third week of the tour. It was then I became aware of having lost touch with three old friends I'd taken for granted - sleep, space, and privacy. You could throw in youth as a fourth, the presence of which may have made up for losing the other three.

One thing for sure, we weren't booked into any five star hotels on that tour. Not that I expected it, but some of the punters out there think it's glamour all the way. Yeah, the dream! The reality for someone at this level is more likely sleeping in the back of a van, a bunk on the tour bus, or if you're lucky, two or three guys to a cheap hotel room.

It's not for me to bitch about it - you've got to start somewhere. But personal space is important to me and there were even times I flashed back to my stint in the Thai prison, especially on waking up at 4am in a room full of guys snoring off a booze binge. At times like that there were always a few confused seconds wondering where the hell I was. The relieved discovery that I was not in the prison, but on a rock tour of Europe, made me kick my own arse for excessive whinging.

Don't get me wrong, the guys in the bands were cool. Yet with most of them in their twenties, I was the oldest muso in the whole party. There were a couple of grizzled veterans in the crew, but most of the band members were just kids compared to an old rocker like me.

It was nearly all guys as well with hardly a female on the tour. A very male sort of atmosphere. This was fine up to a point. The boozing, swearing, metal on the sound system - that was all well and good. But stuff like the body odour, burping, farting, and crude practical jokes - yeah, I found all that funny when I was eighteen too, but now in my forties I just found it annoying.

Still, the last thing I was going to be was some aloof, moody old bastard up the back of the tour bus. If anything, I drank - and sometimes drugged - a little more than normal to be one of the boys and fit in with the whole vibe of the tour. Of course, there was a price to pay the next day when I had to drag my hungover carcass through another show. Adrenalin, music, and contractual obligation pulled me through. And what am I gonna do after the set - go to bed? Well maybe, if I can find somewhere to sleep which won't be disturbed by one of the umpteen band members, crew, fans or hangers-on around the tour. It was often easier to carry on the party a bit longer to deaden my senses to the whole circus going on around me.

In the end, it was straight out fatigue which wore me down. The hangovers were certainly harder to shake off than they were a decade ago. Now they formed an unholy alliance with sleep deprivation with the sole aim of grinding me down into the dust.

They weren't my only enemies. Indeed, I sensed the approach of a 'perfect storm' of adversaries lining up to destroy me. Serious health worries loomed up on one side, financial problems on the other. There were even a few scraps of neurotic energy left to stress over actual music issues, such as writing songs for the next album or my ongoing difficulty singing on stage.

Against this combined attack and in my fatigued state, I began to miss Sandra badly, even to the point of over-idealising our relationship. Absence makes the heart grow fonder and so does distance. Half a world away, I yearned for what now seemed a perfect, near-flawless love affair which had been so recklessly left behind. We'd chat on the phone every couple of days and I'd try not to let on how much I missed her. One night we spoke as soon as I got offstage, still buzzing from the gig.

'Jimmy, is that you? Where are you calling from?'

Her voice sounded cruelly close, as if she were in the next street rather than thousands of kilometres away.

'I'm not sure. Somewhere in Italy.'

'Rome? Venice?'

'Hell no. Some little town you've never heard of.'

'Lucky you - I'm so jealous! You made your millions yet?'

'Sure, Sandra. We're headlining Wembley next week and Madison Square Gardens after that, then we can all retire to the Bahamas. To be honest, I'd trade it all to be sitting at home right now with you and Finzi.'

'I'm worried about Finzi, he's got some kind of feline depression. Last week I found him moping around downstairs, lying on your desk. He wouldn't even get up when I offered him those treats he goes crazy for.'

'Have you taken him to the vet?'

'Of course, but they couldn't find anything. Maybe he's just missing you.'

'Tell him I'll be home soon - and in the meantime I'll get that Skype connection set up so we can all see each other.'

I hung up, a stab of anxiety cutting through my post-gig euphoria. It was silly though to let homesickness kill my buzz. There was a tub full of beers backstage and Jake from Acador still had some of that coke left from last night. I headed back to the party.

As a result, I woke up the next morning - and I use the word 'morning' loosely - with a hangover to die from. This, combined with sleep pitiful in both quality and quantity, was an open invitation for all my ongoing physical ailments to drop in for a briefing.

Most of these weren't yet life threatening, but it wasn't for lack of trying and the smart money was on one of the bastards to get the job done sooner or later. Some were just standard middle age complaints. A crook knee here, a sore back there, that sort of thing. More disturbing was the tightness I felt in the fingers of both hands. Was this the first stage of arthritis? If so, how bad would it get - bad enough to stop me writing or playing guitar?

Another concern was the ringing that sometimes set up camp in my ears, especially after a big gig or a reckless stint on the headphones. This could be the calling card of tinnitus, that feared demon about which I'd heard a few horror stories. It's said that some victims unable to get rid of the constant ringing end up topping themselves in despair.

It wasn't the first time tinnitus had fired a warning shot over my bows. A few years back I'd gone to a Judas Priest show. It was when Rob Halford was out of the band, so it was a small venue, but

Priest seemed to be using the same sound system they'd blasted arenas with back in their eighties heyday. My ears had rung for two days, so I always took earplugs to gigs after that just in case.

Almost as bad was a habit I'd picked up during apartment living in recent years. A few late night beers would send me into listening mode and I'd pump rock songs through my headphones at high volume. The alcohol would deaden any pain on the night but I'd wake the next day with a ring in the ears and fears about how much damage I may have done myself.

See how the demons align themselves to attack you? The alcohol demon and the tinnitus demon work talon-in-talon. But what you gonna do? High volume is an occupational hazard of the rock and metal world. To some degree, so is booze. It's really a question of managing them and getting through as best you can.

With all my afflictions lining up to kill me, I sometimes wondered which of them would end up taking the prize. The reaper bones, I called them, going so far as to write a song of that name. I even pictured some morbid celestial bookmaker up there looking down, framing odds on which one was going to take me out.

And we're still on the minor players. I mean, arthritis and tinnitus were awful prospects but you could never write off the perennial favourites. Heart attack and cancer would always be contenders. Sure, I was only in my forties, but the occasional lines of blow and Lou I was doing did bring heart attack into the frame, especially with the fine platform laid down by the awful sleep and diet habits of the rock touring life. As for cancer, that's one bounty hunter that will always be in the frame somewhere.

AIDS was not really a contender, given my faithfulness to Sandra, but the grim bookmaker might see it as an outside chance if me and Sandra couldn't go the distance.

Outside of disease, there was a whole bunch of long shots that might end up scooping the pool - bus accident, electrocution, terrorist attack, or God knows what else. It's crazy to worry about such things but the older you get, the more morbid you feel about the looming end.

Whatever the odds, the cause wasn't helped by giving in to the drug and booze temptations of the road and indeed of the wider world. Whatever possessed me to make life even harder and more dangerous than it already was?

Then answer me this - what was the big idea of inventing intoxicants in the first place? If there was a god who created the world, including its drugs and alcohol, then what kind of god was that - a kindly deity who gave us drugs as recreation, or as consolation against life's pain? A sadistic prankster who gave us that which makes us feel good but ends up killing us? A stern disciplinarian who uses temptation to weed out the morally weak? Or, if this is some godless existentialist universe, are drugs simply one more hazard to negotiate in a chaotic world?

I talked it over one morning with our drummer, Dave, after another bender had seen us wake up bleary eyed and mournful. We'd pulled into a park somewhere while our bus had repairs. Sitting on a park bench under a tree, we killed some time while the job was done. I'd grabbed a couple of beers, hoping to hair-of-the-dog it. Dave sat silent beside me. He was not yet thirty but looked forty-five in the harsh morning light. He closed his eyes and stretched his long drummer arms, trying to ease the pain.

'Why do we keep doing this to ourselves?' said Dave.

'Because we're human,' I replied. 'Drugs feel good, humans like to feel good, so we take drugs. Stands to reason.'

'There's nothing good about a hangover. That's my last binge of the tour.'

'Come on mate, that's no attitude. Get back on the horse. Here's another beer for breakfast.'

'Piss off, Jimmy - that's the last thing I need. I'm on the wagon til Sydney.'

'Well, Davey, if you're going to turn into some kind of monk that's your business, but good luck fitting in with the rest of this crew around here. Whoever heard of a monk drummer? We're rock stars, this is what we're *supposed* to do. And never mind that, we're physical beings. I never could stand those spiritual types who pretend they don't have a body that likes to feel good. That's the type thinks meditating in a cave all day's the right way to live. Pretending they're not alive, denying their nature and the world. If they hate the world so much that they want to leave, why don't they just kill themselves and get on with it?'

'It's always the extremes with you, eh Jimmy. Who said anything about being a monk? I just don't want to end up the next Bonham or Keith Moon.'

'Sure, and granted that's two of the best to ever destroy a drum kit, rest their souls. But here's some trivia to set your mind at rest - both of them died at thirty-two. What are you, twenty-nine? You're good for another three years! So drink up.'

'Look mate, if you don't get that beer out of my face I'll pour it over your head. I've got better things to do with my life than end up another rock casualty.'

'Alright, have a coffee then. Funny thing though - you know what they put on the exit papers for the likes of Bonham and Moon? Death by misadventure. What sort of a phrase is that? You'd think it fits mountain climbing, canoeing, or a bunch of other healthy pursuits instead of bending the arm. Healthy? Point of fact, it's the ordinary things are the most dangerous. Like getting into a motor vehicle on any given day. There's plenty more die on the roads than OD on drugs. They should make cars illegal. Where's the push for zero tolerance on driving?'

'It's not just about dying young, is it? It's quality of life. Here's another day with things to do, places to go - and a hangover for a stowaway to slow us all down.'

'Sure, Dave, sometimes I wonder how much I could have achieved in life if I'd never drunk a beer or smoked a joint. Then again, some of my best moments were when I *have* achieved something and celebrated by doing exactly that - having a beer and a joint. That's the perfect work / life balance right there.'

Dave looked wistful.

'If only we could celebrate with a lemonade and a run around the park like when we were kids. We're bound to pay for all this in the end. There's got to be a toll.'

I opened the bottle of beer and took a small sip.

'Yeah maybe - who really knows? It's all guesswork. There's always a battle going on in my head. Is it worth the fun of getting high for what you lose in health and productivity? It's a war between the present and the future, and who's master I don't rightly know. Is it worth feeling good today if I'm going to feel bad tomorrow? Is it worth partying hard this year if I'm going to pay for it in thirty years?'

'Or to look on the bright side, you might get hit by a bus in twenty years before your tab's due.'

'Exactly. Pay the reaper before the piper. Not a bad plan, not as silly as it sounds. That's one way to beat the rap.'

'But what if you're unlucky and you *don't* get hit by the bus? What then?'

'I know, Dave, that's what bothers me. It's not so much me I'm worried about. If accounts are due and I have to check out early, so be it. That's the deal you make when you sign articles and enter this whole way of life. It's Sandra who worries me. Straight as a die she is, doesn't even drink. She'll probably make eighty and why should she be denied the love and companionship she's earned? It ain't right, mate. I've tried to give up the drinking and dope smoking just so I can go the distance with her. Trouble is, it's all imaginary. The future's a long way off and we might never get there. Sure, I want to be there for her, but whenever I think of saving myself for this remote, hypothetical future, there's always the thought that the merest puff on my pipe will get me stoned in the here and now. Only now is real.'

Dave put a sympathetic hand on my shoulder.

'Don't be too hard on yourself, mate, there's plenty worse than you. Look at all those rock star books coming out these days where they take the confessional. Some guys were doing coke with breakfast or going through bourbon by the caseload.'

I nodded.

'Sure, I'm an infant next to those guys, thank God. You know what really worries me though? Lung cancer.'

'You don't even smoke.'

'Not cigarettes but it's all the dope over the years. I had the fear put into me from a young age. These health freaks came to our primary school once, trying to scare the kids off smoking. It half-worked. They scared me but I smoked anyway. Funny thing is, the only thing sticks in my head from that day is this bullshit stat they told us - every cigarette you smoke takes fourteen minutes off your life.'

'Fourteen? Not ten or fifteen?'

'It's some kind of statistical average, I suppose. But fourteen minutes - how about that? So every time you light up a fag, there it is - fourteen minutes of your life burning away right in front of your nose.'

'I wonder how many minutes a joint or a bong is worth?'

'Exactly. And what about Yul Brynner - remember those ads he made just before the lung cancer did for him? "Whatever you do, don't smoke." That was his whole message boiled down to five words - and him lying cold in the grave while the ad's running hourly on TV. Or maybe he was cremated and went up in smoke himself. Anyhow, you don't forget something like that.'

'Never saw it myself.'

'Before your time, mate. And still people don't listen. Every now and then you hear the same regret from not-so-aged, dying men. There was a guy on the news only last month. Cheated of his retirement years with his beloved wife and wishing he could go back in time to warn his younger self off the fags. But really, how was he to know? Like I said, it's all guesswork. It does make you think - too much, really. Gets so bad that every time I'm lighting up in the present moment I'm wondering if there's some future, aged me sending back those same sorrowful pleas to quit.'

Dave stood up and walked back to the bus, the matter unresolved. I was left to ponder it on my own.

This whole drug struggle was bad enough in ordinary life. On a rock tour of Europe, the problem was amplified. The responsible thing was to keep my health and longevity in mind, for the sake of my 'marriage' if nothing else. Yet with Sandra far away and a general air of hedonism soaking the atmosphere, the drugs and booze certainly had the upper hand in the struggle. As mentioned, most of the guys on tour were in their twenties, keen to party hard and - unlike me - young enough to get away with it.

For me, the partying was also a way of adapting to the forced sociability of touring with a bunch of bands and crew I didn't know. It's no fun to hang around drunk and stoned people when you're sober, so I'd get out of it just so I could stand the people I was travelling with.

There's also the sheer tedium of much of life on tour. All that waiting around. You wait to load in the gear, you wait for sound check, you wait to go onstage and then for the bands after you to finish. You wait to go back to your room, to travel onto the next town, to arrive and book into the next cheap hotel. It never ends. Lucky for me I was a reader, so books were an escape - but the main escape was the old drugs and booze.

Another thing that killed me was the hours. Not the amount, but how they were ordered. You know, I'm really a morning person!

My brain works best and I do my best work in the morning. So that was really going to work on a rock tour, right?

It's a big ask to be a morning person in that environment. Let's say the show runs from 7-11 pm. You get to bed by midnight at the earliest and have a lousy night's sleep. At best, you'll wake up at 9 or 10am, or later if you've been partying the night before. So there's the best part of the day gone. You're part of the tour, so you need to adapt to the hours other people are following. Sure, if you're Led Zeppelin or Pink Floyd you can escape to your private jet or a five star hotel. But an up and comer? Forget it. It's a long way to the top, but not that far to the bottom.

Drugs and booze weren't the only temptations on the road. What about those famed groupies? At this level, in this genre of music, they weren't exactly wall to wall, but there were certainly a few. Only problem was I couldn't touch them, much as the temptation was very real. I could hardly expect fidelity from Sandra without promising the same in return. Believe me, there were times I wished I was single. Being a little older, I seemed to attract some of the more mature, intellectual types. One time I invited a beautiful girl back for a game of Scrabble, but after I fluked 242 points for the word 'zingiest' on a double-triple word score, she started taking her top off and I had to kick her out quick or I would have caved for sure.

So there I was - groupies I couldn't screw, sleep I couldn't get, and booze I shouldn't drink but did anyway. A real paradise! The one consolation was the huge stacks of money I was making. Right?

You kidding me? Although the tour was mostly drawing good crowds, our band was on a set weekly wage - which was nothing mind-blowing once you took out travel and living expenses. The idea had been to make up the difference through merchandise and CD sales. While we did sell a few t-shirts, Lighthouse XIII was not yet big enough to do any serious business in that area. As for CDs, yeah we sold some, but the whole business of selling CDs was way down on what it was ten or fifteen years ago, since people started downloading or streaming music off the internet.

Let's go over that list again. Groupies I couldn't screw, booze I shouldn't drink, sleep I couldn't get, and money I didn't make. So it was that I found myself on about week ten of the tour, pulling in to yet another rock venue with yet another hangover, about to do yet another version of the same show we'd done fifty times before - and I began to wonder if this whole Groundhog Day was really my cup of herbal tea.

There's no denying it - I am sounding rather a whinger at this point. Yet looking back, I am trying to trace the processes by which my soul gradually soured and led me to the path of evil. Strangely enough, once I did turn to the dark side and accept the Maelstrom, it's striking how much better and easier life became. At this point, however, my soul was not yet corrupt and I continued the forlorn struggle of a good man trying to make his way in an evil world.

Some people who've made it to the top in various fields put their success down to hard work. That's fine if you're an athlete or an executive, or in some other field where work is easily defined. Yet I've found that a lot of 'work' in the artistic fields is nothing to do with art, but rather entails a lot of bullshit networking, schmoozing, and mandatory self promotion. So how much of this 'work' are you prepared to do? How much sucking up, hand shaking, and trumpet-blowing can you stomach?

In the rock game, is the whole touring lifestyle also part of the 'work' you're obliged to take on to get ahead? If so, just how much of staying up all night, hanging round crappy nightclubs, semi-compulsory alcoholism, hangovers and fatigue are you prepared to cop? How much of the whole grinding slog of a lifestyle can you handle to make your cherished dream come true? And in my case, at my age, the answer was... not that much.

Christ, I probably could have done it in my twenties! At that age you have the resilience, the energy, the youthful enthusiasm.

You can get used to that whole way of life as a youngster and work your way up to the higher levels. Starting out as a grumpy old man in my forties was another matter entirely.

I decided to get in touch with Ted Hoffman, my manager, the one who'd set up the whole deal in the first place. He'd made only one visit to the tour and that was weeks ago. I emailed him to request a meeting. He replied that his next check-in would be in Germany. By the time the tour rolled around to Berlin, Hoffman sent me a taxi and I was being driven to his hotel. One thing for sure, it was the first five star hotel I'd seen for a long time. It was called the *Hotel Alexanderplatz* and Hoffman had a luxury suite on the 12th floor. I looked around me in wonder, so opulent was the suite compared to my recent lodgings.

Hoffman was in his element. Silver haired and wearing an expensive suit, he looked like a CEO on an overseas business trip. I felt shabby by comparison, yet Hoffman pretended not to notice. He was all smiles and gave me a welcoming hug.

'Jimmy - great to see you again! How are you finding the tour?'

'Love the music side, Ted. I'm a bit burned out on the rest of it. All the travelling.'

'That's life on the road - it's always tough at first. Never mind. All the sales targets and feedback I'm getting are spot on. For the next tour you can look forward to an upgrade.'

'The next tour? I hate to seem ungrateful but I'm about ready to chuck in the towel. This touring caper's not for me. It's a young man's game.'

'Missing a few home comforts, eh? What happened to your girl - did she end up flying out?'

'It was nice of you to offer that, Ted, but Sandra couldn't get leave from her job. And there was no one to look after the cat. He hasn't been at his best and she was worried about him.'

'Who knocks back a trip to Europe because of a cat?'

'Not me, as you can see. Here I am.'

'More power to you, Jimmy. You must be rapt to finally get some kudos for your music. You're killing it, by all accounts.'

'Sure, it's what I've always wanted. Don't think me ungrateful, but three months is a long slog.'

'Three months? That's nothing. Maiden and Metallica used to go out for two years at a time.'

'They were young blokes in their prime.'

'Age is a state of mind, Jimmy. You're only as old as you feel.'

'I must be about sixty then. How about this? When the tour winds up, I'll go home and make another album and just focus on selling records? Instead of doing these long tours. That's probably a better way for me to make a quid out of all this.'

'I hate to break it to you, old boy, but those days are gone. Ever heard of Napster? You don't make money off record sales now. Since downloading started, it's not about albums anymore. The money's all in live shows and merch.'

'I've made bugger all from this tour.'

'You will though, after you've paid your dues. The next tour and the one after that you'll start to see some serious coin. You've got to get onto some bigger tours and also start headlining a few shows of your own.'

'How long's that going to take, Ted? I'm jack of living on a tour bus already.'

'That's not you talking, Jimmy, it's the fatigue. You're at the back end of the trek and all you can think of is home. Wait and see, a few weeks sitting round the house and you'll be itching to get back out there.'

'You reckon?'

'Sure - and speaking of fatigue, I've got some brilliant news that'll make all the difference. I've found you a singer.'

'You what?'

'I did mention Damien, remember? He wasn't available but I've found someone better. Ivan de Vangelus. Heard of him?'

'Don't think so - and jeez, Ted, I'm not sure I can stand a singer. Divas the lot of 'em. Ivan de what? What the hell kind of a name's that anyhow?'

'Be like that if you want, but you're only holding yourself back from going to the next level. You're exhausted, sure - and why do you think that is? You're taking on way too much. Guitar, songwriting, and vocals as well? That's a heavy load. Ivan will take the weight off and free you up to do what you do best.'

'Well, maybe.'

'It's a game-changer. Wait and see - a couple more tours and a good album and you won't be sleeping on a tour bus anymore. You'll be camped out every night in rooms like this.'

'So where is this guy, anyway? Do I get to audition him before he joins the band - or is he already in through some kind of executive management decision?'

'Since you ask, he's joining the tour for the last two weeks. Not to sing. Just to hang out, watch you play and get a feel for the show. Then you'll go home, take a break, and start writing the next album. How's that?'

'Yeah, maybe Ted. I suppose we can limp our way to the finish line if there's only two weeks left.'

'That won't cut it, Jimmy. I need you at your best. You can't afford to have a bad night or the punters won't come back and see you next time. And that brings me to the other piece of good news - I've got you a couple of special shows to finish off the tour.'

'Like what?'

'I'll let you know as soon as they're confirmed. So don't let yourself down. Tell you what I'll do. You're clearly exhausted so here's what happens. We blow off the Koln date - the other bands can do the show without you. I'll book you a nice room here for a couple of days so you can rest up and get your strength back. Then you come out all guns blazing and end the tour with a bang. How's that?'

'Two nights here, Ted? I'm sold. Thank you very much.'

'For us at Solar Eclipse Management, the well-being of the artist is our prime concern. It's our duty of care. I'll phone reception and book your room now.'

Ted was as good as his word. That night was the first in a very long while that I got to sleep in a private room without the whirr of a bus engine and the sound of twenty other guys mumbling and shuffling down their personal roads to oblivion. And as I sank between the sheets in that luxury bed I was, for a brief and merciful time, able to forget all about my dream come true.

# 12
# Hemispheres

So, it's a couple of days later and I'm back on the horse. It's amazing what a good night's sleep can do. I met Hoffman in one of the hotel restaurants on the 12th floor, not far from his suite.

'You look terrific, Jimmy. Why not stay a bit longer?'

'What about the tour?'

'It won't hurt to miss another show. It's not a major city. You can rejoin them at Dresden, then it's back here in Berlin for the finale.'

'Are you sure?'

'I insist. Now listen up - I've three pieces of news and they're all good. The tour's running an extra three weeks, you've got a headlining show, and your new singer's joining us for dinner.'

'Uh... say what?'

'Well done son - you've made it!'

'Wait a minute, Ted. I never agreed to a new singer. You said he was just going to tag along for a while. Who the hell is this guy?'

'I told you - Ivan de Vangelus. He's perfect. Twenty-five, looks like a Greek god, super voice, and loads of charisma. A real rock star, the whole package.'

'Never heard of him.'

'He's certainly heard of you. He loves your music - he's already learned all the words.'

'Yeah? I suppose we can at least try him. There must be *something* wrong with him. Some kind of attitude or personality problem. There always is.'

'Come on, Jimmy, none of us are perfect, are we? I mean look at you - too stubborn to let yourself go to the next level because you're scared of losing control. A lazy guy not prepared to pay your dues and put in the hard yards of graft to get to the top. You were ready to quit the tour three days ago.'

'Lazy? I'm handling guitar, vocals, song-writing and a fair chunk of the promo to boot - so I'm not exactly shirking. If by lazy you mean I don't like being crammed into a tour bus for three months, drinking myself to an early grave while my marriage falls apart ten thousand miles away, I'm a regular three-toed sloth.'

'I'm not going to discuss your private life, Jimmy. I'm interested in your music - and this is my whole point about getting Ivan. He'll take the pressure right off. Let's be honest - you're a much better guitarist than a singer. Even if you *were* a great singer, you're too old to appeal to a younger, mainstream crowd. With you upfront, the band will never get out of the lower leagues and small tours like this one.'

A waiter came over with an expensive bottle of wine which Hoffman must have ordered before I arrived. Hoffman continued his spiel as our glasses were filled.

'On the other hand, get Ivan in and it's a game changer. Hit albums, a global audience, and headlining tours where you get to stay in hotels like this. Your girlfriend can chuck in her job and come with you. Or if she's not into it, dump her and find someone else. Or have a new girl in every city you play.'

'You make it sound so easy, Ted, but how long's it take to get to that sort of level?'

'Not as long as you think. You've already laid a platform with the hard work you've done so far. Give us a new album with Ivan and leave the rest to me. By this time next year you'll look back on this as the turning point.'

'I don't know, Ted.'

'Well I do and I won't let you wreck this for yourself. So here's what happens. Ivan takes over vocals for the rest of the tour. There's no better way to audition a guy than in front of a crowd, is there? If you're not happy, kick him out - but if he nails the job, we go ahead with that new album.'

'Fine. Do we have to extend the tour though? Three more weeks, you say. I was counting on being home soon.'

'You need to see if Ivan can cut it live. If he does, it'll give you both a huge shot of confidence for making the new record. The smart thing is to let him settle into the job. On top of that, I'll throw in a cash bonus as a sweetener. Two thousand Euros. That's for you, not the band.'

'What about Dave and Viv - no bonus for them? They want to get home too.'

'Who cares? Those guys aren't at your level. I'd say as soon as the tour's done, get rid of them.'

'A bit harsh, don't you think? They're mates.'

'What do you think this is, Def Leppard? I've no time for one-armed drummers or for those who play like them either. This is a business not a charity.'

'How do I tell Sandra about the tour extension? She'll hit the roof.'

'Your girlfriend? Here we go again. When are you going to grow a pair, mate? I thought you were an Aussie. You think the Young brothers let a woman stop them going on tour? No one ever told Malcolm or Angus what to do.'

'Angus's wife was Dutch. Sure, it'd be a whole lot easier if my girl was European but Sandra's never lived outside of Australia. She's not telling me what to do, it's just that... well, look at it from her side. Why would she stay with me if I'm never there?'

'And there's your answer. Forget Sandra, she's only holding you back. We need to get you a classy European girl. Regenerate your life. New album, new singer, new girlfriend. Why don't you move over here permanently? Australia's a million miles from everything. Aha, here he is - someone I'd like you to meet.'

I turned around and there he was - Ivan de Vangelus, a classic young rock god if ever there was one. He was like Robert Plant's better looking cousin - not in his specific looks, but the level of beauty. Style-wise, the Zeppelin singer was an apt point of reference. In the 21st century, rock stars come in all shapes and sizes, with varying lengths of hair, or no hair at all. Ivan was a throwback to the pre-punk 1970s when rock stars were identifiable by a great mane and a shirt unbuttoned to at least the chest.

Ivan lived in the same zone once frequented by Plant and his guitarist, Jimmy Page, that point where masculine and feminine beauty meet. For some, the idea of androgyny suggests an image of a short haired woman in a suit. The early-seventies version was a 'pretty' young man with great flowing locks and flashy attire. It was shocking for the time, at first drawing many a derisive comment from the mainstream. Perhaps the macho posturing of such singers was meant to dispel any doubts about their sexuality.

While not naturally dark-skinned, Ivan was the type who tans without effort in the right climate. His hair, on the other hand, had started dark yet lightened a touch under the same conditions. He looked as if he'd spent six months on a Greek island. His eyes were as brilliantly blue as the sea in those parts, and he had the type of natural comeliness which draws the eye and holds it to the point of rudeness. I found myself staring, as transfixed as anyone else.

As I took in his physical divinity I steeled myself for the accompanying 'attitude.' Yet to my surprise, I found no trace of the expected arrogance or vanity in our brief chat. Although his voice had resonance enough to grace a theatre stage, he spoke quietly during that initial meeting.

'Great to finally meet you, Jimmy,' Ivan said, taking my hand. His handshake had none of the ludicrous hand-crushing machismo which as a pro-guitarist I'd come to despise. It was a firm, simple grip with no hidden agenda.

'Ted tells me you already know our songs.'

'I got the lyrics off your website. I'd be honoured to jam with you guys some day.'

'You'll be doing a bit more than that, mate. Ted wants you to take over vocals for the rest of the tour.'

Ivan looked at Ted, who smiled paternally back at us.

'Alright lads, granted I haven't had time to discuss this with either of you - but trust me, this is my job. I'm looking at you two and I see sparks. This is going to be one hell of a partnership. Don't take my word for it. Let Dresden be your baptism of fire. Any comment from me will be redundant after that.'

Despite myself, I was excited and sensed unimagined new horizons looming up in ahead. Hoffman told us about the headlining gig he'd booked for one of the last nights of the tour in Berlin. Ivan said he was well and truly up for it. As the three of us chatted over dinner, it was clear Ivan had done his homework on the band. He seemed to know our music inside out and only wanted to give it a new dimension. in At the end of the meal, we shook hands again and I departed with a sense of renewed optimism, tempered only by dread at the thought of the coming Skype call to Sandra.

There was a sort of reading room not far from the restaurant. I'd spent time there during my two day rest stop. I'd brought my laptop tonight with the thought of working on some lyrics after dinner. Yet as it was now nearly 10pm and the place was deserted, I decided to get the Skype call over with before going back to my room.

I turned on my laptop so Sandra and I could see each other. As the computer's camera panned to the left, there too was Finzi, the beloved grey cat. He looked a little thin but I fancied it was the camera angle that was unkind. At the sound of my greeting, Finzi looked into the camera. Whether he could see me onscreen, or only recognised my voice, he let out a series of enthusiastic meows.

The camera panned back to Sandra. Her face seemed older, her smile a little forced.

'Hi Jimmy - we can't wait for you to get home.'

'Me too.'

'Only seven more days!'

'Uh, look Sandra, there's something I have to tell you. I really hate to say this but the tour's been extended. Just three more weeks and that's it.'

'What? Oh no. I thought you wanted to come home.'

'I do, there's nothing I want more. Just hear me out. Remember Ted Hoffman, our manager? Get this - it's massive. He's got us a headlining show. Not only that, we're trying out a new singer - he's amazing. So I won't have to worry about vocals anymore. Even better, I'm getting a two thousand Euro bonus for the extra shows - not a bad way to finish the tour, eh!'

Sandra's hands went to her face. There was a long pause through which the only sound was Finzi's famously loud purr. Finally, Sandra looked up again.

'I'm happy for you, Jim, really I am - but this isn't the life I want. I can't have a relationship on Skype.'

'What are you talking about?'

'I've been thinking about it with you so far away - and you know what? I realised I hoped the tour would fail. So selfish of me.'

'Come on, it's only three more weeks.'

'Then how long til the next tour and the one after that?'

'Fine, I'll pack it all in then.'

'Why should you? It's your dream.'

'The dream and the reality are two different things. That's what I've learned. To be honest, if we'd had this conversation three days ago I would have been on the first plane home. I'd had a gutful of it all. But now Hoffman's got us this singer and a headline show - and the bonus money. How good's that? I'm not coming home to a job, am I?'

'I know.'

'If we can make an album with this new singer, it could be the one to break us. I make a million and we retire.'

'So you'll be off on another long tour then.'

'Not a long one. Maybe a month or two.'

'Come on. If your album sells, you think your manager won't have you out on the road half the year?'

'I'll just say no.'

'Like you said no to the tour extension? Look at Finzi. It's killing him. Can't you see how thin he is? He's not well.'

'Look, one more month and I'm back. Please, just be patient. Try to understand my position and be a little more supportive.'

'I wish all the best for you, Jimmy, really I do, but our lives seem to be going in different directions. Perhaps it's best to make a clean break.'

'No Sandra, don't say that. We're both at the end of our ropes so it's not the time to make any rash decisions. Look, the hell with this, I'll tell Hoffman to shove the tour and I'll book a flight home. Any chance you could just lend me the airfare? I'm skint. See, if you'd only wait the three weeks, the bonus will cover my flight home. Just three weeks, please. Then we'll sort all this out. I'll know if the singer's any good, we'll see how the headline slot goes.'

'I don't know, Jim, maybe.'

'Don't give up on us yet. We can work this out, I swear. Come on, you and Finzi are my world. You're all that matters.'

I hung up with a sense of violent anxiety and a looming desolation. Hoffman's timing was impeccable. Just as I'd been about to escape from the tour and save my marriage, here he was dangling a brilliant lead singer and a desperately needed cash bonus in front of my face. The cash was the killer. I swear that if I'd been able to afford a flight home, I would have booked it then and there, and the devil take Hoffman and his fancy singer. Yet my credit card was already stretched to breaking. Suddenly it was as if my two day rest stop had never happened and I was back in my state of exhaustion from the tour bus.

I was still on the 12th floor of the *Hotel Alexanderplatz* where Hoffman's suite was located. I crossed to the window and looked down at the people rushing about on the street far below. It would be instant, you would think. You'd certainly hope so. Would the moment of agony be worth it to end the nightmare my life had become? Who would really miss me anyway? The world would go on just fine without me. My parents were too old to be much damaged by it. They weren't long for this world themselves. I'd lost touch with most of my old friends. Even the so-called fans would quickly move on. But Sandra. I could see her face when she heard the news. The raw, naked grief. The sense of complicity she would carry. No, she didn't deserve that. I must either face up to losing her, or go back to Australia for good and give up all this music nonsense.

The rock and roll dream, eh? Some dream! What a ridiculous illusion. All those years ago, it had been the *music* I'd fallen in love with. It was the music that mattered. Everything else - the touring, the drugs, the tiresome and relentless campaign to sell your 'product' to the world - none of it really had anything to do with the music itself. It was all just a load of peripheral rubbish.

Still agitated after the Skype call, I began browsing the internet. Through force of habit, I checked out a music site and read a news item of a type which had become quite familiar. It was some big rock star complaining he couldn't make a living selling records anymore due to people downloading music for free on the internet.

He was probably right. Most of the CD shops had gone now, as had the bookshops. Retail in general was suffering. Many once thriving industries faced radical change at best, extinction at worst. Their survival would depend on how well they adapted to the rapid changes brought on by the internet. Only the strong would survive this process of evolution.

I sat there reading the article, slowly shaking my head - and that's when I felt it. Not just the rage, but the power. The *magic* power. Yes, it was unmistakeable. Though the Vortex Winder was a good ten floors below in my room, I felt it stirring from the dormancy of recent months. No screen was visible upon which magic words appeared, yet I knew the nature of the power bestowed upon me. The power to rant. Yes, that's what it was. The power for vengeful rant.

Of course, there are those who would say the power to rant is one I was born with and often prone to, needing no help from a magical talisman.

I can't really deny it. The fact is that I *do* - on rare occasions - veer off into the odd rant, but only for a good cause. Yet what I felt now was far stronger. This would be no ordinary tirade. The power of the Vortex Winder surged through my being, giving a turbo boost to my natural propensities.

Reading the article, I saw the truth of the matter. It was clear that my present predicament was, to a large degree, the fault of internet piracy. If only I could have stayed home to make records instead of being forced to go out on tour! In the present day and age, that was no longer possible. Now Sandra was threatening to leave me if I didn't rush back to Australia. Hoffman's titillation of my ambition was pulling me the opposite way. I was dangling like a puppet, being pulled from one side of the globe to the other in a deadly tug of war.

Under such a strain, it's little wonder my frustrations exploded into the ether of cyberspace. I logged into the forum to vent my rage.

# 13
# Extinction.Net

The news story read as follows.

> Jeff Wilding today announced he is quitting music, citing 'fatigue.' In a statement on his website, Wilding says, 'The music industry today is nothing like when I started out in the 1980s. I feel lucky to have lived through those times. Downloading and streaming of digital content on the internet has changed how the game is played. It is no longer feasible to spend money making high quality recordings as your main saleable product. It's all about touring and the live show now.
>
> Yet with family responsibilities, I no longer have the will to go on the road for long stretches of time. As a result, it is not a realistic option for me to continue as a professional musician. I want to thank all the fans who've stuck with me since the eighties. Rock forever!'

There was a comment section leading off from the story. It began with a few tributes from fans. 'Sorry to see you go, bro.' 'Thanks for the memories, Jeff, you rocked.'

It wasn't long before a couple of trolls hit the board. Someone calling himself 'Pyro' wrote 'Aw, what a shame. Time to get a real job you old fart.' Another one - '8Ball' - wrote, 'Always knew this guy was only in it for the money. I thought you play music cos you love it, right?'

That was enough to make me jump in. Before we go on, I should explain that the dialogue that follows has been cleaned up considerably. Not the swearing - most of that came from me anyhow - and not the malice and spite from the trolls. That's been retained. It's the grammar, spelling, and articulation of concepts that's been touched up. In its original form, it was of such a dire standard that readers may have found it hard to follow. I've tried to make it more intelligible.

One more point - we must recall that the events of this story took place a few years ago, about a decade into the 21st century. At this time, CDs still existed, though they were in decline as a medium for recording and selling music. Streaming services like Spotify were on the rise, but not yet in full swing. Downloading of music was all the rage. That is, taking free digital copies of songs and albums from the internet onto a home computer.

Since that time, CDs have become almost obsolete. Downloading has declined a little, and streaming is the main way people listen to music. The following dialogue took place at that point in time when these processes were in transition. CDs were still alive but dying out, downloading was king, and streaming on the rise but not yet ascendant.

I logged in under the user name 'Silva' and joined the chat.

**Silva** – Another one bites the dust - way to go downloaders! There's another dead rocker's head you can stick on your wall.

**8Ball** – His music sucked since the nineties anyhow. About time he got a job.

**Silva** – So you don't think what Jeff does - sorry, did - is a proper job?

**8Ball** – Playing music, partying and banging hot chicks. Give me a break. Some of us have to work for a living LOL.

**Silva** – There's a lot more to it than that. I'm in a band too - you got any idea how expensive it is?

**8Ball** – Waah! I'm sick of hearing you guys cry about it. Nobody said you had to be in a band. You chose to make a living playing music instead of getting a proper job like the rest of us. What's wrong - run out of money for blow? Try getting up every day and going to work for a change.

**Silva** – Ah, the envious spite of the 9-5 worker. At least that's one thing that hasn't changed since the eighties. Just like in the old Dire Straits song 'Money For Nothing' where the worker complains about rock stars getting money and free chicks for 'doing nothing.' Looks like that guy finally got his revenge. Now he can get his albums for free - steal them instead of buying.

**Pyro** – Who's Dire Straits? Never heard of 'em. I'll download that song for free right now.

**Silva** – Don't waste your spite on those guys - that's one band who don't need any more royalties. Lucky bastards put out the *Brothers in Arms* album at the dawn of the CD age and sold a warehouse-full on novelty value.

**Pyro** - No way I'm ever buying a CD again. I'm done with being screwed over paying twenty bucks for a piece of plastic that costs fifty cents to make.

**Silva** – Hey dumbass - you're not paying for the piece of plastic. You're paying for studio and production costs and the years of preparation it took to put the music on there. You think albums emerge fully formed on pieces of plastic?

**Pyro** – Whatever.

**Silva** – Recording's expensive. If no one buys albums anymore, how do bands pay for the cost of making them?

**8Ball** – If you need money, get a job like the rest of us.

**Silva** – Gee, OK. Do I get to keep my fulltime music job too? When do I fit that in?

**8Ball** – If you're doing music cos you love it, you'll find a way. Do it in your free time.

**Silva** – Yeah, cos making great music is something you can toss off in that spare hour after work, right?

**8Ball** – So there are no office or construction workers or doctors who play music in their free time?

**Silva** – Sure, like a doctor - after a sixty hour working week - is going to pop out the next *OK Computer* or *Dark Side of the Moon*. Or a construction guy's going to down tools and go off to do a rock gig three nights a week. When's he fit in the world tour - on the weekend?

**8Ball** – There's holiday time, four weeks a year.

**Silva** – Alright, cos touring is nothing but a holiday anyhow. It must be so restful going back to the day job after spending your four weeks annual leave on the road.

**8Ball** - Playing music isn't work. Work is when you go to a hospital or a factory eight hours a day every day. That's why you get paid. For playing music onstage with fans cheering you on - why should you get paid for that?

**Silva** – Well, gee, I mean those big Marshall amps cost money, you know. Ever been in a band yourself?

**8Ball** – Yeah when I left school I was in a band for a while. We never toured but we played local shows. We recorded some songs at home and gave them away free. I was just rapt people wanted to hear them. That was my attitude. It was a hobby and I never expected to make any money out of it. I've got a proper job for that.

**Silva** – So you're a hobbyist and you're telling pros like Jeff Wilding how to do their job. It might be a hobby for you. It's not for him - it's a goddamn art form and a profession. Problem is that making quality art takes hours and hours of painstaking work over months and years. It takes time, and time costs money.

**8Ball** – Go on tour fulltime then and make a living that way. The days are gone when you guys could put out a record every two or three years, sit on your ass and make a million bucks for doing nothing. You think you can live in your big house, party and screw hot chicks while the rest of us have to get up every day and go to work? I am not here to fund your rock star fantasy lifestyle. You have to go on tour? Good. At least you have to get up off your lazy ass and go play for the fans, if you can call that work LOL.

**Pyro** – Yeah Silva, he's right. I've got a real job and it pays great by the way. I bet I've got more money than you, jerk off. What's the name of your band? I just want to make sure I download all your stuff for free.

**Silva** – Well here's the thing, Pyro, you've probably never heard of my band. We're low down on the food chain. I'd love to have a piece of this rock star fantasy life 8Ball is on about, but that's all it is to me - a fantasy. I've never made one fucking dollar out of my music, you moron. Have a go at Jeff if you want, but for a small band trying to rise up the divisions, what chance is there now? It was hard to make a living in music twenty years ago, now it's almost impossible.

**Pyro** – No one made you become a musician. It was your choice.

**Silva** – So how many people do you think are going to make that choice now? I don't know who'd want to make music their career these days. What do they get out of it - the chance to go into debt so they can entertain thieves like you? Eventually there won't be any good bands left. The next Zeppelin or Metallica probably can't even get off the starting blocks these days.

**Pyro** – Hey, Mr. Serious Artist. Don't tell me you're only in it for the money?

**Silva** – How could I be? Like I said, I've never gone even one dollar into the black. So tell me, 8Ball, I'm dying to know - where is this rock star life you keep talking about? Where are the millions, the hot chicks, the easy life and the rest of it? Hell, I must be doing this all wrong.

**Pyro** – Must be because your band sucks.

**Silva** – Yeah, that's got to be it. Or maybe I just picked up the wrong textbook when I went to muso college. Instead of the rock star fantasy textbook, I must have picked up the one where you learn how to slog away for years for nothing, ruin your personal life, get screwed over by your 'fans' and retire in debt with a broken body.

**Pyro** – Waah, cry baby. Don't you get it yet? I'm not buying your CDs - suck it up fag. If you want to make money, go on tour and maybe I'll come and watch your crappy band if I have time.

**Silva** – OK Pyro, we know you've got a job, you said so yourself. What if you had to take your job on the road - say, go on tour six months every year to do it? Not only that, you have to do permanent night shift and live in a tour bus with all your workmates. Would that be cool? By the way, you might have to consider your wife and kids. Wait, what am I saying - you probably still live at home with Mum and Dad, right?

**Pyro** – So what?

**Silva** - You do? Oh big surprise. Major surprise. Try to *imagine* it then. You're married with a couple of kids. How long's your marriage going to last if you're away on tour six months a year? Your wife's going to love looking after young kids while you're out on the road banging those hot chicks, right?

**Pyro** – If you don't like it, stop moaning and get a real job. If you don't like touring, then don't be a musician.

**Silva** – Yes, I probably *will* be following Jeff into retirement soon. I could stay in music if you guys paid for the albums you download - but clearly that ain't gonna happen.

**Pyro** – If people aren't willing to pay for your music, it can't be worth anything. Goods or services are only worth what your customers are prepared to pay for them. Market forces define their value. That's a simple economic law of the business world, if you can follow it dumbass.

**Silva** – It's a glib argument - and total rubbish. For example, take three of the bestselling albums of all time - *Thriller, Back in Black* and *Dark Side of the Moon*. They've each sold over fifty million copies. If they came out today, they wouldn't sell even half that. Not because they have any less intrinsic value, but because people like you can steal them and get away with it. Your silly little pseudo-economic law means nothing.

**Pyro** – The digital age is here to stay. Downloading is a fact of life. Everyone does it, it's normal. Stop living in the past. Adapt or die.

**Silva** – I'll die then. Fuck you and your world. I won't adapt to it. For all its faults, the old world was better. Kids today have no idea what it was like to buy a new record back then. These days, every track's been leaked or previewed online long before the record comes out. In the old days, you'd have no idea what a new record would sound like, or even look like. You'd pick up the record or CD from the shop, get it home, and put it on excited and intrigued as hell. You'd study the cover art, the lyrics. It was a real trip.

**Pyro** – Whatever you say, Grandad.

**Silva** – Funny thing is, when I was a kid we looked down on singles. Singles were for pop fans, not rock fans. It was all about the album back then. An album was a massive artistic statement. Not anymore. Now you guys just download one or two songs and stick 'em on your laptop, or your phone for Christ's sake! There's no sense of 'the album' as an artistic statement anymore. We've gone back to the single - what a joke. I'm glad I lived through the age of the album before it was killed by Generation Download. And

I'm glad I'll die soon so I don't have to live in the music world Generation Download has created.

**Pyro** – What are you waiting for? Double up on your medication, Pops, that should do it.

**Silva** – If only people would still pay for everything they download, like on iTunes, instead of file sharing with the world. That would work - but it would depend on an honour system. Some chance. I can't say today's generation has no honour - that's too harsh - it's more like they have no idea. The cultural consumer age has reached its peak. Everything comes out of a magic tap now. Hey, you want to watch a movie or a TV show - just click on this link and it'll pop up on your screen. You want to know something - google it. You want a new album - download it. It all pops out by magic. So you don't understand that the awesome new movie you just watched cost millions of dollars to produce.

**Pyro** – I'd buy music if I could afford it, but I have bills to pay.

**Silva** – Don't tell me mum and dad are charging you rent?

**Pyro** – No, idiot, I don't pay rent. I have car payments to make. I'm saving for a trip to Europe and every week I have to pay into a retirement fund. Those are serious bills I need to take care of. Music is a luxury item. Why should I pay for that? You should be grateful people even want to listen to your stuff. It's a privilege for you to be able to play for us - you're lucky we even care.

**Silva** – Words fail me. Just give me the fucking gun and I'll kill myself now.

**Pyro** – If you stop being angry for five seconds you might realise we're on the same side. Everyone knows the music business is a huge rip off. Record companies have been swindling people for years, not only the fans but also the bands. They've been ripping *you* off. Every time I download an album free, I'm staging a protest against those corporate scumbags.

**Silva** – Oh, *I see*. Why didn't I realise that before? Your concern is for the *artist*. You're standing shoulder to shoulder with the muso against his corporate overlords.

Like hell! You've got some kind of nerve trying to spin your petty theft into a noble act of defiance. You think you're a rebel defying the corporate world? Gimme a break. Sure the record companies and managers abused their artists back in the day, but at least the artist got a small royalty. When you download the album, the artist gets nothing. You ain't no rebel - you're just another thieving corporate bastard to me.

**Pyro** – Sure I download a lot of albums. I'll never buy an album blind again. What if I don't like it? Why should I get ripped off with two good songs and the rest filler?

**Silva** – Waah, who's the cry baby now? You might not like every album or book or movie you pay for. Want a tissue?

**Cat Girl** – I agree with Pyro. I download just to try something out. If I like it, I'll sometimes go out and buy the album too.

**Silva** – And do you actually do it, or is it just something you mean to get around to one day?

**Cat Girl** – Sometimes, but there's so many new releases you can't get them all. By the time I'm ready to buy it, it's already on the computer and I've heard it so it's time to move onto the next one.

**Silva** – Yeah, why would you pay ten dollars to iTunes if you've already got it in your album library by then? It starts off with good intentions, but that's as far as it goes.

**Cat Girl** - I try and support the artist by seeing them live if they come to my town, or buying a T-shirt.

**Silva** – How on earth do you fit all these bands into your busy schedule? You must be going to two or three rock shows a week!

**Cat Girl** – Not on my wages. Ticket prices are outrageous these days. And the t-shirts - forty bucks for a cheap black t-shirt, don't think so. Most of these bands suck live anyhow. They look tired and bored like they're just going through the motions. I don't really go to live gigs much anymore.

**Silva** – It's cause and effect. Why'd you think those ticket prices and t-shirts cost so much? Got to make up for those missed royalties somehow and touring's not cheap to begin with. As for being tired and bored, try playing the same songs four nights a week for six months and see how fresh you are.

**Stringer** – Hey Silva, I'm in a band too and I don't agree. You're romanticising the old days. The old days sucked. You had management and record companies screwing their artists big time. Bands were treated like cash cows and forced to tour into the ground while the managers stayed home and skimmed the cream. Even if you got signed, the record companies owned the rights to your masters. They'd lend you money to record and do promo, then you'd have to tour for years to pay them back and get out of debt.

You couldn't get played on the radio unless you made songs that fit their formats. Albums were expensive to buy because the retailers and distributors had to take their cut, along with the studio, marketers and the rest. If you weren't signed to a label you might as well not exist. It's much better now. These days anyone can record an album. You don't need a record company to give you permission. You can bypass shops and distributors and everyone else taking a cut of the profits. You can sell direct to your customers and promote your music anywhere in the world through the internet. It's awesome.

**Silva** – Sure, you've got a point. I know the whole issue is more complex than I make out. I also have to admit my band only got its break because of the internet in the first place with a song on YouTube. We wouldn't have put out an album in the old days cos we would never have got past the record companies. I'm seeing this whole thing through red-tinted glasses right now. We're at the end of a tour and my head's done in. I've got family problems and can't even afford the flight home. So, you actually like touring?

**Stringer** – Yeah, but it's not for everyone.

**Silva** – It's not for me. I'm a dinosaur who'll be extinct soon, wiped out by the climate change caused by technology. Looks like you'll adapt and ride on through. What pisses me off is freeloaders like Pyro who don't understand how hard it is to make a good album and how much work goes into it. You spend a year and thousands of dollars making it and he spends thirty seconds downloading it for free. Then he says it sucks.

**Pyro** –Stop hiding behind your user name, Silva. Tell us the name of your band already so I can steal your music.

**Silva** – Why would I reveal my identity? Why would I say any of these things in public? You morons would just drum up a witch hunt like you did against Lars from Metallica over the whole Napster thing. Lars was totally right in what he said but he got vilified online, lectured on moral issues by people who were basically thieves and parasites themselves.

**Pyro** – At least tell me where your wife lives so I can make a house call while you're on tour. Like you said, you've got problems at home and you can't even afford the airfare home. What a loser!

**Silva** – Why don't you give me your address instead and I'll come round and give you the info personally?

**Pyro** – Yeah come over fag and I'll show you all the albums on my computer that I never bought. There's thousands, I never even heard most of them yet. Yours is probably on there too.

**Silva** – Let's have your address then. Or at least tell me where you work so I can go there and demand that you do your job for free. Oh that's right - then you wouldn't be able to make your car payments and your retirement fund, would you?

**Cat Girl** – But that's the great thing about the internet - freedom. The internet gives us free speech and free expression.

Like Stringer said, anyone can make music nowadays and reach out to the other side of the world to people they'd never meet.

**Silva** – That's a very different sense of the word free. Like I said, just cos it's free to get a movie or an album, it's not free to make. If no one pays to consume it, in the end that means no one's going to pay to produce it. There are long term consequences. Movies, albums, books don't get funded, so they don't get made. Or they're cheaply made, so the quality suffers. Book and record shops close down, newspapers go out of business, people who work in these industries lose their jobs.

**Cat Girl** – Maybe some of those industries will die out. That's technology for you. It's evolution. Progress. You can't stop it and you can't go back.

**Silva** – Sure - a lot of these old businesses are bound to go extinct. The internet must be one of the most effective killing machines ever devised. It kills the old ways of living without effort or intention, without seeing or caring, simply by existing. Parasites like Pyro go along for the ride. He reflects the apathy and indifference of the net, and adds a note of malice into the mix for that personal touch.

**Pyro** – Thanks, Silva. By the way, did I tell you that you suck? So does your wife. I just made a house call and paid her ten bucks to blow me. She said she's gonna put it towards your airfare home. Hang in there. A few more and you'll be on that plane.

**Silva** – Chalk one up for the internet tough guys then. Maybe one day we'll meet in real life, Pyro, then we'll see who sucks.

I logged off and shut down the computer. Then, thoroughly spent, I returned to my room on the hotel's lower levels. Before going to bed, I dug the Vortex Winder out of my luggage, expecting to see the small screen lit up with an explanation of the 'power for vengeful rant' as I'd sensed it to be at the start of my internet rave.

Yet there was no explanation. No description, either cryptic or direct, appeared on that screen. The Vortex Winder lay dormant, as dead and lifeless as it had been since the tour began. Whatever had caused my rant, the Vortex Winder had nothing to do with it.

# 14

# The Price of Dominion

I rejoined the tour at Dresden. The rest of the tour party did not seem unduly fazed by the extra three weeks. If there were a few grumbles, they were only an undertone in the overall mood. These young road dogs were by now attuned to the grinding rhythm of tour life and seemed to take it in their stride.

The Dresden after-show was a big one. Ivan came out and sang the last three songs in our set and killed it. Buzzing from the triumph, we partied hard with the boys from Crank Hammer until the early hours. This helped block out my anxiety about affairs back home in Sydney.

By the time of the Leipzig show, Ivan was ready to make his full debut with us. Any nerves I felt were offset by relief at having the vocal burden lifted from my shoulders. The weight of attention was now directed at Ivan. I was free to pace moodily around the stage firing off guitar riffs, or to briefly take centre stage for my solos. I relished the chance to take a role that was, if not secondary, at least that of evil genius behind the scenes rather than front of stage show pony. Let the punters drool over the young king Ivan. As chief riffmeister and composer, I would always be the real power behind the throne.

Any enthusiasm about Ivan was played down in phone calls to Sandra. I told her the band's new addition had done 'OK' and 'quite well under the circumstances' in his first outings with the band. Any talk that he was a rock god in waiting would have seen Sandra jump to the conclusion a world tour was imminent. This could have killed our relationship then and there. I wanted to keep Sandra in a holding pattern for the next three weeks rather than provoke her into rash decisions. Then I'd go home to Australia, clear my head, and work out how best to balance my two worlds.

If this couldn't be achieved, I'd at least work out which world was to take the ascendancy.

Sandra had not pressed the points raised in last week's call. Nor was she overly interested in Ivan's performance. Indeed, the ups and downs of the band were never a matter of much concern to her. Her ambivalence, indeed almost hostility, toward the band had been made clear with her confession to hoping the tour would fail. At any rate, she seemed more worried about Finzi lately. The beloved cat had still not regained his former lustre, despite the vet not having found any definite ailment.

Before long, the tour had rolled through Magdeburg and on to Berlin, the site of my mid-tour rest stop. Hoffman was still holed up on the 12th floor of his posh hotel, which is where Ivan and I met him when we arrived. Upon hearing how well Ivan was doing, Hoffman said little. Any I-told-you-so comments were made redundant by his faintly smug smile. A small raise of the eyebrows was enough to convey a 'see - what were you worried about?' message.

Hoffman had set up a headlining show for us in one of the small to mid-size Berlin venues. This was a side-show to the main tour. Apparently the phone song 'SMS' had been quite popular here and our ballad 'Leuchtturm' had won us a few points as well. It's normally the European bands who try singing in English, so for an English speaking band to at least title a song in German got us a little attention.

The idea of headlining a show may have been overwhelming if I was still on vocals. The fact that we now had a genuine rock god on board gave me confidence. For his part, Hoffman did not hesitate to stress the magnitude of the occasion. A headlining show in Berlin. It was no stadium, just a small theatre, yet still a high point to have on your CV and the gateway to bigger and better things. Maybe the next time we came we really would be playing a stadium.

Buoyed by the prospect, I was a little less guarded in my next Skype chat with Sandra. This was the most positive I'd felt for months. To celebrate the career breakthrough, I'd taken an advance out of Hoffman's bonus money and rented a cheap hotel room. It wasn't much, but at least I had quiet. On the morning of the show, in the privacy of my room, I fired up the Skype connection to share the good news with my beloved. Sandra's face appeared on the monitor. She was neither smiling nor frowning. Instead, her face wore a blank, passive expression as if she'd just finished a twelve hour shift at work.

'Well, Sandy, just a few more days, then I'm going to stay home for a month and not see a living soul except you and Finzi.'

'Hi Jim. Where are you this time?'

'Back in Berlin. Tonight's the big one.'

'Good luck, love. I know how much it means to you.'

'Where's Finzi?'

Sandra paused for a second, her face blank.

'He's at the vet's. He still wasn't well, so it seemed best to take him in. They're keeping him overnight for observation.'

'That's no good. Do they know what's wrong with him yet?'

'They're not sure. Let's not worry about it now. We can talk about it tomorrow after your big show's over.'

'God, I hope's he's OK. It would break my heart if anything happened to him.'

At that, Sandra's poker face crumbled.

'I'm sorry, Jimmy, Finzi died. A few weeks ago they found a tumour. I didn't want to worry you, so I didn't say. Yesterday, the vet said he was too far gone and they couldn't do any more for him. He was in pain. It wasn't fair to keep him alive any longer.'

'Oh no, Sandra.'

'I'm really sorry. I wasn't going to tell you before your big show. It just came out.'

'I can't believe it. Are you sure there wasn't anything they could do?'

'I got a second opinion.'

'Why didn't you tell me before? I would have come straight home.'

'There was nothing you could have done. I just hoped you'd be here in time to say goodbye to him. That's why I was so upset when they extended the tour. Three weeks. Finzi didn't have that long left.'

'If you'd told me I would've been on the first plane home. Tell me, were you there for him at the end? Did he die peacefully?'

'I was there, love. He didn't suffer. He just lay there calmly - even managed a little purr. A soft purr and I could feel his chest vibrating. I held his paw and stroked him. When he got the injection, he looked up into my eyes... and then he was just gone, Jim. He didn't suffer. It was very peaceful, I promise you.'

Sandra began crying again and I followed. After a while, I looked up and said, 'That's it. I'm not doing the show. I'm coming home tonight.'

'No, Jimmy, don't do that. Go out there and play a great show.'

'I can't.'

'Do it for Finzi.'

'I want to come home now. Nothing else matters.'

Sandra looked up through her tears and spoke gently but with firmness.

'I've put you through terrible stress of late. I haven't been very supportive. You deserve better than I can give.'

'What are you talking about? You *have* been supportive. Look at how you protected me over Finzi. What you must have been through the last few weeks. It's not fair to leave you alone with what's happened.'

'I'm so proud of you, Jim. You've really made something of yourself. You can't turn back now, you just can't. Not for me, not for Finzi, not for anyone. It's *your* life now. Perhaps it's for the best what's happened.'

'Don't abandon me, Sandra - not now. First Finzi, now this. I can't bear it.'

'Maybe now's the best time - get all the pain out of the way at once. A big dose of pain, lots of tears, then we can both mourn properly and heal and come out the other side.'

'No, it can't happen like this.'

'Maybe we take a break for a year or two, like last time. Then, who knows? Let's not talk about it anymore now. Go and get ready for your show and I'll call you tomorrow and make sure you're OK.'

Sandra's image disappeared from the screen and I was left alone with my agony. After pacing round the room for a few minutes, I sat down at my laptop and composed a letter of resignation to Hoffman.

Dear Ted,

I want to thank you sincerely for all you've done to help me and the opportunities you've offered to advance my music career. Without you, I could never have got this far. The tour of Europe has been an amazing experience, unforgettable and eye opening. I only regret that one thing I have learned is I'm not cut out for this sort of life. I wish that were not true, but sadly it is.

I have only just learned of some very upsetting events back in my family home. I am frankly devastated and regret that I am unable to fulfil my playing commitments tonight and for the rest of the tour. If I could do it, I would, but in my present state there is no way I can walk onto a stage and give the performance that the fans have paid for.

I strongly regret the professional disruption this causes and understand that I must forgo any financial bonus you had promised. I do ask on compassionate grounds that you allow me to borrow a one way airfare home to Sydney, which I will repay at the earliest opportunity.

You may be wondering what factors have prompted my decision. Apart from my temperament and ongoing health and financial problems, some clues may also be found in an internet forum which I engaged in last week about music downloading. You will find my comments under the username 'Silva' and as for the other contributors, if you look at the views of a guy named 'Pyro' you may realise why I see little future in this career path.

Once again, I deeply regret any professional inconvenience I have caused and that I have let you down after all your kindness and help.

Regards,
Jimmy Brandt.


I posted a link to last week's internet discussion then sent the email on to Hoffman. I decided to take a bath, then go out to the pubs of Berlin and drink a toast to Finzi.

I had barely begun to dry myself, when the phone rang.

# 15
# Haste

'What's up, Jim?'

I was back in Hoffman's hotel room, sinking deep into a leather sofa.

'Sorry Ted, that's it for me. I'm done.'

'But why? Just when we're on the verge of a breakthrough.'

'You know what they say, Ted. Home is where the heart is, and that's where mine is now. It's certainly not here in Berlin tonight. My cat died and I wasn't there to say goodbye to him.'

'Again with the cat? We've got a headlining show and you're cancelling because of a cat?'

'It's not just that. Sandra's left me. Three months ago I had a happy home. Now there's nothing for me to go back to.'

'Then don't go. Your future's here now.'

'Thanks - but I'm going home to make up with Sandra. If you could just lend me the airfare, I swear on my honour to pay you back as soon as possible.'

'What's your honour worth if you cancel tonight? Do you know how many people you'll be disappointing? Whatever you decide to do once this tour is over, there's no way we're missing this show. You'll let down a whole lot of people who've helped you - management, the promoter, your band mates - and most of all, yourself.'

'I'm sorry but there's nothing I can do.'

'There is, actually - get over it. This whiny self-indulgence has got to stop. So your cat died and your girl left you. Great - go write a song about it. But to deny yourself a career highlight and the fruits of your hard work? It's totally disrespectful to your talents and the opportunities you've been given.'

'You're right, Ted, but I just don't have the heart to do it. My strength is completely drained. The way I feel, I can hardly lift a guitar pick, let alone a guitar.'

'The promoter's going to lose a lot of money if this show falls through. It's not fair to him after the risk he took for your sake. So let me make it absolutely clear to you, Jimmy. If you don't do this show, not only will I not be lending you an airfare home, I'll also regard you as personally liable for all monies lost and I'll sue you into oblivion. Even if you do run off home to your wife, you'll be in debt for the rest of your life. Think she'll take you back then?'

'Threaten me all you like, Ted, it won't make any difference. You can push me onto that stage with a cattle prod and I still won't be able to raise a pick in anger. It's just going to make the band look even worse and the crowd angrier if the show gets cancelled after five minutes.'

'My, my, Jimmy Brandt, you really are a piece of work. I've tried appealing to honour, to vanity, to greed. I've tried reason, threats…'

'Compassion might have been worth a shot.'

'… and here we still are. I've appealed to your sense of professionalism, your regard for others. Looks like we'll have to resort to some alternative methods of ensuring the show goes on.'

Hoffman produced a transparent plastic sachet containing some white powder.

'What's that - blow? I'll pass.'

'Not blow, just a bit of the old Lou Reed to see you through tonight. It's real quality - the best. Take some of that an hour before kick-off and you'll be punching through walls to get out there.'

'You reckon?'

'Yes - now snap out of this ridiculous mood. Do this show tonight like a pro, then tomorrow we'll talk about the future. But let me down here and you'll find out you can sink a lot lower yet. This ain't rock bottom by any stretch.'

'OK, Ted, at least for the sake of the airfare money. I'll give the speed a go, but if it turns out nothing happens on stage, don't say you weren't warned.'

'I'll be coming to the show personally to ensure you reach peak performance.'

Hoffman took strict measures to ensure I was not left alone for the rest of the day. He took me to lunch in the hotel restaurant, forcing me to eat something when I showed no appetite. He booked me a private room on level two of his hotel so I could rest for the gig, and told a security guy from the tour to keep me under constant surveillance.

Hoffman returned that afternoon and ordered me to shower and dress for the show. He accompanied me in a taxi to the theatre, then to a private dressing room where he watched me warm up with some classical guitar and a few scales on the electric. An hour before we were due on, he laid out a big line of the speed, produced a one hundred Euro note, and forced me to suck it up.

In a few moments, I looked up and saw the world anew. The scales I'd been mechanically drilling doubled in velocity. I looked up at Ted and grinned.

'Jimmy, my boy!' said Hoffman, clapping me on the shoulder. 'You're back. What did I tell you? You're going to play the best show of your life tonight.'

'Try and stop me!'

The dressing room lights were zinging with energy. Vortexes of electrical current zapped around the room. The sounds coming from my practice amp were mighty, and I awoke from my stupor to the reality of the situation. Here we were in Berlin about to play a headline show! We had a brilliant new singer and there were hundreds or perhaps even thousands of people out there who'd paid to see us. This was the stuff of my dreams!

I began speed-babbling to Hoffman and his eyes glinted with conspiratorial fervour. Together we would take over the world and rule it through music. There would be nothing but glory from here on in.

'I tell you what, Ted, we're going to blow this place apart tonight. I'm going to destroy that crowd singlehanded to avenge Finzi's death.'

'Who the hell's Finzi?'

'Only the finest cat who ever walked this Earth. Somebody get me a hat, by Christ, so I can take it off to him.'

'Of course - the cat. How could I forget?'

'It wasn't my fault he died. I didn't even know he was sick. How could I? Mark my words, Ted, that cat loved me to death. If he could have understood what a rock concert was, he'd want me to get out there tonight and kick the arse of every German in that goddamn hall!'

'Absolutely right, Jimmy. I think that's a very sound hypothesis.'

'As for that black-hearted wench, Sandra, let's see what she says when Lighthouse XIII's the biggest band in the world and I've paid off a thousand mortgages without even trying, while she's still chipping away at the old nine-to-five.'

'That's the spirit.'

'Best goddamn cat in the world, Ted. I'll challenge any man to a duel who says otherwise.'

'Fire up, old boy! And speaking of world's best, look who's here.'

The new singer, Ivan, came into the dressing room. We high-fived and did a line of the speed together, then wrote a new song on the spot. We called it 'Net Kill' at the time, but in due course its proper title would be 'Extinction.Net.' Fired with a manic sense of potency, we ordered the drummer and bass player into the room to roughly learn it so we could premiere the song tonight.

As show time approached, I could barely restrain myself from storming the stage singlehanded. I was aware of my usual pre-show nervousness yet instead of seeing it as some kind of difficult work colleague to be managed, I viewed it as an enemy of the state who was able to be beaten, crushed and destroyed by the titanic confidence engulfing my being.

I fidgeted with manic intensity over my stage gear. Tuning my guitars, checking my amp settings, my picks, and other bits and pieces. I rewrote the setlist several times before settling on the final version. And if the guys in the lighting crew were going to complain about the changed running order, I'd make sure I personally fired their lazy arses right after the show.

Finally, the lights went down and our intro tape began to play. The four of us took our places on the darkened stage, then we exploded into life with the first song, 'Vortex Winder.'

Aware that I was in a heightened state, I made sure not to play too fast, particularly on songs begun by the guitar like 'Black Art' and 'Waves Upon Waves.' Up the tempo on songs like that and I would have paid for it come solo time. Instead, I focused on locking in with the drums and bass. In any case, there was ample chance to play fast when we debuted a rough version of 'Net Kill' and when the song 'Elijinx' got its first ever live performance with vocals. It had always been too big an ask to play and sing that one myself, yet with Ivan giving a vocal performance that surpassed my recorded version, I was free to deliver a frenzied execution of the riffage. It was only during the slow middle section that I looked up to see Hoffman side of stage with two thumbs up, leering triumphantly.

It may have been a drug-enhanced review, but I thought Ivan's vocal performance was outstanding. He seemed to have everything from the guttural lows of Lindemann from Rammstein to the near operatic highs of Halford from Priest. On songs such as 'Life Line' and 'Spark' he took the original melodies an octave higher and elevated the songs themselves as a result. As for charisma, I had a bizarre flashback to my uni presentation with Jacinta Lynton, when every eye in the room had been drawn to her. The same phenomenon was at work here, yet magnified tenfold in the intensity of a rock concert.

I didn't mind. Unlike the time with Jacinta, my moments of glory were also plentiful. During the solos for 'Spark' and 'LHXIII' my guitar soared majestically to fill the whole of the theatre. The setlist tonight was:

1. Vortex Winder
2. Black Art
3. Trade Winds
4. Z Club
5. Waves Upon Waves
6. Life Line
7. Spark
8. Mountain Gods
9. Extinction.Net
10. SMS
11. Temporary Kingdom
12. Leuchtturm
13. Between the Stairway and the Highway
14. Elijinx
15. Oceanus
16. LHXIII

By the time we came offstage after the second encore, I was dripping wet from ninety minutes of peak level performance. A gaggle of well-wishers greeted us all backstage with handshakes and high fives. I skulled a stein of beer and topped it off with a long toke from a joint. This induced a sudden nausea, but I rode it out for ten seconds before surging to the crest of a wave of intoxication.

From somewhere among the crowd of people, Ted Hoffman emerged and took a firm grip on my hand. Looking deep into my eyes, he grinned with exultant and fiendish delight.

'Hey Jimmy, what was that you said? I didn't quite catch it. Something about cancelling the show, was it?'

'I owe you big time, Ted. You and your medical supplies. And now the show's over, it's top up time. Can you help me out?'

'For you, sir, anytime. How about we make port of call back at the *Hotel Alexanderplatz*?'

'You don't have any with you? I want to party on here.'

'Finish your drink while I send for the car. We'll be there in ten minutes. A quick hit and you'll be back for the after-party.'

'Right you are, Ted. Let's go then, there's not a moment to lose.'

'Your wish is my command, sir. Just grab hold of that young colossus over there and we'll be off.'

Following his gaze, I spied Ivan, who was adorned by a couple of buxom, blonde Berlin stunners. He seemed put out at having to leave, yet Hoffman insisted and he acquiesced with a sulky look. Within minutes, the three of us were sitting in a taxi heading back to the *Hotel Alexanderplatz*. My head seemed to be orbiting my body among the city lights of Berlin and my heart was beating like butterfly's wings.

Back in Hoffman's suite on the 12th floor, the three of us sipped room service champagne, then Ivan and I did a line of the magic powder. With his good spirits restored, Ivan sat there grinning at me. Hoffman, who had abstained, listened indulgently to our drug babble for a few minutes before calling time.

'Mission accomplished, gentlemen. Time for your humble manager to turn in for the night. It's a good night's sleep then world domination, strictly in that order. You boys go back to your party - and look out for each other. We take care of each other in this band.'

By the time we made it back, the party was in full swing. It was wall to wall booze, crew, and girls. I soaked up the atmosphere for a while, but before long I had the urge for solitude. I walked out into the cool night air and bathed in the relative peace of the city. It must have been after midnight and the streets were fairly empty.

Finding a quiet bar, I had a drink and reflected on the chaotic swirl of recent events. Finally, I was able to raise a glass to the memory of Finzi, the beloved cat who would never be forgotten, no matter how crazy it all became from here. It seemed my life was evolving rapidly through its own momentum, which relieved me of the burden of choice if nothing else.

Good old Finzi - and dear Sandra. I wondered how she was doing. It would be daytime in Australia - perhaps I should call her. She'd hear me happy and triumphant, in contrast to the wretched state of our last conversation. It would be good for both of us. She'd see that everything was going to be fine, even though we would now lead separate lives. When the band had conquered the music world and I'd retired to a country estate somewhere, Sandra might even feel a tinge of regret at having cast me aside.

I returned to the hotel room Hoffman had booked for me on the second floor of the *Hotel Alexanderplatz*. On the way, I picked up two containers of takeaway food, wolfing down one of the meals there in the street and taking the other with me. When I arrived back at the hotel, the room was silent, such that the ringing in my ears from the gig was heightened. In my euphoric state, this didn't bother me. It was part of the job to deal with minor health matters. Why complain, given the amazing night I'd just had?

I dialled Sandra but there was no answer. After the third attempt, I gave up. Never mind. The hotel room was tremendous. While not as luxurious as Hoffman's 12th floor suite, it was kingly enough. I was struck by the miraculous nature of the room's facilities. How extraordinary that I could move the bathroom tap handle slightly to the left and cold water came out. Then, just by moving it to the right, the water became hot. How thoughtful the hotel people were to offer such a service to their guests.

I showered, then dried myself with the towels and hair dryer provided. I was overcome by the sense of an intangible kindness - the feeling that there was someone out there, some force or spirit, looking out for me. How lucky I was to have been given this room. It was filled with wonders. For example, that big TV over there. It allowed me to stay in touch with the adventures of my fellow humans all over the world. I would never turn into one of those 1970s style rock stars who threw TV sets out of hotel windows. Acts like that could only result from the desensitisation brought on by alcohol abuse. I might drink my share of booze but it would never blind me to the value of the world around me.

I vowed to stop being so negative from now on. I was truly blessed. From this point on, I would make the most of my good fortune and help make a better world. Music itself could be a force for good. Indeed, why not get out the guitar right now and work on songs for the new album?

I jammed for a while then noticed it was 3am. Better turn in if I was any chance of making it through the next day. I settled in between the lush, heavy sheeting of my bed at the *Hotel Alexanderplatz*.

And couldn't sleep a wink.

Although my body was shattered from the day's extremes, each time sleep asked for admission, the same *thou-shalt-not-pass* answer was sent back by the sentry on command. Neither would my mind settle. It raced in endless circles around the events of recent days and prospects for the future.

I became uncomfortably aware of the too-fast beating of my heart. I'd ignored it earlier but now it began to alarm me. My inner hypochondriac rose up in a panic. What kind of fool takes amphetamines in his forties? It was a real risk once you got older. Wasn't it the bass player from The Who that had that coke-triggered heart attack in his hotel room a few years back? What was I thinking tonight when I doubled up after the gig?

At the same time, I became aware of a looming emotional desolation. It was as if a thick fog was forming within my blood and bones, shrouding every portion of my being within a blinding, dispiriting mist. I was utterly alone. Sandra was gone. Sandra, the only person in this world who really cared for me. And Finzi was dead, his beautiful green eyes closed forever, his vibrant purr never to be felt or heard again.

I was struck by the finality of it. I would never see Finzi again. Not ever. Sandra too was lost, this time for good. There would be no new resurrection. Even in the unlikely event that we *did* get back together, we would still grow old and die. There was no escaping that.

My nightmare from the garden came back to me. The awful vision with its premonition of loss. It was no longer a nightmare from which I could awaken. Here in the surreal surrounds of a Berlin hotel room, it had become a horrifying reality, a waking nightmare with no exit.

I lurched out of bed, for the room was suffocating me. I threw open the door and saw a carpeted hallway with a sequence of identical doors to the left and the right, at front and behind, stretching to infinity like an Escher drawing. The corridor went on forever.

Lunging back inside, I called upon the memory of a Buddhist retreat from years before when I'd done little but meditate and walk around in the Australian bush. That week had brought a deep sense of calm. I tried to recreate that now - yet the attempt to sit and meditate only exacerbated the ringing in my ears and my racing heart.

In a final attempt at salvation, I pulled the dormant Vortex Winder from my luggage. It was as dead as it had been since leaving Australia three months before. The little screen remained blank, quite empty of any words of wisdom, encouragement, or power. Throwing it roughly onto the bed, I called on my mentor who had bestowed the useless device upon me in the first place.

'Iolango! Why do you forsake me now when I need you most?'

My bitter rebuke prompted no miracle manifestation. Instead, the sudden rage gave rise to a sharp sensation in my chest and with a cry, I fell face down onto the thick carpet beside the bed.

*So this is how it ends*, I thought. I was going to die, right here in this hotel room. Dead of a heart attack and only in my forties. Killed by the speed which had poisoned me as surely as if it were arsenic, and by my own hand. Self destructive to the bitter end.

Face down, I waited to die and in this act of resignation found a brief respite. There was nothing more to be done except wait for the further jolt of pain which would expel my consciousness from my body, or perhaps extinguish it altogether. Yet somehow that train refused to pull into the station. It could only be a matter of time.

Feeling myself barely able to move, it was an act of major exertion to turn over and lie on my back. I could see the clock now. 4am. Why was I left hanging? End it, for God's sake. I hovered on the verge of my demise, certain that any further attempt at movement would send me over the edge. Still, perhaps if I could wait it out, someone from the tour party would come to fetch me in a few hours and take me to hospital.

More time passed and death was still waiting in the wings, toying with me. All I could do was lie still and wait. I was left only with my own thoughts and emotions for company. Yet these were all of the bleakest kind. I tried to call upon happy memories for comfort, but even those thoughts of friends and accomplishments which would normally sustain me proved useless.

In hindsight, I surmise that the speed had produced a dire bodily reaction. The natural chemicals that enable a sense of stability, pleasure, and well-being had been destroyed. They'd been used up, negated, or overpowered by the invading substance. The speed had elevated my physical state to dizzying heights of euphoria. Now I was feeling the imbalance rectifying itself to horrendous effect.

I can barely convey the desolation in which I was now entombed. It was as if any ability to feel the simplest sense of contentment had been revoked. All my past accomplishments were drained of value. Even the sense of pride I normally felt in my battle against harsh odds seemed futile. The whole enterprise of my existence past, present and future, was empty and doomed. The universe itself was a place of pain. Suffering was everywhere and all hope was lost.

The smallest and most innocuous item was enough to cause sorrow. After an age lying crippled on the floor, I managed to inch my way along the carpet on my belly like a snake, and had the idea that eating something might make me feel better. This thought alone, with its vague sense of kindness, seemed unbearably sad. Struggling to my knees, I retrieved the second of the two meals I'd bought at midnight. The first had, of course, been wolfed down in minutes in my frenzy of a few hours before.

I opened the plastic container to find some kind of cooked food inside. A white plastic knife and fork lay on top of the container, wrapped up in a paper napkin. I found a steel knife and fork in a drawer in the hotel room and threw the plastic ones away. Yet in my desolate mood this struck me as deeply sad. The plastic knife and fork had been created for only one purpose in the entire world and that was to enable someone to eat this meal. Here I was, negating their entire *raison d'etre* and discarding them into the bin, their purpose unfulfilled.

The meal was a chicken curry. Who doesn't like chicken? And so - how many individual chickens had died over the years because of my gluttony? Yes, I always felt some token guilt, but never enough to make me a vegetarian. I was a selfish and murderous creature, well representative of my kind. Humanity was a species of carnivores. To satisfy our ravenous appetites, we had systematically set up farming and killing machines with the sole aim of satisfying those needs. It was a horror beyond belief, able to be lived with only through a conscious act of denial.

I put the meal down, fell back to the floor, and begged for the heart attack to relieve me of existence. Instead, there was a soft knock on the door. And at that point I still had not the faintest idea that, within a few hours, I would be about to kill a man.

# 16
# To the Dark Side

Ivan entered the room. In escaping from the corridor's infinite doors, I'd forgotten to lock my own. When his knock went unanswered, he came in and saw me flat out on the carpet.

'Jimmy, what's wrong?'

'I OD'd on the speed. Get me to a hospital, quick.'

'Better not do that, dude. What are you going to tell them? It's drugs. You could get deported for that.'

'Just get a taxi. Or an ambulance.'

'I don't speak the language, bud. What's hospital in German?'

'It's *Krankenhaus. Bitte das Krankenhaus anrufen, schnell*! I mean, hurry!'

'*Krankenhaus*! That's a funny word. Tell you what, I'll take you up to Mr Hoffman's room. He'll know what to do.'

With my right arm around his shoulder, Ivan dragged me to the lift. I was breathing heavily as it ascended to the 12th floor. The torturous trip ended at last with Ivan banging on Hoffman's door. He opened it a minute or two later.

'What's wrong with Jimmy? I thought I told you to keep an eye on him.'

'I can't watch him all the time, you know. There were some band-fan relations to take care of.'

'Right then, Ivan, leave him here. You can go back to your room.'

Hoffman walked me over to a sofa bed by the far wall, where I collapsed and lay breathing rapidly, my hands twitching. Hoffman frowned. He laid a pillow under my head and covered me with a blanket.

'Jimmy Brandt, as I remarked only yesterday in this very room, you certainly are a piece of work. What have you done to yourself this time?'

'It was that speed, Ted. Never again. It's evil. You should flush it all down the toilet.'

'So what happens if you have another touch of performance anxiety? It did its job. A little too well, clearly. You shouldn't have had that second dose after the show. Remember that for next time.'

'Next time! Ted, if I survive this, I don't know if there'll ever be another Lighthouse XIII gig. But one thing you can be sure of - if I die here in this room the fat lady has definitely sung.'

'Die? What are you talking about?'

'Feel my heart. It's beating so fast. I could have a heart attack any minute. Maybe I already have.'

'Good Lord, Jim, you do worry so. Even if you do die, why should it be the last Lighthouse XIII gig? Now Ivan has proven himself, I'm sure we could get another guitarist to carry on your legacy.'

'What? Over my dead body!'

'Well, clearly. Think of it objectively. With the wonderful songs you've written, a new band, and Ivan's star power, Lighthouse XIII would undoubtedly go on to conquer what's left of the music world.'

'Are you insane? What's wrong with you, Ted - why are you talking like this?'

'Calm down, Jimmy! If you're genuinely concerned about having a heart attack, stop working yourself into such a lather. Get a grip on yourself.'

'Just get me to the hospital, please. *Bitte das Krankenhaus*!'

'Oh splendid! You're speaking German. Always a good idea to learn a few phrases in the language of the country you're playing - goes down well with the locals. And a lovely phrase it is too. Takes me back to the last months of the war.'

'What's wrong with you, Ted? Come on, I need a doctor!'

'Listen, Jimmy, how's it going to look if you're taken to hospital for a drug overdose? Just when the show was such a success. It's not on, not after such a triumph. No, we're going to ride this one out, my boy. Don't worry. I'm here for you. I'll not leave your side. When you're better, we'll have a proper talk.'

'You only care about the band. It's always about the band, never about me.'

'That's really not fair. I've become quite fond of you, in spite of all the trouble you've put me through. Now what can I get you? A hot drink?'

'The phone. I want to call Sandra.'

'That's unwise. The last thing you want is for her to see you at death's door like this. Again, it's just not a good look. Tell you what - I'll give you something to make you sleep. Your recovery is all about rest at this point. It's really the best medicine.'

Hoffman mixed up some kind of powder in a glass of water. Then, tilting my head upwards, he put the glass to my lips. Within minutes, it took effect and I drifted off into a hazy, troubled sleep. Images appeared and disappeared so I could not tell if I was waking or dreaming. It was a parade of disturbing memories - the day in our Blue Mountains garden, chaotic scenes from the tour, Sandra's face on the Skype call, the prison in Thailand, and the looming swell of a tsunami. I woke in fright several times, yet Hoffman was always there to quieten me and nurse me back to sleep.

At last I awoke in the grip of a paralysing languor, feeling as numb as if I'd slept for three weeks. I felt quite unable to rise from the bed and lay there comatose. Hoffman was still at my bedside. As he peered down at me, his blurry features slowly came into focus. Though my mouth was drier than the Sahara, I managed at last to greet him by his true name.

'Elijinx.'

'Jimmy. Do you have *any* idea what the time is?'

I tried to answer but could only manage a cough.

'Come now, lad, don't splutter at me at this time of night. Here, drink some water. That'll loosen your tongue.'

I took a long swallow and composed myself.

'So, the band's been managed by Elijinx all this time. No wonder my career's been going so well and my life so badly. Why didn't I realise?'

'It's your depth perception. Your species has such a boundless capacity to be superficial. Take another look.'

It was indeed an odd sensation as I peered up at him. On the surface, Hoffman's face was quite different to the other guises in which I had known Elijinx. Yet by making a small perceptual adjustment, I saw through to the face behind the face - and in that I recognised him. Having now seen it, it was as if the two faces, the inner and outer, merged into one. The real recognition, of course, should have come from his behaviour. In the several years since our last meeting I had relaxed my guard. There had been nothing in the way of eternal vigilance going on.

'Well - this time evil wins, Elijinx.'

'What do you mean *this time*? In this world? Don't tell me you're going to chalk one up for the underdog.'

'You're right - what am I saying? Even Iolango admitted the Maelstrom is in the ascendancy.'

'So when are you going to align yourself with the winning side? Your track record really is very poor. Look at you. Homeless, wifeless, kicked out of your university. Friendless, penniless, and lying here on what could well be your deathbed. Yet still you pledge yourself to so called good and the Vortex Winder! Where has your allegiance ever gotten you? Even the band only succeeded because of my direct help and intervention.'

'It's your help that's *put* me on this deathbed. If I'm to die in Berlin, it's your doing.'

'And a wonderful place to die, it is. Although I concede, it's certainly changed since I was last here, during the war. They were such heady times.'

'Don't tell me you had something to do with all that.'

'Once a manager, always a manager. A rock band, a *Reich* - it's much the same thing. In all humility, I can't claim to have had much input there, but I did offer some encouragement from the sidelines. Let humanity be its own creator. As I said, at Solar Eclipse Management it is not our place to usurp the role of the artist. Our job is simply to offer guidance and moral support. That project was most intriguing, and in some ways a success. Heady times indeed and the final days were extraordinary - a frolic in a thunderstorm.'

'Why do you bother to get involved at all?'

'As I told you once before, my aim is simply to hasten the processes of history to their natural conclusion. Humanity's inherent evil is well proven. Clearly you're doomed, so rather than draw the whole thing out *ad nauseam*, why not speed up your destruction and make room for someone else to take your place?'

'Fine - whatever you say. I'll be long gone before any of that happens.'

'Jim, Jim - always the pessimist. Listen to you. You can't handle life on the road. You're going to die. You won't live to see the final extinction of humanity. Why are you always so negative?'

'That's just me, I suppose.'

'It needn't be. There's hope for a young lad like you yet. Smart as paint you are, I knew it as soon as I saw you. It's up to me to step in at this point as your manager. You know what your main problem is?'

'I'm too negative?'

'You're conflicted, permanently divided against yourself. The constant petty arguments going on in your head. Will I travel the world as a rock star and have an extraordinary time, or will I stay home and have a boring life hanging out with the cat? Will I recruit an amazing singer who'll make the band famous, or keep mumbling into the mike myself to keep some illusion of control? Will I align myself with Iolango's stuffy moralistic rot, or turn to the dark side with Elijinx and enjoy myself for once? Really, Jim, it's exhausting just being around you.'

'So you want me to join with you in evil. Is that it?'

'In a sense, but remember we use these simplistic terms for convenience. These definitions are highly subjective. I mean, you seem to see working a regular job and sitting round the house with your wife as good. I see it as an evil waste of your talents. Jimmy the Good is a tedious bore - no one wants to know about him. Jimmy the Evil is a far more interesting character. What's that TV show you like - the one on your blog about the serial killer?'

'*Dexter.*'

'Ah, *Dexter*. That's the one. A wonderful man with the courage to embrace his own evil - and beloved around the world as a result. Dexter Morgan the forensic expert who solves murders, then goes out and murders people himself. But what if he was Dexter Morgan the forensic expert who did his job and went home to watch football on TV? No one would care about him. He wouldn't be loved in millions of homes, as he is now. I tell you, Jim, it's better to be an anti-hero than a non-entity. You know it lad, don't deny it. You're smart as paint and no mistake.'

'You already said that. Think I don't know what you're doing, Elijinx? That's the second time you've quoted *Treasure Island* at me. You're trying to tap into my childhood psyche to sway me to your cause. By the powers, you're surely Silver to my Hawkins...'

'... and you may lay to that!'

Deathbed or not, I laughed along with him.

'Think of it though, Jim' said Elijinx. 'You always sided with Long John in that tale. You were supposed to cheer for Livesey, Trelawney and Smollett. Yet you'd go a fair way to find a more privileged trio than them. The voyage alone showed it plain enough. The toffs resting up in their plush cabins standing to make a fortune on the back of the seamen's hard labour. Any hint of a rising up for a share of the spoils and the poor devils would have been flogged back to their natural born subservience. Second offence and they would have been hung from the yard arm like common pirates.'

'Which they were.'

'And more power to them! Why, it should have been a regular French Revolution on board the *Hispaniola*. Don't tell me you didn't want to see that smug Doctor Livesey cast into the deep. Yet these vile oppressors were on the side of good. Good? Turn away from the light, Jimmy, I beseech you!'

'You have Silver's powers of persuasion, Elijinx, I'll grant you that. What would you have me do?'

'Stop this self-division. Give me your heart and your hand. Where has your adherence to good ever taken you? Did it get you your PhD or a fair hearing in that court of appeal - or did you just come up against a latter day version of Livesey and Smollett?'

'And what of your fight against Pyro and the other downloaders?' Elijinx continued. 'Yes, I read the argument. Join me and I'll show you how to win it in reality, not just intellectually. Where do your fine ideals and arguments get you in any practical sense? Good has no power in this world. Even the famous Sandra abandoned you. Leave this false alliance behind. Embrace evil, which is the true good, as well you know. Live the rock star life which is your rightful destiny.'

All this while, even in my present state of duress, I'd been assessing Elijinx's case and finding it hard to disagree. My allegiance to what I considered good ideals had served me poorly in the chaos of recent events. Now, as had happened once before at the summit of his island, I experienced that perceptual shift in which black and white flickered, merged, and realigned themselves. I saw Elijinx not as a villain, but as an agent of reason, wisdom, and justice. Yet what he was asking was still beyond me physically, if not conceptually.

'Perhaps I would join you, Elijinx, but the task is too great. Look at me, two breaths from death. The spirit is willing but the flesh is weak.'

'Take my hand, accept the Maelstrom, and you'll be a new man. Born again from the fires of extinction, rising from your own funeral pyre like some black hearted phoenix. The Maelstrom will restore you to the vigour you possessed as a young man in your twenties. No drug will ever harm you. Nor will any love scar you, no music deafen you, no debt bankrupt you. You will be a god among men, dominant and indomitable. Your adversaries will cower before you, the world will yield in your direction.'

'What have I got to lose? I've lost everything already. I'm on the verge. Tell me more. You're right that the path of good has led me nowhere.'

'Of course it has. Good has no sway in this world, that's plain. It is the evil who occupy all the positions of high office in the world of human affairs. The Maelstrom is ascendant to the end, until humanity's last breath. Join us and take a share of the spoils. Cease this upstream struggle and remake yourself in harmony with the true way of the world.'

Could I do it? I had resisted once before, now I saw less and less reason to repeat that decision. My recent struggles flashed before my eyes: the PhD travesty, Finzi's death and Sandra's abandonment, the hard slog on the road, the downloading debate, and at last the drug overdose. Where was my great mentor, Iolango, in all this? Where was the Vortex Winder? I'd been betrayed and abandoned on all sides. Yes, it was high time for a change of allegiance. I looked up into my manager's eyes, and with some effort, raised my hand towards him

'I believe you speak truly. That is the world as I've known it. So it is and will always be. I accept your offer.'

Elijinx extended his hand and passed me an arrow-shaped piece of obsidian. Smooth on its surface and sharp at the edges, it fitted perfectly into my grasping hand.

'Welcome, Jimmy. Here is your individualised portion of the Maelstrom. Keep it ever close. It will protect you and bestow upon you your rightful supremacy.'

The resurrection was immediate. On accepting the Maelstrom, I felt my vigour returning, my strength flooding back. The reaper's hand, so close above my head, retreated. I sat up from my death bed. Stretched and stood up. Laughed. Picked up the room's TV set and lifted it above my head. Then, as a courtesy, raised an inquiring eyebrow at Elijinx. He opened his arms wide, palms upward, and I threw the TV against the wall where it smashed and fell in pieces onto the floor. Elijinx clapped, as if applauding a toddler's first triumphant steps.

'By the powers, this is the start of something, Jim. Yet there's one more task to make your rebirth complete.'

'Name it.'

'An act of genuine destruction. Smashing TVs is old hat. By the way, a heads up. Don't ever smash any guitars onstage. Hendrix and Townshend did it in the sixties and anyone doing it since just looks silly. So, let us proceed. One more task will complete your transformation.'

'I'm ready.'

'Follow me.'

We walked through to the next room of Elijinx's hotel suite, the one leading out to a balcony overlooking the Berlin streets twelve storeys below. Darkness had again fallen. I must have slept through an entire day since the crisis of the night before.

A young man was tied up on the couch, gagged and bound. He looked to be in his mid-twenties. The guy was dressed like a stockbroker, yet a couple of days' growth and an anxious expression ruined his good looks. I looked askance at my new mentor.

'What's all this, Elijinx?'

'I believe you're acquainted with this fellow, Jim.'

'Hardly.'

'You know him as a Mr Pyro, I believe, while he may remember you as Silva. You've only met him online.'

'You don't mean to say - the chat group from the other day?'

'The very same.'

'How on earth did you trace him and get him here?'

'The internet is nowhere near as anonymous as these people think. We did have to fly Mr Pyro in from New York but it was really no trouble, I assure you. He's here to answer for his crimes directly. Remove his gag.'

Elijinx pulled an evil-looking knife from a drawer and handed it to me. I took it without hesitation and advanced on the prisoner.

'Well, well, Pyro. Did you bring your keyboard?'

I pressed the blunt side of the knife against his face and severed the gag to bestow free speech upon him once more. A long trail of saliva came away from the side of his mouth as the gag was removed.

'What's this all about?' he asked, making a miserable effort to seem calm. 'This is some kind of mistake.'

'Yeah, big mistake. Tell me, Pyro, what's your real name?'

'Pyro? Who's this Pyro? My name's Matthew Wright. There's some ID in my pocket. Check it out. Who are you?'

'I'm Silva. We met last week.'

'I've got no idea what you're talking about.'

'Come on, Matthew, you heard what my colleague said. You can't have forgotten our spirited online debate on the ethics of illegal music downloading. I believe when we parted, you offered to engage the sexual services of my wife so I could pay for my plane fare home.'

The fellow looked shocked, yet he was going to try to talk his way out of it.

'What do you mean? That wasn't me. You've got the wrong guy.'

'We traced the discussion to you,' said Elijinx. 'What you've said is on record. There's no point denying it.'

'Stop wasting our time,' I said. 'It was you. We know it beyond any shadow of doubt. You're Pyro, Matthew.'

'Come on, dude, I was only trolling. I didn't mean any of that stuff.'

'So you don't really believe music is a worthless profession?'

I'm a music lover, I swear. I've got thousands of songs.'

'Which you stole.'

'Not all of them.'

'So you don't have hundreds of free albums stolen as illegal downloads off the net?'

'Sure, I've got a few. Who hasn't? But I've also got heaps of CDs that I bought. Let me go home and I'll prove it to you, I promise.'

'That's reassuring, Matthew. Perhaps I misjudged you.'

'Can I go please?'

'Maybe - but how do I know you're not going out to molest my wife like you were bragging about online?'

'Come on, dude, it was a joke. I was trolling! No one means anything they say on the internet.'

'I think you've got that backwards, Pyro. People say *exactly* what they mean on the internet. It's anonymous, so there are no consequences. It's what they say in real life that they don't mean. So, you've come all the way from New York. You know where you are now? Berlin. Looks like we saved you the airfare for that trip to Europe you were planning. So, Elijinx, do we let him go now?'

'Come on, Jim. I didn't fly this fellow across the Atlantic for a briefing. He's your means of full initiation to the Maelstrom.'

'What do you mean?'

'Do to him what he tried to do to your music career.'

'Ignore him? Treat him as worthless?'

'Don't be coy. You know what you have to do. Do to him what he and his kind have done to the music industry.'

'Meaning what?'

'Erase him, Jim. Destroy and erase. Use him as a blood sacrifice for your own ends.'

'Blood? That's a step too far, surely.'

'Come now, don't fall at the last hurdle. What would Dexter do? He selected those who deserved to die as a result of their callous crimes and he did it without a shred of regret. It empowered him and made the world a better place. They were justified murders. Now you can do the same. You have the chance to despatch one of those who helped kill music. How many future Led Zeppelins have been aborted or stillborn as a result of his actions? He deserves to die.'

'I've no intellectual quarrel with you, Elijinx. There's no counter argument to what you're saying. The fellow deserves to die, that's plain enough. Yet to have the blood on my own hands? I'm no killer. Or at least, so I've always thought.'

'You've no idea yet what you may or may not be. It's all beliefs. This fellow also thinks himself no killer, yet that is what he is. Duty is duty. Don't let a misplaced sense of pity stop you. Look into your own heart, then show him the compassion he showed you online last week. If nothing else, think of your happy home and what's become of it thanks to the likes of him.'

At that, the memory of the online debate came rushing back. Elijinx was right. This vandal did not deserve to live. He'd stolen music with complete disregard for its value and its source. Music! He'd steal my own too without a second thought, given the chance. Music, which was my own child, near enough. That which I'd nurtured since its very conception. Which I had honed and polished, over long years, from embryonic spark to a state of maturity. A state to which the likes of Pyro should pay reverent homage. Instead this philistine had placed his grubby, sacrilegious hands upon my child and molested it, laughing all the while. Then having had his brief, vacuous thrill, the serial rapist had discarded my creation and moved on to his next vile molestation. And he expected us to feel *grateful*? Oh yes, he deserved to die.

'Music's a luxury item. Why should you pay for it? I should be grateful you even want to listen to my stuff. I'm lucky you even care. That's what you said, wasn't it Pyro?'

'Please, whatever I said, I take it all back. All of it. I was wrong.'

'Too late, Matthew. Finzi is already dead.'

And as I spoke those words, my mind was made up. Yes, I would kill him. I'd kill him gladly as a public service. Yet not like this with the fellow bound. I advanced upon him to cut his bonds. Matthew stood up shakily then tried to run for the door. Yet having been bound for some time, his legs failed him and he sprawled upon the floor.

I hauled him skyward. He was taller than I expected, taller than me and no weakling. Yet it was no effort to seize him by the throat with a single hand. I pushed him back against the wall, then released him so he could hobble towards the only exit within reach - the balcony.

The fellow had clearly not known he was on the 12th floor, for the sight of the city street far below caused him to turn and try to bolt back into the room. He had no chance. I seized him again and forced him backwards to the very edge of the balcony and tilted him over, so he was looking back over his own head at the city. Then I pulled him up to face me once more. Elijinx looked on all the while, yet seemed uneasy at my hesitation and urged me to finish the job.

'Come on, Jim, this is no time for a stay of execution. Do your duty. What say we download this fellow onto the pavement?'

'So it will be and let justice be done,' I said, before turning back to the condemned man.

'Pyro. You destroyed my career and my marriage, and you killed Finzi. I pronounce upon you sentence of death - and may the Lord have mercy on your soul.'

I lifted Matthew Wright off the floor of the balcony and prepared to throw him to his doom. Yet on the point of release, my hand was stayed by a brief intervention, a piercing bell-like chime that broke my focus. This was no external sound but some kind of internal alarm. For a moment, it was enough to jolt me from my murderous frenzy. I saw afresh the street far below and heard Matthew pleading for his life. I paused, unsure what to do next, pulled Matthew back from the balcony edge and relaxed my hold upon him.

Then Ivan de Vangelus loomed up from behind and finished the job I had abandoned. Matthew Wright tumbled backwards over the balcony and, with a horrendous shriek, fell streaming to his death on the pavement twelve storeys below.

# Part Three

# 17

# Black Phoenix

Oh the awkward angles of the overthrown! Even from our lofty perch, the damage was clear. Four squares of pavement turned into a modern artist's canvas, and young Matthew spread out on it like so much paint.

I stared sideways at my new right hand man, perpetrator of the act - and there in that remorseless grin gained revelations about the man and our relationship. I saw that Ivan was not the vacuous pretty boy I'd supposed, but something more sinister, and clearly a good deal further down the path of corruption than me. The look he gave me spoke of complicity. A complicity I had neither sought nor imagined, yet which was now irreversibly mine, blood-bonded by the events of the last twenty-four hours.

'Come lads, let's not loiter unduly,' came the command at our backs.

'There's not a living soul down there, Mr. Hoffman,' Ivan answered.

'It's only a matter of time. Both of you return to your rooms and stay there.'

Ivan and I left the balcony and made for the door of Elijinx's hotel room - only to have our puppet strings jerked to attention once more.

'Jim, you go first. Ivan, stay a while. No need to be seen together just now.'

Duly commanded, Ivan dropped back while I returned to my room alone.

I paused at the threshold. What a pilgrimage to the Maelstrom I had made. A dying man had staggered from this room, bathed in some filthy Lourdes, and returned to it a killer, transformed and reborn. I paced the floor and tried to make sense of the onslaught of recent events, most vivid of which was the demise of one Matthew 'Pyro' Wright, former internet troll and music lover.

The most striking feature of my mood was the absence of guilt. No shred of remorse clouded my thinking. Not for the late Mr. Wright, in any case. Intellectually, I knew I was complicit in the murder of a man and had come within an ace of delivering the fatal blow myself. Yet aside from a mild unease at the chance of being caught, there was a pronounced sense of detachment. I'd seen the fellow struggle on the balcony edge, heard the fading death shriek, and seen the sprawled manikin on the pavement - yet I was unmoved. I who had once pity enough to save a lowly, contemptible cockroach from a urinal was now complicit in a man's death without a hint of regret.

I became aware of a newfound reptilian coldness within myself. It was not a complete novelty. Until now it had been a small shadow dormant in the caverns of my mind. It loomed a good deal larger now. Yet why, after all, should I care about this Matthew Wright? He was a stranger. Strangers die every day. His death had all the meaning of a statistical foreign death on the evening news.

And I had killed him. Ivan may have delivered the *coup de grâce*, yet without me engaging Matthew in moral combat on the internet, he would never have been caught up in the whole chain of events to begin with. Our argument had been a spiteful meeting of minds in which he showed a contempt for my happiness and well-being. He killed me in his mind, as if we were anonymous soldiers on a virtual battlefield. Now I had killed him rather more completely - and cared not one jot. The fellow had been no creator. Technically, he was not even a consumer, merely a loathsome parasite, passively riding the wave of technology like some spineless jellyfish. Now that wave had dumped him twelve floors down, his demise was a nothing, to be mourned by no one. Even if there was a family somewhere at the end of my computer mouse, they had only themselves to blame for raising such a repulsive evolutionary dead end.

Really?

I tittered at this monologue which seemed to come from a foreign voice in my mind. Such arctic hate was a surprise. Yet I realised it was merely my own voice unfettered by its usual constraints. Curious, I crossed to the mirror of my room and saw a face recognisable but subtly transformed. There was a new steel in the familiar features, a fresh vigour and resolve. Yet if I was indeed born again, as Elijinx had intimated, then what had become of the man I once was? And as I gazed into the mirror at a spot over my left shoulder, there he was, still stretched out on the carpet.

I turned to examine him. The fellow certainly looked familiar. Yes, I remembered him now, this naive, conflicted soul. Where had his idealism ultimately taken him but to a sordid, anonymous death in a hotel room? Now he lay pitifully prone on the spot where his struggles had ended. The blue eyes stared into nothing. What a confused, love-weakened fool he had been, never able to unify himself into a single powerful entity.

I knelt beside the body. Even as I looked down at him with a certain scorn, some memories of that former life made a last visitation. His loves, his forlorn struggles, and the tangle of events leading to this spot. Journey's end. A tear fell from one pair of dead eyes to another, and with that gesture the apparition faded. I rose to my feet a new man, rising from the ashes of love and the ruins of defeat - and thus was the Black Phoenix born into his time of dominion.

A short time later, I breakfasted at a Berlin cafe. Elijinx sat across from me, a fatherly smile beaming forth as we confirmed our partnership.

'No more doubts, Jim. This is no acquiescence but an alliance. The terms are the same as always - power, pleasure, and world domination in exchange for the proverbial soul. Don't take the last part literally. It's purely a figure of speech. When you serve the Maelstrom, you serve yourself.'

'And for my part, all I need do is corrupt the world a little more and tilt it towards your fabled collapse.'

'Well, it's coals to Newcastle, dear boy, but every little bit helps. We all have a part to play in the great struggle and as I told you before, think global act local. You'll find your journey hence meets with a good deal less resistance. Now you've aligned your ambitions with nature and how the world really works, you'll be rowing downstream from here. So what's your next move, now you've come of age?'

'My next move? I'd say as soon as the mandatory orgies of intoxication are over, it'll be heads down to finish the new album. It's all about the band now and, Maelstrom or not, I'm no blushing debutant. My reign will be short and sweet. Ten years at the top and a well earned retirement. An album every year for the first five, old school like the seventies. A couple more to sign off, then a final world tour and a double live album to say goodbye.'

Elijinx nodded

'Old school through and through. Between your work ethic, your talent, and Ivan's charisma, there's not a force on Earth can stop you.'

'What of Ivan though - will he go the distance?'

'You're blood brothers now. You'll walk that road together to the end.'

'How long has he been one of your protégés?'

'There wasn't much effort on my part. He ingested the Maelstrom with his mother's milk.'

'He's not getting the lyrics, you know. They're mine.'

'Of course, Jimmy - it's your band. Ivan's no numbskull. He knows we all have our role to play. You're the music, he's the face. Just do what you do best and let him get on with making moral corruption a marketable product for a mass audience.'

'Amen to that. As to practical matters, when do we leave Germany?'

'I thought you liked it here.'

'It's time for a new phase. We'll clean the slate, eh. New band, new album, new country.'

'Anywhere in particular?'

'How about England? I can speak the language and I've never been there. Maybe not London but somewhere nearby. When we make a few quid, I wouldn't mind one of those country estates the seventies rock stars used to ponce around in like lords. Surely some of those old bastards must be nearing extinction after what they put their bodies through back in the day.'

'Not a bad idea, Jim - it could be a real passing of the torch. Leave it with me. Ivan for one will tag along. As for the rest of the band, have you taken care of it?'

'My very next appointment.'

So it was that I met that afternoon with my old band mates Dave and Viv in the *Biergarten* of a local hotel. They slouched in their seats, the four month slog almost at an end. Just a couple more days of the familiar dead travelling time before home. Dave looked restless, his long limbs outstretched, fingers beating a fidgety rhythm on the table. Viv, with his black spiky hair and tatts had begun the tour looking the goods, but had put on weight and was going to seed. I ordered a round of beers and laid them on the table.

'I want to thank you two guys for all you've done. Who'd have thought we would come this far? The Blue Mountains to Berlin - what a trip.'

'It's all down to you, bro. You and your songs.'

'You're too kind, Dave. A frontman's only as good as his backing boys.'

'So what about Ivan - still guesting?'

'He's in the band now - the official singer of Lighthouse XIII.'

'Alright!' said Viv. 'No offence, but you were never really a metal singer.'

'It's funny, isn't it Viv? As soon as someone begins a remark with 'no offense' it's bound to be something offensive. Don't forget, you were offered the mike yourself back in Sydney. Considering I made up all the bass lines, you had plenty of time left over if you wanted to have a crack at it.'

'I'm not knocking your vocals, mate. It's just that you're such a good guitar player. You should stick to what you do best.'

'That's why we hired Ivan, ain't it. But why even say it? You wouldn't say it to Mustaine. You wouldn't say it to Lemmy. They're no great shakes either. So why say it to me?'

'Come on, Jimmy, he meant nothing by it,' said Dave. 'It's been a long tour and all we want to do is get on that plane tomorrow. So let's have a few beers, a few hours kip, then get out to the airport.'

'I'm not going.'

'What do you mean?'

'I don't have a home in Australia anymore. That's all in the past. The band's moving to England so we can finish the new album.'

'Eh, what the fuck? That's the first I've heard. How about asking us before you make major band decisions?'

'What's your problem, Dave? Don't know about you, mate, but I'm done playing the Penrith Tavern and the Wagga Wagga RSL club. We're way out of that league now. So if you're not ready to take the next step, there's no gun to your head.'

'Be reasonable, Jimmy,' said Viv. 'I've got a missus and a mortgage back home.'

'I respect that, Viv. So if this is your resignation speech, let's drink up and shake hands like old comrades with no hard feelings on either side.'

'Whoa, hold up there partner. We'd better talk this through and figure out what to do.'

'Partner? You're a glorified employee.'

'Whatever you call us, me and Dave put in the hard yards with you the last six months. That's worth something.'

'Like I said, thanks for everything you've done and I mean that. But the bottom line is I wrote the songs, I put up the money to record, I did all the business right down to that dumb YouTube clip that kicked off this whole circus. And what the fuck did you ever do, Viv, except turn up and go along for the ride?'

Viv straightened in his seat, jaw tensed and fist clenched, ready to lash out. It looked like four months of road tension was about to find a release - until he wised up to the easy grounds for dismissal this would be. Viv slumped back in his seat with a grin and the polite, forced laughter that follows an unfunny joke.

'Jimmy, you're bang on, mate. I'll put me hand up for that one - but why didn't you say something? I love this band. We'll make this a fresh start, alright? I'll go above and beyond from now on, just watch me.'

'You'll move to England and commit to the band fulltime?'

'Maybe. If that's what it takes.'

'And you, Dave?'

'Give me a few weeks to tie up loose ends in Sydney, then I'm back for the long haul.'

'Well guys, that was a hell of a quick conversion. Are you sure you're up for it?'

'I can't speak for Viv but I know I'll never get a better shot than this. I can't walk away from it - not after the other night.'

I took a long drink from my beer glass. It was one of those tall glasses popular in Germany. For a moment, my face was hidden behind it. Dave and Viv thought themselves unobserved and exchanged a glance. I put the glass down onto the table, paused, then looked across at my drummer.

'OK Dave. There's still one thing bothers me. Something you said on the bus a while back. Might have been the Brussels gig, or was it Eindhoven? Any rates, I don't remember a single name or a face from that night, but that one thing you said.'

'Oh yeah?'

'You said Black Sabbath weren't a metal band. They were hard rock. Your exact words.'

'Did I? I don't remember.'

'What did you mean by it? I've been mulling it over for weeks and it still makes as much sense as a holiday to Afghanistan.'

'All I meant was, well, they're hard rock.'

'Yes, you said that - but what does it mean? What is metal anyway? Distorted guitars, heavy riffs with tritones and minor thirds, dark lyrical themes and images. Sabbath invented all that. Back in the day, they were the *benchmark* for anything heavy - and you've got the nerve to sit there like a young pup and say they're not metal!'

'It's not really metal by today's standards, is it?'

'Why? Because they didn't tune down an octave and put bullshit blast beats in every song? Because Ozzy didn't sound like Cookie Monster talking into a toilet after a whole pack of Tim Tams? Sabbath invented all that down-tuning stuff anyway. Don't forget Tony Iommi had to get that heavy tone with 1970s amplifiers before there were eight hundred different distortion pedals invented.'

'Exactly my point,' said Dave. 'Playing styles and technology have moved on. It's not Sabbath's fault. They were heavy in their day but it's the 21st century now. That's why I call them hard rock, not metal.'

'Right,' I replied. 'So let's re-evaluate all of history by the standards of today. I suppose Genghis Khan wasn't much of a warrior because bombs and artillery weren't invented in the 13th century. What a pathetic wannabe warmonger he was!'

'What's it matter anyhow? I love Sabbath. Bill Ward's one of my favourite drummers. I would've gone to the reunion tour if he'd been part of it. I guess they hired a session drummer so they could cut Bill out of the profits. More money for them. That's what these reunion tours are all about.'

I shook my head, sadly unsurprised by what Dave had said.

'From one piece of idiocy to another. This juvenile cynicism where you think everything's about money. Did you ever think human motivation runs a little deeper than that? I reckon for those guys it was about artistic fulfilment and career closure. One more album and tour with Ozzy before they die, a thanks and farewell to the fans. You think Tony Iommi needs any more money? I doubt it. Apart from that, he had cancer for Christ's sake. What good's a million quid when you've got a year or two to live? Might as well be a hundred million, don't make no difference.'

'Why cut Bill out of it then?'

'Maybe they figured a sixty year old former alcoholic and heart attack survivor would struggle to get through two hours a night playing drums. I really don't know. It's all speculation and I'm not going to sit here and pass judgment without knowing the facts.'

'You reckon Bill couldn't cut it - what about Ozzy? He was struggling big time on some of them YouTube clips from the tour.'

'Yeah, but he's Ozzy, he's the singer. No offence, but Bill's just a drummer. Like you, Dave.'

'What's that supposed to mean?'

'Here's one for you, mate. How do you know if there's a drummer at the door? The knock speeds up.'

'That's real good coming from you, Jimmy. You sped up half a dozen songs the other night. What were you on?'

'Hey, the gig was a bit edgy. That's rock n roll, mate. You want to sit there and play to a click track? Sorry, wrong band. It's a live gig. Me and Ivan wrote that new song in the dressing room half an hour before show time.'

'I could tell. Oh and Jimmy, how do you know there's a guitarist at the door? Answer - there's never a guitarist at the door. Why should he have to leave his bedroom to go to you?'

I laughed, resisting the urge to expound further on the subject of doors and their possible imminent uses for my band mates.

'OK, Dave, forget Sabbath. Let's move on to your buddy there, Viv. I reckon he's topped you for lunacy. I once heard him say Slayer sold out back in the nineties. So Viv, what the hell did you mean by *that*?'

'I don't want to discuss it.'

'Doesn't a sell-out mean they commercialised their sound? I'm scratching my head then because *Divine Intervention* and *God Hates Us All* are two of the least commercial records I've ever heard. You must mean *Diabolus* - but how's that a sell-out? It was still far too heavy for normal people to listen to.'

'They went nu-metal cos it was popular. *Diabolus* and *God Hates Us All*, both of them. Tuning down, groove type riffs and Tom Araya's almost rapping on one track. Even the production is nu-metal. They were following trends of the time to be popular, trying to sound like Slipknot. That's a sell-out in my book.'

'Well Viv, Slipknot passed me by and I don't have a clue about production, so I've no idea what you're talking about. If they put out an album with no guitar solos I'd get your point. You'd have a right to be angry about that. But those three records still sound like Slayer to me. Beats me how that's any kind of a sell-out. If you can pick it, you're just too high ranking a lieutenant in the Sell-out Awareness Gestapo for me.'

'They lost me after *Seasons*, anyhow. I was done with that band since then.'

'So you're the type who thinks *Show No Mercy* is better than *Divine Intervention*.'

'It is.'

'And *Kill Em All*'s the best record Metallica ever made.'

'I wouldn't say that.'

'I know your type. The old stuff's always better than the new stuff for the likes of you. Nostalgia til death, that's your creed. Ain't no woman on Earth will ever be better than your high school sweetheart. The old stuff is the right stuff. So let's have horrible low budget production, tinny guitars and drums, and dumb apprentice songwriting. Three cheers for punk rock values. Let's all have a few beers, put on the rosy glasses, and talk about the good old days when we peaked at twenty-one and went downhill ever since.'

Viv stared at me and his knuckles whitened against the table. Still, he could not resist a reply.

'That's typical of you, Jimmy. You pick up on some little point and blow it way out of proportion. Exaggerating everything. Putting words in guys' mouths that they never said or even thought of. I never said the first album is the best. It's mostly a band's third album, if you want to know. That's where hunger, potential, and experience meet in the middle. *Master of Puppets*, *Reign in Blood*, *Number of the Beast*. Even *The Queen is Dead* or *The Eminem Show* if you want to get outside of metal. But they all sell out sooner or later.'

'Viv, Viv, there you were making a great point and you had to go and ruin it at the end. As soon as an artist does anything different, you guys call it a sell-out. I call it artistic growth and pushing your boundaries - which are only imposed by the fans to begin with.'

'You can't change your core sound.'

'What is a sell-out anyhow? Someone who's popular? Way too simplistic. Someone who waters down their style to appeal to a mass audience? Getting close but still not right. To me, a sell-out is when an artist, in order to be popular, changes a particular piece of work in a way that violates the essential character of that work.'

'Like *Load*?'

'No, strangely enough. If Metallica got bored with thrash metal and wanted to experiment, then maybe *Load* was true to itself and their intentions. If *Master of Puppets* had been watered down that would've been a different story, but that album went gold on its merits. Tell you what would be a sell-out though. I'm writing a new book. Know what it's called? *The Maelstrom Ascendant.*'

'The what?'

'Exactly. It's a bad title in a way. Too long, too wordy, not catchy enough. They say selling books these days is all about selling them online, and what you need for that is discoverability.'

'Come again?'

'Discoverability. It's a new marketing term that means the ease with which people can find your product online. For that, *The Maelstrom Ascendant* is a terrible title. It doesn't mean anything at first glance. People can't say it, let alone spell it - so they won't be able to google it. But the fact is, that's the title of the book. It sums up the essence of it all. Maybe I should call it something simpler which people can find - now *that* would be a sell-out. To dumb down the title just so people can google it. To sacrifice the essence of the work in the name of sales. I'll hand in my badge before I dumb down the book for some bullshit marketing concept.'

Dave and Viv exchanged blank looks after my rave, and made no reply. Finally Dave broke the silence.

'As usual, Jimmy, I've got no idea what you're talking about but let's get back on topic and sort out this major band decision you've made on behalf of Viv and me about moving to England.'

'Sorry, Dave. I don't think it's going to happen. I can't work with people who think Sabbath weren't metal and Slayer sold out.'

'You got a problem with people having opinions of their own? Look at you - up on your little soapbox ranting about crap no one else even cares about - and as soon as someone disagrees, you hit the roof.'

'I don't have a problem with people having opinions, mate. I do have a problem with people having *idiotic* opinions. Money's the root of all human motivation. The old stuff is always better than the new stuff. Everyone's a sell-out. I thought people only typed this rubbish on the internet and now I'm hearing it in real life from people I actually work with. *Unglaublich!*'

'Still with the German? You're not impressing anyone, you know.'

'Sorry Dave, the English word 'unbelievable' just doesn't convey the spittle-tinged intensity of my outrage.'

Again my two colleagues exchanged looks.

'You've really cracked this time, Jimmy. I knew you were gradually losing it all tour but you're a borderline nut job now.'

'*I'm* the nut job, am I? Well, Davey, I'm not the one spouting rubbish about Sabbath and Slayer. The hell with this. As far as I'm concerned, both of you can pack your bags and leave now.'

'Don't worry, we're out of here. Let's go, Viv.'

'A pleasure doing business with you, gentlemen. Enjoy your flight.'

My two former colleagues walked off in disgust. After a few steps, Viv turned around for the last time.

'What happened to you, Jimmy? You used to be a nice guy.'

'Vivian, there comes a time in every man's life when he must stand up against life's bastardry and say, "Enough! I'll take no more. It's my turn to begin dispensing the bastardry instead of receiving it." And gentlemen, for me that time has come.'

Dave and Viv shook their heads sadly and departed. I returned to my hotel with the firm conviction that better days were ahead.

Yet who'd have thought? When I got back to my room, there it was on the bed, come back to life and daring to glow at me like it had never been away. I laughed.

'Look who's back - if it ain't the Vortex Winder! And where were you in my hour of need? Where was the noble Iolango?'

There was some writing on the tiny screen. I didn't bother to read it.

'A new magical power, perchance? How thoughtful. Where have you been the last four months when I was killing myself out on the road? Where were you when I lay dying on this very floor two nights ago? Too late, Iolango, too late.'

I took hold of a chain around my neck. From it hung the piece of black obsidian Elijinx had given me, my individual portion of the Maelstrom. The obsidian had been hidden beneath my shirt but now, in a deliberate gesture, I raised it up for the Vortex Winder to behold.

Then I turned away, packed my belongings and checked out of the room, leaving the Vortex Winder abandoned on the bed.

# 18
# Rookwood

'Now, that's more like it.'

My request for a country estate had been half in jest, but Elijinx had taken me at my word. Rookwood wasn't perfect but it would do. This stately manor lay in silent repose an hour's drive from London. While the house had clearly seen better days, it had been kept in fair condition for the sake of the sale. The lawns were presentable, the indoor pool and the bar operational, and the main bedrooms ready for habitation. There was a library upstairs and a recording studio downstairs. The living rooms had been done up Tudor-style. What would Sandra think of me now?

Some of the smaller rooms looked like they'd been unused for years and fallen into a state of disrepair. Much like the seller's career, but let's not be unkind. There's no need to name names. Suffice to say the 1970s was a very long time ago.

'Never tell me I don't look after my clients,' said Elijinx. 'It's just as you requested.'

'It's a dream but how do you know whoever buys it will agree to renting it out? They might want to move in.'

'You don't rent a place like this. It's an ideal base for operations for the next ten years - and a steal at three million pounds. I urge you to buy it without hesitation.'

'Buy? What - *this* place? I was begging funds for a plane ticket last week. How do you expect me to enter the property market?'

'Never mind how. Just place your hand on that talisman around your neck.'

I grasped the Maelstrom. The black, arrow-shaped piece of obsidian fitted easily into my hand. Its subtle emanation flowed into my fingers and on through my being. I dallied on the verge of an enchantment. Elijinx continued speaking, his voice seeming more distant yet more immediate.

'I told you, Jim. Once you embrace the Maelstrom all things are possible. The ordinary limitations no longer apply. Listen. Listen to the voice inside your head. That is the voice of the Maelstrom. It will convey the nature of the power available to you.'

The Vortex Winder had taken the form of a technological device, right down to the appearance of written words on a screen. This Maelstrom was a different kind of artefact. No words appeared - yet there was no mistaking the message I heard internally, no doubt of the gift on offer. It was wealth. I knew with certainty that lavish opulence would soon be mine. The Maelstrom told me; so it would be.

I took my hands off the artefact and the sense of conviction faded. Common sense reasserted its grip. I opened my eyes to face Elijinx.

'Well, I'm half a believer, but how is it possible?'

'I've found you a buyer for the film rights.'

'What film rights?'

'For the book, of course. Your *Vortex Winder* book.'

'The book! I'd almost forgotten it existed. Why would anyone want the film rights for that? It only sold a couple of hundred copies.'

'Come on, Jim, you're not in Hicksville, Australia anymore. We're dealing with people who can see past the end of their noses. Speculators who are five years ahead of the trend, not ten years behind. The investor coming here today believes in you deeply. Or at least, the man he represents does.'

'You're saying they'll pay enough for a down payment on this place?'

'Forget the down payment. Sign off on this and you can buy the place outright. You'll be setting up camp here next week.'

'You can't be serious.'

'The investor is meeting us within the hour.'

'I've got to say, Elijinx, this all feels very unreal. A week ago I was more or less bankrupt. Now I'm to be an English lord of the manor because some investor wants the film rights to a novel which sold less than two hundred copies.'

'I'll say it again. Once you embrace the Maelstrom all things are possible.'

'Doesn't it bother you that a film of *The Vortex Winder* will lead to your exposure?'

'What, some fairytale? No one's going to take it seriously. This investment offer, on the other hand, that's as serious as a heart attack. As your manager, I'll nut out the finer points of the deal and all we need's your thumbprint. So let's have an embargo on the old Jimmy Brandt stubbornness. You'll smile and shake hands with our fine investor. No haggling, no conditions. You won't even open your mouth. Just sign the contract and walk away.'

'Don't worry, this one's a no-brainer. The book's done nothing for me. If some billionaire wants to waste his money, I'll take it.'

A silver Mercedes pulled into the drive and made its way towards us. It slowed to a halt. The driver got out, walked round the back of the car, and opened the rear door on our side. An imposing, well-dressed man of African appearance exited the vehicle. When he stood up and joined us, I had to tilt my head slightly upwards to meet his gaze. He looked to be in his mid-fifties. Shades of silver in his hair and a formal, expensive-looking suit gave him the air of a statesman.

Elijinx introduced him as Mr. Zambeko. When we shook hands, I had the sense he could crush mine if he wished. Yet there was no such macho posturing from the man. With a firm grip and a small bow, he professed his honour at meeting me. Elijinx told me to take a walk while he looked over the contract.

I left them to it and wandered the grounds as if in a dream. If this reversal of fortune was legit, I should have turned to the dark side years ago. Improbable as this event seemed, I supposed it was not impossible. Plenty of the idle rich had nothing better to do than squander their money on sport, the arts, or whatever else took their fancy. Several of the English Premier League teams had private, foreign owners. If Elijinx had managed to snare one, all the better for me.

While there is no denying I was possessed by a great avarice for this house, I was not so overcome as to lose all regard for the fate of my book. I would sign the contract, of course, as long as we could establish a few minor ground rules for the adaptation. Yet when I returned to the meeting and saw that the offer was four million pounds, it was hard to maintain a poker face. I tried to keep my voice calm.

'Well Mr. Zambeko, this seems very fair and as long as we can write a couple of simple clauses into the contract, there's no reason we can't sign off on it now.'

Zambeko and Elijinx exchanged glances, as if this was just what they'd expected.

'Naturally, I'd love to see *The Vortex Winder* as a film,' I continued, 'as long as it bears a fair resemblance to the original. We all know how disappointing it is when a book is changed so much you can hardly recognise it onscreen.'

When he replied, Zambeko's voice was deep and tinged with some kind of African accent, yet his English was rather formal and precise.

'You have nothing to worry about, Mr. Brandt,' he said. 'My client is an immense fan of your book. You may rest assured that any film version will retain the essential truth of what you've written.'

'Excellent,' I said. 'So if we could just put that in writing, I'm prepared to sign right away.'

Zambeko stared down at me. There was a hint of condescension in his reply.

'You do understand, I hope, that film and literature are two different art forms. No film can reproduce exactly what is on the page. You should not try to impose such a burden, unless you intend to stifle any creativity a film may have. The director is not a servant to the author. Actors are not mere puppets reciting lines.'

'Sure, Mr. Z. I'm not so vain as to think I know better than a director what makes a film work. Still, that doesn't mean it's a case of anything goes.'

'If the client I represent did not believe in your book, I wouldn't be here. While every effort will be made to reproduce your story faithfully, some changes are inevitable.'

'I've no doubt whoever ends up directing it will do a fine job. I just want to make sure we're on the same page, so to speak.'

Zambeko paused and held my gaze for several seconds. I made sure not to drop my own. Zambeko's eyes were deep brown, almost black, so that the pupil was barely visible.

'What is it you want?' he said at last.

'All I ask is to write the script, have final say in casting, and power of veto over any major cuts and changes to the storyline.'

'I see. And have you ever written a film script before?'

'No.'

'It is entirely different to writing a book. Do you understand that?'

'Oh come on, how hard can it be?'

Zambeko and Elijinx again exchanged looks. Elijinx decided it was time for some divine intervention.

'Mr. Zambeko, excuse me while I take a few minutes alone with my client. Let's take a walk, Jim.'

Soon Elijinx and I were pacing briskly through sunlit fields.

'Are you out of your mind?' he said.

'I'm as keen to sign as you are,' I replied, 'but you can't expect me to give him a blank cheque to ruin the movie.'

'That's essentially what he's giving *you*. Four million pounds and you've got the nerve to quibble over casting.'

'It's crazy anyway. Why would anyone pay so much money for a film option?'

'It may seem exorbitant to you. For the man he represents, four million is little more than spare change. He probably spends as much at the casino.'

'That's what worries me. If it means so little to him, I should definitely keep some control over how my story's portrayed. What about the *Harry Potter* author? She had executive control over how they made the movies.'

'You idiot! JK Rowling was a worldwide publishing sensation with millions of books sold. You might be half a rock star but you're a zero in the publishing world. You haven't even cracked five hundred sales.'

'So I should just sign the book away?'

'Yes, of course. Look at you - you're homeless. Last week you were suicidal and begging me for a handout. Now here's a mansion dangled in front of your outstretched fingertips - and you have the nerve to talk about keeping control. Just take the money and run.'

'I suppose you're right.'

'So this is what happens. I do all the talking. You smile politely, shake hands, and sign the contract I negotiate for you. If you so much as open your mouth, I'll strangle you myself.'

'Fine. Go on then.'

'Don't worry, I'll put in a word for you. Your book won't be thrown to the wolves. Let's hurry back and close the deal before he changes his mind.'

Soon Elijinx and I were back at the meeting point.

'Mr. Zambeko, my client is ready to modify his terms. We accept your offer as long as the following conditions are met. Jimmy won't write the script but he'll co-write it with an experienced script writer. He will act as an advisor on casting. He won't interfere with your making of the film but he requests consultation if it comes to any major changes to the plot or tone of the film.'

'How's that, Jimmy?' Elijinx asked.

I nodded. Zambeko also seemed satisfied.

'That all seems very reasonable. Gentlemen, we have a deal.'

We shook hands on the matter and I signed a letter of intent. The official contract arrived the next morning. Within a week, I also signed the deeds to the estate and took up residence.

Rookwood was now my home and the official headquarters of Lighthouse XIII.

# 19

# The Five Food Groups

Embrace the Maelstrom and it will set you free.

Now awakened, I looked back at the life I'd been living and it seemed frail and fettered. How enfeebling was conscience. The old band would have been dumped long ago but for loyalty. The rock life should have been fully embraced but for an addiction to home comforts. The fleshy fruits of the road could have been tasted except for qualms about love and ethics. Now the game had changed. Freshly unfettered, I was at liberty to embrace the bacchanalian feast laid out before me.

My life became comprised of two pursuits. One was the quest for musical immortality, the other, the habitation of a twilight world of self indulgence. I served the Maelstrom and in so doing, served myself.

I grasped the talisman and felt its message reverberate. 'Freedom from consequence.' That was the essence of the power bestowed upon me. I knew that, within reasonable bounds, I could sin with impunity. For me, intoxication was not followed by hangover. Fornication led not to disease or unloved child. And as there had been no sequel to Matthew Wright's swan dive, it seemed also that murder did not lead to the gallows.

Maelstrom or not, I was rarely actively malicious. If harm was done, it was only from letting events run their natural course on the world's downward spiral. It was as impersonal as gravity, and if I passively rode that current it was hardly my fault it all ended in tears.

I had a number of short term affairs, for example, mostly with curious or star-struck fans of the band. On the surface at least, I took pains to treat these girls well. I was polite, good natured, superficially friendly - yet in all truth I cannot claim to have been kind. None of these liaisons were going to end in marital bliss, nor any other kind. Yet unlike in my previous life, I was no longer much concerned about the effects of my actions on others. It was simply a matter of taking what was on offer. While there was no active cruelty dispensed, there was a passive cruelty in allowing these affairs to even begin. There would be no happy-ever-afters here.

Bodily closeness is so superficial, a taunting illusion. Even the physical matter itself is full of empty space. There was always a point on the path from go to woe where the girl would sense the remoteness of the man touching her. She'd try to come nearer, only to draw back after glimpsing the abyss within her 'lover.' The affairs never lasted long after that.

As for the band, there was no need to go looking for new members. I simply stole the rhythm section from Acador, the band who had headlined the European tour. While Jake and Amos had tended to be standoffish for much of the tour, they'd been rather friendlier since Ivan joined. Tipped off about a possible vacancy, they'd witnessed our Berlin triumph. As soon as Dave and Viv had their notice, the talented rats jumped ship. The rest of Acador weren't too thrilled but that band was never going to the top league anyway. Not to mention their singer, Symon, had snubbed me from the outset, so I wasn't bothered to have scuttled his vessel.

Finding a second guitarist was a much bigger problem. Given that there are more unemployed guitarists than drummers and bass players put together, the reason for this may not be clear. Yet guitarists are almost as troublesome as singers, due to the ego problems common to the profession.

Playing the guitar well takes a lot of skill, and that often comes with a package deal that includes pride, ambition, and the will to create. Yet the last thing I wanted was another artist with a strong personality in the band. You don't want some new guy coming in, imposing his own style, and trying to write half the songs. To be honest, I just wanted a flunky who'd shut up and play live the second guitar parts I'd overdubbed in the studio.

When you record a song, one guitar is rarely enough. You always want a second guitar, not just to fatten up the sound but to add more layers. The problem for lone guitarists - from Zeppelin to The Who to Pantera - is that when you play live, who is going to play those extra parts? I'd battled on by myself until now but most of the songs still needed that extra guitar onstage.

Lighthouse XIII songs are not all that hard to play, but they are hard enough. It was no job for mugs. Indeed it would take a good guitar player to pull it off. With that ability would come the usual personality problems. I did not yet have the status of a Dave Mustaine who could hire a virtuoso while denying him any real creative power. I had to let prospective guitarists think they could express themselves in the band. Otherwise, no one would join. So, I was forced to hire someone, privately resenting them all the while. In light of this, one may understand, if not forgive, my appalling treatment of Oliver Sims, the guy who finally got the gig. I said I was rarely malicious. This time was an exception.

He pissed me off from the get go. I'd been holed up all day auditioning guys in a London studio. Not one of them was up to the job. So when it turned out Oliver could really play, there was no choice but to hear him out.

The first thing he did wrong was bring Suzy. Who brings their girlfriend to a job interview, for Christ's sake? By a cruel twist of fate, this pretty, buxom brunette looked rather like Sandra as she may have been at about twenty-one. It was really too much.

The guy was quite pretty himself. One rarely uses that word for a man, yet Oliver had the type of delicate, slightly feminine beauty that reminded me of Randy Rhoads, Ozzy's first guitarist. Randy had been blond, of course, and possessed the aura of an old soul. Oliver was dark-haired with a look of virginal innocence whose veracity I did not doubt - girlfriend notwithstanding. He and

Suzy had the air of the young Christian couple sworn to chastity until their natural lusts were sanctified through marriage. What on earth were they doing here?

Oliver wheeled in a huge amp and, with shaking hands, plugged in his guitar. The amp emitted a wild howl of feedback. Oliver turned round to apologise, blushing prettily beneath his shoulder length dark hair. By Christ, with the right makeup job he could pass for a Japanese schoolgirl and no mistake. I winced and bit my lip.

'Why don't you have one of these beers, mate? It'll settle you down.'

'No thanks, Mr Brandt, I don't drink.'

'I'll have yours then. And lay off the Mr Brandt stuff, we're not in school. It's a rock band. It's Jim or Jimmy to you - and you're Oliver, right?'

'Or Ollie if you like. This is Suzy.'

'She's your guitar tech?'

'Oh no, my fiancée.'

They giggled coyly as if laughing afresh at some cutesy in-joke. I was clearly expected to chuckle along in sickly collusion. Stony faced, I got on with the professional matter at hand.

'Which of our songs have you learned, Oliver?'

'All of them.'

'Well, talk about Shamus the Show Off. You only had to learn four. You can't possibly know all our songs.'

'But I do.'

'That must have taken you a while.'

'Not really.'

'You're a cocky one, son.'

'Sorry Mr. Brandt, uh Jimmy. I don't mean the solos, just the riffs and song structures.'

'Warm up on an easy one then, like 'SMS' if you know it.'

He played it right too, even down to the string muting and vibrato. Already he was way ahead of the other five applicants that day. He stopped playing just before the solo.

'Come on, Oliver, you know the solo, don't you? You needn't pretend - I bet you really did learn them all.'

The fellow looked sheepish and proud at the same time, quite an achievement.

'Don't hold back then, give us your best. Tell you what, let's do another song. Think of a number between one and twenty and I'll tell you what song it is.'

'Seventeen.'

'Seventeen? That would be 'Waves Upon Waves.' Let's have it then.'

The little bastard nailed it, solo and all. He was probably better than me, to be honest. In the studio I'd had to record the song in sections due to playing mistakes, but he pulled it off note perfect in one take.

Big, big deal. Performing and composing are two different things. Lots of guys can play, very few can write. Anyhow, this kid might be useful in the short term to get us out of a jam.

'Well played, sir. Let's do one together.'

I strapped on my Gibson Explorer and hit the opening riff to 'Temporary Kingdom.' Oliver came in at exactly the right time and wouldn't you know it, he was tighter than a kiwi on payday. Despite myself, I began to feel excited and a little upset. This wasn't meant to happen so easily. I tried to temper the happy mood by injecting a sour note of realism. I turned to the young man's fiancée, who I'd been ignoring all the while.

'Well, Suzy, how would you feel about your boyfriend becoming the second guitarist in Lighthouse XIII, away from home six months a year touring the world? It's a tough road for you and him both.'

She beamed. 'I'll support him one hundred percent in everything he does!'

'How very galling. Aren't you a little worried about the road life with all its temptations? The drugs, the girls, and the rest of it?'

'My Ollie doesn't do drugs and he'd never look at another girl. I trust him completely.'

'That's right, Jimmy. Why would I ever look at anyone else when I've got a girl like Suze?'

'Is Suzy the first girlfriend you had?'

'And the last. We're getting married at the end of the year.'

'I see. Well, I am going to have to think about this and call you later. I need to get back into the studio to work on the album.'

'Can I play you something then? I've a few riffs you can use.'

'Really? You're a pushing lad, Ollie. In the band two minutes and already trying to write half the album.'

'Oh no. I just thought you could use a couple of riffs somewhere. I wouldn't even want any royalties.'

'The album's fully written. The job advertised is for a touring guitarist, not a songwriter.'

'I assumed I could write songs as well.'

'Lots of guys assume that until they actually try and do it. Now don't give me that look, Oliver. No one's ruling anything out for the future. You come on tour with us, build up some chemistry. When the next album's due we'll hear some of your riffs. Let's leave it there, I'm due back in the studio five minutes ago.'

When the happy couple had left, I cracked another beer and cursed my bad luck. The fellow was perfect. He was a younger, perhaps more talented me, and the youthful Sandra clone was just fate putting the boot in. No way she was coming on tour with us.

But what could I do? We needed a second guitarist for the live show. Irritating though he was, Ollie was the man for the job. Well then, he could stay on for the new album's world tour, then go the same way as Matthew Wright for all I cared.

I closed my eyes and grasped the black arrow head hanging round my neck. The Maelstrom would know what to do. I listened and the voices spoke, telling me what special power was on offer. 'Corruption of the Innocent.' How fitting.

The next day Oliver came out to Rookwood - without the girl. The taxi rolled up the drive and he got out wide eyed.

'This is awesome, Jimmy. You really live here?'

'Yes, I've been here a while. Maybe it'll inspire you to put your head down. Put in the hard yards, Ollie, and you could end up somewhere like this too.'

'I'll do whatever it takes.'

'That's the spirit. Right, here's the big picture. Next week you're here 24/7 for boot camp. The week after, we join the rest of the band. We're putting out an EP and doing a short tour to break in the new line-up. If everything's cool, we'll hit the road for a six month stint flogging the new album. Are you with me?'

Oliver stood there grinning like a jackass.

'It's too late to use any of your riffs on this album,' I continued, 'but if you get through the tour, you've got a license to write two songs on the next one, and a deal for a solo album to boot. Don't worry - there won't be any of this five-years-between-albums rubbish you get from other bands. We're doing it old school like in the seventies - a record a year. Life is short, you know.'

'Alright!'

'Now, Ollie, here's the thing. You're smart as paint but you still need a lot of work to make this gig a success. Not so much with the music, that's all fine. It's your personality that worries me. You're greener than a seasick frog and if we're not careful, the road's going to eat you alive. That's the whole point of boot camp next week. It's not just to polish the songs but to harden you up for the tour. With a lot of hard work and my guiding hand, I reckon we can get through this. So let's be drinking a toast to the new venture, shipmate.'

'I told you, Jimmy, I don't drink. You got some coke or something?'

'Steady on mate, we'll start on the coke next week. Still, that's encouraging to hear. This sure ain't no temperance society band - get that through your head for a start. A teetotalling rocker's not going to cut it round here. Now, if you want this job you'll have a drink with me to seal the deal - and I'll not take no for an answer.'

'If I have to, just the one.'

'That's the spirit. So let's smash a bottle over the hull and launch this voyage!'

The following week, Oliver moved into Rookwood. He'd carefully packed and prepared everything he thought boot camp would entail. Once he'd unloaded his gear in an upstairs bedroom, we went down to the recording studio and began perfecting songs for the live show. The young fellow was a touch overawed to stand on the threshold of his life's ambition, but I tried to set him at ease. Comrades in arms, we put our heads down and got the job done. Then came the night and stage two of the enterprise. We went in to the bar and sat down on opposing lounge chairs. When Oliver had settled in his seat, I fixed him with a stern and appraising look.

'Now Ollie, here's where the real work begins. Like I said, there's nothing wrong with your guitar playing. It's your personality that's the problem. You're a boy in a man's world. Look at you - never had a drink. About to marry your first girlfriend. You're a natural innocent. In fact, you remind me of a much younger me.'

Oliver didn't reply, so I continued.

'You're a good kid but you'll see things out on the road that'll shock you. If you're not prepared, it could break you and send you out of the game altogether. We can't afford to lose an artist of your calibre. That's why I'm asking you to trust my guiding hand, shipmate, as I toughen you up for what lies ahead. So tell me, have you ever heard of the five food groups?'

'Sure, we learned them at school.'

'Good. Of course, your school days weren't so long ago as mine but I remember them too. Took it to heart as a lad and here I stand before you, the results plain to see. Never mind your fancy fad diets and all that bilge. I've seen a million of 'em and what we learned in primary school still holds up. The five food groups for healthy eating. Fruit, vegetables, meat, dairy, grain. The key to life and health.

Now, when it comes to being a rocker, or in fact being a man of any real calibre at all, there's also such a thing as the five food groups of vice. Booze, drugs, gambling, porn, and heavy metal. These are the five pillars of a healthy manhood. Get a handle on them and they'll see you through to your dotage.'

Oliver shifted uneasily in his seat and tried to assess whether I was joking - yet my expression was deadly serious.

'You know, Ollie, there are some women don't believe in the five food groups. They'll try to deny a man his natural province, keep him weak and pliable, and in some cases emasculate him entirely. That's the kind of woman to steer clear of. The good news is a man living on a healthy mix of the five food groups will automatically repel that sort. He'll attract a girl who understands that a man is only defined and sustained by the vices in which he partakes.

What's all this got to do with you, Ollie? No offence, but I've a duty to speak plain. You're weak. You've led a sheltered life and unless you harden up double quick, the road's going to eat you alive.'

'But Jimmy, I don't drink or do drugs. That's a big part of why Suzy likes me.'

'I know that, mate, and the bottom line is Suzy's the reason I'm doing all this in the first place. You kids are getting married soon and I won't let anything get in the way of that. Fact is, though, you'll see a lot of vice out on the road. Gorgeous young girls taking their tops off in the front row, hedonism galore, enough drugs and booze to sink an army. You go out there all babe in the woods and before you know it, you'll find yourself waking up dead drunk in a hotel room with a naked girl under each arm. What's Suzy going to think of you then?'

I pursed my lips and shook my head.

'I won't let that happen to you, Ollie. Forewarned is forearmed. The road will throw a lot up at a young fella like you. Know your enemy, know your temptations. That's my defence. We'll go through the five food groups overall, with a special attention to drugs, doubtless the most insidious of the bunch. The work we're doing now is your defence against all that. Think of it as an inoculation. The doctor gives you a little shot of the disease so your body can manufacture a resistance. That's exactly what we're doing this week when it comes to drugs. We'll try all the usual suspects in small doses so you'll be safe from harm. Ain't nothing gonna creep up on you that you haven't tried and don't know what to expect.'

'Gee, I don't know what to say, Jimmy. I've always been a bit of a square peg.'

'No kidding! Still, you're young, there's time for you yet. Mind you, I can see the doubt in your eyes, shipmate. Maybe you don't want a bar of what I'm preaching and if so, go join one of them straight edge groups and we'll shake hands with no hard feelings on either side. But a square peg won't fit into the new Lighthouse XIII. The only straight edge you'll find around here's a blade on a mirror. And if there's one thing you need to get through your head sooner rather than later, in rock n roll you don't just clock in, play your set, then collect your pay check. It's a lifestyle, an attitude. You live it 24/7 or don't do it at all.'

Oliver looked away, trying to reconcile his personal values with his commitment to passing boot camp. I let him stew for a moment, then steamed ahead before he could reach a conclusion.

'Right, let's kick off with an inventory. Oliver Sims and the five food groups. Never mind the heavy metal, we'll check that straight off the list. The booze, though, you're a regular vestal virgin there if I'm not mistaken.'

'I don't drink. You know that.'

'We certainly don't want it getting out of hand, but keep in mind you'll be hanging with a bunch of guys out there. Support bands, crew, media, fans. If you can't learn to accept a quiet beer every now and then, you'll stick out like a priest at an orgy. What's more, these hand pressing sessions can get pretty dull and you'll find a beer or two takes the edge off. And let's be frank, lad, you're a great guitarist but you're not quite the sparkling conversationalist, are you? A couple of beers will get you out of your shell.'

I walked over to the bar and took a six pack of beer out of the fridge, opened two bottles and handed one to Oliver.

'At the same time, we don't want you to go in with zero tolerance, get pissed on two drinks and make a goose of yourself. You're representing the band here. So we'll build up your resistance bit by bit. There's one beer for starters, get that into you. Then you can have a couple more before curfew. Three's your limit today, but we'll up the dosage by one each night this week. You'll be up to a full six pack by Thursday and come Sunday, you'll be able to handle nine beers without raising a sweat. Once you do nine you'll be fine - that's my motto. Moving on to the next group though, how are you with drugs?'

'Oh no, not for me, thanks.'

'Fine - that's just as it should be. And I'll level with you, Ollie, just between you and me, and as long as you don't let on to the boys in the band. I won't have a bar of drugs myself. You and me are alike there, we're regular peas in a pod. I know you're no druggo, son. My only concern is you're going to walk offstage one night buzzing from the gig. Some clown's going to offer you a dodgy line or a pill and you'll be too caught up in the moment to say no. Next thing you know, it's yours truly ringing the grieving fiancée, and it's sombre looks all round and weeping and wailing enough to break your heart. And all for the want of a bit of pre-tour prep! No, you won't be any kind of vestal virgin by the time we hit that road. Have a toke of this for starters. A gateway to bigger and better things. That's the way lad and don't mind a bit of coughing. That's your entry fee for the ride.'

Hesitating, yet swept along by my sense of conviction, Oliver accepted the joint.

'I suppose one little puff won't affect me much.'

'Course not. There you go, shipmate.'

Oliver inhaled, coughed, then looked up a few moments later with glazed eyes. I gave him the thumbs up.

'Well done, son - and I see contact has been made. That grin of surprise has slit you ear to ear. All hail the sweet leaf. How's that for a good start? It's only Monday and we're already powering through the steps. Tuesday's eccy night. Wednesday we'll put you to the acid test. Thursday's a regulation coke binge. Friday we'll speed headfirst into the weekend and slow down with some mushies on Saturday.'

'Wow, what happens on Sunday? Heroin?'

'Heroin? What do you take me for? We'll take Sunday off for a day of rest, by the powers! It's straight edge Sunday. Apart from the nine beers, of course. So there's our week all mapped out and it's heads down from here, son. We'll practice by day and party by night, and if all that don't battle-harden you for the road, I don't know what will.'

'Gee, Jimmy, I don't know what to say. My head's spinning. But I've finished my three beers already. Is it cool to have another?'

'And that, my young friend, is exactly the sort of rookie error I'm here to protect you from. Sure, I could let you have your fill - and the next thing we know I'm scraping your vomit-stained carcass out of bed in the morning and how the hell do we suit up for day two of boot camp? Moderation, my friend, all things in moderation. As soon as we're done here, you're off to barracks, soldier. So let's wrap this up and push on with the other food groups. How are you with porn?'

'I've seen it, of course - who hasn't? - but Suzy doesn't let me watch that stuff. She'd flip out if she knew you wanted me to watch it.'

'And that's the thanks I get for trying to save your marriage! Suzy's not seeing the bigger picture here. Tell me, Oliver, what are you going to do when you float off that stage one night and there's half a dozen red hot nymphs wanting a piece of you? I hope to Christ you're a saint, cos you're gonna need to be with that nubile crew in your face and Suzy nothing but a faint voice on the end of a phone line.'

'Can't I bring her on the road?'

'You're on probation, lad, this is no time for making demands. Once we get through the trial tour, we'll look at it. Anyhow, according to ship's articles, wives and girlfriends can come out for set periods, but we can't carry an extra body for the duration. It's out of the question. So I repeat, what are you going to do when the nymphettes are there in 3D and Suzy's a J-PEG on your laptop?'

'How do I know? I've never been on tour.'

'Exactly. You don't know, because you've never experienced it. Well, make no mistake, if I ever catch you violating your marriage vows with one of them girls, I'll be on the phone to Suze before you've had time to pop a condom. I'll tell you what you do when the time comes. You go back to your hotel room, or your bus bed or wherever you can find a private spot, turn on your laptop and log on to some internet porn. Beating ain't cheating and porn's the only real protection against these temptresses. You can feast your eyes, then look deep into Suzy's with a clear conscience.'

'I guess it makes sense if you put it like that.'

'Course it does. Right, what else? We've done heavy metal, booze, drugs, porn. The other one's gambling. For my own take on it, I don't hold much with lotteries and casinos. Sports gambling's my racket. Used to be, any rate. The Black Art's good for many a lost weekend and you may lay to that. Why, back in my heyday I'd set up a brace of sporting bets, watch a few games, and count the money rolling in. When all's said and done, gambling's the least important of the five food groups of vice. Still, I like to think it rounds out a man's character and applies the finishing touch.'

I stretched. My work was almost done.

'Well, I reckon that's covered it and not a moment too soon by the look of you, shipmate. It's lights out, and we'll rendezvous at 0800 hours. Before you clock out completely, I'll leave you with one last thought and a warning. There'll be a final exam next Monday night to round off the week and if you want to earn your stripes, you need to show mastery of all five food groups at once.'

I stopped, as Oliver had fallen asleep. I left him where he fell. As long as he was up in time for day two, it was no concern of mine where he slept.

So, to cut a long story short, you've got to hand it to him. Ollie was a fine student. Did he pass his final exam a week later? Did he what! Come Monday night, I walked into the exam room and he'd laid out a nice little tableau to prove his manhood.

There he was sprawled on the couch in my games room. Football on the TV, hardcore porn on his laptop, a six pack of empty beer bottles on the table, next to that a bong and a sachet of coke - and heavy metal music blaring out all the while. I marched up to my protégé, saluted him, and extended my hand in congratulations.

'Now you are a man, Ollie. Welcome to the band,' I bawled above the general hubbub.

Oliver tried to stand and return my salute, but could only clutch at my hand, before falling back onto the couch unconscious.

I turned off the heavy metal music, the football and the porn, put away the bong and the booze - and still poor Ollie just lay there.

'Let's see you play 'Waves Upon Waves' in one take now! Ha ha ha ha ha...'

Ollie moaned, but did not awaken. Boot camp was over. Bring on the tour!

# 20
# High and Mighty

The High and Mighty tour was a four week jaunt through Europe and the UK. Its purpose was to break in the new line-up and generate some buzz for the coming album. A four song EP of the same name came out to mark the tour. It was Ivan's vocal debut on record and featured one song from the new album, 'High and Mighty,' and a re-recorded 'Z Club' off the last one. It also had 'Mountain Gods' - a track I feel is underrated - along with a comedy song about downloading called 'Retro Stereo.' The EP was available on CD and for digital download. For the purists, a limited number of vinyl copies were pressed as a vintage collectible.

All of a sudden, there was a real buzz around the band. Put it down to the last tour, the charisma of Ivan, or the power of the Maelstrom itself. Whatever the cause, Lighthouse XIII had become a hot name to drop. We were on the point of transition from the underground to the mainstream. The *Vortex Winder* album started to sell, as did the *Waves Upon Waves* EP, along with the new one. Suddenly the media wanted to know us, our gigs started to sell out, and there was a dark, potent energy pushing us forward.

You can see it in publicity shots from the time. Ivan dominates the frame, his decadent beauty shining forth. You'd pick him for a lady killer, without guessing he had the capacity for actual murder. I am to his left, detached and aloof, smirking slightly. Ollie, virginal, angelic has been allowed into shot to draw in the teenager crowd. In reflection of their onstage roles, Jake and Amos glower away in the backline. Jake's bandanna and tatts are a bit too LA for my taste, but no doubt they suit him. Amos, the drummer, is all long limbs and aggression. The Lighthouse XIII image stands transcendent over us all.

The new line-up was gelling so well there was little need to rehearse once the tour kicked off. Offstage, the boys also bonded through music, partying, and the time honoured practice of 'hazing the new guy.' Hazing - a harmless rite of initiation through practical jokes - is a custom common to many fine organisations. It is, of course, well established that terrorising the newest members of a group is a terrific way of integrating them into that group.

The old me had been a critic of the practice but the new me was far more a traditionalist. There were three newbies in the band but as Jake and Amos were hardened rock hacks, the obvious target was Oliver. We'd prank him by placing a room service order for 2am. Or by sending a stripper or callgirl to his room. To his credit, Ollie always sent them away.

The ongoing jape, however, was a continuation of the booze and drugs theme begun during boot camp. This was my idea but the rest of the guys were in on the joke and played along. I called an official band meeting in the library at Rookwood the night before the tour.

'OK, you guys, listen up. Our golden reign starts now - so seize the moment. This tour, I want everyone who sees our shows so blown away they buy the new album the first day it's released. Even the downloaders, by thunder! The next four weeks, I need two hundred percent from the lot of you.'

Jake and Amos nodded, Ivan scowled, and Ollie beamed as I continued the spiel.

'I like to think this band stands for something - well, here's our mission statement. Forget all the fads and phases in music. We're bringing back traditional rock values - sex, drugs, and rock n roll. Make sure you guys are ticking all three boxes daily. Ollie gets an exemption from the sex cos he's engaged but I expect the rest of you to pick up the slack. Now don't give me that sulky look, fellas. If I had a fiancée like Suzy, I'd never touch another groupie either.

That's his luck and more power to him. Just be sure you make up for it in the other two areas, Ollie.'

'So... drugs and rock n roll?'

'That's right. Let's show the world that rock values still mean something.'

'We owe it to the kids,' said Jake.

'We're role models,' said Amos.

'Exactly!' I proclaimed, thumping the table in affirmation. 'The kids look up to us. We can't let 'em down.'

Oliver looked confused, as he had ever since day one of boot camp.

'So because we're role models, we've got to take drugs?'

'Precisely. Me and Ivan were talking about it just the other day, weren't we, Ive. You said it best - we're *alternative* role models.'

Ivan put his hand on Oliver's shoulder and stared deep into his eyes.

'It's like this, Ollie. You've got your regular role models - your sports stars and supermodels. Throw in your lawyers and politicians as well. But what about the kids who can't aspire to those heights? Not every kid can be a footballer or a supermodel. Not every kid's smart enough to be a lawyer. Most of them just want to have a good time. It's our job to show them that's OK. The kids are sick of being pressured into high achievement. That's where we come in - the alternative role models.'

'Spot on, Ive,' I said. 'So I want every one of you fellas in a state of intoxication for the next four weeks. In fact, Hoffman and me decided to make if official. We're gonna have random drug tests. It could be at one o'clock in the morning or four o'clock in the afternoon, you won't see it coming. Anyone found without some kind of intoxicant in their system will have a case to answer.'

'Don't you trust us, Jimmy?' said Jake.

'I *want* to trust you, Jake, don't get me wrong - but you and Amos have just come on board. Trust is something you have to earn. Some of you guys I hardly know.'

I raised my eyebrows in the direction of Oliver, then continued.

'That's the whole point of this tour. To get to know each other. To break in the line-up and get everyone on the same page.'

Oliver piped up again. 'I can't take drugs every day. Is it OK if I just do it on the weekends?'

'Come on, son. This is the High and Mighty tour, not the Straight and Pissweak one. Every day's the weekend in rock n roll! You might have aced boot camp but don't get cocky. You're still on trial. Stick it out, lad, if you can get through this, you'll receive full membership of the band and a place on the world tour.'

'Will there be drug testing on the world tour as well?'

'No, that'll be a six month slog and we'll ease off. You'll have to pace yourself. But for this little stint, I don't think four weeks of intoxication is too much to ask. Once you've proved you can handle it, you'll be fully inoculated against an OD or an addiction when the real tour begins.'

So it was that at random intervals, Monty, one of the crew guys, was set up as an official tester. All the boys in the band pretended to give a urine sample and Ollie had to go along with it. Soon after, Monty went through roll-call with the 'results.'

'Ivan - coke and ecstasy. Jimmy - marijuana and acid. Jake - coke, ecstasy and speed. Amos -mushrooms and meth. Oliver - marijuana and coke. Everyone - booze. OK guys, you're in the clear.'

Monty was just making these up. The 'urine samples' were nothing more than apple juice, scotch or whatever we could find to put in the bottles. Ollie, however, took the tests with deadly seriousness - and I got Monty to run a real drug analysis on his sample so I could keep tabs on Ollie's progress. Sure enough, it was only a couple of weeks before he let the side down. One day in Prague, I was forced to call him into my hotel room.

'Oliver, how are you holding up so far?'

'Good thanks, Jimmy.'

'Nothing to report? No problems?'

'Nothing.'

'Anything you'd like to get off your chest?'

'No, it's all good. How about last night, eh!'

'What a night! What were you on, mate? Acid or something?'

'I popped an eccy before the show and washed it down with a few beers and a joint.'

'That's odd, because according to this morning's drug test you were straight and stone cold sober.'

'Huh? What do you mean?'

'Monty double checked the results and there was no trace of any booze or narcotics in your sample. How do you explain that?'

'Gee, boss, there must be something wrong with the test. I was wasted, honest. You saw me yourself.'

'Really, Oliver. You know what hurts me the most? It's not the sobriety, it's the lying. Here I am trying to build a relationship of trust and you turn around and throw it in my face. How are we supposed to work together if you can't be straight with me? I mean, if you can't be honest with me? You're not the only second guitarist I put through boot camp, you know. There's two guys on standby. Maybe you'd better pack your bags.'

'Oh no, Jimmy, give me another chance.'

'So you admit you were sober last night?'

'I had a headache. I just wanted to get through the show.'

'You had a headache? Jesus Christ, son, do you know how many kids out there look up to us as role models? Here we are busting our balls trying to put across a classic bad boy image and you're up there poncing around like some kind of virginal choir boy.'

'Sorry Jimmy, I swear it won't happen again.'

'A team's only as strong as its weakest link, Oliver. I didn't need Monty's test kit to know there was something wrong with the vibe last night. I walked round that stage testing you all one by one. Jake was speeding deluxe but he never missed one note on his bass. Ivan knocked off a whole bottle of Jack. Amos did a line off his snare before his drum solo. All present and accounted for. Then there's you over on stage right giving off the stench of sobriety with every note. You're about as rock n roll as a Devonshire tea! Why don't you come out tonight in a cocktail dress and play the ukulele?'

'Give me another chance, boss.'

'I don't know, Oliver. I just don't know. What you do in your own time is your affair, but this is work time. Is it too much to ask you to stay intoxicated for four weeks of your life?'

For the next show, Lighthouse XIII effectively reverted to a one guitar band. Not because Oliver was sacked or didn't show up. He was just so out of it I had to relay a message to the mixing board to cut his guitars out of the mix altogether. That was until he passed out halfway into the show and we had to haul his drunken arse offstage. The next morning, he again fronted up at my hotel room, this time in Budapest.

'What am I going to do with you, Oliver? You're a piece of work and no mistake. What happened?'

'I guess I over-compensated.'

'No kidding! I've got to hand it to you for effort and clearly your heart was in the right place - but that doesn't mean commonsense has to go out the window. There's stoned and there's Syd Barrett. I mean, come on. You've still got to be able to play your instrument. What did I hire you for?'

'Sorry, Jimmy, it won't happen again.'

'I'm getting a bit sick of your apologies, Ollie. Look, son, here's what I'm going to do. Don't tell the guys but I'm giving you a free pass for the rest of the tour. You want to be straight edge for the next two weeks? Fine. The drug tests will go on but I'll clue in Monty to turn a blind eye. As far as the other guys will know, it's business as usual. We can't afford to let them down. And don't forget, your fiancée will be out for the last weekend of the tour. Until then, just make sure you turn up to the show on time and do your job. As far as I'm concerned, you've got the gig. You're in for the world tour.'

'You mean it?'

'Welcome to the band, son.'

We shook hands and embraced, and my young protégé went on his way with the spring back in his step. As promised, we kept up the facade of doing the urine tests. Except it was no facade. I kept tabs on Ollie's results and, just as I'd suspected, he passed with flying colours. Almost every day he returned a positive reading for booze, speed, blow, meth, or whatever other drug was going around. Just as I'd guessed, his choir boy image was all an act, probably forced on him by his uptight, goody two-shoes girlfriend. Secretly, he was a little drug tart all along. It was fine with me as long as he didn't screw up onstage again.

Strangely enough, by this stage of the tour, the band had started copping some flak over the alleged pro-drugs message of the tour's theme song, 'High And Mighty.' One radio interviewer in Manchester really took me to task. It was a bit of an ambush, really. After a few friendly warm-up questions, the woman, who I'll call Helen, went on the attack.

'Do you ever feel uncomfortable with the pro-drugs message your band is promoting?'

'Pro-drugs? What do you mean?'

'You're calling it the High and Mighty tour.'

'That's nothing to do with drugs. It just means the band's riding high on a wave of popularity and we feel pretty good about it.'

'I'll quote you the song lyrics. "Then we ride on high. High and mighty. Even the pure will die, sooner or later. Ride on high." What about that?'

'That could mean anything. Really, Helen, aren't you taking those lines a bit out of context?'

'Out of context? It's the chorus.'

'Look, fair play to you, I can see where you're coming from. There is an insinuation there. I see how you might misinterpret it.'

'There's nothing to misinterpret in verse two? "Life is short, so make it shorter. Drink, smoke, or snort, what you ain't oughta." You're blatantly encouraging people to take drugs.'

'It may seem that way on the surface, Helen, but you're conveniently ignoring verse one. 'Choose your vice, don't let it choose you. Know the price, one day accounts are due.' If that's not a warning about the dangers and consequences of drug use, I don't know what is.'

'Really? It's mixed messages at best. As you're calling the song 'High and Mighty' it's not much of a warning. You're telling people to take drugs. How do you think parents feel about their kids hearing that when they look up to you guys as role models?'

'Role models? We're a rock band, for Christ's sake. Who said we're role models? Alright, I'll answer you this way. 'High and Mighty' is an attitude song. It might seem pro-drugs but it simply reflects the values of people who choose a certain kind of lifestyle. We're not judging, we're simply observing. I am neither endorsing nor condemning those values.'

'I find that hard to believe.'

'I mean look at the song 'Highway to Hell' by AC/DC. That's an ode to hedonism and self destruction if ever there was one - and it's one of the best songs ever written. As we know, Bon Scott was dead within a year of writing it. Do you think the kids don't make that connection? Maybe you should give them the benefit of the doubt - they're not as dumb as you seem to think.'

'The fact is you're glamorising drug abuse. There are plenty of kids out there who aren't going to make a sophisticated analysis of these issues. All they'll think is that drugs are cool because the guys in Lighthouse XIII said so. Doesn't it bother you to have a few ruined lives on your hands?'

'Oh come on, we're just a rock band. You're overestimating our importance. Go back to verse one and it's undeniable this song is a warning about the dangers of drug use. If you're going to put me on the spot, let me take the confessional of my own free will. I had an awful OD myself a while back and haven't touched a drug since.'

'Is that right?'

'Frankly, Helen, I think there should be testing procedures in music like there are in sport. Random drug tests in studios and backstage, that sort of thing. Musicians found with drugs in their system should face lengthy bans. That would solve the problem. If it was up to me, I'd have a Royal Commission go back through popular music of the last fifty years, and any album proved to have been written or recorded under the influence of drugs would be placed on a banned list and removed from sale. So if you want to know my opinion of drug use, shove that in your pipe and smoke it.'

'That's a very extreme measure, Jimmy. Surely it would wipe out a lot of the great music from the 1960s and 70s.'

'About time too. We could clear the decks for some new stuff. While we're at it, the classic rock radio stations could do with a clean out. Not to name names, but it's well known some of those easy listening bands from the seventies were total coke fiends. *Those* are the sort of artists you should be worried about. They pretend to be clean cut and wholesome when in reality it's sex and drugs all the way. A disgrace, really, and the sooner that filth is off the air the better.'

The rest of the tour passed without incident other than a series of intense shows at sold out venues. Our star was massively on the rise - of that, there could be no doubt. I'd go out in public in disguise and see Lighthouse XIII t-shirts everywhere. Albums and merch were flying out the door. Everyone was namedropping us at every chance. We lapped it up deluxe as our carnival rolled on unstoppable. The band's dark energy drove us forward and everyone was swept up in the general fervour.

Oliver himself stopped resisting and surrendered to a higher power. He accepted the Maelstrom as his personal saviour. He did not call it by that name, nor was he aware of the forces behind the scenes that shaped his character. Nameless though it was, Oliver gave in to that mighty power. The rest of his tour was a wild ride of sex, drugs, and rock n roll. So much so that when his fiancée showed up for the last days of the trip, she found him passed out dead drunk in a hotel room with a naked girl under each arm. The upside was that they saved a fortune on their wedding and I had a fine guitarist and comrade to take on the world tour.

All hail the Maelstrom, ascendant to the end. To the end. The end. To the bitter end.

# 21

# The Jack Lynton
# Memorial Award

Ever since the move to England, the band had been working on the new record. And I do mean *the band*. Ivan rarely showed up to rehearsal. That was fine - at least he wouldn't interfere in the lyrics. This allowed me to write about recent events. 'Haunted' and 'The Price of Dominion' mourned the loss of Sandra and Finzi. 'Quitter' and 'Death Bed Regrets' showed different sides of ambition. 'Black Phoenix' reflected my turn to the dark side, and contained a couple of secret allusions to Pyro's sorry demise which had sealed the deal.

It is a curiosity of the album that the song 'Moonlight Tiger' was called 'Frostbite' on the original release. Of course, 'I For An Eye' did not appear at all, given that I had yet to compose it. These tracks only appeared when the album was re-released some time later.

In due course, the record was done. Jake, Amos and I spent many weeks developing the songs at Rookwood, before recording them in London. While Ivan contributed little to the rehearsal stage, his actual performance was top class. When I heard the final mixes soon after the High and Mighty tour ended, I could not have been happier.

*The Maelstrom Ascendant* was intended as our breakthrough album and that's exactly what it was. In the end, it was by far the most popular of our first three albums, outselling both *Vortex Winder* and *Waves Upon Waves* (this later release was an expanded version of the first EP with several tracks added).

The Maelstrom world tour was all set to kick off with a headlining run through Europe. Yet when Elijinx emailed me the tour info, I was none too thrilled with the support band. Not bloody

Acador again! They must have found a new rhythm section since I took Jake and Amos, but I was in no mood to renew acquaintance with their idiot singer, Symon. He'd snubbed me for much of the last tour when they were headlining over us. There'd been nothing direct, just a general air of condescension. In a way, it would be an act of spite to take them out with us now that we were a much bigger deal than them. Yet spite is a hard emotion to sustain. I had no wish to see him day in day out, nor did I want to give his band any kind of professional leg up. I'd already stolen his drummer and bass player. That was revenge enough. There was no way those idiots were coming out on tour with us.

I placed my hand on the black arrowhead around my neck in search of inspiration. This time the Maelstrom surprised me. The voices in my mind were loud and clear. *Idealism versus cynicism. Kill Matthew. Kill Matthew. Kill Matthew.*

Of course! Instead of taking Acador out again, why not give some young unknown band a chance? I now had the power to pluck a band out of obscurity and help make their dreams come true. The more I thought about it, the more it seemed like a brilliant idea and an act of philanthropy as well. I logged on to the Lighthouse XIII website and placed the following message on the homepage.

## Support Bands Wanted For European Tour

Hey guys, Jimmy here. Anyone ever heard of 'The Matthew Effect?' It comes from an old bible quote which says 'To him who has, more will be given, and from him who has not, even what he has will be taken away.'

What it boils down to is 'the rich get richer and the poor get poorer.' We all know that one, right? You're either a somebody or a nobody. A have or a have-not. The Matthew Effect is all over the music business.

When you first try to get gigs, they ask, 'how many gigs have you played?' When you're after a record deal they say, 'how many records have you sold so far?' The hardest thing in this business is getting a start.

So that's what we're offering - a start. Lighthouse XIII is running a competition where the winners get to support us on our European tour. If you've got an album recorded but you're unsigned, we'll also put it out on our label, Momentum Records.

Before you start sending in your band bios, photos, and websites, stop right there! All that stuff will get thrown away or deleted. This competition will be a blind audition based on one thing only - the quality of your music.

See, we're not interested in your networking and list of contacts. We don't care who you know in the music business - DJs, journos, or other rock stars. We don't give a damn how many Facebook likes you have, or if you won Battle of the Bands because you dragged the most friends to the venue to vote for you that night. We don't care if you're pretty, cool and popular, or ugly, uncool and unknown. Forget all that rubbish - we only care about your music.

All you have to do is send in three songs that your band has recorded. It might be on a CD, as long as there's no name or photo on it. Or it might be an mp3 audio file as long as there's no link to YouTube or your website. And I promise you this - I, Jimmy Brandt, will personally listen to every song that's sent in. I won't just listen to one of your three songs, and I won't turn it off after ten seconds if it sucks. If you cared enough to invest all that time creating a song, the least I can do is hear it out.

The winning band will then tour with us as our support act.

I listed an email address for mp3s and a mailing address for CDs. As long as bands got their entries in and paid the £125 processing fee, there was no reason this couldn't be the big break they were all looking for.

A few days later, Elijinx was on the phone.

'You know, Jimmy, it might be an idea to check with management before you go making major decisions about the tour.'

'What's up?'

'Your little brainwave about the support acts. Beautiful idea, fine philanthropy... but who has time for that? You *do* realise the tour kicks off in three weeks? Didn't you get the dates I emailed?'

'The only thing I saw was bloody Acador as the support - which ain't gonna happen, that's for sure. How come we're touring again so soon? The album's not out, is it?'

'Pre-orders are high and it hasn't even leaked yet. One week to go - then the sooner we get out and tour it the better. There's no time to mess about with the support acts. Acador's all set to go.'

'No way that little prick Symon's going out with us. But point taken, we'll fast track the competition for the support slot. We get any entries yet?'

'Yeah, you could say that. There's 122 entries already emailed.'

'Alright! So hold on a second, let me work that out. With the processing fee of £125... wow, that's over £15, 000 of tour profit before we've even kicked off. Fifteen thousand pounds! You should be thanking me.'

'I'll certainly thank you for listening to all those songs yourself. That's 366 songs so far - and you've made a firm promise to listen to them all - and all the way through. Remember?'

'Oh yeah, I forgot about that. Hmm, let's see if it's worth it. £125 for every three songs. I'm still earning £42 a song. Guess it's decent money for about four minutes work. That makes £625 an hour. Fine - just email them through and I'll get stuck in.'

'Get on with it then. There's a load of CDs as well. I'll drop them off tomorrow.'

'The more the better. Bring it on.'

Well, I gave it a try. I must have got through as many as thirty songs that first day - even the ridiculous twelve minute epics. That meant there were only another 336 songs to go. I'd slogged through another twenty the next morning when I heard Elijinx's car pull up outside. He marched into Rookwood with a suitcase, raised it above his head, and let a rainbow of CDs cascade onto the marble floors of the Rookwood lobby.

'There you go, Jimmy! There's 323 CDs here from all over Britain and Europe, and another 612 new entries by mp3 on the website.'

'Brilliant! So - 323 CDs, 612 mp3 entries and 122 from yesterday - that's 1057 entries. 1057 times £125? Now wait a minute, I've got the calculator right here. And the results are in. £132, 125 in entry fees. Over a hundred and thirty thousand quid! We don't even have to go on tour now!'

'You do, actually. You've got three months of dates in Europe and the same in the US. Make sure you sort this lot out and pick a winner by Monday. How many of those songs have you gotten through so far?'

'About fifty.'

'I see. With 1057 entries you're going to have to listen to another 3000 songs in the next 5 days. What's that, 600 a day? At 15 songs an hour, if you go 24 hours without stopping, you're still only getting through 360 songs a day. Tricky.'

'Oh for fuck's sake, I don't have to actually listen to them, do I?'

'You made a solemn promise on the website.'

'That's before I knew there'd be so many entries. Tell you what, let's get Ollie and Ivan and the other boys down to help out. And we'll cut it down to one song per band and if it sucks after five seconds we'll bin it.'

'That just won't do. You promised to personally listen to each song in full. As a man of your word - words that have not just been spoken, but actually typed and released into the public domain - you're going to have to follow through. That is, unless you want to refund all the entry money and put Acador back on the tour.'

'No way. Not after all the hard work I've put in listening to the fifty songs so far. Look, here's what we'll do. I'll drive into the village and pick up a dozen portable CD players. I'll set them up in a circle and run twelve CDs at a time, then walk around the circle and pick whatever stands out over the general hubbub. That'll just leave the mp3s.'

Elijinx laughed, either at the absurdity of the suggestion or because I seemed serious in making it.

'I think this farce has reached its endpoint, Jimmy. Let's get real. There's no way we can take out just anyone as a support act. Sure, Lighthouse XIII is popular, but it doesn't hurt to have a couple of other buzz bands bring in their own crowd too. Everyone will assume they're there for the headliner. So forget this ridiculous contest and let's pick an appropriate support.'

'So I don't have to listen to the 3000 songs?'

'Of course not. You've got to get in shape for the tour.'

'Oh thank God for that. Do we have to refund all the entry money?'

'Don't be absurd. I'll get the girls in the office to check out all the bands who entered. Check their websites, Facebook pages, how many gigs and records they've done, how hip and trendy they are. Then as long as they're not actually a better band than Lighthouse XIII, they're a chance. We'll pick the top twenty prospects and invite a rep from each band to an awards dinner here at Rookwood next Monday. At the end of the night, we'll announce the winners.'

'Fine - so what do I do now?'

'Bin these CDs for a start, then write a new letter for the website. Make sure you run it by me this time. You've caused enough trouble already.'

'And put us a hundred grand in the black before the tour's even begun. Don't forget that.'

As soon as Elijinx had left, I sat down to compose the following letter.

### And the Finalists Are...

Hey guys, Jimmy here again. No more entries please!

I want to thank you all for what you've contributed. Both the quality and the quantity was outstanding and my only regret is I can't take each and every one of you out on tour. Anyhow, the good news is we've got the top twenty finalists. They're all invited to an awards night next Monday, when we'll announce a winner. This is going to be a very special award. It might even turn into an annual event.

It's called the Jack Lynton Memorial Award. Jack was a colleague of mine a few years back. He came from a background of harsh poverty but worked his way up through sheer grit and determination, and made it all the way to the top. In these days of nepotism and networking, Jack made it on talent and hard work alone, only to die of a fatal heart attack on the job just a week after he started.

As Jack lay dying in my arms, I swore an oath to one day create a scholarship to honour his name. That's why it's going to be such a huge thrill to meet all you finalists next week and hand one of you the inaugural Jack Lynton Memorial Award.

The following Monday, a band member from each of the twenty finalists was picked up in London, in conditions of grave secrecy. Their phones were confiscated, and the finalists were brought to Rookwood in a coach with covered windows. After all, I didn't want any of the losers to know where I lived. No further correspondence will be entered into and all that, if you know what I mean.

On arrival, everyone was invited into the great banquet hall at Rookwood for the celebratory feasting and drinking. It was a fitting conclusion to a wonderful initiative.

Before dinner, Elijinx and I held court in the 'throne room,' granting a private audience with each band rep so they could present us with goodwill gifts to increase their chances. I also took a few of the guys on a tour of Rookwood. They were awestruck by their proximity to the rock stardom they'd always desired.

They all seemed eager to become friendly with me. It just goes to show that human nature is inherently generous and kind. A couple of the boys busted out some big lines of blow, which we snorted right off the lush green felt of the snooker table in the games room. This was followed by an impromptu game of indoor football, during which I scored an astonishing twenty-two goals! Everyone applauded. I hadn't felt this popular since the Chica Boom days.

Finally, at the end of the night, everyone was gathered in the great hall of Rookwood once again. The room hushed. I walked onto a stage set up at the front of the room, and spoke into the mike.

'Hey comrades, what an epic night! It's been my personal honour to meet and party with each and every one of you. And much as I'd like to stand up here and rave, that's the last thing you want to hear. Let's cut to the chase and find out who won.'

I paused for dramatic effect.

'The inaugural Jack Lynton Memorial Award winner has been chosen. But the other nineteen of you, don't get downhearted. The US tour's coming up and plenty more tours after that. So if you're one of the losers, hang in there. This ain't over. In the meantime, we'll adjourn to the bar, drink each other's health, then shake hands and say goodbye with no hard feelings. Right, let's get on with it. I'm proud to announce that the winner of the Jack Lynton Memorial Award is... Acador!'

A thick, tense silence filled the room. Within it jostled frustration, suspicion, and fifty other emotions, none of them good. Finally, a grudging ripple of applause began, building up in volume until it almost seemed real.

Symon, the lead singer from Acador, strode up to the stage, positively beaming, and tried to embrace me. I shook his hand condescendingly, then directed a look of the utmost malevolence into his eyes. He staggered back as if assaulted. I was still holding his hand and dragged him violently forward again.

'Steady on shipmate. You'll soon get your sea legs!'

Then it was free drinks all round, metal over the PA, and before long, a coach with covered windows taking twenty dreamers back to London.

Never mind guys, there's always next year. Until there isn't - and then the fat lady has sung.

# 22

# Diva Land

*The Maelstrom Ascendant* record was released. Was it a good album?
Yes. Was it a big success with the music public? Yes. Did that entitle
Ivan and me to carry on like prize divas? Ah... no.

Still, what you gonna do? The Maelstrom itself said I had a free
pass to Diva Land. I could hear the voices loud and clear. With
the album out and the world tour begun, the timing was perfect -
perhaps even a little redundant. If there was ever a time to embrace
my inner diva, it was now. No invitation was required.

It was soon clear that Ivan had received the same dispensation.
In those early weeks of the tour we were two divas on show, both
in career best form. Sometimes we harmonised in beautiful duet.
At other times, we battled like feuding rappers trying to outdo
each other. The diva wars were amusing for a while. The demands,
the ridiculous riders, the high strung tantrums. Never mind the
music, diva-dom was an art form in itself.

The tone was set in Athens on the first night of the tour. Ivan
was given a fine room on the second floor of the hotel - lush carpets,
all mod cons, and a balcony with stunning views of the Parthenon.
The only problem? It was a twin share. When Ivan found out he
was rooming with Ollie, he had a fit. Who could blame him? How
are you supposed to sleep with that drunken fool snoring in the
background, or twitching away all night on a drug comedown?

To his credit, Ivan's tantrum was not immediate. It was prefaced
by a polite phone query to Steve Johnson, the tour manager.
Johnson had been hired to oversee the day-to-day running of the
tour. Elijinx had better things to do than run round after us, so
Steve was the man in the hot seat. Well, the poor guy tried to
calm Ivan down until he foolishly let slip that I'd been given a
private room on the floor above. By the time the bedding, the TV

and all other portables from Ivan's room were in the swimming pool two floors below, Johnno was hammering on his door begging forgiveness. You've got to hand it to him - Ivan always did have a talent for throwing things out of hotels.

Ivan was rewarded with a private room right above mine. So, having mostly slept through the prior commotion, I was woken just before midnight by a self-satisfied voice from the balcony above. Some idiot was on the phone. The fellow ignored my shouted request to keep it down, so I thundered upstairs to find that the guilty party was none other than our star vocalist. Pushing past him into the room I was further outraged to find he'd been given a deluxe suite equipped with a bathtub and a mini-sauna. What's more, as his room was a full storey higher, his view of the Parthenon was far superior to mine.

There was only one course of action to take. I returned to the pitiful room I'd been given and began depositing its contents into the swimming pool three floors below, where they joined Ivan's in a state of soggy disgrace. The mattress itself was the last thing to go. Before long, Johnson was hammering on my door this time, the hotel manager by his side.

I opened the door. Johnson's shirt was unbuttoned at the top, as if he'd gotten dressed while half-asleep. His thinning hair was made more obvious from the sweat brought on by the Athens heat. He had the harried and jaded look of a man who's been coerced into going through fatherhood for the second time, in his fifties, against his better judgment. In this case, the children, were five rock stars. He glanced at the hotel manager beside him, then turned back to me.

'What's up, Jimmy?'

'What's up? Why don't you think about it for a minute, Steve, and let me know if you come up with any theories.'

'Calm down, mate. This guy's threatened to kick the whole band out of the hotel if there's any more ruckus. I've already had to pay him extra to let us stay til morning.'

'Can you blame him, Steven? This whole shebang's only just kicked off and if this is an example of your management skills, I have grave concerns for the rest of the tour.'

'What exactly is the problem?'

'Tomorrow's the first show and I'm stressed enough as it is. Yet here I am getting woken at midnight by Ivan's bullshit phone call, thanks to you putting him in the room above mine. And what do I find when I go up there? A bathtub and a sauna. Take a look around my room, Steven. Where's my sauna? Help me out buddy, maybe you can find it.'

'I had no idea what the rooms were like.'

'Isn't that your job? We all have a job to do on this tour. Mine is walking onto that stage and bringing joy to thousands of people. Yours is organising a decent hotel room so I can go to the gig fresh and happy. Do you think you can handle it?'

'Jimmy, it's late. Why don't we sort this out in the morning? I'm sure Ivan won't mind you taking a sauna in his room if you really need one.'

'At this time of night? Are you out of your mind? I've had just about enough of this. Get me Hoffman on the phone right now.'

'Come on mate, we're only here one more night. It won't happen again.'

'I spent six months making that album. That twat turned up for two weeks at the end to sing - and I wrote the lyrics anyway. If anyone's getting a sauna it's me.'

'Point taken. Now is there anything else you need?'

'I'd like to move to the balcony room two floors up.'

The hotel manager, a grumpy looking fellow, chose this moment to intervene.

'That room is taken.'

'Well I certainly can't be expected to sleep here now that my mattress is in the pool. I'm going to need a room upstairs on the floor above Ivan's.'

There was a pause while the manager went through some kind of internal struggle. It looked like he was as pissed off with Johnson as I was. Finally, he came to a solution.

'509 is free.'

I ignored the hotel manager and turned back to Johnson.

'Steven, take my gear up there at once. I'm prepared to forget about what happened tonight, but unless you lift your game dramatically this is going to be a very long tour.'

The next morning I headed down to the breakfast room and opened my laptop. As I was checking email, Ivan entered and inspected the breakfast buffet laid out at the front of the room. One table held fruit, bread, cold meat and cheese. The next displayed a wide selection of miniature cereal packets, along with pots of coffee and orange juice. Still, our singer seemed unable to find anything to his liking.

'Got any Coco Pops?' Ivan asked the girl in attendance. The girl looked like a local but spoke good English, which was her bad luck as she was forced to converse with him.

'Everything we have is on the table, sir. Or you can order something from the menu.'

'I'll have some Coco Pops. That's my order.'

'If it's not on the table, sir, we don't have it.'

'But I want it.'

The girl turned and glanced at the cereal table.

'There's toasted muesli. How about that? We also have Rice Bubbles, Sultana Bran, Special K, Fruit Loops, or porridge. And look, there's some Cocoa Puffs!'

'Cocoa Puffs? Oh no, they're awful. I want Coco Pops. What kind of a hotel is this, anyway?'

'Whatever is on the table, sir, that is what we have. But if you prefer, there are many fine cafes in Athens which may suit you better.'

Ivan greeted this jaw-dropping display of insolence with the only possible response. He upended the cereal table, sending porridge, muesli and umpteen mini packets of cereal to the floor, along with pitchers of milk, coffee and orange juice. With a resounding crash, they formed an unholy mess on the floor. The other patrons in the room looked up in alarm.

'Just an omelette then,' said Ivan, 'with some buttered toast on the side. I'll be over next to that gentleman with the laptop.'

As soon as Ivan sat down beside me, I gave him a stern warning.

'I'd think twice about eating that omelette, Ive. They might not be inclined to dish up their best after that little display.'

'It's their job.'

'They're people, not vending machines. Some of them have feelings and they can be spiteful if provoked.'

'So? What are they gonna do about it?'

'An inside tip for you, pal. It's just possible they might do something to the food. I'd give it a miss myself.'

'You serious?'

'It's been known to happen in these situations - and I can see by that look of righteous rage you're starting to get my meaning. Now then, don't go upending this here table for an encore. Why not be the bigger man? Revenge is a dish best served cold, so leave your frigid eggs and toast here for them and we'll go and find one of those nice cafes. That's the way to make a moral statement as to what you think of the service here. Cold and haughty does it.'

'Wise council, my friend. Let's go.'

We stood up and left the room. As we approached the glass doors in the hotel lobby, I saw the manager from last night walking to the breakfast room with a face of thunder. I sniggered and nudged Ivan.

'Uh oh. Looks like Johnno's gonna cop it now!'

We laughed, pushed through the exit doors, and walked into brilliant sunshine. What a glorious day to be alive!

With time to kill, we spent the morning on a short tour of Athens, paid respects to our fellow gods at the Parthenon, then I adjourned to my upgraded hotel room to prepare for our first show.

It was a monster. As we walked onto that darkened stage, there was a palpable sense that hell was about to be unleashed. Still in darkness, I played the opening riff to 'Black Phoenix.' When the band and the lights kicked in, there was an ungodly roar from the crowd as we manifested in front of them like devils at a sacrifice.

By the time the tour rolled on through Italy, Johnson made sure that Ivan and I were always given rooms which were not just of commensurate quality, but in fact identical. His commitment to the ideal of equality would have done a socialist proud. Yet now that we were left with no real cause for complaint, we applied our talents to the increasingly ludicrous riders that were part of our tour demands.

For those who don't know, the 'rider' is the list of items a band asks to be given at each show. Early in our diva period, a typical Lighthouse XIII rider might include three cases of an obscure brand of imported beer, a dozen bottles of expensive wine, a fruit platter with no yellow fruits, a seafood platter with no shellfish, and various other requests as picky as they were extravagant.

Now really, that was pretty tame, but as the tour went on, Ivan and I began to make our own demands which Johnson had to include in the official band rider. As competing divas, we always took note of what had been added at each show so we could up the ante for the next one. If Ivan ordered a bottle *of Chateau Margaux* 1979 for one gig, I'd order a 1978 for the next. Not that I had any idea if this was a superior vintage but I'd be damned if Ivan was going to one-up me in any shape or form.

We expanded the rider to include services and entertainment, along with various rules and conditions. Ivan insisted a masseur had to be provided. I added an acupuncturist. I wanted a vocal coach to help me with backing vocals, so Ivan asked for a guitar tutor, even though he only strapped on a guitar for three songs each night.

The demands became more and more outlandish. Ivan requested a martial arts trainer travel with us to help him physically warm up each night and pull off the David Lee Roth style high kicks he performed onstage. In response, I picked up a 'juggling consultant' in Belgium on the grounds that juggling balls backstage helped quieten my mind and reduce stress.

Ivan ordered that table tennis had to be set up backstage at each show. I asked for a badminton court. Ivan wanted a model railway at one gig, so I needed a mini car racing track for the next. The rider arms race escalated - yet no matter how demanding we were, the band's popularity continued to rise. We were at the peak of our powers, pushing the limits of what was possible. Thus, we set a positive example to show the kids what could happen if you believed in your dreams.

On the more practical side, we wrote in some strict rules and conditions. For example, no one was allowed to shake my hand within six hours of show time. I'd had a gutful of macho guys squeezing the hell out of them. After all, my hands were my livelihood. Ivan followed suit by demanding no one talk to him within three hours of the gig, to save his voice. He soon extended this to say that no one was allowed to even *look* at him while he was in the venue. Not even I could top that, so I tried to mock him instead.

'So that's no talking and no looking, Ive, have I got that right? What if we need to discuss the setlist?'

'Just slip it under my dressing room door, Jimbo. The setlist is your job. It won't bother me what songs we do.'

'OK, but how are you going to play table tennis backstage if your opponent can't look at you?'

'They should be watching the ball. Isn't that what they say - play the ball not the man?'

'One last question - if you don't like people looking at you, what are you going to do when you walk onstage in front of a crowd of ten or fifteen thousand? They'll be not only looking but staring. That's what they've paid for.'

'And that's what *I'm* paid for - to be looked at. Damned if I'm going to do it in my time off as well.'

Strangely, one of Ivan's next diva demands was for a local portraitist from each city to paint him before the show. This would definitely be a breach of the no-looking rule. However, Ivan granted each painter a special exemption. Unfortunately, there was one night in Venice when young Ive dozed off mid-session, then woke up confused. When he saw the painter with brush in hand, Ivan snarled 'what are you looking at?' and assaulted the poor devil. Not for the first time, Johnno had to dip into the tour funds to fend off a lawsuit.

Ivan's portrait fad didn't last long. What began as a painting in each town quickly degenerated into a five minute 'street sketch' and finally a photograph. Then he lost interest altogether.

Meanwhile I'd been pondering how to further up the ante in the diva stakes, and came up with the idea of having themed backstage parties. We'd been visiting some of the old castles, for example, so I suggested a medieval theme for one show, complete with knights in armour, royal banquets, and court jesters. This, by pure coincidence, offered a golden opportunity to show off my amazing juggling skills, with which my juggling consultant Philippe had been helping me.

We were in Sicily when Ivan had the idea of a mafia theme night. Johnno thought that was unwise so we changed it to 1920s American gangsters. I followed up with a 1960s hippie theme for the next gig. Ivan changed it to punk the night after. I suggested science fiction for the next show, before Ivan went back in time to the days of ancient Rome, dressing up as Caligula himself to lord it over proceedings. How appropriate. Yet, to his chagrin, I trumped him with an impeccable Julius Caesar outfit.

Continuing in this vein, I ordered a 'seven wonders of the ancient world' setting, with miniature replicas of each wonder to be reproduced back stage. It was a super idea but the end result fell short of expectations - and I sure let Johnson know about it.

'Is this the best they could manage, Steve? Granted the pyramid's nicely done. Likewise the Temple of Artemis and the Colossus of Rhodes. But a few plot plants strung up from the ceiling does not a Hanging Gardens of Babylon make. I've seen better hanging gardens at my grandmother's house!'

'I'm sorry to hear you feel that way, Jimmy - but shouldn't we focus on the actual show rather than all this other stuff ?'

'The show's fine. We've got it down pat. In fact, that's the problem. It's starting to feel like Groundhog Day around here. These theme nights help keep it fresh and make each show unique. Did you ever think of that, Johnno?'

'Point taken, but you should see some of the emails I'm getting about your riders. These promoters are trying to book a rock show, not a fancy dress party.'

'It's their job to satisfy the artist. Without the artist there is no show - never forget that. Anyhow, it's your problem, you handle it.'

'Well, at least you've got to be happy with your Lighthouse of Alexandria.'

'Yes, credit where it's due, it's superb.'

It was indeed the Lighthouse of Alexandria which triggered my next inspiration. I issued a decree that an ice sculpture of a lighthouse was to be freshly made for each show, with a XIII carved in the front. Johnson gritted his teeth but complied. With each passing week, he'd been slowly losing patience with our demands.

I suspected the job had become too much for him. Indeed, he seemed to be approaching a breakdown.

Sadly, it all came to a head in Rome. Johnno totally lost it and had a tantrum that would have done a toddler proud. It all started with one of his characteristic displays of negativity, which had been bringing the whole tour down for several weeks. I was in my dressing room backstage, watching funny cat videos on YouTube on my laptop. Johnno knocked on the door, a grim look on his face.

'Jimmy, I've just had an email from the accountant. The tour profits are way down on budget projections. We're not even close.'

'How come? All the shows are sold out.'

'We're spending way too much on all these theme parties and the extra people on the payroll.'

'Take it up with Ivan. He's the one hiring all the bogus hangers on.'

'It's not just Ivan, is it? What about you?'

'What do you mean?'

'Jimmy, please. Have you seen the size of your entourage? Don't you think this is all getting a bit crazy?'

'I'm sorry you feel that way, Steven. I didn't realise having the band at peak performance level meant so little to you.'

'Of course I want the band at peak performance level. Why wouldn't I? And I get that there's some value in a masseur and a vocal coach. But accounts has just sent over the latest payroll and - please enlighten me - why in God's name do you need to hire a juggling consultant?'

I closed my laptop and turned to look at Johnno.

'Why does Ivan need a martial arts instructor?'

'I agree. It's a ludicrous waste of money. He says he needs someone to help him warm up for the show.'

'That's why I need the juggling consultant. There's nothing like a good juggle before a show. Twenty minutes with three balls in the air and my mind is clear, and my hand coordination is as sharp and steady as a surgeon's.'

'So you like to juggle - fine. That doesn't explain why we need a fulltime juggling coach on the road with us.'

'I'm about to make the difficult transition from three to four balls. Philippe is easing me through it. His guidance is invaluable. If you did your research you'd realise he's one of the top jugglers in Belgium, probably even in Europe. Like me, he's at the top of his profession - which is more than I can say about you. You're supposed to be running the tour and you can't even balance a budget.'

Johnson's face flushed red.

'How can I? With the entourage you and Ivan are dragging around with us we're going to have to hire another bus soon. I mean look at this payroll. A masseur, an acupuncturist, personal chefs, vocal and guitar tutors, costume consultants. Why do you need a costume consultant? You're wearing the same stage clothes every night, far as I can tell.'

'It's not for the show, that's for the theme parties afterwards. I simply adore Holly's work. She made me up as the most wonderful Julius Caesar at the Roman orgy party last week. I quite put Ivan's Caligula to shame! Everyone said so. You should have seen Ivan's face - it was priceless.'

'I'm not paying someone to dress you up for a goddamn toga party. Jesus Christ, you wrap yourself up in a sheet and stick a few leaves on your head. My six year old daughter could do that for you.'

'I really doubt that, Steven. Holly's a seasoned pro.'

'Why don't you get Philip to dress you? I mean, your hugely important juggling warm up is only half an hour a night, right? What does he do the other twenty three and a half hours of the day? Does he help load in and out? Does he run the lights?'

'It's *Philippe*, Steven. He hates it when people call him Philip. It's offensive. Please try and be a little more sensitive to people's feelings.'

'OK, Jimmy. I'll put that right at the top of my urgent list for the rest of the tour. The last thing I'd want to do is hurt the feelings of your juggling consultant. Is there anything else I should know? Oh for Christ's sake, why am I even having this conversation? I'm supposed to be running a rock tour, not a fucking circus!'

'I think you're being rather horrid, Steven. There's an important show to perform tonight and you're putting out all this aggression and negativity. How am I expected to go onstage?'

'I'm so sorry to have upset you, Jimmy. Maybe you can organise a kids' birthday party to cheer yourself up. You can invite your chef, your masseur, your vocal coach and the rest of the clowns on the payroll. Philippe can turn up and serve cupcakes and lemonade. Meanwhile, I'll get on with the actual job I'm paid nowhere near enough to do 24/7.'

Steve's attitude was starting to annoy me. I was about to deliver a withering reply when there was a knock at the door. One of the road crew wheeled in a trolley containing something hidden under a sheet.

'Your ice sculpture's here, Jimmy.'

'Oh how marvellous!' I cried in delight, clapping my hands. 'Bring it over.'

I lifted the sheet to behold a wonderful likeness of a lighthouse with XIII carved on the front.

'Oh, it's simply stunning! Don't you think so, Steven? Nearly as good as the one at Bologna. My spirits are quite restored just by looking at it. I do believe I'll be able to go onstage after all.'

'It *is* nice, Jimmy, I'll give you that.'

'So let's put our little tiff behind us, shall we? Let's not have any more of these boring chats about the accounts. I simply yawn whenever I hear them. I'm sure it will all come out just fine in the end.'

'I hope you're right, mate, but we really need to show a little more fiscal responsibility. It's my job to make sure this tour runs smoothly and ends up in the black. You want to have a Roman orgy party? Fine, one night won't break the bank. But we can't live like that every night. Understand?'

'Of course not, Steve, tonight's the NASA party with a space theme. We've hired a gravity-free chamber - it'll be a scream!'

'Oh no. How much is that going to cost?'

'Is that all you ever think about - money?'

'It's my job. Look mate, I'm sorry but we're going to have to make a few cutbacks for the rest of the tour. Don't have a meltdown, so to speak, but we need to talk about these ice sculptures. Look at this invoice. 1250 Euros!'

'So?'

'I'm not saying it's not worth it, especially if it makes you happy. It's a beautiful sculpture. But this business about getting a fresh one made up in each city - that's not on. We're going to have to whack this one in the freezer and take it around with us from now on.'

'I'm afraid that's impossible, Steven. I get a fresh infusion of energy every time there's a new one. It's the symbolism that counts. The ice sculpture sits at the back of the stage and by the time the show's over it's melted away to nothing. It's an allusion to the Buddhist concept of impermanence and that these good times aren't going to last.'

'If that's the symbolism it's highly appropriate, but it's got to stop. It just doesn't make economic sense. We're not paying out 1250 Euros every show, it's ludicrous.'

'I don't think it is.'

'Come on mate, we should be making gazillions off this tour and we're blowing it all on a bunch of bullshit.'

'How dare you!'

'I don't mean the ice sculpture itself, but getting a new one made every night. It's insane. I mean, do you buy a new amp every show? Of course not. So from now on, this is it for the rest of the tour. Either that or get rid of Philippe and some of the other freeloaders.'

'I'm sorry Steven, that simply isn't possible. Philippe is indispensible and unless I get my fresh lighthouse every night, I won't be able to perform. Hey, hang on a moment - what's this? Oh no, I don't believe it.'

My eye had been caught by the inscription on the front of the lighthouse. No, surely not. It couldn't be. Yet there it was.

'Well, if that don't beat all,' I said. 'Here we are in the Italian capital and they can't even get their own language right.'

'What's the matter now?'

'Look at it. They've written a V instead of an X. VIII. I've never heard of a band called Lighthouse Eight, have you?'

'I wish to Christ I'd never heard of one called Lighthouse Thirteen.'

I shook my head, appalled, and began pacing round the dressing room.

'This is a dreadful omen, Steve. The energy just doesn't feel right. I'm afraid we're going to have to cancel tonight's show. Go and inform Ivan at once.'

'Holy mother of God, over a fucking ice sculpture? Get a grip on yourself, Jimmy. I've had a gutful of this rubbish. Will ya do something for me, mate? Remember back to when you started out in rock n roll. You probably had a cheap second hand guitar and a dodgy amp. You were lucky if you ever got a gig or if anyone gave a damn enough to listen to you. And just think - you never had a masseur or a personal chef or an ice sculpture then, did you? And definitely no juggling consultant! Look at you now. What happened?'

'You're really not being very supportive. I'm an artist, you know.'

'I don't have time for this. It's hard enough running a rock tour at the best of times, let alone babysitting you and Ivan and cleaning up Ollie's puke into the bargain. For Christ's sake, Amos is the least trouble of the lot of you and he's a drummer! From now on, this tour is going to be conducted with a little more professionalism or let's just call the whole thing off. And I'll tell you something for nothing, Philippe's off the payroll. As far as I'm concerned, he can take his juggling balls and fuck off back to Belgium!'

'Then how am I going to make the transition to four balls, Steven? Did you ever think of that? I think you're being simply horrid. Well guess what? I'm quitting the band. There, are you happy now?'

I pushed the ice sculpture over onto the floor where it broke into a thousand pieces. Then I burst into tears and ran out of the room.

Ten minutes later, Johnson found me sitting in the backstage bar drinking a schooner of beer. He came up looking nervous and put a tentative hand on my shoulder.

'Alright, Jimmy?'

'Ah Johnno, sit down, mate. Let's have a drink together. I'm just having a couple before I go and do my warm-ups.'

'So you're doing the show?'

'Of course, why wouldn't I?'

'You're not quitting the band?'

'Quitting the band? Why would I do that? Stop being such a drama queen, Johnno. Let's sit down and have a beer together like men.'

'OK great - and how about we compromise on the ice sculpture? Let's go with a new one every four shows. What do you reckon?'

'Oh no thank you, Steven. Ice sculptures are so last week. They bore me.'

'Eh? You mean it? Well, if that ain't Mother Mary's latest miracle. I must visit the pope and thank him personally. That's €1250 a show we'll be saving.'

'You hang onto that money though, mate. It might be an idea to save it all for the last show of the tour and get a giant Stonehenge sized ice sculpture onstage. It'd be a nice way to go out.'

'Uh... OK Jimmy, whatever you reckon. Let's talk about it in a few weeks.'

'Right you are, Johnno. Anyhow, I must dash. There are some Italian bottoms that need a good kicking. Ciao.'

I headed off for my dressing room. Oh Diva Land, Diva Land. Those were the days! And just like the Roman Empire, who could have thought they'd ever come to an end?

# 23

# Ivan the Terrible

At the time, the Diva Wars made up one of the most amusing periods of the whole tour - but it suddenly got old for me. Almost overnight, it stopped being funny and turned into a drag. This prompted a Maelstrom check. Sure enough, the message came through loud and clear that diva season was over. With a sigh, I gave up being a prima donna and returned to ordinary levels of obnoxiousness.

To my surprise, Ivan did not. All this time I assumed he'd been singing from the same hymnbook as me. How else to explain his conduct? So when his high throttle diva-dom continued unchecked, I realised his behaviour was nothing to do with any short term powers bestowed by the Maelstrom. No, that was just him.

Now that we were out of sync, his conduct became increasingly irksome. It was the little things at first. The way he seemed to be constantly on the phone. The habit of taking his shirt off in public at the slightest provocation, or with no provocation at all, in order to display his ripped and tattooed physique to all and sundry. The indignant 'what are you looking at?' glare when all and sundry actually looked. The need to always have the loudest voice in the room. The habit of taking centre stage in photo shoots, or hijacking band interviews to give cringe-worthy answers.

There wasn't much I could do about it. If we didn't see eye to eye, it was no great wonder. There was the generation gap, for a start. Ivan was nearly twenty years younger than me. Apart from that, he was a lead singer. Say no more.

I did try to take on more of the media requests but with the band's rising popularity, it was no easy burden to shoulder. The album was selling well and being downloaded, legally or otherwise, in great numbers. The live shows were phenomenal. Musically, we were on fire. The rhythm section was tight, Ivan was in fine voice, and Oliver managed to rein in his drug use until after the show.

As the tour went on, however, Ivan's singing remained great but his sinning began to grate. Every time we boarded a plane, it was a lucky dip how obnoxious he'd be this time around. For one thing, he was obsessed with trying to score with an airline hostess on each flight. To my disgust, it actually worked on occasions. There was nothing subtle about his 'courtship' techniques. Indeed his conduct, if coming from an ordinary man, would have been deemed the crudest harassment. His rock god looks and growing fame somehow made it acceptable.

Call me unromantic, but an airline toilet doesn't seem the most ideal site for a sexual tryst. Or maybe they used some kind of crew area back there, who knows? I wasn't that bored on the flight to ever find out. But seeing him come back from these hook-ups with a smug look on his face was irksome indeed. I'd sink lower in my seat and go back to my book. Thankfully, there were also plenty of times the air hostesses gave him the short shrift he deserved. I'd still sink into my seat, this time from embarrassment at his antics and the damage to the band's reputation.

The guy certainly had a rapacious appetite for women, which I'll concede was hardly a first for a rock star. It's nobody's business until someone gets hurt. For me, it only became a concern when the damage landed on my own doorstep, quite literally, one night in Seville. Around midnight there was a soft knock outside my room. I threw the door open savagely, expecting to see Ollie begging for drugs. Instead it was a weeping girl of about eighteen who'd been sent down from Ivan's room. Through her tears and broken English, I deduced he'd seduced and reduced her to tears after a liaison. The bastard had thrown her out when he finished and some other girl showed up to replace her. When she became weepy, Ivan fobbed her off on me.

I offered the lass a kindly word and a signed T-shirt, then called her a taxi. This apparent good guy act rang hollow, for I was not Ivan's moral superior by much. Back at Rookwood, I too had gone through a succession of girls, if not quite so quickly and ruthlessly as my colleague. In replacing one girl with another on the same night, he merely offered a time-lapse version of what I'd done over weeks and months at Rookwood after first turning to the Maelstrom.

Another day, I was heading off for a swim in the hotel pool when I was struck by the urge to stop by Ivan's room. It was a strange impulse given that I'd begun to avoid the guy. He answered the door wearing only a pair of shorts - but he wasn't the only one topless in the room. I entered to see two pairs of budding breasts bobbing over two pairs of bended knees. It seemed I was just in time.

'Girls, how lovely to meet you. I'm sorry, but some urgent band business has come up. I'm going to have to ask you to step outside and come back in a couple of years.'

When they'd gone, Ivan turned to me in surprise.

'What are you doing, man?'

'Did you check their IDs?'

'No. Why would I?'

'You idiot. You could wind up in the can for that.'

'They were into it.'

'That's not the point. What about you? If you're depraved enough to do it, that's one thing, but if you're silly enough not to realise the consequences if you get caught, that's a whole new level of crazy. Use your head, mate.'

Ivan's behaviour was becoming a problem and his sexual antics were only the half of it. His whole bad boy persona quickly became tiresome. I suppose there was a certain mileage to be gained from it, cliché though it was, as long as it didn't go too far. Yet it was one thing to annoy members of the general public, quite another to mistreat actual fans of the band. It was an alarming trend that looked set to worsen. At Cordoba, we were booked in for some kind of signing event at a record store. If we'd known how big the album and tour would turn out, we'd never have bothered, but this had been set up months ago by a radio station. These events can be awkward. They're meant to bring band and fans closer together, but isn't the whole point of having rock star mystique about keeping a distance between the two?

This time we were stuck with it so we had to front up. The fans are eager and awestruck so you have to smile and be nice for hours at a time. This is not always easy if you've been up for hours after the show the night before. Still you can't let them down by being surly.

So there were Ollie, Jake, and Amos doing their duty but the main man was a no show. We had to make up a cover story about him being caught in traffic. After half an hour, there was a commotion up the back of the venue. A frazzled Steve Johnson had collared Ivan and dragged him along. Ollie shifted to the seat at the end and Ivan took his rightful place beside me. He sat there in shades, sulky and withdrawn, as a parade of adoring fans presented their merch for him to sign. None of them received eye contact or any words beyond a grunt. To compensate, I tried to give each fan a smile and a few words.

Not long after this, Ivan started showing up late for gigs. I was in my dressing room at the Madrid show when word came through that he hadn't arrived at the venue. After the signing fiasco, this was fresh cause for agitation. When he was still absent at show time I was ready to tear up the dressing room. By the time he finally materialised, we had to go on an hour late.

Nothing was said after the gig. My body language alone must have conveyed exactly what I thought of his tardiness. So when it happened again at Pamplona, I was speechless for a different reason - sheer disbelief. It was not only the disrespect shown to me and the other guys, he was actually ruining the whole energy of the show.

I know from experience how these rock shows work. A lot of the people who go to them are intoxicated, whether from a joint, a pill, or a few beers. If that's your go, the idea is to time the dosage so your buzz peaks around the time the headliner comes onstage. I learned this the hard way as a youngster at a Van Halen show back in the day. My friends and I were so pumped to see the mighty VH we made the mistake of starting the party at 3pm. While a fine afternoon was had by all, by the time Eddie and co hit the stage at nine our race was run. I lasted four songs before fizzling out into a soggy mess.

Ever since, I'd timed my run a good deal more carefully. There was strictly no drinking before 6pm. You'd have a beer or two on the way to the venue, and a couple more once you got there. Then the canny thing to do was find a quiet spot before the support band, or halfway through their set if you weren't fussed on them. A quick joint or a pipe and your buzz would peak just as the headline act hit the stage.

This was all carefully planned to optimise the whole live rock show experience - which is why Ivan's tardiness was a spanner in the works. Everyone was primed to go at the designated show time but the starter gun couldn't be fired. You could feel the crowd's energy even from backstage - their excitement, their growing anticipation. It was a volatile state of mass emotion which sought release in the power of a rock show. Yet that volatility could quickly sour if the release was withheld.

That's exactly what happened at Barcelona. It was an outdoor gig and as luck would have it, sweltering night followed scorching day. The crowd wasn't quite capacity but it was certainly well oiled, thanks to the conditions. With impeccable timing - if I may say so ironically - Ivan chose tonight of all nights to be ninety minutes late onstage. Oh, he was in the venue, he just wouldn't leave his dressing room until he was 'ready.' The prima donna barricaded himself inside and ignored all pleas to come out.

Given the turbulence of the crowd, this fresh diva turn was the last thing we needed. Sufficiently enraged to take matters into my own hands, I grabbed one of Ollie's spare guitars and smashed it against Ivan's door. Yet my valiant act was to no avail and we could hear the twat sniggering from inside, even as he feigned some 'urgent' pre-show vocal warm ups, without which he 'could not perform.'

Venue security put a stop to my righteous rage and I was urged to employ sweet reason and other non-violent methods. A fine idea, but Gandhi himself would have been stumped by this scoundrel. By the time we finally hit the stage, a sinister energy had engulfed the crowd. Many of the venue's seats were torn up, some people were injured, and an undertone of violence permeated the whole show. If we'd been any later, an actual riot may have occurred. As a postscript to this fiasco, the band was hit with a hefty fine for violating the terms of the contract, and the odds of us ever returning to that city were remote.

I did not trust myself to confront Ivan that night. It was only two days later when we reached Paris that I felt calm enough to summon him to my hotel room for a sit down. I'd been given a luxury room with city views, a piano, and an ensuite containing an enormous bathtub. Yet these comforts were all tarnished by my growing rancour towards Ivan. We had to have it out before the tour went any further, that much was clear.

Ivan was due to front me at 3pm. At 3.30, he strolled into the room, his shirt unbuttoned to just below the navel and a gold medallion suspended above it.

'Jimbo!' he exclaimed with faux-camaraderie, high-fiving me, before sitting down at the piano. Striking a Freddie Mercury pose, he launched into a sentimental jazz ballad with heartfelt lyrics about his own deep concern for world peace.

'That's for the next album,' he announced grandly after the song came to an end.

'Is that so?' I replied. 'Bit soon for a new album, ain't it?'

'The early bird catches the maggot. Olly's got some riffs, I've got some piano songs. We're on our way.'

'It's a hell of a stylistic departure, shipmate, that's all I'll say on that one. And speaking of early, we need to talk about what happened the other night.'

Ivan swivelled round on his piano stool to answer me.

'How good was it, I ask rhetorically. Edgy. Violent. The show of the tour so far. But next time save the guitar smashing until you get onstage, alright?'

'Next time I'll be smashing it over your head if you pull another stunt like that.'

'Jimmy, me old mate. Am I reading too much into this or do I detect the merest hint of antagonism?'

'You cunt!'

'Yes, I'm definitely getting something now.'

'Not only did you make me and the other lads look bad, we could have had blood on our hands and be sitting in jail cells by now. That joint was two degrees away from meltdown. It was a sauna from the get go and that mob had nought to do but self lubricate while you were beating off in your dressing room.'

'Hey, it was a hot day. That's an act of God, it's not my fault. Maybe you should have booked an indoor with air conditioning. Take it up with Johnno. That's his department.'

'If you ever go on more than half an hour late again, we're going to have a problem. A big one.'

'Yeah? What you gonna do? Tell you what, why don't you give me a one-gig suspension and go back on vocals yourself? See how good the show is then. I don't know why you're so uptight lately. Are you back on the blow again?'

'You're driving me to it. Put it down to workplace stress.'

'Work? It's not really work, though, is it? It's a party - and for a party, it's always best to be fashionably late.'

'Not when you're hosting it, you clown!'

'You know, Jimmy, your attitude is all wrong. You think of this as a job. You think everyone has to do what they're told and clock in on time, like it's a factory or something. This is rock n roll, man. We're supposed to be rebelling against all that. If the people in the crowd have got a problem with it, they shouldn't be there in the first place.'

'It's alright for you. They have to go to work the next day.'

'So do I.'

'Well, Ivan, the thing is most of those guys have to start work at 9am, not 9pm like us. Ever think of that?'

Ivan turned back to the piano and began an extra schmaltzy version of 'Sorry Seems To Be The Hardest Word,' making cow eyes and kissy lips at me over his shoulder from time to time. Luckily for him, none of Ollie's guitars were lying about the place. I suffered in silence through his vile rendition and made an effort to claw back my equanimity. If I gave in to present impulses, the entire world tour would come to an end then and there. I vowed to shut my mouth, for at least as long as it took to pack a quick cone. Finally, the woefully insincere ballad came to a stop. With an effort I mustered a smile and outstretched arms.

'Ivan, my friend, let's down tools and reboot this whole conversation. Come on - what happened to us? We used to be mates. Let's have a toke of this here peace pipe and talk about better days. You and me have stood shoulder to shoulder in front of ten thousand, every one of them chanting our names. We're bonded through that for life, so let's not be falling out over a little mid-tour fatigue. Look, I apologise. You know what I'm like. I get a bit uptight sometimes, what with the album, the tour, and as you rightly pointed out, a bit too long on the old ski slopes.'

'Have you ever thought of rehab? It might be just what you need.'

'Yes mate, I've thought about it, but you know what they say - rehab is for quitters. And there's another three months of this carnival to go.'

'Some counselling then? We've already got a masseur on the road. Why not a therapist? Maybe that dude from the Metallica movie is free.'

'It's touching to see your concern for my welfare, Ive, but we're not that far down the road to damnation just yet. I reckon we can still talk this out among ourselves. Let's have it out like men, a full airing of grievances to clear the air.'

'Are you sure you can handle it, Jimmy?'

'Whatever it takes, shipmate. What we have is too good to squander, so we'd best not let any grudges fester. Better to call a spade a damned shovel than hit each other over the head with one.'

'Or a guitar, right? OK, buddy, you take first shot at it. My hands are in the air. Like I just don't care.'

'Well, Ivan, let's kick this off right and accentuate the positive. You're a rock god with charisma to burn, and a set of pipes to put Gillan or Dickinson to shame. You can conquer a crowd, and when you take your shirt off it's enough to make a man turn. Without you, this band would still be playing the toilet circuit in lower Estonia. I take my hat off to you for all that.'

'Why, thank you, Jimmy. This is probably a good point to end the discussion.'

'At the same time, you have this pathological need to be a complete dick.'

'And there goes our window of opportunity. You had to go on one sentence too long!'

'So if we're airing grievances, Ive, let's put them under two columns. Column one is 'do you *have* to do that?' and column two is 'you *can't* do that.' So let's start with column one - ain't none of these a hanging offense on its own, but add them all up and there's a case to answer.'

'Fire away.'

'For starters, there's your constant need to draw attention to yourself. Parading round with your shirt off, for instance. No one minds if we're at the beach or onstage. But walking down the main street or in a shopping mall? And your need to take an entourage of bodyguards and hangers on with you everywhere you go. You're a rock star - we get it.'

'Isn't that what you pay me for?'

'There's a time and a place. You don't have to showboat 24/7.'

'Just trying to enjoy myself. This ain't the nineties, bud. If you want me to mope around in a flannel shirt with a face like I'm sucking lemons, too late. The good ship Grunge has sailed and sunk.'

'So has eighties glam rock. Why don't you think about what you say onstage? *Yo motherfuckers, this is The Price of Dominion. Let's rock.* Really? That's a song about heartbreak and you intro it like it's some whorehouse party anthem. I'm cringing over there scared of what you're going to say next. And where do you get off asking girls in the crowd to lift up their tops? Did you ever read any of these lyrics you're singing? Cos if there's even one song with a sexual innuendo then I'm David Lee Roth.'

'You were definitely right about being uptight, Jimbo.'

'If those girls want to take off their tops, fine, do it back at the hotel. You're tarnishing the reputation of the band with these lowbrow antics. All I ask for is a little dignity.'

'You know what your problem is, Jimmy? You asked for a rock god to front your band, got it, then complained. These 'antics' are part of the package. What you really want is a lapdog like Ollie, or worse, a clone of yourself - someone as po-faced as you who'll take all this as seriously as you take yourself.'

'Yes, ideally.'

'Only problem is, it wouldn't work. It takes an extrovert to front your band, so take the good with the bad and stop your moaning.'

'That's what I *have* done. I've compromised myself enough. All I ask is you do the same. Just keep some of your habits on the down-low. Do you have to try and score on every flight? Hell, what's wrong with reading a book for once?'

'Not my cup of tea, mate. Each to their own. We've all got to compromise and accept each other as we are. You read your book, I'll find my own in-flight entertainment.'

'This is all minor stuff though, let's move onto the type two offenses. You know, the ones you just *can't* do. For starters, you can't fire people. You tried to fire Johnno in Warsaw cos the promoter ordered the wrong brand of imported beer. Who's going to run the tour next week if you do that?'

'I was just giving him a scare.'

'And you can't be rude to fans. I don't want to hang out with them either but you've got to be polite. See, if we bump into one, it's just a moment to us but they'll remember it forever.'

'Are you done yet?'

'Finally, being late for the gigs has got to stop. You're ruining it for everyone. I'm all psyched up for the show and the last thing I want is to sit around waiting for you. It's killing the whole vibe.'

'Sorry, Jimbo, but I'm an artist and what I say goes. Delivering high quality art isn't like delivering a pizza. I have to be in the mood - and if I'm not in the mood by show time then the show will just have to wait. Don't forget that without the artist, there *is* no show. That's just the way it is.'

'You reckon? I'm bored with that whole sensitive artist spiel. It's a scam, nothing more - just a way for selfish people to pass off their character flaws as something more noble. Yeah, I know I was as bad a diva as anyone a while back, but my head wasn't right. I've had a gutful of the whole diva complex. Supermodels, sports stars, A-listers - to hell with the lot of them. It's no license to forsake the basic kindnesses. As for the show, we may be artists but this is a business. Let's have a little professionalism. There were twenty thousand there the other night and we were all on Greenwich Mean Time last time I checked.'

'But there's a whole routine I need to go through to give the performance the punters have paid for. Dinner, a massage, meditation, vocal warm ups. There's a couple of hours right there.'

'So if show time's at nine, kick off your warm ups at seven. Do what you have to, as long as you're ready to go on when we are. You can't have twenty thousand people waiting for you.'

'Apparently I can. The question is, who's master, them or me? And if the crowd thinks I'm some kind of puppet who'll jump to order, I'm not and they'll learn that the hard way. I'm the artist. I'll perform when I'm ready and not a second before. The crowd has to go with my flow. So what if I toy with them a little? Tease them, fire them up - that's what they need. Enough of that and it brings on the kind of inferno we got in Barcelona.'

'An inferno now, is it? What are you, a singer or a pyromaniac? I saw the look in your eyes the other night - couldn't read it then but I get it now. The firebug loving his work. You sick son of a bitch.'

'Who me?'

'I wondered why you're such an ass, but it's no mystery. It's for only one reason - you can get away with it. You could be anything and this is what you choose. You can pretend you're a sensitive artist, or a rebel living outside the rules, but you're just another bastard on the crest of a wave.'

'Are you done, Jimmy? Then it's my turn to vent. Every word you said might be true, but get this through your head - I don't care. This may be a temporary kingdom, but it's mine and I'll rule it as long as it lasts. Sure, we're neighbours in dominion and from one kingdom to another, we've a handy alliance. Don't deny you're just as addicted to all this as am I, and I'll wager the price you paid is the same. Don't be sermonising to me, comrade. That's typical Jimmy Brandt, always browbeating guys, lecturing, moralising. Rock's biggest curmudgeon. I ain't buying it, bud. Don't come riding your high horse into my kingdom. I know a thing or two about you. I know about your little talent quest for the support slot. I know about your string of girlfriends. I've a fair inkling what you did to Ollie. You treat him like a dog.'

'He *is* a dog.'

'That dog will come back to bite you. Reckons you broke up his marriage. What do you say to that? She was a tasty one, though, that fiancée of his.'

'No. Don't tell me. Surely you didn't?'

'I had a go at it but she wouldn't come round. Left in a flood of tears.'

'Then there's some shred of hope left for humanity. Even *I* wouldn't have stooped that low.'

'Never mind your moralising, it's a bit late for that. You're going to have to change your attitude, Jimmy. Give up on the idea you're the ringmaster round here. You ain't running this show. Get that through your head once and for all. I do what I want and go onstage when I'm ready. You daren't fire me. You can't go back to the way you were, and you'll never get a better singer than me. I've ruined the band for other singers. You know it and the punters know it. That's my crowd now and I'll do what I want with them.'

'Is that it, mate? Are you finished?'

'I've said my piece. Do you get it now?'

'Do I get it? Well, I can see you're no numbskull, Ive, and I'll grant there's something in what you say. But if you think you've got a blank cheque from now on, forget it.'

'We'll see.'

'What say we call a recess? It's getting late and we've said enough for one day. I reckon we'll pick up the thread tomorrow.'

'Fine and in the meantime I'll show you something to help you get the point. A picture's worth a thousand words, you know.'

With this, Ivan left the room without a backward glance. I didn't understand his parting remark until my phone beeped a few minutes later. Ivan had sent me a video. I hit play and watched it with a chill of recognition and a growing sense of alarm.

I saw the inside of Elijinx's hotel suite in Berlin. Then myself, clearly recognisable, my hands around Matthew Wright's throat. Hauling him to his feet, pushing him against the wall, then holding him backwards over the edge of the balcony. There was a cut in the video and the next shot was a zoom on Matthew's mangled corpse on the pavement below. At no point did Ivan or Elinjinx appear in shot. It was a damning montage and no mistake. If this fell into the wrong hands it would be the end of me.

My predicament was far worse than I'd imagined. It was bad enough to be beholden to Ivan's talents. It was worse to be locked in a power struggle for control of the band. Yet to go on with him holding the incriminating footage like a gun to my head? It was unthinkable. If he'd been insufferable before, he'd be completely out of control now - and there was not a single goddamn thing I could do about it.

# 24

# The Old Swan Dive

Oh, to think as you've done me, Ollie. Making me cancel the tour a month early. I never saw it coming, not for a moment. Such was my focus on the threat from Ivan that I failed to see the other turncoat among us. Sure, there'd been the odd mumble of discontent from stage right but I wrote it off as static within Ollie's general drug babble. As long as he did his job onstage, who cared? So when he started taking a few little verbal shots at me, it seemed nothing to get het up over. Not at first.

Look, there's no denying I botched the solo in 'Spark' the third night of the US tour. Still, it's not for Ollie to point it out after the gig. Nor is it his job to complain that I sped up verse two of 'Oceanus.' So by the time he started listening back to tapes of the show and whining that his guitar was too low in the mix, it was time to call this pup to heel.

The next morning, most of the band and crew were at breakfast. One of our crew wheeled in an old Marshall amplifier and speaker box over to where Ollie was sitting. The Marshall logo had been removed and replaced with 'Oliver.' That wasn't the only piece of Brandt intervention. I walked up and made a big show of examining the settings on the amp.

'Well, lookee here, fellas. Ollie's got his own custom amp, just like Nigel Tufnel from Spinal Tap. Nigel's amp went to eleven cos ten wasn't loud enough, and I'll be damned if Ollie's don't stop at six. I reckon that explains your problems with the mix.'

There were a few uncomfortable titters from around the room. Oliver didn't join the chorus, just sat there sulking. It was poor sportsmanship on his part.

'Come on lad, give us a smile. Surely the hangover's not *that* bad.'

Oliver upended his bowl of Cocoa Pops so that soggy brown blobs went all over the table.

'And that's why you're on second guitar to begin with,' I continued. 'Call that a tantrum? Me or Ivan would have had that table out the window by now.'

Ollie rose to the challenge and upended the table, including the breakfasts of the drummer and a couple of the crew, before storming from the room. I turned to Steve Johnson at the next table and shook my head sadly with a '*see what we have to put up with?*' look. Judging by his expression, Johnno felt the same way.

Yet somehow the joke had fallen flat. No one made any effort to clear up the mess, and an awkward mood prevailed for the rest of the meal. I sat there poker faced, finally giving up on the small talk and resigning myself to staring at my laptop through sunglasses.

Well bugger me if the *next* morning at breakfast I'm not getting the cold shoulder from the rest of the room. Maybe it was a paranoid delusion, but there was a definite vibe of the sort you don't want halfway through a voyage. And look who's sitting together like schoolgirls at recess - my two best mates, Ivan and Ollie, along with that twat from Acador. Sniggering and talking behind their hands like they'd just bought their first packet of tampons.

Ollie was becoming a problem. As for Ivan, his diva antics had shown no sign of abating since our arrival in the US. As I'd feared, he was getting worse, coming onstage later and later, treating fans and crew alike with disdain. If not for that accursed video, I'd have thrown him off a hotel balcony myself by now. Finally, I requested a sit-down with our absent manager, Elijinx. He agreed to check in when he could, but would not be pinned down on a date. That meant I was stuck with Ivan's antics in the meantime, and had little choice but to feign indifference.

In the midst of such a cold war, I resolved to remain unflappable, but the less I flapped the more my enemies tried to goad me. Prank warfare began to escalate - and instead of instigating them as was only proper in my role as band leader, I started copping a few myself. I'd open my hotel room door at 1am to find random hookers trying to gain entry. It was a dominatrix one night, a male masseur the next, or whatever other insult they could conjure.

In one case of especially bad taste, some awful Julie Andrews lookalike showed up in a Nazi nun outfit. She was wielding an acoustic guitar with the words 'Gibson Explorer' scrawled on it in black marker pen, and putting out a very poor rendition of 'Edelweiss.' I guess that was Ivan's way of telling me to go fuck myself. As with all the other hookers, I told her she had the wrong room and sent her on to Johnno's.

Then there were the puerile food pranks. Bags of flour over the dressing room door or rotten eggs under it, that kind of rubbish. Once again I held fire and stored it in the memory banks for the looming reckoning day at tour's end.

It was only when the show itself was affected that the line was crossed. We always closed with the song 'Elijinx' before the band came back on for the first encore, 'LHXIII.' My solo in the latter was one of the highlights of the night, yet in Seattle it was nearly a showstopper for another reason. I was centre stage about to launch and my amp cut out. So there I am in the spotlight looking a prize goose - and guess who's ready to step into the breach and play my signature solo note perfect?

No sooner had the house lights gone up than I seized Ollie with Thor-like fury and thrust him halfway out the nearest second floor window.

'Hookers, flour, eggs... that's all in a day's work, shipmate - but when you mess with the show you're for the swan dive. It was you scuttled my amp, right?'

Oliver looked up at me, pleading for his life.

'I'd never touch your gear, Jimmy. I was just trying to cover for you.'

'Really, Oliver? The first encore, my solo spot. Ivan put you up to it. Don't try to deny it.'

'Jimmy, it wasn't me, I swear. I haven't even spoken to Ivan for days.'

Looking past Ollie's face at the hard ground below, it struck me he should get the benefit of the doubt. No point jumping to conclusions and throwing the baby out the window with the bathwater. Besides, we'd have to find another guitarist to finish the tour. I dragged him inside and clapped him very hard on the back.

'My apologies - didn't mean to keelhaul you there, Ollie. Truth be told, you saved the show tonight. You're the man for a crisis, and no mistake. Come and have a drink in my dressing room and we'll clear the air on all this.'

Back in the sanctity of the rooms, we opened a beer each and again I clapped him on the back, if a little softer this time.

'I don't tell you this enough, Ollie, but your contribution's been impeccable. You're up for a promotion, right enough. So let me apologise and not just for dangling you out of that window. My little gag with the amp the other week - that's all it was, a gag. A laugh among lads. No need to take it to heart. So let's shake on that and drink up, alright?'

'OK, boss. After all, there's still two months to go. We can't be brawling among ourselves.'

'Right you are, mate, couldn't have said it better myself. What say we start thinking about the next album? Don't forget you've got a license for two songs. Hell, let's make it two and a half and go for a co-write to boot!'

'You mean it?'

'Sure - so what have you got? Give me a showcase.'

I handed Ollie one of my spare guitars. He let fly a long blast of complex riffage that recalled some prog rock monstrosity from the seventies. I'd downed the best part of two beers before it ground to a halt. Jumping to my feet, I grasped his sweaty hand in mine.

'Put it there, comrade! I've not been so dumbstruck since the Jack Lynton Memorial tryouts. Still, let me hold off on a verdict 'til you've had the chance for an encore in the morn.'

I thought about it overnight. The next day, Ollie's repeat performance in my hotel room confirmed my suspicions. The boy could play but he was no riffmeister. His output had only two styles. It was either hook-less virtuosity or pedestrian rock riffage that lacked the spark or point of difference to make it onto one of our albums. But how to relay the message without inciting another mutiny?

'Ollie, there's the good news and the bad news. The good news is I'm hearing a very strong solo album. The bad news is I'm not hearing any Lighthouse XIII songs.'

'Huh? You saying it's not good enough?'

'If anything, it's *too* good. Trouble is, most of your stuff's too fast for the human ear to follow. It's suited to a small boutique venue - a jazz club, or something that size. That style gets lost in an arena. It'd sail up into the ether like so much lighter flame.'

'That's not what you said last night.'

'I didn't say anything last night. I had my suspicions and they were right. You're a great athlete on the guitar, Ollie - far better than me - but where are the catchy riffs? The strong musical statements?'

'What about this?'

Oliver reprised some of his pedestrian riffage on the spot, then looked up to meet my rueful gaze.

'It's not bad in its own way, but it's too old school for me. Weren't all the pentatonic riffs used up in the seventies? And please - was that a 'four chord song' in there? The old I-VI-IV-V? I'll go back and work in the Public Service before I ever lay down one of those. Sorry mate, I just don't know if your songwriting's going to work in this band.'

'Why not let the public decide?'

'Because they're about as loyal as a gossip mag with a new editor. We can't afford to follow a strong album like *Maelstrom* with anything subpar. One weak release and we're done. Where do you and Ivan get off thinking you're going to take over writing duties? Between his soppy piano ballads and your hook-free shred fest, you'd turn Lighthouse XIII into a totally different band. One the fans won't recognise. Hell, I can hardly recognise it myself.'

'Maybe I should hand in my notice.'

'What you do at the end of tour's your call - but don't even *think* about skipping out early. That'd be breach of contract and you liable for all money lost from missed shows. To say nothing of the ethics of it.'

'Don't lecture me on ethics, Jimmy. You made me a drug addict, broke up my marriage, and now you won't even let me have my two songs. How's that for breach of contract?'

'Eh? Where's all this come from? Made you a drug addict? I gave you a pre-tour inoculation against all that. If you're going to go all Motley Crue on me, don't be pointing the finger anywhere but yourself. Did I tell you to become a junkie? Cos if there was even one needle on that boot camp, then I'm Kurt Cobain.'

I shook my head in disgust.

'As for your marriage? If your deal's kipping three to a bed, wait til your fiancée's out of town. That's my advice. I warned you internet porn was your salvation, but did you listen? Anyhow, I did you a favour. You're too young to get married. I saved you a world of pain in the long run. And the album? The two songs are still yours but give me a song not a solo. Mentoring ain't mollycoddling. The ball's in your court.'

Oliver took that ball and went home. He upped and left without another word. We ignored each other on and offstage for the next three tour stops. Given the balance of power, it was a poor excuse for a cold war. Russia vs Australia circa 1970, or some such comical mismatch. Fine - I only had to wait out the tour and he'd be gone.

But by the time we crossed into Albuquerque, New Mexico, he was making a pilgrimage to my hotel room begging forgiveness. Oliver with the olive branch.

'Sorry, boss. I thought about what you said and you're right.'

'Really? What changed your mind?'

'Ivan gave me a few home truths. Told me to put away my ego and do what's best for the band.'

'Ivan! Well if that ain't the clincher. What else did he say?'

'He told me to accept that I don't know it all. I'm young and still got it all to learn. You're the master, I'm the apprentice, so I should be learning while I can.'

'I see. Maybe I've misjudged him. Him and you both.'

'If you accept my apology, all I ask is the chance to learn songwriting from you.'

Now, the most obvious part of Ollie's about-face was not his admission of the truth, but the transparency of his motives. It's all very well offering the old peace pipe if you're not so clearly also clutching a wrench behind your back. That white flag had a black spot on it all along.

Still, if he wanted to play Gale to my Walter White, so be it. I'd go along with the charade for now. It was plain enough Ivan meant to oust me from the band. Laughable but true. It was also plain he'd roped in Ollie as my successor - except Ollie's failure as a songwriter had put a dent in the scheme.

So now they expected me to take this humble pie at face value when it was clear they were going to shove it into my *own* face at the first opportunity? As if I'd make myself redundant by training up a rival! What was the correct strategic response? The cold shoulder? A scornful diagnosis of their motives? Far better, methinks, to string these bozos along until I could deal with Ivan's possession of the incriminating footage. Then I could fire both of them and start again with a clean slate.

I extended my hand.

'Well done, son. It takes a big man to admit he was wrong. I accept your apology. Let's begin training tomorrow. Boot camp part two.'

So began our weekly sessions, ostensibly to impart the secrets of songwriting. In reality, it was a process of bamboozlement and obfuscation. I led him a merry dance. I mean, how was studying the history of jazz going to help Ollie write a good Lighthouse XIII song? We were nothing like a jazz band. But just because I'd slipped the odd major or minor seventh chord into a couple of our songs, I convinced him it was a worthwhile step.

At other times, confusing Ollie was as easy as setting up an effects rack on his amp, getting him to drop acid and ordering him to play the five note theme from the *Close Encounters* film over and over with different effects. That kept him engrossed for hours, and as far away from quality songwriting as ever. I capped off that session with some classic Spinal Tap type BS.

'You want to know the secret of my sound, Ollie? The real secret.'

'Sure, boss.'

'Listen up then. You're not going to believe this, but here it is. You know that signature sound of mine, the one that's on all our recordings? No one's ever been able to copy it. And the reason? Before I tell you, swear an oath it will never leave this room.'

'I swear.'

'Then here it is. I tune the guitar down to E flat. That's step one. Then I put a capo on the first fret. That's step two. That's it - that's how I get my sound.'

'No!'

'Hard to believe, but there it is. That's my secret.'

For non-guitarists, let me explain. My 'secret' entailed tuning the guitar down one semitone, then raising it back the same amount by attaching a clamp-like device called a capo. Thus, it sounded exactly the same as before I tuned down. It was utter nonsense, yet Ollie was far enough gone on the drugs to take it seriously, at least until the dose wore off.

At other times, I'd confuse him with a half truth. For example, the day I urged him to change instruments.

'You know one of the biggest problems for songwriters who play guitar? It's the guitar. Every song they write sounds like it was composed on six strings. That's how to get into a rut. But what's the best Van Halen album? In my book, it's *Fair Warning* - and you know what? Most of those songs were written on piano, then transposed for guitar. Maybe that's why it's so great.'

Was this true? I'd read it somewhere in a guitar mag so maybe it was. Still, that's ignoring the fact that, unlike Oliver, Edward Van H was a master songwriter as well as a player. Even if Ollie did somehow break out of a rut via a change of instrument, it would be months before he'd find out one way or the other. By then he'd have his marching papers, long before we made it back to the recording studio.

When it comes to obfuscation, mixed messages always help. One day I'd advise Ollie that a classic song needs a bipartite structure with a modulation into the subdominant key in the middle eight, and a metaphorical lyric expressed in Iambic pentameter. The next day I'd tell him he was over-thinking it and make him listen to Bob Dylan and AC/DC.

After a couple of weeks of this, Ollie was still no closer to coming up with a decent rock riff. But by the time I finally caught up with Elijinx in the quiet backroom of a Boston cafe, it turned out the mutineers' plans were further advanced than I'd thought.

'Well, Elijinx. For once, your face is the same, but it's been so long since we met I hardly recognised you.'

In truth, Elijinx looked exactly the same as he had at Berlin - an affluent, silver-haired businessman in his late fifties. He might have been taken for a CEO reluctantly meeting one of his poorer relatives who was looking for a handout. He ignored my remark and stared soberly at me across the table.

'I understand there's some kind of problem, Jimmy. What's up?'

'Where have you been? The tour's a shambles.'

'What do you mean? All the dates are sold out.'

'Rumour has it you're our manager. If you came out with us, you'd know what's really going on.'

'Please. As if I'm going to hang out with you artist types and your petty whining. Third world despots are less troublesome. It's Johnson's job to deal with all that.'

'Did he say anything about Ivan? His behaviour?'

'He said you've both been carrying on like a couple of prize ballerinas. Yawn.'

'That guy's got to go.'

'Who, Johnson?'

'Ivan, of course. I've had a gutful of him.'

'Have we reached the point yet where it's you or him? You know, either he leaves or you do.'

'Don't be ridiculous. It's not me or him. It's him. This is my band.'

'Ivan seems to think it's the other way round. Here - you'd better have a read through this. I intercepted it three days ago.'

Elijinx handed me a sheet of paper with a printout of some kind of typed IM exchange. At first I couldn't make head nor tail of it.

**Hoe** - Hey bud, cracked it yet?

**Arabella** - He won't give it up. He's still stalling, like I don't know what he's doing.

**Hoe** - That's Julie for you, arrogant as ever. Get on with it. I've had enough of him. Find out his formula so we can move on without him.

276

**Arabella** - What if there is no formula?

**Hoe** - That's your problem. I'll give you 3 weeks max. If you can't crack it, we go to Plan B, the songwriting contest.

**Arabella** - Is that legal? What if we get sued down the track?

**Hoe** - As long as it's in the terms and conditions, there's nothing they can do. Julie pulled the same stunt getting the supports.

**Arabella** - Come on, give me more time on Plan A first.

**Hoe** - I told you 3 weeks and that's it. Try this. Get him to do some co-writes, then he might open up to you. Offer to take a lower royalty. I bet that's what he's worried about. Who cares? He won't be around to collect any.

**Arabella** - So I offer him all the royalties?

**Hoe** - He won't buy that. Ask for 60/40 then let him beat you down to 80/20. Apprentice rates. Let him think he's got the upper hand.

That was all. I looked up at Elijinx.

'What's all this then? Who's Arabella?'

'Come on - pretty obvious, isn't it? Ollie, brolly, umbrella, Arabella. Ivan, hoe. Jimmy, Julie.'

'Julie, huh? Guess that explains the Julie Andrews lookalike in the Nazi nun outfit. What a nerve!'

'Julie - it suits you. And you wonder why I don't hang around the tour.'

'What's this about the royalties? "He won't be around to collect any." And what's this contest?'

'Let me give you a briefing. As you probably realise, Ivan's gunning for you, and Ollie's lined up to step into your shoes. All he has to do is learn to write songs. That's Plan A.'

'What's Plan B?'

'They're going to run a songwriting contest on the website. For a small processing fee - say £125 - unsigned bands get the chance to write a song for the next Lighthouse XIII album. They have to send in three original songs, then Ivan will pick the best. It's the Jack Lynton Award all over again.'

This was enough to propel me out of my seat. For several seconds I was too outraged to do anything but pace around the cafe's backroom in a state of disbelief. Eventually I sat back down, looked at Elijinx, and shook my head.

'I've got to hand it to him. That's one way to solve the problem. Still, there can't be many royalties in it if they're using outside writers.'

'That's where the terms and conditions will come in - in the very fine print. All songs and riffs submitted become property of Lighthouse XIII, who have first option and rights for all future usage. If a hundred bands send in three songs each, Ivan and Ollie have three hundred songs to choose from. All they have to do is take the best ten and there's the new album. With the amount of unsigned talent out there, the top ten songs out of three hundred should be pure cream.'

I bounced out of my seat again. The plan was as brilliant as it was evil. Still, I would never have touched it. Ivan must have had two Maelstroms hung round his neck.

'The bastards! It's theft, plain and simple.'

'Is it any worse than the Jack Lynton?'

'Far worse. I'd never do that to a band. With the Jackie L, we only got their hopes up for a support slot, but stealing a song is like stealing a child. No way this goes ahead. How'd they ever get it through their heads I'd have anything to do with this?'

'Exactly, Jimmy. They knew you wouldn't - and what conclusions do you draw from that?'

'You don't mean...?'

'Let's just say I wouldn't be sharing any hotel balconies with Ivan anytime soon.'

'Like that, is it? Well, well. I promise you this, Elijinx. If anyone in this band's doing the old swan dive, it won't be Jimmy Brandt, and you may lay to that. This is a mutiny needs crushing, double quick. Maybe tonight. If only he didn't have that footage.'

'What footage?'

'That night in Berlin in your hotel room. I've seen it with my own eyes. The cursed downloader, Pyro, my hands around his throat, then him all over the pavement. Ivan's got it on his phone. He's been holding it over my head since Europe or I'd have buried him by now.'

'Is that so? Intriguing. Let me think on this awhile and we'll come up with a counter scheme.'

I relaxed a little. At least Elijinx was still on my side.

'Between the two of us,' I said, 'we'll come up with something. We've been around a bit longer than young Ivan and I reckon we'll outlive him too. Still, how do we play it from here?'

'You've read the transcript. Oliver's got three weeks to winkle out your trade secrets. That leaves a couple more again before the tour wraps up. My guess is there's a tragic accident waiting to happen during the last fortnight. It would make a perfect launching pad for their Plan B, wouldn't it?'

I slapped my thigh with a thunderclap that followed a flash of insight.

'Not just a launching pad, a rationale! By the powers, my demise makes the perfect excuse for their shameful contest. They'd probably name it after me too. The Jimmy Brandt Memorial Songwriting contest.'

'Dead right, Jimmy - I never thought of that! What say we pull the rug out from under these turncoats? We'll make the New York show our swansong next week and blow out the last month of the tour. Then go home and clear our heads.'

And so it transpired. The New York show was phenomenal. There were all manner of weird undercurrents filtering into the vibe. Ivan and Ollie both made a point of smiling at me like we were comrades in arms. I smiled back, all the while wondering if this might be the band's last ever show. Our setlist was as follows.

1. Black Phoenix
2. High and Mighty
3. Trade Winds
4. The Price of Dominion
5. Quitter
6. Life Line
7. Spark
8. Extinction.Net
9. SMS
10. Death Bed Regrets
11. Temporary Kingdom
12. Between the Stairway and the Highway
13. Vortex Winder
14. The Maelstrom Ascendant
15. Mountain Gods
16. Retro Stereo
17. Elijinx
18. LHXIII
19. The Ephemeral and the Eternal

And that, for the moment, was all she wrote. By the time Ivan and Ollie heard the tour was being cut short a month, I was already back at Rookwood plotting my next move. I only hoped it wouldn't be my last.

# Part Four

# 25

# I For An Eye

I returned to Rookwood with the sense that somehow, somewhere along the line, things had gone a little awry.

Where did it all go wrong? I'd begun the world tour a conqueror. Yet by tour's end, I'd been forced to flee a palace coup at the hands of my singer and second guitarist. That would have been unthinkable a few months back when Ivan seemed to be the band's saviour. Now we were in a state of war. He'd recruited Ollie as an ally, only to be thwarted by the guy's failure to usurp me as a songwriter. I would have sacked the pair of them and moved on but Ivan's possession of the damning footage meant that the axe I had to grind I could not wield. I would have to think this through very carefully.

Given my confusion and sense of peril, it's no wonder I became so involved with the Volant Society. While browsing the library at Rookwood one morning, I came across Edward Bentley's great book *Lunar Luminous*. After skimming the first few chapters, I looked again and found some of his other books, including first editions of *Volant Voyeur* and *The Oversight*.

Bentley's work reminded me of the Hartford Papers, the material I'd studied for my PhD. Yet it was no carbon copy. Bentley had his own style and slant on the matters Hartford had discussed. For a time, I forgot my own battles and immersed myself in the man's work.

His first books had been published in the 1970s, so it seemed likely Bentley would be dead or retired by now. However, a Google search revealed that he was still active, living and teaching in London at the  head of a group called the Volant Society. With few commitments and my life in a state of limbo, I resolved to pay them a visit.

At the listed London address was an old bookshop. Most of the books dealt with esoteric subject matter of one sort or another. Ed's wife Myra was behind the counter that day, although I did not know her identity at the time. She made no comment when I brought her husband's most recent book, *Wings of Eternity*, to the counter.

'I think that completes my collection,' I said, stretching the truth a little. 'If only Mr. Bentley could sign this, it would be perfect.'

Myra said nothing but slipped a card into my hand along with my change. I had an odd sense she'd been expecting me all along. The card listed coming meetings of the Volant Society, the first of which was set for the following week.

I returned the next Thursday to find fifteen to twenty people milling around the shop. Shortly before 8pm, Myra took steps to remove a handful of these, the ordinary customers. Those who remained - the Volant Society members - had already begun to move in ones and twos down a flight of stairs to the cellar. Feeling rather self conscious, I insinuated myself into the group.

The cellar had the same dimensions as the shop but seemed more spacious due to the absence of books. The shrine at the front was dominated by Myra's classic painting of the Eye over the Moon. Her other paintings were along the walls. Several had doubled as covers of Bentley's books - I recognised *Volant Voyeur* at once - yet they were much more striking at this size. Abstract or realistic, the core element was the invocation of power, or illumination. One could say they suggested nature worship, yet the insinuation was to super-nature.

The room was lit by candles and scented with incense. There were enough half open windows to ward off any sense of claustrophobia. The windows opened at the base of street level and the occasional pair of legs could be seen walking past, as if they were independent entities not attached to bodies.

A circle of cushions was laid out around the room. When almost all the members were seated upon them, I took a place at the back left of the circle. At a bell from Myra, the members struck up a chant. This was all quite familiar from time I'd spent in various 'Eastern' style groups in Sydney. Chanting, candles, and the rest of the mystic trappings were no novelty.

When the chanting had gone on for some time, Edward Bentley appeared at the foot of the stairs. Despite the passage of time, I recognised him - but only just. The photo on the back of his books showed a charismatic man in his thirties. By now, of course, Ed must have been pushing seventy. The neatly trimmed black beard from the photo had lengthened and turned snow white. He could have pulled off a *Lord of the Rings* cameo without much bother. In spite of this, a trace of the youthful Ed Bentley remained.

The chanting continued while Ed walked round the circle, placing his left hand on each person's head for a moment in turn. When he reached me, Ed showed no surprise. He touched my head, lingered a moment as if somehow reading my thoughts, then moved on. At last he finished his rounds and took up his place at the front of the circle.

Edward welcomed us all to the meeting with some jovial remarks, then greeted each member by name. This made me even more self-conscious about my status as an outsider so when it came to my turn, I felt obliged to make an introduction.

'I'm Jimmy. Perhaps I should say a few words about myself.'

'No need,' replied Edward. 'I feel you're an old friend and we met a very long time ago. Let's assume we've known each other for years. Don't speak. Just be here and go along with the experience.'

We began a period of meditation. Again, this was no novelty to me, except for the use of music. A few minutes in, I was surprised by the evocative swell of a violin melody. Opening my eyes a crack, I saw no violinist. The music was coming from surround speakers at the four corners of the room.

Before long, some soft percussion entered the piece, then more instruments. The music evolved seamlessly, adding layer on layer until it reached a climax of sorts, then stopped abruptly. When I opened my eyes, everyone was gazing at Edward Bentley sitting at the head of the circle in some kind of trance. After a long silence, Ed pointed at a woman on the other side of the circle and gave her a message which meant nothing to me but seemed to make a great deal of sense to her.

Edward repeated the process twice more with other members then, to my surprise, the next message was for me. He fixed his gaze upon me and spoke in sonorous tones:

From mountains blue to mountains white

One heart in day and one in night

The bond between you died on that table


They owe you allegiance who seek to depose you

The golden tongued thief who means to expose you

Many faces lie, the multi-face speaks true


Come to the Eye in supplication

Seek your deliverance and salvation

Moonflight the eternal illumination


Bentley closed his eyes again, then turned his attention to someone else. His words meant little at first hearing. It was only when I examined the transcript later at Rookwood that their meaning hit home. The Volant Society had the practice of taping and transcribing all of Ed's pronouncements. The first two stanzas, at least, were a direct reading of my recent past. As I pored over his words, their uncanny accuracy convinced me that Bentley was the man to guide me through my current crisis.

I returned to the Volant Society the next three Thursdays. My real wish was for a private audience with Ed but he seemed to speak only in front of the group, either in casual banter or in the cryptic verse style of his trance statements. I stuck it out for a month to show I was no fly-by-night, then entreated Myra to ask Edward for a session.

The request was granted more easily than I'd expected, and a meeting set up. The following Sunday, I went downstairs to the cellar once more, where Edward was holding court. This time he sat on an armchair, rather than the usual cushions, with another set up across from it. Smiling, he gestured at me to sit down.

'Welcome Jimmy. What can I do for you?'

'Thanks for seeing me, Mr. Bentley. As you know, I'm in a bit of strife at the moment.'

'Call me Edward - but what makes you think I know anything about you?'

'Some of what you've said in the meetings has been... uncanny.'

'Really? I don't remember much of what I've said in trance.'

'You're telling me things about my life I'm hardly aware of myself. How do you know so much about me?'

'It is the Eye that knows, not I. Possession of the Eye makes it possible.'

'I only wish I had it myself.'

'Isn't that why you're here? The entire aim of the Volant Society is to attain the Eye. That is our whole *raison d'être*, and all of our rituals and practices are directed to that end. Myra said you have all the books. Surely you've read *Lunar Luminous*.'

He pronounced luminous with the stress on the second syllable. For a moment, I wondered if I should confess to having exaggerated my knowledge of his work.

'I've read *Volant Voyeur* and *The Scarlet Triumvirate*. I'm halfway through *Lunar Luminous*.'

'That's really the one you should have started with. All the fundamental doctrines of the Volant Society are laid out in its pages. If you've picked up anything from what you've read so far, you'll know that the world we live in - the ordinary three dimensional world - is the tip of a much larger iceberg floating in a vast sea.'

I raised my eyebrows and looked around me. Edward smiled and continued speaking.

'The human being exists in much the same manner. We are far more than we know. The ordinary human self - the you and I who are speaking now - belongs in this world and is fully suited to it. There's nothing wrong with that. Indeed the main purpose of the ordinary self is to function in the world that we know.

Yet there is also a deeper portion of the self which equates to the iceberg and swims freely in that sea of which I spoke. It is that self and that deeper realm we so ardently wish to reach. But oh how the ordinary self struggles against the knowledge of its roots. That is the perennial struggle, for the ordinary self knows that reaching the deeper realms entails its own destruction, or at least its minimisation. And how the proud and egocentric self resists that minimisation! Here at the Volant society, we do not shirk this destruction, we embrace it. We know that to attain the Eye we must sacrifice the I.'

'So it's an I for an eye.'

'Exactly, Jimmy. You see, our philosophy embraces the whole self. The waking self has its role to play, while the deeper self has a more profound role. From a greater perspective, neither self contradicts the other.'

'You know what your stuff reminds me of? The Hartford Papers. Ever heard of it?'

'Of course. Fran Stuart's work. I visited her group in the seventies.'

'You're joking! Really?'

'I was living in the States at the time so it was easy enough. Hartford was one of my first teachers. I won't deny he's an influence. But ultimately, Hartford merely spoke the perennial truth, which we all come to sooner or later. Ah, the seventies - they were heady days indeed. People speak of the sixties as the great Utopian decade and say the seventies was a comedown, but that's not the case. There was just as much excitement and experimentation going on in the seventies, as long as you knew where to look.'

'I certainly wish I'd been around then. They had the best music, the best drugs. Er, sorry.'

Edward laughed.

'Don't apologise. We all did it back in the day - and why not? There are many roads to the Eye. Some may be illusory but you never know until you try. Open experimentation was the rule in those days. Still Fran Stuart was no drug user as far as I know. She was a natural mystic. I had a lot of time for her.'

'I wrote a PhD thesis on the Hartford Papers.'

'Is that so? I'd be very interested to read that. And what are you doing now - still writing?'

'No, I'm a musician. In a band called Lighthouse XIII.'

'A musician, eh? I've certainly known a few of those in my time. I'm a bit out of touch now but London was the place to be in the late-sixties and early-seventies. They were glory days indeed. If you're a musician, perhaps you can compose a quarana for us.'

'You mean that music you play during the meditations? I've been wondering about it.'

'As I said, there are many paths to the Eye. Study, meditation, drugs, sex magick to name a few. I've always found music a wonderful aid. That's the whole point of the quaranas. They're a vital part of the ritual. The quaranas offer an atmospheric ascent into the higher realms of consciousness. I learned the practice in Africa but adapted it to my own tastes.'

'I like the way they're not too bland, unlike most of the New Age music.'

'That's the mistake people make about spirituality, isn't it? The spirit isn't bland or wishy washy, not in its essence. The spirit is a mountain, a volcano! A quarana can be any kind of music from the most delicate harp strings to the heaviest rock music.'

I nodded my approval. I was warming to Edward by the moment.

'That's right up my alley then,' I said. 'My own music's on the heavier side.'

'Really? Then I challenge you to compose a quarana yourself. See what you can come up with. The Volant Society is always open to new inspiration.'

'Sure, why not? What does the name of your group really mean though?'

'It was the Voyant Society originally. To do with vision, as in clairvoyant. Volant is more suggestive of flying. The word itself describes wings extended in flight. You can see it in Myra's picture on the altar - a pair of wings traversing the moon towards the distant Eye. Moonflight is the state to which we aspire. It's the pathway to the Eye.'

'Moonflight?'

'The occult symbolism is rather obvious. The sun represents the waking world and the self's normal perception. The moon represents the hidden domain of true knowledge. During Moonflight, you move through that secret realm and fly directly into the Eye. Attaining Moonflight and then the Eye is the entire aim of the Volant Society. That's the whole point of the quaranas and our other rituals. What we do here on a Thursday night is a very mild form. You should really come on one of our weekend retreats.'

'Do they happen here too?'

'Oh no, we have an estate out of the city. That's our retreat centre.'

'Really? Whereabouts?'

'It's up north near Essex.'

'I have a house out that way myself. A place called Rookwood.'

Edward Bentley raised his eyebrows.

'Rookwood! I know it. In fact, I've been there many times. It was quite the gathering place for musicians in the seventies. Did you know that?'

'That's no surprise considering who used to own it.'

'Indeed. I could tell you a few stories from those times, believe me. Rookwood has a wonderful energy. It can be rather erratic, yet it's highly conducive to creativity and accessing the hidden domain.'

'You and Myra should come out one night for a visit.'

'We all should. Old Rookwood, eh. You know what, Jimmy? It might make a splendid site for a ritual, if you're receptive to the idea. Perhaps when you've composed your quarana?'

'I don't see why not. But tell me, what do you actually see during Moonflight?'

Edward leaned forward, and spoke with quiet intensity.

'We see the world as it really is, beneath the surface world of appearances. We see the past and the future, our origins and our destiny. Each of us sees our life afresh as one illusion among many. One we can change and control. There's very little knowledge that can't be attained through Moonflight if the conditions are right.

We can contact the dead, or those yet to be born, or those entities in the higher realms. If you have a question, you may ask it and expect to be answered. There are no horizons during Moonflight.'

'Then I agree to the ritual. I'll go to your retreat, then return the favour at Rookwood.'

Edward smiled and leaned back in his armchair.

'Thank you, Jimmy. I do not need to contact the Eye to know you are troubled. Your thoughts are full of confusion. The dark and the light battle within you. You cannot tell friend from foe, or how to proceed. No one is more needful of Moonflight than you.'

'It's true I've lost my way. And if, as you say, Moonflight allows us to contact the dead or those in the higher realms, perhaps I'll use it to contact Hartford himself. Could I do that?'

'It's certainly possible.'

'I need guidance from someone. Why not Hartford? He can advise me on what to do.'

'I support the intention, Jimmy - but a word of caution. You cannot enter Moonflight with preconceived notions of what you will find. That contradicts the entire endeavour. To attain the Eye you must destroy the I - as you so aptly put it yourself. No, to attain Moonflight and the Eye, you must let go in the most wholehearted way possible. Do not hold on to the tiny, waking self which holds you back. On the contrary, you must allow it to be annihilated to enable the higher self to come to the fore. It is only then that you'll find the knowledge you seek.

So by all means, request a meeting with Hartford and he may indeed appear to you. Yet he may not, and you might experience something quite different and unexpected. Moonflight can never be pre-ordained.'

'I understand, Edward. Whatever happens, I'm excited now. I haven't picked up a guitar since we came off tour but I'm going home to start on the quarana tonight.'

'Then go well, Jimmy, and may the Eye go with you.'

# 26
# Moonflight

The Volant Society's retreat centre was less than an hour from Rookwood. I drove out on the Friday night and settled in for the weekend. As it turned out, the retreat was really just an extended version of the Thursday night meetings - meditation in the morning, followed by a discussion of Edward's philosophy in the afternoon. The focus was his latest book, *Wings of Eternity*.

I fidgeted through the discussion. I was simply biding my time, waiting for the Saturday night ritual, wondering about Edward's famous Moonflight and whether I could achieve it. Ed had told me not to get my hopes up for the first attempt. He advised me to use the weekend simply to get a feel for the quaranas. Ed had chosen some of the best quaranas from his collection to inspire me, although with a definite rock music slant.

At last it was time. In preparation for the ritual, all participants drank a cup of herbal tea laced with Mendara, a mild hallucinogen related to the peyote family. According to Edward, this allowed the ego to loosen its tight grip on perception. If that was the aim, it succeeded. I felt a loosening of the tightly woven basket of beliefs, thoughts, and habits that normally made up my identity. It all began to dissolve in a warm pool of euphoria. I rode the quaranas like a surfer cresting a wave, sensing an elevated state of consciousness almost within my reach.

Almost. Yet although Moonflight was not attained, there's no doubt I was on the verge. At the same time, I'd seen several of my colleagues in a state of great rapture, such that I became all the more determined to achieve the same state myself.

I returned to Rookwood the next morning and resumed work on the quarana. I conjured some riffs, lyrics and a solo, then invited Amos to record drums. There was no need to bother with Jake, or of course Ollie. Ivan was left out of the loop altogether as I reprised my former role as a singer. Within three days, the song 'I For An Eye' was recorded. When he heard it, Edward seemed genuinely excited.

'This is a tremendous quarana!' he proclaimed. 'You've mastered the form at your first attempt.'

'Thank you, Edward. I only hope it appeals to Hartford as much as it does to you.'

'You never know. I imagine the vibrations from that tune would resonate through the entire spiritual realm. If Hartford doesn't hear it, someone else will.'

'Maybe Randy Rhoads will come and check it out.'

'Who's that?'

'He was Ozzy Osbourne's first guitarist when Ozzy went solo after Black Sabbath. A genius. He was killed in a plane crash in 1982.'

'What happened to Ozzy himself?'

'He's still alive and touring, surprisingly.'

'Is that so? To anyone who knew him in the seventies that must come as a miracle surpassing even the virgin birth. Now, remember what I said. We must never prejudge what will be encountered in Moonflight. The ego's need to control is never-ending, yet it is precisely that need which will keep you earthbound. The only way to the Eye is to surrender your control, to allow the ego to be annihilated.'

'I understand. As for the ritual, my song is only five minutes long. What other music do you plan to use.'

'Why don't you take care of that, Jimmy? Let's make it a real rock oriented ritual. I suggest you make up a shortlist of songs, then we'll finalise the running order together.'

'I'd love to.'

'With your own song taking pride of place as both the opening and closing piece. The first listen will familiarise us all with the song, which will help make the second a launch pad into Moonflight.'

The ritual was set for the next full moon, ten days hence. I settled in at Rookwood, waiting impatiently, holed up in the library reading Edward's books in front of the fire.

At last the day came. It had been a bitter winter, but the night itself was fairly mild. The air was crisp, yet not so harsh as to force one to dash instantly indoors on arrival. As the ritual's attendees arrived at Rookwood one by one in their cars, they had time to pause and gaze in devotion at the full moon, on the way to the house. That moon seemed supernaturally large, its power immense in the minds of its devotees.

I joined the other Volant Society members in the back lounge. Not for the first time, I noted their seeming normality. They came from various backgrounds and professions, all of which were left behind once they walked through these doors. 'It matters not what mask we wear in the world,' Edward had said. 'All facades are discarded in search of the Eye.' I did note that there were no young members. None younger than myself, at any rate. Still, we had all been young once.

Before the ritual we drank our Mendara tea, then filed into the drawing room, one of the largest rooms at Rookwood. I had prepared it in imitation of the bookshop cellar. Candles, a circle of cushions, and a vacant space in the middle. Nature abhors a vacuum. Super-nature adores one.

By the time we had all taken our places, the Mendara had well and truly done its job. Unknown to Edward, I'd taken a double dose, so avidly did I seek Moonflight. The sense of exhilaration had already set in as I took my place to the left of Edward in the circle. Then the music began.

'I For an Eye' kicked off the set. I could not resist a peek at my fellows to gauge their reaction. Given the average age of the group,

I feared the tune might be too heavy for them, but it seems Ed's rituals had trained them to expect the unexpected - and educated them in various styles of music. Mind you, some of them were probably veteran fans who came up with the great rock bands of the 1970s. As the set of songs rolled through its phases, I sensed that many of the members were affected in the desired manner. Yet I was too engrossed in my own experience to pay them much heed. This time I went to the summit and beyond. By the time 'I For an Eye' made its encore at the end of the set, my consciousness was tripping giddily up and down the runway. As the song reached its crescendo, my thoughts dissolved in a lunar alchemy until at last I flew...

...and went nowhere. I was still in the drawing room at Rookwood - but the other Volant Society members had vanished. I was alone in an empty room. The furnishings had also changed, a fact made more obvious because the room was now illuminated by broad daylight.

I removed my jacket, for the day was sweltering. Then, crossing to the windows, looked out on a summer day. The gardens were in full bloom. What had become of the midwinter night?

I saw bed upon bed of flowers. The grounds at Rookwood had never been very well kept in my experience, yet here were clear signs of a nurtured environment. My eyes ran left to right over flower beds red, white, violet and yellow - and in that last bed, a grey cat lying in the sunlight. As I saw him, the cat raised his head and fixed green eyes upon me. Finzi! Surely not - yet the resemblance was enough to send me hurrying out the side door and into the garden.

It felt like mid-afternoon. The grey outlines of the winter landscape were nowhere to be seen. Instead, the lush green of the lawn and trees suggested the height of a classic European summer. I walked quickly alongside the flowerbeds, then saw the cat disappearing round the front of the house.

By the time I reached the front garden, however, there was no sign of him. I went to the very end of the driveway before giving up. It was only after reaching the front gate that I turned around and took in the spectacle of the house itself. Compared to the semi-dishevelled state in which I had bought it, this Rookwood was immaculate. It looked to have been recently painted. None of the windows were cracked. The whole building seemed sturdy and smart, in contrast to the somewhat decrepit air possessed by the Rookwood I knew.

A well-preserved, retro-styled Porsche pulled in at the gates, passed me, and rolled down the driveway. At the end of the drive, it pulled up alongside a number of other flash cars parked on the right-hand side of the house. It was then that I noticed a faint murmur of voices coming from the back garden. My curiosity piqued, I walked back past the house and rounded the corner, to find some thirty or more people milling about on the lawn.

Feeling strangely self-conscious, I was glad to have dressed smartly for the ritual yet still felt drab among the flamboyantly attired crowd - and of course there was nothing to be done about my hair. It was only to my neck. Almost every other member of the party, male and female, had it past the shoulders, and in some cases halfway down to the waist.

A stage had been set up at the rear of the garden. There was a drum kit at the back, a PA at the front, and three or four amps on either side of the drums. Most striking was the sight of a number of vintage 1950s and 60s electric guitars - all in pristine condition. They must have been worth a fortune.

The whole experience was dreamlike yet highly vivid, as lucid dreams are said to be. My inclination was to stand back and observe. Yet Edward had said the idea of Moonflight was to go along with the experience fully. Shyness would get me nowhere. I approached a group of people gathered a short distance from the side of the stage.

They were sitting cross-legged on the grass, holding wine glasses or other drinks. In pleasingly retro fashion, some of the girls had strewn flowers in their hair like hippies. Almost everyone was smoking cigarettes. Barely had I sat down on the grass myself than one of the girls offered me a smoke as well.

'Groovy party, wasn't it?' she said. 'What time did you get to sleep?'

Groovy? What a dated piece of slang. It was so old-hat I hadn't even thought to resurrect it for our hippie theme party on tour.

'No idea,' I replied. 'I don't remember.'

'Scandalous,' she said, with an exaggerated raise of her eyebrows. 'But I'm sure you're not alone there. I certainly wasn't when I went to bed.'

I didn't pick up the *double entendre* until her neighbour, another hippie girl, gave off a high pitched peal of laughter. They looked fresh out of high school. A long haired, bearded man put a possessive hand on the second girl's waist. He looked a little older than the rest of the crowd and I sensed he was struggling to balance the concepts of ownership and freedom. He was about to say something when the party was distracted by the sight of someone walking onto the stage. The fellow looked familiar but I couldn't quite place him. Our little group stood up and moved in front of the stage for a better view.

It was then that I noticed someone lying comatose in the shade of a tree about ten feet away. This guy definitely looked familiar. Indeed he bore an uncanny resemblance to Ozzy Osbourne as he appeared on the inside cover of the *Paranoid* album - and there he was dozing under a tree like Carroll's Red King.

'What happened to *him*?' I said to no one in particular.

'He challenged Keith Moon to a Rolls Royce race,' answered a deep male voice from behind me. I turned around to see a charismatic looking man with a short black beard.

'Oh really - who won?'

'As neither of them finished the course we'll call it a draw,' the man replied. 'Although considering the amount they'd drunk it's a miracle they're both still alive. I'm not sure where the cars ended up. Fortunately for Ozzy he can't lose his license, given that he never had one in the first place.'

'Ozzy?'

I peered at the guy dozing under the tree. He looked like Ozzy alright - at about the age of twenty-two.

'Who did you come down with?' my new friend asked. 'I didn't see you earlier.'

'Er... I came with Ozzy. Gave him a lift. I'm Jimmy.'

'Oh, I thought he came with Graham. Anyway, pleased to meet you Jimmy. With a name like that, you probably play guitar. Is it J-I-M-I or J-I-M-M-Y?'

'Just your regular Jimmy, as in Page, not Hendrix.'

'Got it. Nice to meet you Jimmy, as in Page. I'm Edward.'

And so it was. Edward Bentley, looking just like the picture in his books but a few years younger again - and some forty years younger than I'd seen him earlier tonight at the ritual.

'What's your tipple, Jimmy? Go inside and help yourself. These cats are going to start jamming soon.'

I did as Edward suggested and walked into the back lounge of Rookwood, the same room where I'd sipped my Mendara tea with the Volant members a few hours ago, if I could still think in those terms. Yet now the room was done up with eastern style rugs and tapestries. Psychedelic posters were stuck on the wall alongside a couple of framed Escher sketches. Several people were sitting around talking, a haze of smoke over their heads. For some reason, everybody seemed determined to be smoking their heads off at this party. Hadn't anyone heard of lung cancer?

Underneath one of the Escher pictures was a bookcase containing a great many paperbacks, many of which I'd read. I was delighted to find a copy of *The Constant Nymph*, Margaret

Kennedy's early 20th century classic, which I'd thought to be long out of print. Next to it was an even greater surprise, a copy of *Hartford Speaks*, the first published volume of the Hartford Papers. Yes, this was it, the one with the famous set of pictures of Fran Stuart speaking as Hartford.

The book was in remarkably good nick. My own copy was falling apart. I was about to examine the front pages to see if this was a new edition when my attention was drawn by a familiar sound which I'd not heard for many a long year. It was strangely exciting, if only through associations of memory. There was a sudden stab of noise, then a loud, irregular crackling that lasted a few seconds followed by the full, rich tones of an electric guitar. Oh yes, a vinyl record on a record player.

Putting the book back on the shelf, I followed the sound and found a huge stack of old vinyl LPs leaning up against the wall. How striking they looked - far better than CDs, let alone the thumbnail size pictures you get on Spotify or iTunes. Whoever owned this collection certainly looked after their records. Most of these LPs were more than forty years old but perfectly preserved. As I flicked through the pile, I noticed that the owner was rooted firmly in the past. He seemed to have lost interest in music after about 1972. There was a stack of old Beatles, Stones and Dylan records, but hardly any from the mid-seventies onwards. Understandable for the Beatles, who broke up in 1970, but the other two artists had continued making records up to the present day. There was also a mint condition copy of *Led Zeppelin IV*, as there was of Sabbath's *Paranoid* and *Master of Reality*. *Who's Next* by The Who was in equally good nick.

Such was my fascination with the pile of vintage rock LPs, that it took a strong and familiar fragrance to divert me. Someone in the room had lit up a huge joint. Oh well, when in Rome. I stood up and insinuated myself into the loose circle which had formed around it. I was placed about three people to the right of the joint's current position.

Soon after, the guy to my left took a toke on it. He said something in a thick Brummie accent as he handed it to me. I stuck the joint in my mouth, then noticed I'd been given it by Geezer Butler, Sabbath's legendary bass player. His hair was well past the shoulders, his moustache was almost to his ears, and he looked no older than twenty-five. My jaw slackened and the joint fell on the floor. I picked it up at once, took a toke and handed it to Keith Moon on my right. The Who's drummer took it without a word and went on chatting to Zeppelin's John Bonham on *his* right. Everyone in the room looked impossibly young and richly alive.

I may have been slow but I finally got it. Through the process of Moonflight I had travelled back in time to Rookwood in the early 1970s. Now that the penny had dropped, I gazed in awe at the luminaries around me. Many people in the room I did not recognise and some rang only the faintest of bells. Yet as I went round the circle, there were many I could identify. There was Jon Lord from Deep Purple. Next to him was John Entwistle from The Who chatting to Mick Taylor from the Stones. Then Hendrix's bass player Noel Redding, Paul Rodgers from Free, and then Ivan.

Ivan?

Ivan de Vangelus?

Apart from his clothes, Ivan looked exactly the same as he had on the recent US tour. His presence was totally incongruous with the present scene. As soon as the shock wore off, I remembered we were enemies. I ducked out of his line of vision but it was too late - he'd seen me. Yet he showed no sign of either recognition or interest. Somewhat insulted, I left my place in the circle and walked right by him. Again, nothing. So I addressed him directly.

'Ivan! What are *you* doing here?'

My singer looked at me blankly, then without a word turned back to resume talking to Paul Rodgers.

At that moment, a loud electric guitar cranked up from the back garden. Through force of habit, most of those in the circle gravitated towards the noise, filtering outside in twos and threes.

John Mayall, leader of the Bluesbreakers, was onstage with a few mates. After they'd played a couple of songs, I heard murmurs in the crowd that Clapton had showed up and was about to go on, but this proved unfounded. It turned about to be Jeff Beck instead - fine by me. Then to my great surprise, Ivan got up and took over the mike, letting rip on a couple of blues numbers. I got the definite impression that Beck and several of the other rock stars knew him. They had the elitist musicians' air of treating him as a peer while looking down on everyone else.

Beck left the stage and handed his guitar to some guy I didn't recognise. The new guy cranked out the riff to Free's 'Alright Now.' Ivan pointed at Paul Rodgers and told him to get up onstage with him. Rodgers sang the first verse and Ivan the second, both of them harmonising together on the chorus. Ivan showed off a high pitched bluesy wail reminiscent of Glenn Hughes, yet Hughes himself was not in attendance. If I was right about the date, he had not yet come to fame as a member of Deep Purple's Mark 3 line up.

As if in tune with my thoughts, Ritchie Blackmore was next to walk onto the stage, but just as the Deep Purple maestro strapped on his white Stratocaster guitar, the vision began to fade. The people in the garden began moving faster as in a sped up film. The stars realigned themselves and day became night. Now the air had an Autumn feel. I was alone in the empty garden, yet there was music coming from the house. I turned to go inside.

The house looked much the same, although the vinyl LPs had been tidied away and some of the pictures on the wall had changed. The sound of chanting came from the drawing room. Easing open the door, I beheld a familiar sight - Edward Bentley at the head of the circle and a group of collaborators around him. Edward was still a young man. The circle was populated by long haired men and women. As they all had their eyes closed, I took the opportunity of slipping quietly into the circle and joining the chant.

This was clearly a nascent incarnation of the Volant Society. In fact, a prominent piece of seventies-style art proclaimed it the Voyant Society. The painting showed an all-knowing eye, but there was no sign of the moon. Perhaps Bentley's philosophy was still in development and this fledgling version of the group had yet to adopt the lunar symbolism.

I looked around the circle in search of the illustrious figures from the party. Yet, with one exception, none of the early-seventies rock stars were present. That exception was Ivan. He was seated two places to the left of Edward, eyes closed, chanting along with the rest of the hirsute truth seekers.

What the group lacked in maturity, it made up in enthusiasm. The intensity of the chant was greater than the relatively sedate fare served up by the 21st century group. Although the members had closed eyes, I could sense they were all under the sway of hallucinogenics. The chanting was unbridled, no doubt encouraged by the Indian raga LP playing on the record player at the front of the room. That style had been all the rage since the Beatles' late sixties excursion into Indian mysticism. With its repetitive, hypnotic drone, it was just the sort of piece to fit Bentley's concept of the quaranas.

The chanting increased even further until I fancied some kind of external energy was about to manifest within the circle. With a shock, I sensed that this ritual might be a conjuring of some sort. Whether this was true, I would never know - for the scene faded at the crucial moment.

The third and final stage of my Moonflight began back in the garden. It was night and this time there was no doubt of the season.

Spring was proclaimed by every budding blossom which thrust itself forward under the luminous glow of the full moon. A heady, natural intoxication filled the air as if all living beings, regardless of age, were young again and brimming with potential. I was swept up in the mood of invigoration, and this served as some preparation for the scene that awaited in the house. I opened the door of the drawing room to a new ritual, and found the congregation of the Volant Society circling the room as naked as they were born.

There were six men and six women, along with Edward Bentley himself, chanting manically, marching round the circle with a strange mix of discipline and abandon. Bentley was beating a drum in time with the music coming through the speakers. There was a woman in front and behind him, for the sexes were alternated around the circle. Ivan was at the opposite side of the circle to Edward. It was not the first time I had seen Ivan naked, but it was a touch disconcerting to see it again in such a context. Again, I did not recognise any other member of the group.

While there was no actual fornication going on, the air was charged with eroticism. What was it Edward had told me? 'There are many roads to the Eye. Study, meditation, drugs, sex magick.' Something like that. Sex magick? From what I knew, this was a practice in which the power of sexual orgasm was conjured but withheld, its energy diverted to other ends. Perhaps the group was using that withheld energy to attain Moonflight, for I saw that the lunar symbolism now figured highly in the group's imagery. The latest official painting revealed that the Voyant Society had become the Volant society. Yet the imagery had changed. In an overt display absent from Myra's 21st century painting, an archetypal witch on a broomstick was silhouetted against the full moon, flying towards the distant yet looming Eye.

Like the intruder I was, I watched the scene from the doorway, unsure what to do next. At that moment, Edward Bentley turned his gaze in my direction. It was a gaze of such intensity that it felt like a physical force - and then I was lying on my back in the middle of the circle. It was midwinter once more, and my eyes were still locked into the gaze of Edward Bentley. Those eyes burned just the same, yet this time from the white-bearded visage of an aged occultist. Edward was forty years older and I had returned to the 21st century.

# 27
# Edward

'Who is Ivan de Vangelus?' I asked him at once.

'Not now, Jimmy,' said Edward. 'Don't try to speak. It is dangerous to come out of Moonflight too quickly. We'll speak of this tomorrow.'

I accepted his advice for my head was spinning. Far better to process my experience alone before discussing it. It was not until 3pm the next day that I found myself once more armchair to armchair with Edward at the Volant Society headquarters in London. I gave him a detailed account of what I'd seen, from first to last. He seemed undaunted by anything I said. On the contrary, he seemed rather excited.

'Jimmy, what a wonderful Moonflight! You're making me feel terribly nostalgic.'

'So what I saw - were these actual historical events or hallucinations?'

'I'm not sure you need to make the distinction. What is life, in any case, but a dream?'

'You know what I mean.'

'You say you saw Ozzy Osbourne asleep under a tree in the garden, like Lewis Carroll's Red King. Then we may echo Carroll in asking whose dream it was. Were you dreaming of Ozzy or was he dreaming of you?'

'Yes, but in factual terms - did you attend a party at Rookwood in 1971 in which Ozzy Osbourne and Keith Moon had a Rolls Royce race around the grounds?'

'My dear boy, it's certainly possible. I don't remember it, but it sounds highly plausible. Good Lord, I was on so many hallucinogens back then. We all were. I'm not sure what I remember from those times.'

'Well, did you go to a summer party with all those rock stars I mentioned?'

'Probably. I mean, I don't remember any one specific party like that, but that's only because there were so many. I told you before, Rookwood was quite the hangout for musicians in those days.'

'Were those guys members of the Volant Society?'

'Oh no, not at all. Sabbath, for instance. Despite their image, they wouldn't have a bar of the occult. They were just four guys from the midlands.'

'What of the final ritual I saw? Was that some of your sex magick?'

'As I said, there are many roads to the Eye and my word, we explored every one of them. We're a little past that now.'

Edward patted his stomach modestly.

'It was certainly a memorable scene.'

'You must remember, Jimmy, this was the seventies. Experimentation was the norm - indeed, it was almost mandatory. They were glory days. I'm not ashamed of anything we did back then.'

'Then tell me straight. I saw your altar and the painting at the ritual. Is the Volant Society a coven of witches?'

'That's a little melodramatic. You're taking it all far too literally. We were just young people having fun. There's a rich symbolic tradition associated with all this, and we made full use of it. Black magic? White magic? Good and evil? I've been walking that line all my life. It's in the eye of the beholder. And my, how times have changed. I saw white magic and paganism magazines at the newsagent the other day.'

'Whatever else it was, Moonflight was certainly an amazing experience - but what am I supposed to take from it?'

'Moonflight gives you exactly what you need. Think back over what you saw. What is the overriding question that stays with you?'

'That's pretty obvious. It's Ivan. As I told you, he's the singer in my band. So what the hell was he doing in Rookwood in the early 1970s?'

'You're sure it was him?'

'Yes.'

'Well, Jimmy, this one has me baffled. Naturally, I looked you up when you said you were a musician - and I certainly did a double take when I saw Ivan's face on your website. It's an uncanny resemblance, no doubt. Still, these things have been known to happen. Apparent doppelgangers, whether through genetic relation or sheer coincidence. The man I once knew looked just like your singer. Frankly, I surmised that Ivan might have been one of his bastards. That seemed the most likely explanation. He was hardly the celibate type. Yet after what you've seen in Moonflight, perhaps there's more to the story.'

'So you know who Ivan is?'

'I don't know who he is, but I know who he was, so to speak. Anton Carew. He was the brightest star in the firmament in his day. He could match all the great rock singers - Plant, Rodgers, Daltrey, Gillan, and the like. Given time, Carew would have outshone them all.'

'Is that right?'

'You know, Jimmy, history seems terribly factual, yet the history we know is only a thin line of events on the surface of what might have been. As the saying goes, we only remember the winners. Consider that party you attended. The likes of Zeppelin and The Who are now enshrined in rock's canon. Yet there were probably others at that party who could have gone as far, but for one reason or another didn't. What are they now but tiny footnotes in rock history? There's no more left of them than a handful of news cuttings turned yellow in a scrapbook in someone's attic. Or a faded picture on the back of an old LP that not even the second hand shops will bother selling. Like these, for example. I brought them in especially for you.'

Edward handed me two records. In contrast to the mint condition of those I'd seen at the party, these were faded and scuffed. *White Midnight* had come out in 1970 and *White Midnight II* in 1971.

'That's Carew's old band. Take a look at the photo on the back cover. The guy in the centre of that group. That's Anton Carew in his prime.'

'No, that's Ivan de Vangelus. He's a dead ringer at any rate. Only difference is I've never seen a smile like that on Ivan's face.'

'Anton Carew had every reason to smile in 1971, I assure you. He was wealthy, he had girls hanging off him left and right and, as I said, he was *the* up and coming rock singer of the 1970s.'

'So what happened - drug overdose? Car accident?'

Edward shook his head and sighed.

'It's a sad story and as I played a part in it, the guilt has been with me to this day - although I too was a victim. If I hadn't escaped in time, I may even have suffered the same fate as poor Anton. As it was, I was forced to seek asylum in the USA. I spent the best part of the seventies there.'

'That's when you went to Fran Stuart's group?'

'Yes, among many others. I kept a low profile and didn't dare show my face in Britain until the turn of the decade.'

'Go on.'

'It happened at one of our rituals. You've seen it yourself, Jimmy, so I won't elaborate on the details. We'd been experimenting for some time and making huge advances. Some of the forces conjured were immense. As far as Moonflight is concerned, those times were probably the pinnacle we've been trying to recapture ever since.

As you saw, Anton Carew was a willing participant in those rituals. He came out regularly with his girlfriend of the time, a young lady named Elizabeth Morgan. Sadly, Elizabeth didn't quite have the constitution for it. She overdosed on a bad batch of acid one night and tried to find Moonflight by leaping out of a top floor window at Rookwood. It was a gross misinterpretation of the practice. Still, we had no idea what had happened until later. The rest of us were so absorbed in our own experiences we didn't even know she'd gone upstairs.

When we found out Elizabeth had died, there was an immediate meeting of the Volant Society and everyone swore an oath of secrecy. Although we regretted what had happened, we didn't consider it our fault. Life is inherently dangerous, no matter what path one takes. Yet we knew the police and the newspapers wouldn't see it that way.

Despite our oath, somehow the story got out. Or a distortion of the story, at least. It was a salacious scandal that kept the good folk of Britain pleasantly outraged for weeks. The Volant Society was painted as a coven of witches who indulged in drugs and orgies in the pursuit of black magic. And Good Lord, while that was essentially true, the noble ideals and rich philosophy behind it all was completely ignored. We were portrayed in a sordid and tacky light, which I maintain was a gross misrepresentation. The whole thing was sensationalised to the point of farce. I realised there was no hope of a fair hearing from the scandalised public, so I fled the country and travelled the world for the rest of the decade.

Anton Carew wasn't so fortunate. He bore the brunt of it all for a number of reasons. He was young, handsome, and free. He'd achieved wealth and fame at an early age through activities the establishment frowned upon. They relished the chance to come down hard on him, making him a scapegoat as an example to others. They couldn't believe their luck, that one such as Carew had fallen into their hands. Although technically he wasn't guilty of murder, they made him responsible and tried him for manslaughter.

Elizabeth's father was a leading barrister. Although he wasn't allowed to be involved in the trial directly, there's no doubt he had a hand in it. You can imagine the legal profession's vindictive reaction to what happened - not that they would ever admit it, of course. Poor Anton didn't stand a chance. In a spiteful response, the judge put him away for thirteen years with no chance of parole. By the time Anton got out of prison in the mid-eighties, his singing career was done and dusted. Musical fashions had changed out of all recognition. Anton's records had been withdrawn from sale after his arrest, and now no one had the faintest idea who he was. As far as popular culture was concerned, he was a footnote in ancient history.

The last time I saw Anton, he was a wreck. I looked him up a few years after his release, when he must have been nearly forty himself. He was a bitter, broken man. An alcoholic, virtually homeless. He must surely be long dead by now - and that's exactly why I can't square it with the fellow on your website. Is Ivan de Vangelus Anton Carew? It's impossible, but he's certainly a dead ringer. My best guess is that Ivan is one of Carew's bastards - except Ivan's too young. Carew's whoring days were long gone by the time Ivan was conceived. A grandson? That makes more sense. Sometimes the looks can skip a generation.'

'I've heard of that,' I said. 'There's this country punk guy, Hank III. They say he looks just like his grandfather, Hank Williams.'

'There you go then,' said Edward. 'Perhaps that's the explanation. Ivan is Carew's grandson. Either that or Anton made a return to the dark arts and achieved some kind of rejuvenation.'

'I'd ask Ivan directly, except for one small problem.'

'What's that?'

'We no longer speak. We're on very poor terms these days.'

'Then a word of advice, Jimmy - I would be very cautious about this. It's possible there's some link to old Carew we can't even imagine. And one thing I do know, there's some awfully bad karma around that one. I would suggest that this Moonflight has given you exactly what you need. It may be a kind of warning.'

'What should I do then?'

'I don't know, I'm not omniscient. This is something you have to work out and face on your own. Still, I believe the answers are somewhere within that vision you experienced.'

'What I really need is another Moonflight. The first one has given me more questions than answers.'

'Has it? I don't think so. You have travelled towards the Eye now, and Moonflight always gives us what we need. Go away and meditate on what you've seen. I'm sure the answers are already with you. When you find them, come back and tell me. This is unfinished business for me too.'

Edward stood up and we shook hands.

'By the way, Jimmy, there's something I neglected to tell you - Moonflight never ends. Once you've seen that illumination, it will always be with you. You may well need it, for I sense there's a still greater crisis for you to face.'

Edward stared into my eyes.

'And when that time comes, look to the moon.'

# 28

# Lombala

So, last stop Lombala. Fabled isle, lotus land, final destination for the flight of the Black Phoenix. I'd never heard of the place until Elijinx turned geography master one day at Rookwood. There we were in the library looking out over the grounds, him sitting and me pacing, while we decided the fate of the mutineers. I'd not seen Elijinx since our meeting in Boston. So absorbed had I been in the Volant society that, to some degree, I'd been able to put the band crisis out of my mind. Yet with my mentor's return, the whole drama came flooding back.

'Ollie's gone,' I said. 'That part's obvious.'

'Goes without saying,' Elijinx agreed.

'Wants an uprising, does he?' I continued. 'I'll raise him up by the neck. He should have been hung from the yard arm for that New York finale.'

'It would have made a fine encore - but Ollie's neither here nor there. There are hundreds could step in for him now.'

'Dead right. I couldn't have said that a year ago but now everyone knows the score. Still, what of Ivan? He's not so easily replaced. Or handled.'

'The pity with Ivan is it's such a waste. You should have wrung more than one record out of a talent like that.'

'Agreed. Still my hands are tied. Duty is duty, mutiny is treachery. There's no excusing that. But how to get rid of him when he's got that footage?'

'Your hands are doubly tied.'

'It's not all bad news. I've learned a thing or two about Ivan since the tour ended, and I'll wager you've been in the loop all along. So here's a name for you - Anton Carew.'

Elijinx did not react. For one so given to changing his face, he was far less inclined to change his expression.

'So you've found out about Carew? What have you learned?'

I related the tale of the Volant Society, Edward Bentley, and Moonflight. Elijinx listened with polite interest, making only occasional comments to query the odd detail. When I'd finished, he gave me a satisfied nod.

'There you go then, Jim. There's your leverage.'

'So - Ivan and Carew. What's the connection?'

'I'm not sure I should divulge Ivan's secrets just yet. For now, take heart that you've negated that video. Just keep Carew's name up your sleeve and say it out loud next time he threatens you. That'll wipe the smirk off his face.'

'But why?'

'Never mind why. The point is you've got him. Your hands are out of their bonds and around his neck. So wring some more magic from that golden throat.'

'I'd like to squeeze another album out of him, sure - but how can I work with someone who plotted my own death?'

Elijinx shrugged.

'Show me a rock band without conflict and I'll show you a solo artist. Some of the greatest partnerships in rock history have been fuelled by a little creative tension. Why should you be denied what *you* want because of Ivan? Use him, I say. Take him for another album and tour, then do as you wish.'

'I doubt I can stand another tour of duty with Ivan.'

'It'll be different next time. He'll be less inclined to the diva antics with Carew's ghost over his head.'

'Maybe. As for the tour, I can take it or leave it. It's the albums that matter to me.'

'You'll make a lot more money off a tour, Jimmy.'

'So what? A live show's temporary, an album is immortal. Every good album's a comfort on my deathbed - and you're right, Ivan's gifts are too rich to squander on just one record. Ozzy got two records out of Randy Rhoads. Blackmore got three out of Dio. One record's a flash in the pan, two or three are a measure of substance.'

'So there's your answer - and here's how we do it. *The Maelstrom Ascendant* tour ends after one more stop. I've got you a three show package at premium rates. It's a million in your pocket alone.'

'You serious?'

I stopped pacing and sat down. Elijinx continued his spiel.

'We'll film the shows for a concert DVD. Soon as we're done, Ollie's for the high jump and Ivan goes under contract for one more record. When that's in the can, you can do as you like. Sack him, assassinate him - it's your call.'

'Where are these shows?'

'Somewhere very special. Cast your mind back to our first day at Rookwood. Remember Zambeko who signed up your film rights?'

'The African?'

'African, is he? Maybe originally. You never asked me much about Zambeko - where he's from or who he represents. Well, it's Zambeko's master who's booked these three shows. It's the tenth anniversary of his ascent to the throne of Lombala.'

'Thrones now, is it? No wonder you negotiated such a fee.'

'Lombala's no third world nation. Your fee won't make much of a dent in the treasury.'

'Lombala... Lombala? I can't place it. Geography was never my strong suit but I generally have a foggy idea. One of those new Russian states, is it? Some resurrected Slavic kingdom?'

'Wrong continent. In fact, it's on no continent at all. Lombala is an island nation. It sits in the Arabian sea between Africa, India, and the Middle East. It's a wonderful place, Jim. The shows are spread out over a couple of weeks, but don't be surprised if you stay a while longer. There are many go to Lombala end up never wanting to leave.'

I clapped my hands and stood up again.

'I hope Johnno's lined up a decent hotel if we're staying weeks.'

'Johnno handed in his notice after New York, but never mind the hotel. It wouldn't surprise me if his majesty puts you up in the palace itself. He's taken quite a shine to you. So we'll have none of your diva antics, understand?'

'Course not. There'll be nothing like that, not from me. Just make sure Ivan's on the same page. Anyhow, I'm seeing a clear path for the first time in months. We end the tour with these shows in your Lombala, leave Ollie there as a maroon, and use Carew's ghost to prise another album out of Ivan. Now that's management.'

'All settled then. We fly out on Friday. Make sure you travel light - you'll want for nothing where we're going.'

So it was that a few days later I walked up to Ivan and Ollie at Heathrow, my right hand extended, a magnanimous smile on my face. They seemed relieved at the ceasefire, for their minds must have made endless dry runs of speculation on our future these last months. I tried to give the impression normal service had been resumed.

We boarded the Qatar Airways flight to Oman, then transferred to a smaller plane for the last leg. From the air, Lombala looked to be an island paradise. We flew over great expanses of wild terrain, from thick woven jungle to galloping plains. A few smaller towns were dotted around the place, but nature prevailed through the bulk of the visible land. The largest settlement was the capital, Lombala city, sited on the far coast where the journey came to an end.

As soon as we stepped outside the air-conditioned plane, the moist tropical air wrapped us in a sensual embrace, tantalising rather than overpowering. The first person to greet us was Mr. Zambeko himself at the head of a guard of honour. In full military dress despite the heat, Zambeko bowed. His deep 'African' voice boomed out in welcome.

'This is a tremendous honour, Mr. Brandt. Allow me to take your bags.'

'Very kind, thank you.'

Zambeko turned and shouted a military command at one of his underlings. The words were in the native language yet their meaning was clear. Zambeko's kindness was enacted at once.

The five of us were escorted to a limousine. The vehicle set off and our focus turned to the approaching city. We peered out, drinking it all in, from time to time glancing at each other with raised eyebrows, wondering what on earth we'd gotten ourselves into. Even Ivan and Ollie grinned back at me, our feud forgotten for the moment.

We entered the city and drove down tidy streets. Whether modest or grand, all the houses appeared well kept. There were ample gardens and parklands. There was nothing to suggest the chaotic urban sprawl of the cities we normally toured.

We passed quickly through a business and shopping area. Although it buzzed with activity, traffic flowed easily. Before long, we were out of the bustle and back into open space. Our attention was soon drawn by a spectacular section of coast, so that we did not at first notice the palace looming up like a mirage in the distance. Jake was the first to spot it, his exclamation alerting us to the vision.

The Royal Palace of Lombala was bordered by mountains on one side, jungle on the other, and ocean at the rear. It struck me as an eastern version of Germany's *Neuschwanstein*. It had the same sense of having come straight out of a fairytale. As our car approached, we craned our necks up at its crowning turrets far above.

At ground level, the palace was protected by walls several metres high which circled the whole edifice. As I was to learn, any intruder bold enough to scale those walls would only have entered the next layer of protection - the Royal Gardens of Lombala. These gardens were patrolled by the king's fearsome guardians, whose identity was made plain on the Lombalan coat of arms.

I did not discover this, however, until the next morning. Upon arrival at the palace it was almost nightfall and we were each shown to our quarters. As Elijinx had suggested, we were given rooms in the palace itself. I was assigned a suite above West Garden, a fine view of which could be had from my balcony - at least during the daytime. As it was now nearly dark, I concentrated on settling into my quarters.

My spacious suite was made up of three rooms. First, a bedroom with an ensuite, second, a sitting area complete with sofas and a home theatre, and third, a study where I could work. The bedroom led on to a balcony overlooking West Garden. In the near dark, I could make out that the garden extended some fifty or more metres from my balcony to the palace's outer wall. Some way behind that wall was a beach, from which came the sound of breaking waves.

The suite was no slum, that much was clear. I'd come to Lombala with the idea that this trip was an inconvenience, something to be done with quickly. Having seen it, a rethink might be in order. It could be the ideal setting for a working holiday. The thought was interrupted by a knock on the door. I was expecting a palace attendant calling me for dinner. Instead it was Elijinx.

'When did *you* get here?' I asked, rather surprised.

'I've been here for a while. So, what do you think?'

'No complaints at all. How'd you score us a booking like this? The king's really a fan of the band?'

'Very much so. King Tianjan was an admirer even before Ivan joined. After all, he bought the film rights for *Vortex Winder*.'

Elijinx pronounced the king's name as Tee-arn-jun, with the middle syllable slightly drawn out.

'I wonder how he got hold of the book in the first place,' I said. '*Vortex* was no best seller - and it's a long way from Coogee Beach to Lombala.'

Elijinx winked.

'Blame it on the trade winds. Now, listen. I've spoken to the other lads already. I shouldn't have to tell you, but this is royalty. Tianjan's been good enough to put you up in the palace, so there'll be no hijinks of any description. No tantrums, no mess. No swearing or rowdiness. No loud music at the wrong time. No fraternising with the local girls.'

'Did you tell Ivan?'

'He's been warned. Tianjan's a pussycat as a rule but you don't want to rouse him. The Lombalans have moral standards they take very seriously.'

'Don't tell me Ive's got to take a vow of chastity.'

'Chastity no, fidelity yes. Same goes for the rest of you. You're all expected to take a wife for the duration of your stay. That's wife, singular.'

'What do you mean?'

'It's a peculiar local custom of temporary marriage. Zouman, they call it. It's the government's way of managing human nature.'

'Seriously? And this is compulsory?'

'It's expected. Unless you already have a wife at home - which, correct me if I'm wrong - none of you boys do. You'd better go along with it for the sake of good manners.'

'Oh well, when in Rome. When's this going to happen?'

'You'll meet your wives tomorrow and they'll help you settle in. The day after that's the official band welcome, and you've an audience with Tianjan himself in the afternoon.'

'You're making me nervous. Where can a fella get a drink around here?'

'Really, Jimmy? On your first night?'

'Oh alright - if I'm meeting my so called wife tomorrow, I suppose an early night wouldn't hurt.'

'That's more like it. Don't worry, you'll have plenty of time for carousing. All the time in the world.'

# 29
# Lalitha

I slept like the dead that night. Waking at last, I drew the curtains
and looked down into West Garden. Beyond the palace wall at
the rear of the garden, the beach could now be seen a little way
off. I was tempted to enter the garden, climb the wall, and get
to the beach. Yet given Elijinx's warning the night before, such a
move might be seen as impolite. I would check the etiquette of
unscheduled palace departures later.

It was only then that I noticed a couple of leopards snoozing
in the morning sun in the garden below me - a garden into which
I'd been about to climb. What were leopards doing there? I was to
learn the answer to this before day's end.

A palace employee knocked on my door, then led me through
high-ceilinged corridors to the banquet room where the other
boys in the band were already at breakfast. A wide range of tropical
fruits was laid out on the table. They made a good entree, indeed
so good they turned into the main course. I barely had appetite for
anything else.

King Tianjan had not yet put in an appearance, although from
time to time I had a sense we were being observed. Whether it
was the royal eye upon us or simply the curious gaze of the palace
staff wasn't clear. In rock n roll, you soon become used to the stares
of strangers. At any rate, Zambeko was in attendance and said
we were to come to him for any guidance about life in Lombala.
He also informed us our wives would be joining us shortly. As
Zambeko was seated at my own table, I could not resist a mild
interrogation of our host.

'Your system of marriage is a curious custom. Is it traditional
in Lombala?'

'No, it is quite a recent innovation. Tianjan's father introduced it when Lombala became more open to the West. Some say opening the borders did more harm than good. At first it attracted the kind of tacky sex tourism associated with parts of South-East Asia. Tianjan's father considered this an affront to Lombala - its internal values and international image. There were arrests and some diplomatic incidents.'

'It's hard to control that sort of thing.'

'Not if your stance is made clear. The king made prostitution illegal for tourists. Instead, he established the Zouman system in which any unmarried man staying more than a month in Lombala was allowed to take a wife for the course of his stay. This on the condition of strict monogamy, at pain of permanent expulsion.'

'What about female tourists - do they have the same rights?'

'A female tourist is allowed to take a husband or wife, under the same conditions.'

'Your country is a strange mix of the conservative and progressive.'

'Behind our sleepy facade is a well ordered society. Pragmatism is the rule. The king was able to wipe out casual sex tourism at a stroke. We accept the realities of human nature without condoning its excesses.'

'If you'll forgive me, doesn't your system just encourage sex tourism of a different kind? It's marriage minus the hard bits. The honeymoon without the hangover.'

'Perhaps, but why not? At least the tourist is forced to treat his spouse as a human being, not just a sexual object. There are strict laws discouraging any abuse of the practice. Besides, many such marriages have blossomed into lifelong love affairs.'

'Doesn't the custom attract a lot of undesirables? I mean the type of sleazy, middle aged white men you see in parts of Asia?'

'It would, but Zouman is by invitation only. No one is granted a visa to Lombala without a background check to ensure he or she is of good moral standing.'

Zambeko edged forward.

'And between you and me, Mr. Brandt, there are two members of your party who under normal circumstances would not have been granted visas.'

He glanced over at Ivan and Jake at a neighbouring table.

'Your Mr Hoffman has been informed of this. His majesty the king, in his great benevolence, has granted your colleagues an exemption. Mr. Hoffman has let them know where they stand, and the consequences of any transgressions. I advise you to remind them of this yourself.'

'You have my hand on that.'

Zambeko leaned back, but my curiosity was yet unsated.

'How are these marriages made - do a husband and wife choose each other?'

'Zouman is a system of arranged marriage. After our background checks, we select the available wife most suitable. You will soon see for yourself. At any moment, your betrothed will present herself - and the king is confident you will be pleased. He chose her for you himself.'

Barely had he spoken than a bevy of dark skinned beauties entered the room. The group was comprised of two Indians, two Asians, and an Egyptian. This racial mix was not unusual for Lombala. I later learned that due to its location and social policies, Lombala was a sort of Switzerland of the East in its blend of cultures. Nestled between India, Africa and the Middle East, and with Asia not far away, it was indeed a multicultural nation. There was also the native Lombalan type, perhaps most similar to Thai in appearance, as well as a minority of assimilated Westerners.

At the sight of the girls I was struck by a fit of introversion. Then I spied Ivan, with his customary avarice, running his eyes over the entire group. Mindful of Zambeko's warning, I scowled at him and raised a warning finger. Yet when the Egyptian girl approached Ivan and smiled, her radiance was such that Caligula himself would have converted to monogamy on the spot. As I later found out, she called herself Nefertiti after the famed historical beauty - yet surely the original could not have shaded this girl by much.

In purely physical terms, my own bride was not at her level, yet my heart was captured as quickly. The two Indian girls began to walk towards my table. Both were beauties but while one was a little thin for my tastes, the other had a more voluptuous figure. I prayed that the king had chosen the latter as my wife - and the gods were with me, for the waif-like girl passed me by and sat down next to Amos. The full figured maiden came up and introduced herself as Lalitha.

So relieved was I to have the right girl that I kissed her on the lips in rather too forward a manner. She was unfazed, showing no hint of shyness. Indeed she flashed a smile so bright that any covetousness I'd felt for Ivan's bride was quite forgotten. I still recall the classic red sari she wore that day, which I fancied could have graced the most glamorous Bollywood actress.

Lalitha led me outside to the gates of the palace where an open-topped car was waiting. She took the wheel and we set off on a tour of the shimmering delight that was Lombala city. Our enchanting surrounds were enhanced by comments from my betrothed, all delivered in an Indian accent and a pealing, musical voice. She punctuated her remarks with light, flirtatious touches.

I had asked Lalitha about the beach glimpsed from the balcony of my room. When the city tour was over, she drove down a road that ran alongside the western edge of the palace. We pulled up at a sheltered spot close by. The beach turned out to be little more than a narrow and deserted cove, bordered by luxuriant jungle foliage. Invited by the seclusion, a series of rambunctious waves had no reticence about breaching its shores.

We were both sweaty after the city tour but it was Lalitha who, with no hint of modesty, undressed and walked into the sea. I followed and dived exuberantly into that ocean to be swallowed up by the encompassing might of this great natural force.

When we eventually returned to the car, we were dry within minutes. I felt no need to wash off any residue of sand and salt. Instead, we drove straight back to the palace so Lalitha could show me the interior of the king's wondrous abode.

We began on the ground floor and were soon wending our way upwards. What can I say? The palace of Lombala was the sweetest fairytale delight one could imagine. It was a perfect marriage between natural features and human artifice. Each ascending level gave more cause than the last for fresh gasps at the opulence and artistry on display.

A number of staff were on hand to keep the palace functioning. People bustled about like bees at a honeycomb. They occupied every layer of the palace yet their numbers thinned as we ascended, until at last we reached the very top layer, which was almost deserted. At the head of the staircase was an antechamber with a great oaken door set into its far wall.

'The royal chambers,' Lalitha announced.

'Am I to meet him now?'

'Oh no. The official ceremony is tomorrow. Let's go and see the gardens.'

So began our descent back down those winding stairways - and of all the wonders of the palace, none delighted me more than those gardens. As Lalitha explained them to me, I learned the reason for the leopards beneath my balcony that morning.

Some castles have a moat. The Royal Palace of Lombala had a garden. The whole periphery of the palace had been made into a circular garden which, as noted earlier, extended some fifty metres out from the palace walls. One might suppose this had aesthetic value but no practical use, however each section of the garden had been filled with its own variety of the predatory big cats.

This was the meaning of the Lombalan coat of arms, which I'd seen displayed at the front of the palace. The circular garden was divided into four sections corresponding to the points of the compass. North Garden was patrolled by lions and South Garden by tigers. East Garden was the domain of panthers, while my own West Garden was the province of leopards. The coat of arms showed the four big cats in this exact configuration. Anyone seeking unauthorised access to the palace would first have to traverse the lair of one of these royal protectors.

Of these four beasts, like many before me, I had always liked tigers the best. They were the perfect union of power and beauty. The lions, leopards and panthers were all worthy, yet I lingered longest at South Garden to gaze at the tigers.

Sensing my fascination, Lalitha took me into one of the vacant guest bedrooms with a balcony directly over the garden. From here, we could look at the grassy expanse below, where half a dozen full grown Bengal tigers lay at rest. There was even a tiger cub loitering around the edge of the group, playfully trying to attract the attention of its elders, who were having none of it.

This was the first time I had seen a 'little' big cat of any description and I could not take my eyes off it. Lalitha began trying to attract the cub's attention, calling out to it in that musical voice of hers. Soon enough, it looked up to see us smiling and waving. It left its dozing elders and moved in our direction until it stood at the base of the palace wall.

'Isn't that the most exquisite creature you've ever seen?' I remarked. 'Present company excepted,' I added as a somewhat corny addendum. My new wife simply pealed that Bollywood laugh.

'Wouldn't you just love to cuddle it?' she asked.

'If only we could.'

'Why don't we see if the keeper is around?'

'Oh, you're serious? Quick then!'

I hurried past Lalitha and down a flight of stairs, keen to reach the level of the garden before the tiger cub lost interest and wandered away. Lalitha saw one of the garden keepers dozing in a chair and called out to him.

'Ranji, the tiger baby is right at the gates. Jimmy would dearly love to meet him. Could you arrange it?'

Ranji opened the garden gates. Then, having made sure the adult tigers were a safe distance away, he took two steps into the garden, gathered the cub in his arms, and brought him into the palace grounds. The tiger cub was not much bigger than Finzi, Sandra's beloved cat, although the paws were markedly thicker. I could hold him quite easily. The cub seemed delighted to be picked up and put his paws around my neck just as Finzi used to do.

'How old is he?' I asked.

'Two months,' said Ranji.

'Is that all? Then I won't be able to do this much longer.'

Lalitha wanted her turn holding the cub and with some reluctance, I gave him up. The young tiger seemed to revel in the attention. After a few minutes Ranji noticed one of the adult tigers approaching the glass to see what we were doing. Distracting it with a thrown portion of meat, Ranji took the opportunity to thrust the cub back inside the grassy surrounds of South Garden before closing the gate again.

I could not complain. With my day of wonders now complete, Lalitha and I returned to our respective quarters to prepare for dinner and the ceremony that would join us in unholy matrimony for the rest of my stay in Lombala, however long that turned out to be.

# 30
# Tianjan

The morning after, I woke as a married man for the first time in my life. The next surprise of the day was the official band welcome. I'd been expecting a low key affair of tea and sandwiches. To my embarrassment, it was something more like an Olympic Games opening ceremony. There was a brass band and a military parade. Acrobats, dancers and other Lombalan artists cavorted about the palace grounds. It concluded with a twenty-one gun salute - and all, it would seem, to welcome the five members of Lighthouse XIII to its three date tour.

King Tianjan kept his distance from all this - literally. I could sense him far above us, observing the spectacle from the top floor of the palace. When the official welcome came to an end, I was summoned to those lofty heights myself. So began the long ascent to his chambers, a repeat of the journey I'd taken with Lalitha the day before. Up and up round the spiralling stairways until I reached the great oaken door at the threshold of the king's domain.

The door was open. I entered and found the royal chambers every bit as lavish as one would expect. I was more interested in the king himself. Now that I could see him up close, there was no resisting the desire to stare. Tianjan was an Asian prince upon whom nature had bestowed great beauty to complement his wealth. I could not tell his specific ethnicity, but if pushed would guess he was Chinese. He was younger than I'd expected. Indeed he looked barely older than Ivan. For one so blessed, it could only be hoped judicious upbringing had curtailed any urge to corruption. Perhaps Zambeko had served to mentor him. If it was a decade since the coronation, Tianjan must have attained the throne as a young man indeed.

Tianjan was decked out in some kind of golden robe, casual yet flamboyant. The billowing folds gave him a graceful air and lent him animation when he became excited, which as I discovered was no rare occurrence. For the moment, however, he sat on his throne, silent and still. Unsure of the correct protocols, I too stood in silence, waiting for the king to begin the conversation. Yet he simply sat there staring back at me, a strange smile upon his face. I had the impression he'd been waiting for this moment a very long time. When the silence became a little uncomfortable, I decided to go all Dennis Lillee and play the down to earth Aussie, jumping into the conversation with no airs and graces.

'That was a stunning presentation, your majesty. Surely that wasn't all for us, was it? There I was expecting a cold beer and a handshake and you laid that on. What an honour.'

Still the king said nothing, so I blundered ahead.

'Pardon my ignorance but I'm not sure what to call you. I should have asked Zambeko at breakfast. My only experience of royalty is watching *The Tudors* on TV. Perhaps I could call you majesty, as they did King Henry.'

'Majesty will do,' the king replied. His voice was deeper than expected for such a young man. 'And I will call you Jimmy, just like they do in The Book.'

'You may call me whatever you like, majesty. Jimmy will do fine. I've been called a lot worse in my time.'

The king smiled. 'Ah, your Australian humour. So exotic.'

'Exotic, now is it? First time I've heard it called that.'

'Forgive me staring, Jimmy, but this is the most magical moment. It's as if a character in one of my favourite story books has come to life and is standing before me. I am almost speechless with joy!'

'Sorry, your majesty, I don't follow you.'

'You do not know how many times I've read The Book, or had it read to me by one of my wives. Your escape from the prison, the amusing adventures in Germany. Such marvellous tales.'

'Oh, you mean *my* book.'

'And now you are here, you must read it to me yourself.'

'If that's what pleases you. It's the least I can do after your wonderful welcome.'

The king leaned a little closer, an ecstatic look in his eye. His voice took on a low, conspiratorial tone.

'You see, Jimmy. I know your secret.'

Tianjan raised his eyebrows and sagely tapped the right side of his head three times.

'Is that so?' I replied, my mind making rapid orbits through the constellation of consternation.

'I know about your Mr. Hoffman. Who he really is.'

Having dropped this bombshell, the king smiled in triumph.

'Yes, Jimmy. I know who he is, and I know you've been through some deadly scrapes together. It's an honour to call Iolango my friend - and now *you* are here as well.'

'Iolango!' I exclaimed.

I had not heard or even thought of that name for many a month. Why would I? My former mentor had abandoned me long ago. Such was my surprise that it gave me time to stop and think. It was just long enough to strangle the urge to point out the king's mistake. It might be wise to process this surprising conversation before telling the king that the man he thought was Iolango was the latter's arch enemy, Elijinx.

'You see, Jimmy, it was Iolango who first gave me The Book and your wonderful music. It was he who encouraged me to bid for the film rights. Without Iolango, you would not be standing here now.'

'That's quite true. It's all his fault.'

'And that is not all. I know your other secret. The bigger one.'

'Oh yes?' I said, with renewed dread.

'You pretend The Book is a fairytale, but every word is true.'

As Tianjan's mind was clearly made up on this point, I made no effort to dissuade him. Instead I tried a diversionary tactic - which rather backfired, as it happened.

'Well, there you go. I'm busted, your majesty. But here's a secret you *don't* know - I'm writing a new book. A sequel, about my adventures since escaping from Elijinx's island.'

This revelation had an immediate effect on the king. He threw both hands in the air, palms facing me with fingers outstretched. His mouth opened in a cartoonish parody of delight. Then he stood up and surged forward, billowing sleeves all aflutter, and clasped my hands between his.

'This is the most wonderful news! You must read it to me without delay.'

'I regret it is still in the draft stage,' I said, backpedalling hastily.

'Then you must stay here and finish it. I place the entire resources of Lombala at your disposal.'

'That's most generous, majesty, but the band has to get back to England and start work on a new album.'

'Why not do that here too? I'll have a recording studio made for you. You'll be given everything you need. Surely you are happy with Lalitha. I hand-picked her myself. I know the kind of girl you like.'

'Majesty, truly your bounty knows no boundaries. Everything here is so strange and new. Perhaps when I've settled in we can talk about this.'

'Of course. It is ungracious of me to pressure you. Forgive me. At times my enthusiasm overwhelms me.'

'You certainly don't bother with the small talk. I suppose kings are beyond all that. You're straight to the point - and that's just as I like it. Would you think it impertinent if I spoke in kind?'

The king returned to his throne.

'I command you to speak freely.'

'Why are you so interested in the book? Or The Book, as you call it. You even bought the film rights. Why is it so important to you?'

The king sighed a deep sorrowful sigh. A sigh of royal proportions.

'You and I carry a great burden, Jimmy Brandt. You are burdened to reveal the truth and I am cursed to enact it. Iolango has schooled me in this prophecy I must fulfil. The commoner and the king - together we will usher in the end days.'

'Oh, you mean that apocalyptic spiel Iolango and Elijinx are always on about? The great battle between the Vortex Winder and the Maelstrom at the end of the world? Really, they do go on, don't they? Take some advice from a commoner, majesty. If I were you, I'd forget all that rubbish. Why would you bother with all that when you live in this paradise?'

A cloud passed over Tianjan's expression. It seemed that this time my tone of levity had offended him. I had the impression of a volcano about to erupt. Instead he broke into volatile peals of laughter.

'Ah - once again, your exotic Australian humour. The low key manner and down to earth mockery! You bloody bastard, sir! You had me that time. Still, let me answer your question.'

There was a portentous pause while the king gathered his thoughts. He stood up again and beckoned me to follow him. There was a door at the back of the throne room. We walked through a series of other rooms, equally lavish, until at last we came to a balcony offering a stunning panorama of the kingdom. I could see the palace grounds far below, Lombala city stretching out ahead, mountains to the right and jungle to the left. The king turned to me and spoke.

'You believe Lombala to be a paradise. So it is, yet it is the paradise at the end of the world. As I told you, I have read The Book many times, especially your tremendous learned dialogues with Iolango and Elijinx. I know the fate of the world is in the balance, hinged on the great struggle between the Vortex Winder and the Maelstrom. Even the good Iolango concedes the state of the battle. I quote The Book itself - the Maelstrom is in the ascendancy.'

'True. The Book *did* say that and to be frank, there's been bugger all happened since to change it. The ascendancy remains and it's only getting worse.'

'It is with infinite sadness that I concur.'

'Buck up your majesty. How can you have infinite sadness when you live in a palace like this with half a dozen Lombalan beaches around the corner?'

'Because Lombala is the final flowering of humanity before this species dies out - and I am burdened to be its custodian. It's the role Iolango has taught me to fulfil. Yes, Lombala is a Utopia. That was always the intention, to unite the best of nature and nurture. It's a land of natural wonders, bountiful harvests, happy citizens, and enlightened laws. If our species is to die out, then at least let Lombala blossom as one last jewel in the face of its extinction. Since the days of the ancients, the great Utopian ideal has been sought but never attained. Then let Lombala fulfil that ideal at the last. Late, so late, but at least not never.'

'Wow, if things are that bad, I really had better go back to England and get on with the new album.'

'And the new Book, don't forget that. There's really no reason why you shouldn't finish them both here. Still, we won't speak of that now. Let us play chess.'

We adjourned to a sitting room within the king's chambers, where in time to come we would often entertain ourselves. The king brought out a most eccentric chess set. There was a miniature likeness of Tianjan himself as the tiny king on the board. His first wife was the queen. Zambeko was bishop - indeed he was both bishops - and the remaining pieces were fashioned in the manner of the royal guardians. Panther and leopard as the knights, lion and tiger as the rooks.

Tianjan marshalled his forces skilfully, beating me three times in a row. Well pleased, he dismissed me, saying we would meet again 'on the morrow' in that kingly manner of his. I made the long descent down the winding stairways of the palace to my ground floor quarters, where Lalitha was waiting.

My wife seemed overjoyed that I was in such good favour with the king, yet concerned lest I should have inadvertently offended him. She made me repeat the conversation to her in as much detail as possible. Once satisfied all was in order, she resumed her task of acclimatising me to life in Lombala.

It was indeed a charming way of life. Lalitha and I would rise soon after dawn, swim at our private beach, then breakfast on those tropical fruits so bountiful in Lombala. After breakfast, we'd go driving through the city, or out past the city limits on roads through the national parks where the wildlife ran free.

Lalitha insisted on driving inside the city, only allowing me to take the wheel once we had left the city limits behind. She was afraid I'd take a wrong turn and get lost. I didn't mind, as this freed me to sit beside her and take in the city sights.

In the afternoon or evening, I was often invited to the king's rooms for games of chess. Occasionally, he asked me to the read from The Book, so I'd select a chapter or a short excerpt, to which he listened spellbound. To make a variation from chess, we also played Scrabble, a game Tianjan had played only occasionally but now took to with a surprising fervour. Oddly enough, his interest in the game grew into something of an obsession. Indeed it was the cause of our first quarrel.

For those who don't know, Scrabble is a game in which a hundred small tiles are placed in a bag. Every tile is imprinted with a letter of the alphabet. Each player holds seven tiles at any one time, holding them in a rack to keep them secret. The players take turns making words on a board with their tiles, joining to whatever letters are already down. Each tile is worth a certain number of points and the board itself has spots for double letter scores, triple word scores, and so on. The best way to score maximum points is to make a word using all seven of your tiles at once, for this earns a fifty point bonus. If one has a feel for words, the game can be rather addictive.

The king was highly competitive in all the games we played. He loved to win - and win or lose, he was no poker face, for he often flushed angrily at the height of battle. Thus, I thought it prudent to let him have the upper hand most of the time. This was easy enough with chess, as Tianjan was the superior player. Yet I shaded him in Scrabble and sensed his frustration when he was losing. I began to hold back, pretending I'd drawn bad tiles and couldn't play any high scoring words. However, the king was no fool and was soon onto me. If I thought losing had made him angry, it was nothing compared to his rage when he found out I was letting him win.

It happened towards the end of a game when there were less than a dozen tiles left in the bag. I was on 380 points, Tianjan on 368. The seven tiles on my rack were GOERTIV. If I could make a seven letter word, the fifty point bonus would guarantee victory. Sure enough, there was a seven letter word there. Yet I could see the king's face flushing a darker colour and hear his impatient breathing as he tried to establish dominion over his own rack of letters. Judging the mood as I thought best, I shrugged and played the word EGO for six points.

The king looked up in suspicion, sensing something was amiss. Then reaching a judgment, he leaned forward and turned around my rack of letters. He placed my EGO back on the rack so he could see all seven tiles. A few seconds later, he exploded in accusation.

'You had VERTIGO!'

'What? Oh, you're right - VERTIGO. Well done, I didn't see it.'

The king rose to his feet, flung the Scrabble board across the room so that tiles flew in all directions, and upended the table on which it had rested. There was a display case nearby holding three swords, which I had assumed were purely ceremonial. Tianjan drew one of the swords and held the point to my neck.

'Don't patronise me, Jimmy Brandt.'

'Majesty! I didn't see it!'

'A false victory is worse than an honourable defeat. You mock me with the very word you play. Ego indeed!'

'Come on, your majesty. It's only a game. You whip me at chess. I'm a little better at Scrabble but that's only because English is my first language.'

'That is no excuse. Part of my education was spent at the finest schools in England. I should be able to win on merit.'

'I also learned all those weird three letter words most people have never heard of. If you knew them, you'd beat me for sure.'

'Then I will learn them. Now get out.'

The king put away his sword and I withdrew from his chambers.

A couple of hours later, I was dozing on the bed in my room when there was a knock at the door. Lalitha opened it and let off a small scream before prostrating herself on the floor. Tianjan bestowed a benevolent smile upon my wife and lifted her to her feet. I sat up and wondered what was coming next.

The king bowed.

'My dear friend. I am so deeply sorry. Can you forgive me?'

'Forgive you? There's nothing to forgive, majesty.'

'I'm dreadfully remorseful, Jimmy. I get so involved in our games I sometimes forget my poise and my entire upbringing. Understand, however, that you must never again let me win. I must win on my merits, nothing else.'

'Of course, I feel the same way.'

'Let us not play again for a few weeks. When we resume, do your worst. Or rather, your very best.'

I thought nothing more of the incident until a few days later when Lalitha and I were driving through the streets in the main part of Lombala city. Something was bothering me but I could not put my finger on it. Then it hit me.

'Have you noticed the number plates, Lal?'

'What about them?'

'Take a look next time we stop at the lights.'

And there it was. Almost all the cars had been issued with shiny new number plates. The plates were bone-coloured with black letters, just like Scrabble tiles. Instead of featuring three letters and three numbers, all the new plates contained two lots of three letter words - and all of them Scrabble words.

When I quizzed Zambeko back in the palace that night, he answered with no trace of embarrassment, as if this were a routine reform. Either this sort of whimsical madness was normal or Zambeko was a remarkably good actor.

'Oh yes. The king wanted to learn your three letter Scrabble words. All the cars in the capital have been issued with new number plates until he does. His driver takes him around the city for an hour or two each day so he can study and memorise them all.'

With that, Zambeko returned to eating his dinner as if there was nothing amiss.

Sure enough, by the time Tianjan and I resumed our Scrabble a couple of weeks later, he more than held his own, displaying particular mastery of the three letter words. Before long, Lalitha and I saw that the city's cars had resumed possession of their old number plates.

One might accuse Tianjan of ignoring his regal duties. Surely there were urgent political reforms he should have been attending to. Yet considering the Utopian nature of Lombala and the complete absence of social problems, perhaps there was indeed no more pressing task for the king than learning the three letter Scrabble words.

A king must conquer. Would one prefer him to wage war on his neighbouring states? Far better that Tianjan should channel his urge to victory into the drive to obliterate me on the Scrabble board. Such are the battles to be fought when all the real wars are left behind as ugly, distant memories. When all is said and done, a war of words is better than a war of bullets and bombs. These are the wars fought in paradise, the paradise at the end of the world.

# 31

# Lotus Land

One morning, I was relaxing on the beach after breakfast when a familiar voice struck up beside me.

'Jimmy. How are you getting on?'

I removed my shades to find my manager beside me.

'Elijinx? You've been keeping a low profile. Where've you been?'

'Here and there. You boys aren't my only clients. So - enjoying yourself?'

'I'm in no hurry to leave, put it that way. You were right about Lombala. It's got to be hands down the best country in the world. Perfect climate, enlightened laws, and no conflict or suffering of any kind. All races live together in perfect harmony. I mean, look at my wife - she's Indian. But Zambeko's African, and what's Tianjan - Chinese?'

'I knew you'd be happy here.'

'Why wouldn't I be? I've got to ask you though - Tianjan doesn't spend much time governing. He seems to sit around playing games most of the time. Is there nothing more urgent to attend to?'

'The king's a figurehead, more or less. It's Zambeko runs this country. When Tianjan's father died, it was Zambeko who stepped up. Even before that he was the ideas man. This Zouman, for example. He won't take the credit but that was his doing. Tianjan's got sense enough to let him get on with it. Zambeko's the man. He's de facto prime minister, minister for foreign affairs, arts and culture, and head of religion to boot. Calls himself pope when he's in the mood.'

'Pope!'

'It's an affectation of sorts. Not that they're any kind of Catholics round here but for some reason Zambeko fancies the title. It's rumoured he has some history with that mob and got himself excommunicated. Don't mention it though, and if you see him done up in his papal finery, be sure to keep a straight face. He's a proud and pious man.'

'Noted.'

'Old Zambeko's got a few strings to his bow, as you may discover. Stay on the right side of him. Mind you, I wouldn't go upsetting the king either. There's no telling what that one will do if he's roused.'

'I have no intention of upsetting him, I assure you.'

'As long as you uphold that, Jimmy, all will be well.'

Despite what Elijinx had said, I was far more concerned about my dealings with the king than Zambeko. Still, now that good relations were restored, life in Lombala returned to its comfortable rhythms. Long, languid breakfasts followed by briefly invigorating swims, then blissed-out dozes on the beach with my wife beside me. In a strange fashion, it reminded me of the early days in the Blue Mountains with Sandra and Finzi when I had forsaken all ambition. Here I was, a quitter once more, this time with not even a day job to blight my sense of retirement.

The other boys in the band seemed just as mellowed by the island. Our former animosity had dissolved like morning mist into the tropical haze. Indeed we began breakfasting or going to the beach together with our wives, or having sunset cocktails in the various bars overlooking the palace gardens. Ivan and Ollie were a couple of lambs these days and I could just dimly recall that we were enemies.

It was only our bass player who seemed restless. Jake kept nagging about rehearsal and asking when the gigs would be done so we could fly home. He challenged me one evening in the bar at North Garden, when our wives had gone to the bathroom.

'Come on, Jimmy, when's the first show? We've been here for weeks.'

'What's the rush? This is exactly what the band needed instead of the constant moving from town to town. Don't you see how much better everyone's getting along?'

'Yeah, it's great and all, but... I can't put my finger on it. I've never been the type to stay in one spot too long.'

'Then you must learn to adjust. It's a paid holiday. Workaholism is a dreadful disease. That's a vice done up as a virtue if ever there was one.'

'Can't we just get the shows done and leave?'

'Oh relax. Look at that. Do you see that in London?'

I pointed at a pride of lions below and across from us in the garden, sitting on some heavy logs.

'Appreciate that while it lasts. You never know when these magnificent beasts will go extinct.'

Our wives returned to the table, just as a waiter brought over another tray of complimentary cocktails. It was a tough life alright.

The fact is, when Elijinx first told me about the gigs in Lombala, I saw it as a smash and grab raid. Get in, do the shows, collect our pay cheques and leave. But as the days went by, a return to the outside world seemed less and less appealing.

All our needs were taken care of. We had beautiful, devoted wives. The climate was idyllic. What on Earth was there to hurry back to? I began to think - why leave? Why not stay a while longer? The king had put the entire bounty of Lombala at our disposal. We'd have to be mad to go back to the real world with its harsh climate, chaotic nastiness, and general turmoil.

So strong was the holiday feel that I almost forgot the band was expected to play the three shows. Jake's nagging eventually wore me down. With reluctance and considerable effort, I roused myself from my state of torpor and rounded up the lads for rehearsal. It had been a long time since the last gig in New York, so we were bound to be rusty. When we at last gathered for a practice, it was a shambles. It felt like I'd not picked up a guitar for six months.

There was no choice but to postpone the first show until we'd done a couple of weeks rehearsals. From that point, we got into the habit of turning up each morning, or early afternoon, to hammer away at our trade until the old vigour and spark began to shine through once more.

Eventually we got it. At first, it was a brief invigoration, like diving into a wave on a Lombalan beach. Then we learned to sustain it for half a dozen songs, then for a full show. In due course, the band was ready to play.

It was at the show that first night - then the second and the third - that we remembered who we had once been and might never be again. A great rock band, flawed and chaotic and alive. We walked on a wire in a brief, spot-lit moment across the chasms of eternity. Then it was over and I was beset by sadness. Perhaps I knew this line up of Lighthouse XIII had played its last ever show.

I assumed that after three gigs the king would be quite sated, perhaps even sick of us. Yet if anything, he seemed more obsessed with the band - and The Book - than ever. He began to invite me to his chambers for music and drinking sessions. One of his rooms was set up for the sole purpose of listening to music. It was fitted with enormous, state of the art speakers, and of course there were no neighbours who were ever going to complain about the noise!

After a few drinks, Tianjan always tried to make me agree to a fourth show. I was adamant in my refusal. In the realm of my art I insisted on remaining sovereign, and even a king had no right to intrude. There would be no more shows, at least not until the next album was finished.

By way of compensation, I consented to read Tianjan Chapter One of the new book. He seized upon the offer and ordered me to begin at once. I hurried down the winding palace stairways, retrieved my laptop, then reversed my journey, arriving breathless back in the king's domain. Tianjan sat up straight in his throne and closed his eyes as I began to read.

It felt so good to be a quitter. There I was, having given up on my dreams and resigned myself to a quiet life. My guitars were in storage and the Vortex Winder lay dormant, as it had for the last three years. Even Sandra was back on the scene, having forgiven me my madness of the years before.

'Oh, Sandra is back? How wonderful!'
'Yes - she was for a while. Shall I go on?'

Even Sandra was back on the scene having forgiven me my madness of the years before. We'd left the glamour of Sydney's east to live in the unwild western suburbs. After all, that's what she wanted. It was in fact west of the west - in the Blue Mountains out past the city limits. I retired from music, got a real job and settled into a quiet domestic life.

Sandra? The Vortex Winder? Forgive me. I must remember that many readers have no knowledge of my past adventures.

And on it went to the end of Chapter One. When it had finished, Tianjan breathed a long satisfied sigh.

'You must stay here and complete it, Jimmy. Once again, I place all the resources of Lombala at your disposal. I will ensure that you work here undisturbed until the new Book is done.'

'Your generosity is boundless, majesty. No writer or musician could ever hope for a more supportive patron - but surely I should be getting back to England soon.'

'Why, Jimmy? Everything you need is here. You're not married. You have no children. What do you have to go back to except an appalling climate and an empty house?'

The king's comment pulled me up short, for he was quite right. Yet this offered the perfect chance to raise a matter which had been on my mind for some time.

'Once again your wisdom exceeds my own and you have correctly divined the loneliness inside me. Knowing your great generosity of heart, I make one humble request. Will your eminence grant me one boon - the right to take Lalitha home to England as my lawful wife?'

Tianjan's face darkened.

'Lalitha? No, that won't do. It's out of the question - and it matters not whether you ask permission from me, Iolango, or the Vortex Winder itself. Lalitha is a flower native to this island. Once away from Lombala, she will wither and die. Surely she has not agreed to this.'

'I haven't asked her, your grace. But surely there are many natives of this part of the world who move away and adapt. There's no shortage of Indians or Africans in London.'

'They may travel from India or Africa, but never from Lombala. Zouman only applies for the duration of your stay here. Once you leave Lombala, your marriage is dissolved. Lalitha must stay behind for her next betrothal.'

'Majesty, be reasonable.'

'It's nothing to do with me, Jimmy. These matters are beyond my dominion. You might as well try to take the jungle or the ocean back to London with you. I suggest you reconsider. Stay a while longer, finish the new Book and your album. I repeat, what do you really have to go back to?'

'I once again give thanks for your majesty's generosity and concern. May I take a walk and think it over?'

'Of course. Let us meet on the morrow.'

346

I returned the laptop to my room. Then, refusing Lalitha's request for company, began a long, reflective walk through the palace. I explored all parts of that marvellous domain, noting its enchanting opulence and artistry. I paid my respects to the four guardians of Lombala: the panthers to the east, the leopards to the west, lions to the north, and tigers to the south.

I searched for, but could not find, my little tiger cub. So, spotting the keeper, Ranji, dozing again at his desk, woke him up to ask where the cub was.

'There he is, sir,' Ranji replied, 'right in front of you.'

The cub had grown considerably. He no longer stood out from the adult tigers anywhere near as much as he had on first sighting.

'How old is he now, Ranji?' I asked in surprise.

'How old, sir? He has just turned one.'

'One? One year? Are you sure?'

'I am certain. It was his birthday only last week.'

'My, how time flies when you're in love.'

I walked towards the garden and stuck my face against the glass. The tiger cub - if I could still call him that - turned and approached me. When he reached the other side of the glass, he roared softly and stared into my eyes. As our eyes met, I was struck by a remote and fanciful notion, yet one which seemed more plausible the longer I considered it.

This tiger was young. Indeed, so young, he had not even been alive at the time of Finzi's death. It was some time after Finzi died that this tiger was born. Was it possible some kind of transmigration of souls had taken place? Perhaps he had come back to give me a message.

In a flash, I understood. The symbolism was unmistakeable. Finzi had deliberately been reborn here to give me a message that this was to be my new home. The circles of life and love were to be joined once more. I had lost Sandra's love around the time Finzi died. Now the beloved cat had come back into my life just as I realised I was in love with Lalitha, not only for the short term period of Zouman, but for the rest of my life.

My mind made up, I returned to my room, took Lalitha in my arms and kissed her. It was the genuine kiss of husband and wife. I resolved to stay in Lombala at least long enough to finish the new book and album. After that, we would see. Perhaps Tianjan would grant us permission to leave at that point - or perhaps I would make Lombala my permanent home.

I called a meeting of the band, not to force them to stay, but to allow them to leave. Love is benevolent and involves no compulsion. Freedom must always play the decisive role. I marched to Elijinx's room and informed him of my plans.

'I think that's a very wise decision, Jimmy. I congratulate you.'

'Could you round up the other lads and send them to my room? I want to chat to them one by one.'

'As you wish - but Jake's already gone.'

'Gone? When did this happen?'

'He left a couple of weeks ago, right after the last show.'

'I didn't even notice - and what you don't miss you don't need. He's only a bass player. I can do all that myself. You might as well tell the crew to go home too, they won't be required. But I do need a drummer.'

A few minutes later, Amos was sitting beside me on the balcony in my room. The leopards were dozing in West Garden beneath us, and the distant crash of breakers from the beach offered a soothing backdrop to our discussion.

'Amos, I went online today and checked the weather conditions in London. There are pensioners dying of cold. I can't think of a single good reason to go back. Will you stay here and help me work on the new album?'

'I was thinking about getting home.'

'You're no use to me in London. If you leave, I'm going to have to fly in another drummer.'

'Are we still on full pay?'

'Of course. Just stay long enough to demo some tracks and wait for winter to blow over back home. Besides, what have you got to go back to? You've got a beautiful wife here, which is more than you have in London, right?'

'Righto then, Jimmy, I'm in.'

Next to the balcony was Oliver. He had the same vacant look as Amos, yet the air of sullen reproach from the last weeks of the US tour had gone. On tour, he'd acquired the pale, unhealthy look of the drug addict, yet Lombala seemed to have done him good, at least physically. He looked like a beach bum on a surfing safari, with a tan to match.

'Ollie, it's terrific to see you looking so well, but it's time for us to part. I'm staying on here for a while to work on new music. Even if I wanted to, we can't keep working together. You should go home.'

Oliver looked at me for a few moments, then went through the motions of protest. I sensed he was working from muscle memory.

'What about my two songs?'

'I'm sorry, Arabella, but I can't work with someone who was plotting to kill me.'

'What are you talking about?' he said feebly.

'I know all about it. In your defence, I probably deserved it. I've treated you abominably.'

'So you admit it?'

'Sure, I'll take the confessional on that one. I just hope you got something out of this whole experience. You got to travel the world on a big rock tour. You know what you should do, Ollie? Go back and form your own band, then make up with Suzy. You kids were good together.'

'It's a bit late for that.'

'I don't see why. Has she married someone else?'

'No.'

'Well, neither have you. I don't think this Zouman counts.'

'She won't take my calls.'

'Then you must go back on bended knees and beg for a second chance. Tell her you've got the drugging and womanising out of your system. Blame it all on me if you like. Tell her I'm the devil incarnate. I don't care, as long as you set it to rights. See, I'm in love now too, Ollie. Lalitha's put the charm on me, and when you're in love you want everyone else to be happy as well. So Ollie, you go back to Suzy and start over.'

Tears had formed in Oliver's eyes and he leaned forward and put his head in his hands.

'Thanks Jimmy. Thanks for everything.'

'For what - being nothing but a bastard to you? I crave your forgiveness, not your thanks. Now go back to Suzy while there's still time.'

Finally, it was Ivan who took the balcony seat. He sat there shirtless, a medallion hanging from his neck, gold against the tanned skin. Even pacified by the tranquillity of Lombala, I could not resist a facetious greeting.

'Sir Ivan! My old jousting partner! Or is it Hoe these days? I can't quite keep up.'

'Sir James!' Ivan replied, ignoring my question. 'A dubious pleasure as always.'

'See how far we've come, Ive. At each other's throats a while back and look at us now having cocktails with each other's wives. I put it down to the transformative powers of this island, wouldn't you say?'

'Indeed, Sir James. I don't understand it, but my urge to disembowel you has quite gone off the boil.'

'If I may return the compliment, my burning desire to decapitate you with one of Ollie's guitars has faded to the merest flickering flame. I've come over all lovey-dovey thanks to Lalitha. I'm sure Nefertiti's had the same effect on you. So since we've both gone all John and Yoko, what say we call a truce and you hand over that footage of yours?'

'And give up my one defence against your slumbering megalomania? Why would I do that?'

'It's a fair point. Why would you trade in your bargaining chip? There's no way Ivan de Vangelus would ever do that. On the other hand, Anton Carew might.'

For the first time in our acquaintance, Ivan reacted with something less than complete self assurance. For once he was lost for words.

'You hear me, Ive? Anton Carew might. I know all about Carew, don't worry about that?'

'What do you know?'

'Everything. I found out the whole story.'

'Let's hear it then.'

I sighed. He was going to call my bluff.

'Anton Carew was one of the great rock singers of the early seventies until he made the mistake of joining a coven of witches known as the Volant Society. He was arrested and blamed when his girlfriend tried to achieve Moonflight out of an upstairs window at Rookwood during a ritual. He did thirteen years prison as a result of her death.'

'What's all that got to do with me?'

'Come on Ivan, it's over. You're the spitting image of Carew.'

'So, I look some old rock singer from the seventies. What of it?'

'I'll admit I don't know the full story, but there's no doubt someone out there does - and the press would love to get their hands on it, given the right tip off. There'll be some up and comer investigative journalist who's sure to see it as a career builder. But they'll never know, as long as I get that footage once and for all. What do you say?'

'I say it's fact against speculation. The footage is solid evidence, unlike your vague innuendo.'

'If it comes to that, Ive, someone's bound to ask who was holding the camera though, aren't they? And why wouldn't I spill the beans it was you played the key role in that young fella's downfall? Let's get past this petty banter and look at the big picture. You and me, mate, we're in the same boat. Whoever we once were are dead and gone since we turned to the Maelstrom. I became the Black Phoenix and you're Ivan De Vangelus. We've had a good run in this temporary kingdom of ours. What say we resurrect our alliance and start working together like we're supposed to?'

'What is it you want, Jimbo?'

'What do you say we make one more album together and call it quits? We don't even have to tour. Just make a great record and leave it at that. If we can agree to that much, then you'll hit delete on that footage and I'll forget I ever heard the name Anton Carew. Then, when the record's done, we'll shake hands and part company, if not as friends, then at least as professional colleagues and partners in music. What do you say?'

'Fine, Jimmy, as long as you double my percentage on the royalties.'

'Like that, is it? Oh well, why not? Only for this record, mind. So here's what we do. You probably know Jake's gone, and young Arabella will be joining him shortly. Amos will stick around while we make the album. When it's done, you can go or stay as you please.'

'I'd have to run it by my wife first, see what she wants to do.'

'Well, there's a turn up. Then again, with a wife like Nefertiti, I'd do the same myself. Mind you, I wouldn't count on the king granting her permission to leave, if that's what you're planning. Not after what he said about me and Lalitha. Anyhow, that's none of my affair. Let's just get the record made.'

We shook hands on the matter and there we were, Jimmy Brandt and Ivan de Vangelus, mates once more. Who'd have thought? It was onwards and upwards from here, no doubt about it.

# 32
# Moonlight Tiger

Having made my decision to stay, life resumed its agreeable patterns. With Tianjan's encouragement, I began serious work on the new book, a pursuit that became part of my daily routine. After breakfast and a swim with Lalitha, I'd spend the rest of the morning writing. Those distant days with Sandra and Finzi seemed remote and dreamlike now, despite the strange resemblance to my present life. The distance in time and space allowed me to write of those past adventures almost as if they'd happened to someone else, which in a sense they had.

The addition of a purposeful task meant my life in Lombala had now attained the perfect blend of structure and relaxation. I wrote in the morning, then in the afternoon went to the studio Tianjan had built and came up with riffs for the new album. I spent the rest of the day with Lalitha unless summoned to the king's chambers.

This lifestyle drifted on for some time, which allowed slow but steady progress on the work. There was one morning, however, when I was out of sorts. I snapped at Lalitha, who responded in kind. In an attempt to avoid a full blown argument, I left the room, stormed out to the palace gates, and demanded a car.

'Your wife will need to sign for that,' said the attendant.

'My wife won't be coming - and as I'm now a citizen of Lombala, I will be driving today.'

The man was reluctant yet cowed enough by my tone to hand over the keys. I drove off at once, following at first the usual route Lalitha always took through the affluent suburbs. Yet in keeping with the unusual mood of the day, I took a different turning at a familiar juncture.

Before long, I came to a section of the city unlike any other I'd seen so far. The streets were dirty, the houses run down, and many of the inhabitants appeared to be poor, sick, or mad. It was almost like I was back in a normal city, typical of the rest of the world.

When I parked the car and proceeded on foot, the dirtiness of the streets became even more obvious. The shopkeepers had a sullen, guarded air, and judging by some of the populace it seemed well justified.

There was a rumble of voices up ahead and rounding a corner, I came across a group of ruffians gathered in a circle. To my horror, they were staging a cock fight. After being so long cocooned in the sheltered world of the palace, it was a shock to encounter such cruelty.

Beating a hasty retreat, I made for a nearby tavern in search of a drink. I brooded there for the best part of an hour trying to reconcile this place and the cock fight with the idea of Lombala as a paradise. To dally so long was my misfortune, for a worse spectacle awaited. I gradually became aware that the bar patrons' attention was fixed on a TV screen at the front of the room. Another scene of controlled violence was about to appear on that screen. It looked like an execution, for a blindfolded man was being led to an executioner's block for beheading.

Given the archaic mode of despatch, I assumed it to be a televised historical drama. But the action onscreen lacked the seamless construction which is the sign of a scripted, edited drama. It had the clunky, unrehearsed quality of real life. As the participants were native Lombalan in appearance, it seemed that the event was local.

As the axe was raised, the atmosphere in the room tensed and acquired some foul quality I could not define. This execution was no fiction. I looked away at the crucial moment but could not resist a peek at its ugly aftermath. Then, downing the rest of my drink at a swallow, I hurried out and drove off in the car. This awful interlude was not at all what I'd expected from my unplanned excursion. For a few panicky minutes, I was unable to find my way home, until at last a familiar landmark appeared which helped me navigate back to the palace.

That evening when the king summoned me, I told him what I had seen. He was not surprised so much as annoyed, an emotion he managed to control this time.

'I thought Lombala was meant to be a Utopia,' I remarked, in what could only be seen as an accusation.

'Utopia is an ideal,' said the king. 'Lombala aspires to that ideal without so far attaining it.'

'How can capital punishment be part of an enlightened society?'

'Perfection is attained by the elimination of imperfection. Perfect citizens are made, not born. In theory, education alone should be enough to produce them. In practice, there will always be failures.'

'So you just bin them?'

'Only as a last resort. We call it the Option C rule. It's educate, rehabilitate, eliminate. If the first two fail, we move on to the third. It is a three strikes policy, as the Americans call it.'

'Except it's only two strikes.'

'The third strike is delivered by the executioner.'

'It's like something out of the Middle Ages.'

'On the contrary, it is compassion personified. The life ends within seconds and the suffering is over - not just of the death but the life. To live an evil life is suffering in itself. We relieve those so afflicted. Besides you said it yourself in the great Book - you would sooner die than rot away in the living death that is prison life. Do you now recant those noble sentiments?'

'No, not at all. It's true I'd prefer death to a life enslaved. Especially in that prison where conditions were so rank. Can you at least make the conditions bearable within your prisons?'

'Why? These people have failed rehabilitation. What use are their lives in prison when they can only grow old and die? The coffers of Lombala can't sustain such a futile existence. How do you think the rest of the populace enjoys such a high standard of living if not for judicious control of our wealth?'

'It seems so ruthless.'

'These are the burdens of government, Jimmy. What are we to do with these criminals? We can't export them, we can't reform them. So we liberate them. Option C.'

'Surely it's better to let them live, and hope for the best.'

'How then are we to attain our perfect Utopian society? We cannot tolerate evil in our midst. Tell me, these barbarians you saw waging the cock fight - wouldn't you agree they are evil?'

'Certainly.'

'And they should be punished?'

'They should be stopped, at least. Punished too, I suppose.'

'What happens if we arrest them, re-educate them with the belief that cock fighting is wrong, and they re-offend after we release them? What then?'

'I don't know.'

'We eliminate them.'

'Even so, how can you televise such a vile spectacle for the entertainment of drunks in a bar?'

'For the whole of Lombala, you mean. Clearly, it is a deterrent. Justice is most effective when seen in action. It's the old carrot and stick, and one does not govern by carrots alone.'

I had the impression the king was mocking me and that perhaps I deserved it. I left the royal chambers unsure what to believe. My impression of Lombala as a kind of paradise had been dealt a blow, yet the king's arguments had exposed my poorly thought out notions of how easily such a paradise could be maintained.

As it turned out, Tianjan's bid to educate me was not over. A few days later, I was woken at dawn and ordered to the front of the palace. After splashing water on my face and throwing on some clothes, I arrived at the palace gates to see a limousine waiting. Tianjan was inside, sitting on the back seat.

'Majesty!' I exclaimed. 'What pleases you?'

The king sported his enigmatic smile. 'You will see,' was all he said.

We drove away from the palace for a long while, until at last a grand three storey house came into view. My attention was drawn to the sculpture over the gate. It took me a few moments to realise it was a carved phoenix of pure black marble. Still the king ignored my questions and simply beckoned me to follow him on a tour of the premises.

The mansion was a work in progress, yet still exceeded Rookwood for grandeur. When the tour was complete, we returned to the front of the house and its marble sculpture. Tianjan motioned for me to kneel. He drew his sword, a gesture that alarmed me. Yet he merely tapped me upon both shoulders and elevated me to the Lombalan nobility.

'Arise, Sir Jimmy, Duke of the Black Phoenix. When the estate is ready, you will live here and rule this province. It is just reward for your newly sworn allegiance. You'll help me govern - and while you will enjoy the perks, you'll also learn the difficulties of office in the long pursuit of Utopia.'

Somewhat bewildered at the sudden promotion, I decided to wait and see how it played out. As repairs to the mansion were a good way from completion, the matter could be deferred for a while yet. In truth I had little interest in government, but wanted only to resume the easy life to which I was now accustomed. Whether or not the king was serious, I did not know. Perhaps he was merely trying to make a point, as well as punishing me for my rogue mission out of the palace. It was quite possible this was merely a whimsical joke that would never be mentioned again. On the other hand, if Tianjan was serious, then the Duke of the Black Phoenix I would become - and use the position to full advantage.

As it turned out, a more pressing development was about to put a question mark over my future in Lombala. The turning point in that long, seamless haze of days and nights came when Lalitha and I received an invitation to the king's theatre. The gold lettering on the card proclaimed that a special event was to take place three days hence. The formality of the invitation and the inclusion of my wife implied this would be no ordinary night. As for the nature of the event itself, no clue was given. Tianjan always did revel in secrecy, and surprises. Along with grand, whimsical gestures, they were quite his forte.

Over the next two days, my efforts to tease some clues out of the king were in vain. When the big night arrived, Lalitha and I were shown to the Royal Theatre two levels below the king's quarters. It was here that he staged small theatrical events and concerts, and had been the venue for the band's three gigs. For viewing plays and films, it was ideal.

Elijinx was there, as were Ivan and his wife, Nefertiti. Zambeko was in attendance with both his wives, who took seats at the front with Lalitha. I was given one of the three chairs of honour in the centre of the room. Tianjan took the middle place, of course. I was to the king's left with Zambeko on his right. His majesty seemed barely able to contain his excitement. My main mental state was one of bamboozlement and, frankly, fear. I was back in the constellation of consternation, wondering what the blue-blooded lunatic had come up with this time.

The lights went down, engulfing us in darkness. A movie screen came to life at the front of the room. On that screen, a nocturnal street scene appeared. The street looked familiar but I couldn't quite place it. A dashing young man in his mid-twenties came into view, walking down the road, taking the occasional sip from a beer bottle.

The young man approached a hotel, outside which various black-shirted rogues were gathered. He entered the premises to find it crowded and a rock band playing. Ignoring them, he headed for the hotel toilets and noticed an insect floundering in the urinal.

The young man fished the insect out of the water and dumped it outside in the beer garden. As he lit up a cigarette, an older man in a blue robe appeared. After a brief conversation, the older man handed over a device called a Vortex Winder. There was a crash of drums and the guitar riff from the song 'Vortex Winder' burst majestically through the cinema speakers.

All through this opening sequence, Tianjan had been on the point of bursting into fits of giggles. He kept giving me little sideways glances to gauge my reactions. Zambeko was also eyeing me, yet in his more austere manner. On my part, I was so shocked by what I was watching that I'd noticed them only peripherally.

When the theme song came surging out of the speakers, Tianjan could restrain himself no longer and clapped me heartily on the back. I barely felt it for my mind was reeling from the discovery that somehow *The Vortex Winder* had, behind my back, been made into a feature film. Yet as the king and Zambeko were obviously delighted - and clearly expected me to feel the same way - there was nothing for it but to keep watching and pray they hadn't mucked it up.

The early signs weren't good. For a start, the actor cast as Jimmy was far too young and possessed the conventional good looks of a Hollywood star. It was hard to see how this would not upset the dynamics of the story.

The next mistake was not so major but did nothing to allay my fears. The band playing at the hotel was not Nevermore, it was Arch Enemy. Now, I have nothing against the latter band - indeed, I am a fan and own some of their albums - but the change unsettled me, even so.

I hope I may be forgiven for speaking of 'Jimmy' in the third person, yet as I was now watching 'him' on screen, and he bore so little resemblance to the original, there are adequate grounds. As the film progressed, I saw 'Jimmy' have his encounter with the thugs from Chapter Two. Instead of using the Vortex Winder merely to repel them, he went on to deliver a punch and a head butt respectively to punish them for their aggression.

This disturbing and gratuitous violence was followed by an awkward scene between Jimmy and 'Sandra.' The actress playing Sandra, looked nothing like my ex. That may be excused, as the book didn't describe her appearance in very much detail. Yet I rather squirmed at the sight of her, and the scene itself. There seems to be the belief, especially in some mainstream American films, that a young couple can't have a normal conversation unless it is punctuated by a constant stream of kisses, affection, or borderline erotic gestures. So the entire argument about BB King from Chapter Three seemed on the verge of collapsing into either porn or rom-com at any given moment. It didn't make sense.

Then to my sheer amazement, during his period as a pro gambler Jimmy turned out to be a lifelong Manchester United fan, obsessed with betting on the result of games from the English Premier League. In a wildly implausible climax, Jimmy borrowed fifty thousand dollars to bet on United beating Chelsea in the FA Cup final. With Chelsea up 4-0 at half time, Jimmy's goose appeared to be cooked. Yet an astonishing five goal comeback in the second half saw both he and Man United emerge victorious.

Following this debacle, Jimmy went to Germany to meet Freya. Rather than being ten years his senior, as she was in the book, Freya had been cast as a youthful blonde with enormous breasts. And did those breasts get an airing during this cinematic masterpiece? What do you think?

Let's not be over critical. For what it's worth the acting was of a fair standard, many of the locations were right, and the songs were skilfully interwoven at key points of the plot. Yet the story had so obviously been prettied up and dumbed down in the usual Hollywood manner, and for the usual reason. Much of the dialogue had been omitted from the final encounter with Elijinx and replaced by a ridiculous fight scene in which Jimmy simply punches Elijinx out so that he falls into the ocean below. Then Iolango swings by in a helicopter and plucks Jimmy from the rock just as the wave is approaching.

When the lights finally went up, I was almost struck dumb, partly because everyone else in the room seemed so happy. Tianjan was delighted, Zambeko displayed a proud, fatherly air, and Elijinx, despite the onscreen pummelling he had just endured, was grinning with fiendish delight of the most classic kind.

'What do you say to *that*, Jimmy Brandt?' roared Tianjan.

'Majesty, I'm speechless! Why didn't you tell me the movie was in production?'

'I think you know by now my penchant for surprises. Let us take to the bar for a triumphant aftermath of wine drinking!'

'I fear, my lord, that I am too overcome by emotion to trust myself with wine. *In vino veritas.* It may cause me to over-praise the film too candidly. May I have a Royal Pardon to excuse myself and take an early night?'

'Your position is quite understandable, Sir Jimmy. What say we take morning tea in my chambers instead?'

'Thank you, majesty.'

I left the cinema with Lalitha, but feeling a need for solitude, asked her to go home without me while I walked the palace grounds alone. It was now approaching midnight and there were few people around. This suited my mood, troubled and pensive as it was.

An odd thought arose. For all my time in Lombala, I could barely remember having suffered the anger or impatience which had so often troubled me in the past. Ivan had recently remarked on this. At the time I'd seen it as a compliment, taking it for granted that my newfound placidity was a virtue. Now I wasn't so sure. If I had seen this film version of *The Vortex Winder* prior to Lombala, I would have been enraged beyond measure. Yet here I was calm, unprotesting - and lifeless. What was wrong with me?

Perhaps equanimity could be taken too far. There was something deeply troubling about that film and my overly calm reaction to it. It was as if the seas of Lombala were awash with morphine and bathing daily therein, I had absorbed a sufficient dose to keep me in a state of compliance.

The moon was full, casting a lunar radiance over the palace gardens. I began a circuit of the walkways overlooking the four ceremonial gardens, home to those noble beasts, the guardians of Lombala. Looking down into North Garden, I saw the lion pride at rest near the far wall of its territory. I headed to East Garden but the panthers, perhaps having found the moonlight intrusive, had taken cover in their shelter. I continued around the walkway to South Garden.

Two or three of the tigers were at rest under a tree some distance to my left. My tiger cub was with them, yet he was no longer a cub. He could barely be told apart from the others, for he was now almost full size. How long had I been in Lombala? I could only recognise the tiger by his own unique pattern of stripes.

I returned once more to the fanciful notion, conceived when he was half grown, that this tiger was Finzi reborn. That idea had served as a key pillar in the reasoning by which I'd chosen to stay in Lombala. In my present state of unease, fresh doubts arose and old ones resurrected. Nothing was certain now. Although the moon illuminated the garden, my own mind was befuddled as if lost in the worst London fog. Yet somehow I knew the tiger's role was crucial.

When Lalitha first showed me the cub, we had looked down upon it from an unoccupied bedroom just above the garden. I returned to that room now and found it unlocked. I went inside and crossed to the window. There was a bunch of dried flowers in a vase on the bedside table. I removed the flowers and dropped them out the window in the hope of drawing the tiger's attention.

His fellow tigers did not stir but mine was sufficiently alert to follow the sound. He strolled over and I called out in a soft, urgent voice. 'Finzi. Finzi!' The tiger looked up at me, his eyes burning into my soul until I no longer had any doubt this was Sandra's beloved cat reborn. 'Finzi!' I called again.

The tiger began a strange series of movements, taking a couple of steps forward and one to the side. If I'd not known better, I'd say the beast was performing some kind of dance. He continued in this odd manner until he was directly below the window, then stood on his hind legs, placing his front paws up against the wall. It struck me he was about to take a mighty leap into my arms, as Finzi himself had done at our first meeting. Then the tiger backed down and wandered some distance away, waiting to observe my next move.

My mind was made up. With sudden haste lest my courage should desert me, I pulled two sheets from the bed, knotted them together, tied one end to the bedpost, and lowered myself into the garden.

The sheet ended a few feet from the ground so I dropped the rest of the way, making a clumsy landing on the soft earth below. There I was at last, standing on the grass of South Garden. The tiger, who had been watching patiently, stood up and padded across on its enormous paws. It now stood only one good leap away, and it was at this distance that I came to my senses and realised what a profoundly foolish thing I had done. This was not Finzi. It was an enormous, man-eating Bengal tiger, capable of ending my life with a single bite from those mighty jaws. Looking into its eyes, I saw not a domestic cat but a killing machine honed to perfection across thousands of generations of tigers. I was almost certainly dead.

I turned my head to look back at the knotted sheets dangling from the window and was about to make a frantic lunge for safety when the tiger pounced. Soundlessly and with incredible speed, it launched itself, catching me chest to chest in a frontal assault. Its body weight and speed combined to knock the breath from my body. I was smashed backwards into the ground, powerless, humbled, and about to meet my end by the might of this phenomenal beast.

# 33
# Zambeko

The tiger's weight was immense. Any thought of fighting back was crushed by my shocked perception of its dominance. Yet the tiger did not roar. For some reason, the whole attack had been soundless. I would certainly have cried out myself had not one of the tiger's enormous paws by chance landed on my mouth, stifling any outburst. Breathless, I waited for my life to end.

Still, the end would not come. I opened my eyes to confront that terrible head. The beast was toying with its prey. Or perhaps this young Bengal tiger, born in captivity, did not know how to deliver the killer blow. It simply lay on top of me, its green eyes boring into my own. I was close enough to feel its breath against my face and whiskers brushing my cheek

As I closed my eyes and waited for the savage release of death, I was gripped by a dying hallucination. The weight of the great beast seemed to be diminishing ever so slightly. The impression became tangible enough that I opened my eyes once more. There was no doubt about it, the tiger was shrinking. What had been a full grown Bengal tiger had regressed to three quarter size, then half, and was now a tiger cub once more, lying on my chest. And still the master illusionist's work was not done, for as I watched, the cub's stripes disappeared, the orange fur changed to grey, and I was holding the beloved cat Finzi in my arms once more.

I lay there a few moments longer. Whether it was from shock, or a bewildered joy at Finzi's resurrection, I did not know. At last I stood up and turned slow circles in the moonlight, this time feeling Finzi's whiskers against my wet cheeks, hearing his distinctive purr thundering in my ears. I held him a while feeling his chest fur, his little heart beating, and his paws firm around my neck.

There was a moment in which I believed two contradictory ideas. I knew this was not really Finzi, that it was an illusion. At the same time, I knew it was no illusion at all, that the spirit of Finzi had come back from the grave to save my lost soul.

I released the little cat onto the grass of South Garden and he began to change one more time. Soon he had transformed into a man, the good Iolango, whom I'd assumed had long since forsaken me where in truth it was the other way around.

I gazed at my old mentor. It was more than three years since we'd met, but he looked the same as ever. A casual observer would have seen a handsome man in his fifties, yet on closer inspection may have sensed a youthful vitality and ageless wisdom.

Now that the experience had come to an end, I became aware of how exposed we were under the glare of the full moon. There were no curious bystanders, but that could change in an instant. Iolango tilted his head right and I followed him towards a sheltered area under some trees at the rear of South Garden. Out of sight of the walkway, we sat down on a thick low-lying tree branch, leaning against a section of the garden's outer wall.

Iolango reached forward and removed the Maelstrom from around my neck, a position it had held almost unchanged since Berlin. At that, my surroundings came into clearer focus and the first thing I saw was a group of tigers lying at rest just a few metres away. Here we were - two men sitting in a garden among a posse of man-eaters. Yet the tigers made no move in our direction. They simply eyed us with an air of mild curiosity and I had the distinct feeling we were among friends.

I had not seen my former mentor for years, yet my first question concerned someone else's identity.

'So you were the tiger all along. I sensed something about that cub from the start. Can it be that you were Finzi too?'

'No. Finzi is Finzi. He is unique. I merely adopted his form to awaken you from your trance.'

'How did you know about that cat?'

'I've kept an eye on you from afar - and if you'll forgive me, I snuck into your room one day and read the first few chapters of your new book.'

'Then what of the real Finzi? What becomes of a cat after death - is that the end of him?'

'It's complicated. I say to you only this - Finzi lives! The life force that made up your beloved cat goes on. Finzi rejoins the great gestalt of being - but he is not swallowed up anonymous. That cat will go on to many lives and forms. Apart from his essence of true identity, what also survives is the love you and Sandra had for him. That love is immortal and indestructible. It has become part of him and he will carry it in his spirit forever. Therein lies the true meaning of your song - the Ephemeral and the Eternal.'

I slumped in relief, my spirits light as if a long-held burden had been released.

'Why are you here, Iolango? What brings you to Lombala?'

'That is the question you should ask yourself. I'm here for only one reason and that is to awaken you. To awaken the Black Phoenix from his trance.'

'The Black Phoenix! That's right. I was - I am - the Black Phoenix. The bird has flown here to this paradise. I tell you, crime does pay after all. There's no better place to nest. Lombala is the greatest country in the world.'

'Is it?'

'Certainly.'

'Then let me ask you something. Have you ever heard of Lombala before?'

'No.'

'Ever seen it on a map?'

'Can't say as I have.'

'Ever met anyone from Lombala. Anyone who's emigrated to England or Australia or anywhere else?'

'Why would you emigrate if you were born here?'

'Think about it, Jimmy. Doesn't this place seem a bit... perfect? The beaches, the city. The idealistic laws. The different racial groups living in perfect harmony. Look at them. The king's Asian, the first minister's African, and your wife is Indian. Isn't that a bit pat? Even the weather's flawless. I mean, have you ever seen it rain here?'

'What are you saying?'

'Not all hauntings take place in the dark.'

'My head's spinning.'

'You need to leave. The sooner the better.'

'Leave Lombala? Why should I? I'm happy here. Besides, there's too much to do - the album's half done, so's the book. I can't leave Lalitha. Losing Sandra and Finzi nearly killed me, I can't go through all that again.'

'I tell you, Jimmy, Lombala is an idea. Still, I see it's an idea you are not yet ready to part with. If you must go back, then at least try to see through the illusion. Let's meet again tomorrow night.'

'Can we do that?'

'We must. Now, before you return to the palace, hang the Maelstrom back around your neck. I've diminished its power to a degree, but you must keep up appearances. Don't let on anything's changed. Not to the king or Elijinx, not to anyone. Understand?'

'Got it.'

I hesitated, a shade bashful.

'May I ask a favour? Your friends here.' I indicated the tigers in front of us. 'May I pat one?'

Iolango transformed from a man back to his tiger form. He padded across on all fours and nuzzled a secret language into the ear of a tigress, then looked at me. With hesitation and utter reverence, I approached the beast and placed my right hand gently upon her noble head. The tigress made no objection, graciously accepting my touch. I continued the thrilling contact for a minute, then stood up and made my way back to the garden wall on the palace side. I seized the makeshift rope and hauled myself up to the bedroom window, pausing at the top for a last look into South Garden. Iolango and the other tigers lay under the tree as if nothing had happened.

I returned to my room and climbed into bed beside Lalitha. She did not waken but continued to dream, to dream. The next morning I stood on the balcony and saw the beach as usual through its frame of jungle. It was perfect. Lalitha and I frolicked in the surf as we did every morning. Nothing had changed; everything had.

With grave anxiety, I prepared for my morning tea with the king. We would have to discuss the film. From his behaviour last night, it was clear that Tianjan approved of the adaptation. Given its many divergences from the book, this seemed inexplicable and I was bound to have it out with him to some degree. Yet given his capriciousness, there was no telling how this would be received.

I climbed the winding stairways of the palace as I had done many times before. The exertion offered an excuse for my quickened pulse and flushed face. Tianjan was waiting. He glanced pointedly at the royal clock on the wall, then seemed to forgive me being a few minutes late. He smiled and rose from his throne, practically doing a little jig on the spot as if his excitement from the night before had barely abated.

'So tell me, Jimmy Brandt, was that film not the most wonderful surprise you have ever had? It's no wonder you were too overcome with joy to speak last night.'

'Majesty, I still don't know what to say. It was definitely a surprise. I'm not so sure about the wonderful part.'

'What do you mean?'

'Let me ask you then. By your own admission, you've read The Book many times over. How can you accept a film that diverges from it so widely?'

'I know there were changes but the story was essentially the same.'

'Was it? I was making mental notes of all the changes and I lost track after half an hour. This is exactly why I wanted to write the script and have veto over casting.'

'Do you seriously mean to say you don't like the film?'

'I'm sorry, majesty, but no. Why wasn't I consulted? I'd like to have a damn good talk with whoever directed it.'

'Is that so? Then I shall send for him.'

The King picked up his phone and shouted a terse message in Lombalan.

'What happened to that contract?' I continued. 'I was guaranteed a co-write and consultation on changes to the story, not to mention casting. What about Freya? Did not the great Book make it clear she was ten years older than me? She looked about eighteen in the film.'

'Does that really change the story?'

'Probably not. It just seems a bit cynical. I mean, no disrespect to the original, but no way were Freya's breasts that big. What do you think this is - *Game of Thrones*?'

'I've never seen you so animated, Jimmy. This is most out of character. I'm not at all sure this is the correct tone to take with your king.'

'Sorry, majesty, but there are limits. Remember what we discussed before. You are sovereign in all things but when it comes to my own work, it is I who have dominion. What about the cricket scene? It was supposed to be Australia vs England in the Sydney test match. Yet somehow, it turned into Australia vs India! I couldn't believe my eyes. Was that really Tendulkar you got to make a cameo, or just some lookalike?'

'You forget, Sir Jimmy, that funding for this film came from the royal coffers of Lombala. We want to recoup our investment - and with interest. The Indian market dwarfs that of England and Australia combined. Indeed it could swallow them many times over. Tendulkar is quite the deity in India. The merest glimpse of him in the film is enough to guarantee a lucrative bonanza. As a loyal citizen of Lombala, you should be delighted to put your art at the service of your king.'

'Like that is it? I haven't completed my citizenship yet. Perhaps I'll reconsider.'

Tianjan drew himself higher in his throne and was about to cast down a booming rebuke, when he was interrupted by a knock at the door.

'Come in,' bellowed the king, on the cusp of a rage. 'Ah, Zambeko. It is with the deepest sorrow that I summon you here.'

'Majesty?' said Zambeko, surprised. 'What is wrong?'

'It's Brandt. He doesn't like your film.'

Zambeko's nostrils flared slightly. He stopped himself speaking for a moment. Finally, he asked in a low voice that combined menace and hurt.

'What exactly is it that Brandt doesn't like?'

Tianjan and Zambeko turned to me accusingly. I decided to hell with it, and let it all out.

'I've just told your majesty what I think of the casting and the way the Australia-England match has become Australia-India. While we're on the subject of sport, perhaps you'd like to tell me how long I've been a Manchester United fan, because I've come over all amnesiac about it.'

'Oh, is that all?' said Zambeko dismissively. 'You surely didn't think we'd have him betting on a provincial sport like rugby, did you? In any case, we have three different versions of that section. The Indian cut has him betting on cricket and the US version has him gambling on American football and basketball.'

'Are you serious?'

'Don't be so precious, Brandt. It's just the basic idea reworked for different markets. Any other complaints?'

'What happened to Nevermore in scene one? How come it changed to Arch Enemy?'

'As you should know, Mr. Brandt, Nevermore broke up years ago. It made more sense to use a band that is still current.'

'And what's with the inappropriate violence - beating up the thugs in scene two?'

'It's hardly inappropriate considering they were going to do the same to him?'

'So he descends to their level? It's just standard action-man Hollywood crap. The same as that abysmal scene at the end when he has the fist fight with Elijinx. It's rubbish!'

'I thought I made it clear to you when we first met that film and literature are two very different mediums.'

'Yeah, you did. You had a real nerve giving me that spiel back at Rookwood, trying to protect the director's rights when it was you going to direct it all along.'

'Mr. Brandt, I am an artist like yourself. It would behove you to summon up a little more respect.'

'Oh it's *behoves* now, is it? If we're talking respect, you might have had the good manners to consult me. It was even in the contract, I'm sure of it. I demand to see that contract now.'

'It was your Mr. Hoffman who drew it up, so you had better go and see him. I'm afraid we're at an impasse. You have your book and I have my film. Quite frankly, I think I've been able to take your clumsy raw material and improve it considerably. Let's leave it at that, shall we? I'm a busy man.'

With those final terse remarks, Zambeko turned on his heels and exited Tianjan's quarters without even a bow in the direction of the king. Tianjan affected a sorrowful look and stared at me with an air of the profoundest disapproval.

'You have quite a nerve, Jimmy. Zambeko has served this kingdom all his life. He was particularly proud of this film. I'm afraid you've offended him very deeply. He may never speak to you again.'

'If that's the case, I'd better go back to England. Looks like it's just not panning out as we'd hoped. Sorry your majesty, I'm taking Lalitha and going home. My *real* home.'

'I've already told you, Jimmy, that's impossible. Lalitha cannot leave here - and neither can you.'

'Is that so? You may be the king of Lombala but you forget that I'm not one of your subjects.'

'It's not up to me, Jimmy. It is Lombala who decides these things, not I. Lalitha cannot leave because she is part of this island. And day by day, you have been joining with us, becoming part of the place with every thought and act. You have no need to leave. Everything you need is right here in Lombala. Your every want is cared for, your every hunger sated. There's nothing to go back to. Nothing at all.'

'I've never heard such rubbish. What do you think you're on about?'

The bluster in my tone was for my own benefit, to cover up a growing sense of unease. There was something deeply disturbing not just about the king's words, but the detached certainty with which he said them. I decided the conversation had gone on long enough.

'Majesty, if you'll excuse me, I'm going to see my manager about that film contract. Hoffman's got a lot to answer for.'

'Oh yes, Hoffman,' Tianjan said with a laugh. 'By all means go and talk to your manager. Rush away and harangue him, as is your way. Yes, you may leave. Leave! But I tell you this, Jimmy Brandt. You may leave my chambers, you may leave the palace, but you will never leave Lombala.'

I strode out of the king's room in fear and anger and began dashing round and round and around the downward spiral staircases until my head spun. Yet no matter how fast I ran or how far I circled, the stairways never seemed to end and the only word I

could see was the one on my winning scrabble rack from my game
with the king.
    Vertigo.
      Vertigo.
        Vertigo.
          Vertigo.
            Vertigo.
          Vertigo.
        Vertigo.
      Vertigo.
    Vertigo.
      Vertigo
        Vertigo.
          Vertigo.
              Vertigo.
                Vertigo.
              Vertigo.
            Vertigo.
          Vertigo.
        Vertigo.
          Vertigo.
        Vertigo.
      Vertigo.
        Vertigo.
          Vertigo
            Vertigo.
              Vertigo.
                Vertigo.
            Vertigo.
          Vertigo.
        Vertigo.
      Vertigo.
    Vertigo.

Vertigo.
  Vertigo.
    Vertigo.
      Vertigo.
        Vertigo.
      Vertigo.
    Vertigo.
  Vertigo.
Vertigo.
  Vertigo.
    Vertigo.
      Vertigo.
        Vertigo.
      Vertigo.
    Vertigo.
  Vertigo.
Vertigo.
  Vertigo.
    Vertigo.
      Vertigo.
        Vertigo.
          Vertigo.
            Vertigo.
              Vertigo.
                Vertigo.

                  Lombala!

# 34

# The Maelstrom Ascendant

'You!'

'Jimmy, what can I do for you?'

'Show me that movie contract - now.'

'Come in then. I'm not going to conduct a business meeting on my doorstep.'

I pushed past Elijinx into his suite. In a near panic after the long descent from the throne room, I used my fear to fuel the confrontation - but the descent was not yet over. With each step, the mire deepened.

'I suppose you had a hand in that cinematic masterpiece last night?'

'Me, Jimmy? Oh no, I would never interfere with the masterly vision of a director like Zambeko. He got it just right, don't you think?'

'What happened to that contract? You said I'd co-write the script with a specialist script writer.'

'You wrote the book, Zambeko adapted it into a screenplay. If that's not a co-write I don't know what is.'

'You know that's not what it means. What about my consultation on casting?'

'I believe you were mailed a shortlist. Perhaps you were on tour at the time. Now you mention it, I recall there's a good deal of mail for you at the office. It must have been mixed up with the late entries for the Jack Lynton Award.'

'I suppose my consultation on changes to the story is in there too, is it?'

'My dear boy, if you're not going to call into the office to pick up your mail, it's hardly Zambeko's fault. Besides, the last thing he needed was some scribbler dogging his every creative move.

A genius like Zambeko needs complete freedom to execute his artistic vision.'

Once before, at his island summit, Elijinx had tried to goad me to anger. For some reason he was doing it again. Now, as then, I sought defence through laughter. Wild and hysterical laughter. Meanwhile, my tormentor upped the ante.

'The terrific thing about the film is it will reignite sales of your book. Of course, you'll have to revise it considerably before we republish. You're going to have to bring the story much more into line with the improvements Zambeko has made.'

The pitch of my laughter went up a notch.

'Indeed, it may be wise to let Zambeko have a crack at rewriting the book himself. If he can fit it into his schedule, of course. He's a busy man.'

I stopped laughing.

'Right, Elijinx, we're done here. It may surprise you to know I'm back on good terms with Ivan. I think we'll go back to England to make the new record - without any further assistance from you. You're fired.'

'Ivan? Oh, Ivan won't be going anywhere. He's here for the long haul - as are you.'

'Forget it. I'm going back to Rookwood.'

'What makes you think you can return to Rookwood?'

'That house is the one and only benefit I got out of this farcical film deal. Tianjan, Zambeko and you - you can all go to hell. Thank God for Rookwood. I can get some serious work done there with no more interference. Don't even think of bothering me there.'

'If that's what you think, I have some bad news. Rookwood isn't yours. It belongs to Edward Bentley.'

'Eh?'

'Oh yes - and when the rent payments stopped going in after you left England, he gave two months notice to vacate. Your possessions are in storage in the basement waiting for collection.'

'Rent payments? I never made any rent payments. I own the place.'

'I'm afraid not. I did give Edward a holding deposit with the full intention of paying the balance later. We had to hold over most of the four million from the movie deal to bankroll the Maelstrom album and tour. All that promo doesn't come cheap, you know. You would have made most of it back but the extravagance of the tour put paid to that. I was paying Edward the rental for a while but you took so well to life in Lombala, I let it slide. Forget about Rookwood, Jimmy, this is your home now.'

'Like hell. I'm done with this place. There's nothing but treachery and betrayal at every turn. I should have realised the folly of an alliance with you.'

'There's gratitude. After all I've done for you.'

'After all you've done *to* me. So this is goodbye.'

'Oh Jimmy. If only you knew how many times I've heard that over the centuries.'

Elijinx smiled. I turned and left, slamming the door shut behind me.

'Come on, Lal,' I said, back in my room. 'Let's go for a drive. You're the only person I can trust around here. Let's go out of the city somewhere.'

'No thank you, Jimmy,' my wife replied.

'Why not? Why is everyone arguing with me all of a sudden?'

'The king has forbidden us to leave the palace.'

'Has he now? Look, Lal, bugger this. How about coming back to England with me?'

'Oh no, I couldn't.'

'Course you could. What's with all the nay-saying and people telling us what we can and can't do? Let's just up and leave. Next flight out - what do you say?'

'If his majesty won't let you leave the palace, how can you leave the country?'

'It's none of his business - he doesn't own me. Goddammit, that's it! I'm going upstairs to give formal notice of my return to England. First plane available, I'm gone. Either come with me as my wife or I'll leave you behind.'

Lalitha said nothing but laughed that pealing Bollywood laugh. This time it sounded callous. It was the scornful dismissal from a princess who had already rejected one hundred suitors and was about to see off her one hundred and first. Or was it something more sinister?

For the second time that day, I found myself knocking on the king's oaken door. This time, I received a much frostier reception.

'Jimmy Brandt? I did not summon you.'

'What's this about not being allowed to leave the palace?'

'That is correct. You're confined to the palace until further notice.'

'But why?'

'It's your ingratitude. You're given everything a man could want and you're still not happy.'

'I want to go back to England.'

'That won't be happening. I suggest you knuckle down to work.'

Tianjan saw this as the end of the conversation and nodded pointedly towards the door - but I wasn't ready to leave.

'Isn't Lombala supposed to be the last great Utopia at the end of history? What kind of country imprisons its guests?'

'Utopia was an ideal I inherited from my father. I have concluded that it is unattainable, and will always be thwarted by human nature. The only part Lombala will play at the end of the world is to help bring it about.'

'Well, this is a turn around.'

'Yes, I too have become a Black Phoenix of sorts. Long ago, in fact. We are alike, you and I. Both turned to the dark side at the hands of your manager.'

'You mean Iolango?'

'Come now, we both know who he is, and his plans we are destined to carry out.'

'I told you before, I'm not interested in that apocalyptic spiel - and Elijinx is no longer my manager.'

'It doesn't matter. You're working for me now. I am to rule the kingdom at the end of the world. You will remain here as my fulltime artistic director and the chronicler of my reign. You will write me into the new Book. Where were we up to? The end of part three, I believe. Then here's your part four - Lombala, the last kingdom. If your concern is the Maelstrom's ascendancy, let's make it a fitting climax. Forget your diva tantrums. Never mind music downloads or mobile phones. I'll show you real evil. That'll be your part four.'

Tianjan reached for his phone and ordered a car. Soon we were marching out to the front of the palace. A long limousine pulled up, armed guards to the front and rear. The king and I sat in the middle, where Zambeko was already waiting. He seemed to have forgotten our argument about the film. At any rate, he had returned to his usual manner of aloof indifference.

The limousine drove out of the capital into parts unknown. At first, the country we drove through had the lush, idyllic qualities typical of Lombala. It gradually became sparse and barren. After a while, the grass and vegetation died out altogether. The road came to an end under some dead trees on a coastline. We left the car and walked onto the beach, although I had an eerie sense that our party had no real presence here. We were mere spectres and the waves crashed unheard upon that bleak and barren shore. Tianjan turned to me.

'So Jimmy, why bother with that apocalyptic spiel when there's half a dozen Lombalan beaches round the corner? Your very words.'

'I didn't mean this one.'

'No one else meant it either. Still, here it is.'

'Can we return to the land of the living, majesty?'

'Back to the thriving metropolis? Certainly.'

We returned to the car and drove away from the ghostly beach until a town appeared up ahead. It was little more than a shanty town, making the neighbourhood I visited on my rogue excursion seem posh by comparison. Random aggregations of dirty children came out to see the strange, shiny vehicle as it passed. We ignored them and drove on.

We stopped outside a monolithic building in the town. As soon as we entered, I knew it was a prison. My stint in Thailand years before gave me instant recognition. The stench of internment came rushing back. Tianjan seemed to enjoy my discomfort.

'Just like old times, eh, Jimmy Brandt? Wouldn't these fellows love to wriggle out through the drains!'

'Why are we here?'

'It's a reality check. There's more to life than palaces and sunbathing, you know. Behind the glittering facade there are also places like this - which you'll have to deal with when governing your dukedom. Such are the burdens of office.'

'I thought you didn't believe in prisons. Wasn't it only rehabilitation or execution?'

'Here's the rehabilitation, we'll come to the other soon enough.'

As we moved through the squalid setting, some of the prisoners cried out for release. Tianjan and Zambeko walked on imperiously. As the nation's head of religion, Zambeko dispensed a few blessings as he passed.

The next stop was worse. I had never visited an abattoir. Of course, I had always been intellectually aware of where my meals came from. There had been no actual denial, but it was always possible to push the uncomfortable idea into the shadows. Now, it was illuminated by a harsh, stark light. There was no ignoring the sight of these animals being herded through the processes of murder.

This, then, was my punishment for a lifetime of passive, cowardly consumption. You had to hand it to the likes of Morrissey for railing against this whole way of life. He was more moral than I. Yet why was the world so created in the first place, if it was created at all, where creatures stayed alive by eating one another?

'Majesty, please, why are we here?'

'To acknowledge the Maelstrom's endless ascendance. Stop and observe. It is your job to chronicle all this. Mind you, there'll be a fitting postscript once we return to the palace. It will put our species in a better light, so do not lose heart entirely.'

We drove back to the capital. Lombala seemed a darker fairytale now. It was only when we arrived at the terrace above North Garden that I understood the meaning of the king's last remark. A crowd had gathered, the likes of which I'd not seen in Lombala since the day of our welcome ceremony. They cheered the arrival of the king, after which he continued his dissertation for my benefit.

'With power comes responsibility. The wise ruler must govern with an eye for justice and consider the rights of all beings from the highest to the lowest. The abattoir is there for our convenience, yet let us not be presumptuous in our dominion. From time to time, we must give something back.'

A young man was being held captive. His face was familiar and gave me a sense of unease. Zambeko approached me, relishing the chance to explain.

'I believe you're acquainted with this fellow, Brandt. He's the one who signed off on your unauthorised car. It was contrary to orders and a grave breach of security.'

Gaining an inkling of what was about to occur, I turned to Tianjan.

'Majesty, what is this? Please, that was entirely my fault. It was I who insisted on taking the car. He tried to stop me.'

'Don't blame yourself. Without criminals to pay our debts, we would have to select citizens at random. Someone has to make reparation to the king of beasts.'

Before there was time for any further protest, the man was lowered into North Garden using a kind of harness around his waist. When he reached the ground, the harness was released and pulled back up. The man did not attempt to run and the lion pride made mercifully short work of him. It was only the burning eyes of Tianjan and Zambeko upon me that made me conjure, through a great effort of will, a minimisation of my reaction. I withdrew to a place inside myself, offering a poker face to their scrutinising stares. Tianjan seemed satisfied by my stoic response, and concluded the lesson.

'Thus do we make a token repayment to the animal kingdom for our pillage. From the kingdom of men to the kingdom of beasts, here is our tribute. We make pilgrimage to the lord of beasts and humbly ask  forgiveness for our plunder of his subjects. We offer up one of our own in thanks. Placated, he allows us to continue our murderous ways. If the ideal of Utopia cannot be attained, we can at least be mindful of our transgressions against it.'

Tianjan seemed quite serious and, not for the first time, I sensed the unique blend of sanity and madness that characterised all our conversations.

The last two days had been a continual series of shocks. Perhaps, then, I may be forgiven for accepting the king's offer of an evening drink. We adjourned to Zambeko's private quarters within the palace. It was the first time I'd seen them. Given his status as head of religion, I had assumed Zambeko to be a modest and pious man. At least until the night of the film, he had seemed little more than a humble public servant doing his duty. As it turned out, his private quarters were, if anything, more lavish than those of Tianjan himself. Jewels, ornaments, and extravagant works of art were on display throughout. His living room opened onto a long balcony in which West Garden was visible far below, then the ocean out to the horizon. I realised that, residentially at least, Zambeko had been towering far above me for the entire course of my stay.

Any naive impressions of Zambeko as a diffident man were now disproved. As if to underline the point, he made a show of donning his 'papal' robes so he could hold court in his own grand domain. He fairly lorded it over the place and of the many items on display, piety was not among them. We were waited on by topless female servants in a manner befitting some sleazy bordello. Neither Tianjan nor Zambeko batted an eyelid when one such girl came over with a tray of drinks. When a second girl appeared with a tray bearing lines of white powder, I saw our host in a new light. What kind of religious leader was Zambeko if this was how he conducted himself at home?

I recalled reading about a notorious 12th century pope who somehow attained office despite a taste for nymphomaniac ribaldry, boozing, and a range of other unholy pleasures. I'd twice been informed recently that Zambeko was a 'busy man.' As I watched him snort a line of cocaine from the girl's ample cleavage, just how busy was now becoming clear. I was frankly astonished that this evil 'pope' of Lombala had found time to direct my film, given the manner in which he evidently lived. Yet Tianjan seemed quite unfazed by any of this, taking freely of the refreshments on offer. I did not join them, for the second time in two days crying off on the grounds of fatigue. I did query the king on the scene before me.

'If you'll forgive me, your highness, I was told drugs were illegal in your kingdom.'

'For the common man, of course. Yet such are the burdens of high office our load needs to be lightened by any means possible. When you've been inducted into the dukedom of the Black Phoenix, you'll come to appreciate these privileges. And although your formal induction is some way off, feel free to indulge yourself now.'

'Your bounty is truly boundless, majesty, but I will confine myself to a drink. Indeed, it's been a fearfully long day. If your graces permit, I beg leave to take an early night.'

'Again? That makes two nights in a row. Really, Jimmy, you're hardly the most convivial guest we've had on these shores. Oh very well. Finish your drink and be off. Zambeko and I will carry on without you.'

I thanked the king and, before he could change his mind, finished my drink and bowed.

'Bless you, my son,' said Zambeko with a papal gesture.

'Goodnight, Jimmy,' said Tianjan with a benevolent smile.

'My lords,' I replied, bowing once more at the doorway. But they had already forgotten me. I turned on my heel and began to hurry back to my room as fast as my legs would take me.

# 35
# War of Words

Back in my room at last, I pondered my next move. A new meeting with Iolango had acquired fresh urgency after the events of the day. Yet the attempt to excuse myself for a late night walk met with clear signs of disapproval from Lalitha. I felt another screw tightening round my neck, as if my wife had become my personal jailer. I sensed that any attempt at a solo excursion, even around the palace, would be reported to the king. Instead, we went to sleep and it was only when my wife's breathing attained a steady rhythm that I eased myself out of bed. I dressed silently, closed the door behind me and left for South Garden once more.

The tiger was waiting. I hurried into the spare bedroom and, with panicky hands, made the makeshift rope from the bed sheets. After landing with a bump on the grass, I followed him to the same sheltered spot as the night before. Iolango reverted to his human form. Again a group of tigers loitered nearby, mostly ignoring us but also, I sensed, strangely pleased at the visit. It was reminiscent of the way the sociable Finzi had enjoyed the company of Sandra and myself at our Blue Mountains home.

I related the day's events and Iolango listened with careful attention.

'How could I ever have taken this place for a paradise?' I said.

'Your visit here was controlled from the start,' he replied, 'and the rest was enchantment and selective perception.'

'I should have known something wasn't right.'

'You've been in a trance since your defection to the Maelstrom. It's even stronger here. Do you remember I told you the Maelstrom is spread over three geographical points? One is near Sydney at Elijinx's island. I need not remind you of that. The second is off the coast of India, as is Lombala itself. What does that tell you?'

'Why didn't you change into your human form and come to get me when I first arrived here?'

'Your experience in Lombala was a kind of dream and you weren't actively doing harm. Perhaps it was an experience you needed to have. Besides, the trance was too deep. It took a severe psychological shock to wake you. First the film, then death by tiger. Until then, you weren't ready to awaken. Not in the slightest.'

I sighed, partly because of the pain of that awakening. Not for the first time, discovery of the truth had ruined a perfectly good illusion.

'That's true,' I said. 'I was prepared to spend the rest of my life here, until I saw behind the glittering facade. Now I just want to leave - but how?'

'Tianjan won't let you go easily. Why would he?'

'I know. It was bad enough when he was Super-fan. Now he wants me to write the soundtrack to his apocalypse. From Utopia to extinction, it's always the extremes with him.'

'It's the proximity to the Maelstrom. In such a volatile environment, ideas of creation and destruction are taken to their fullest conclusions. Tianjan himself is highly changeable, as you have seen. Still, he seems to like you. Can he be reasoned with?'

'I doubt it. He's like a child and what he wants he will have.'

'He must have a weakness of some kind.'

'I've been musing on it and all I can come up with is his competitive streak and strange sense of honour. He loves playing Scrabble and chess but I'm not allowed to let him win. Apart from that, he can't resist a contest and I recognise a fellow gambler when I see one. What say I challenge him to a game with my freedom for the prize?'

'A flimsy hope, surely. The king's not of a mind to make political decisions on the basis of board games, is he?'

'But that's exactly the sort of king he is. Childish and capricious - as so many of them are, if you think about it. Nothing would surprise me with him. My freedom hinging on a winning Scrabble hand would be far from the top of the lunacy scale when it comes to Tianjan. So how about I give him the album he wants, then challenge him to a contest? If I win, he might be prepared to concede the loss at that point.'

'You really think so?'

'It's the best I can do.'

'Sounds like a long shot. Still, you never know. Let's call that Plan A. Now, as for Plan B, let's go for something much more simple and direct - like a boat on the beach.'

'Well, Iolango, it's always a boat on the beach with you, isn't it? I seem to recall that from last time. Could it really be that easy?'

'With the nearest coastline a day's travel away, I wouldn't call it easy.'

'What if there's an even simpler solution? Remember our escape from the prison - why don't we just turn into birds and fly away, then fishes and swim home?'

'We're too close to the Maelstrom for you to pull off a transformation like that. Even if you could, you wouldn't sustain it for long. You'd never get out of Lombalan waters. No, we'll escape this island as men or not at all. Go and speak to Tianjan and try your luck.'

'I'll give him the new record first, then make my play.'

'And I'll work on Plan B in the meantime. Go well, Jimmy.'

I arrived back in my room and slipped into bed beside Lalitha. Although she feigned sleep, I could feel her fuming on the other side of the bed. The next day her vigilance as my personal jailer went up a notch. It's not as if she was even subtle about it. I was now expected to account for any time spent away from her, and in due course she decided it would be simpler to eliminate the 'time apart' factor altogether. As the yoke grew ever tighter, it brought to mind the stories one hears about women with controlling partners - except in this case I was the 'woman' and Lalitha my captor. In her defence, she may have been under orders from the king, and perhaps the macabre scene in North Garden had underlined the consequence of failure.

It got so bad that trips to the recording studio became the only sanctuary against my wife's control. More than ever, I made a point of banning her from the place for 'artistic reasons.' As a result, the new album came together far quicker than usual, although other factors also played a part. First, as this was a 'commissioned' work, rather than self-motivated, I agonised far less over the songs' finer points and was content to simply bang out a few dark sounding anthems. Second, Ivan had free rein to include a couple of his piano ballads. Hell, if Ollie had been around, he would've got his two songs as well. The ballads weren't too dire and as Tianjan loved Ivan, he'd probably be glad to have them on the record. Of course, the strongest driving force behind the album's completion was my ardent wish to escape from Lombala.

In a matter of weeks, the album was in the can. *From The Slime To The Dust* was the title. Tianjan could change it if he wanted to, I wasn't bothered. It was a decent enough record under the circumstances, although hardly our best work. One of the few songs I'd consider a Lighthouse XIII classic was 'New World Alchemy.' It was an ode to empire builders and despots of all stripes, and of course a veiled shot at Tianjan himself. The album also featured a reworked 'Moonlight Tiger' with its 'correct' lyrics, unlike those which appeared on the original *Maelstrom* record. 'I For an Eye' was another song inclusion, the quarana I'd written for Edward Bentley. I decided that if I ever escaped from Lombala, both 'Tiger' and 'Eye' would appear on a revised version of *The Maelstrom Ascendant* album.

As for the book, I re-wrote part four in a way I hoped would please Tianjan, depicting him as a noble sovereign presiding over the kingdom at the end of the human race. The ending was left open until I could gauge his reaction to the work in progress.

When both book and album were ready to be presented, I made the ascent to Tianjan's lair. It was almost like old times. We had a few drinks and blasted the album through the king's huge speakers. When the music finished, I read him the last section of the new Book. With the show over and the king tipsy and ecstatic, it seemed a good moment to raise the touchy subject of my release.

'I've done everything you asked, majesty. I humbly beseech you to grant me leave to go home.'

It was encouraging to see that Tianjan did not fly into a rage. His mood was unchanged and he even felt at liberty to make a drummer joke.

'Leave, Jimmy? Well, Amos can go. I just hope Lombala can still function as a nation without his intellectual prowess.'

I laughed along in deceitful collusion with the king. After all, Amos was no fool and Tianjan had barely ever spoken to him. Still, if the king let him go that would be one less person to worry about.

'Thank you, highness. That's most kind.'

'But not you and Ivan. You're staying here. We'll all face oblivion together.'

'Please, I have family in Australia. Can you not grant me leave to say goodbye to them?'

'You did that a long time ago, did you not? After all, have you been to Australia since the split with Sandra?'

'It was always going to be my first port of call after the *Maelstrom* tour ended.'

'Yet you made no effort to include Australia in that tour and you've been in Lombala a long time. I find it hard to believe this sudden urgency to return.'

'I had no idea there was so little time left to us all.'

'It's out of the question. Your duty is here as my artistic director and royal chronicler. You're not leaving. Now, let's have another drink.'

'If you're going to detain me against my will, I can't guarantee any future cooperation. Art, like love, can only flourish under conditions of freedom. If you think you'll get anything decent out of me through intimidation, forget it.'

'What romantic nonsense, Jimmy. You'll do exactly as I command.'

'You're wrong there. Still, why don't we look at this from a different angle? What do you say to a little wager? How about a game of Scrabble? If I win, I get to go home. If you win, I stay on in Lombala for good and I'll stop complaining about it too.'

'Scrabble?'

The king's eyebrows arched.

'You'd stake your freedom on a game of Scrabble, Jimmy?'

'Sure, why not?'

'It's an intriguing proposition, I must say - and now we've done the book and the album I'm on a bit of a comedown. We do need something to spice the evening up.'

I was already setting up the board before he changed his mind or got too drunk to play.

'So Jimmy, if you win you get to leave. If I win, you're mine and you'll stop your infernal whining. Is that the deal?'

'That's it, your majesty. Let's draw to see who goes first.'

The game began. In recounting it, I will follow the convention of writing the scores in numerical form and other numbers as words.

I pulled seven tiles out of the bag and prayed for the blank ones which made it easier to score the seven letter words with their fifty point bonuses. If not, at least a good mix of vowels and consonants. To my dismay, I drew nothing but vowels. UUIIAOE. I thought about playing 'eau' for 6 points then decided it was better to miss a turn and chuck the lot. Meanwhile the king got a seven letter word at his first attempt, playing 'bandits' for 76 points. 76-0, what a start!

My next rack was little better. YWFNGAR. I used the 'N' in bandits to make 'granny.' With the 'Y' on a triple letter score, the word was worth 20. Tianjan replied with 'blaze' which would have been worth 16 but as it crossed a double word score it became 32. I was now down by nearly 100 points, Jimmy 20, Tianjan 108.

After my appalling start and his own good luck, the king got cocky and began sledging me in a manner not at all befitting his royal status.

'I thought English was your first language, Jimmy. Perhaps we should have a game in German and you'll show more competence. I will be truly glad not to hear your nagging to go home anymore.'

I tried a bluff.

'Bit early to start gloating, isn't it? This is only game one.'

'What are you talking about?'

'It's a five match series, of course.'

'Who said anything about a series? The bet's on one game.'

'That's how we always do it in Australia. I assumed you knew.'

'Nothing was said about five games. It's out of the question. Now make your move.'

I played 'twirl' for a feeble 12 points and the king followed with another seven letter word - 'realist' for 69. Jimmy 32, Tianjan 177. I was getting absolutely smashed.

My luck picked up a little from there but the horse had bolted. His majesty kept up a steady run of thirty point scores, while the best I could manage was 48 for 'windy.' There was no way I could catch him. What's more, the king kept up his poor sportsmanship to the end. He moved from cocky to pompous to patronising as he reached a score of 465 against my feeble 280. In his final phase of amused condescension, he began offering unsolicited advice about my play. I just sat there steaming, saying not a word other than to announce the meagre scores I picked up from each move. There were only a dozen tiles left in the bag and I was no chance of catching up the nearly 200 points difference in our scores, considering that the average seven letter word, even with its bonus, would be only worth about 70 points. Tianjan had me.

As if to rub it in, the king's extraordinary run of luck continued when he put down yet another seven letter word, in a vertical line down from the very top of the board. It was 'outraged' for 75 points. The more observant will notice that this was actually an eight letter word. As it happened, he used the 'G' from my early play of 'granny.' In using all seven tiles on his rack, he still received the fifty point bonus. Jimmy 280, Tianjan 541. He was nearly double my score. The king downed the rest of his wine at a swallow, then refilled his own glass in celebration. He made no effort to hide his joy.

'That's a PB, Jimmy Brandt! PB stands for personal best, in case you don't know. I've never cracked 500 before. It's my most crushing victory over you yet - oh, what an auspicious day! And you a native speaker and a Scrabble master - yet I have swept you aside as if you were an intellectually disabled baboon come down with dementia! Never mind. As the English say, it's not if you win or lose, it's how you play the game.'

All I wanted was to get 'the game' over with. My letters were QXCTIIU. Another impossible rack to finish with. Pathetic. And that's when I saw it. The miracle. The absolute miracle. No. Surely it could not be. It was impossible. I double checked. I triple checked. There was no mistake.

I used the O in the king's 'outraged.' The first O, on the top line of the board. The one that opened up the Scrabble player's holy grail - the triple, triple word score. The top left and top middle squares are both triple word scores. To reach both squares at once you need an eight letter word - only possible if there is already a tile on that line.

Normally I might have felt some trepidation to make such a move against the king, but so obnoxious had Tianjan been that I relished the chance to knock him backwards off his perch. Slowly, putting the tiles down one at a time, I played the word 'quixotic' on the double triple.

'Right, let's see. This may take a while to add up. The X on a double letter score makes 16, plus the Q is 10 so that's 26 and the other tiles are worth 8 between them. That makes 34 and I'll triple that for 102. Triple it again for 306 and not forgetting my fifty point bonus it rounds out to 356. That might be just enough. So it's Jimmy 636, your majesty 541. Never mind, your PB is still intact, even if I have topped it by nearly 100 points!'

The king sat there disbelieving, opening and closing his mouth like a guppy. He challenged the authenticity of the word but found it in the dictionary. He double and triple checked my scoring - and all the while his face of thunder scowling back at me. I kept a close eye on him. Factor in the alcohol and there was no telling what he might do in his present mood. Finally, all he could come up with was to copy my own failed gambit.

'Let's move on to game two, Jimmy. It's best of five.'

'Oh no. We've already established that.'

'You wanted best of five.'

'You overruled me in the most emphatic fashion. I've won my victory fair and square, so let's shake hands and say goodbye.'

'You're not leaving! You cheated!'

Tianjan's face was flushed. I fancied he was about to throw a five star toddler tantrum at any moment. Yet having won my miracle victory, I wasn't about to back down now.

'Cheated? How could I?' I said with a smug and infuriating calm.

'Those tiles were marked.'

'Marked? What rubbish. They were the last tiles left in the bag. Even if they *had* been marked, did I force you to leave that O on the top rank?'

'Show me those tiles!'

'There, I'll hold them up for you. Take a good look. See, front and back, no marks, not that it matters. In fact, I think I'll take these tiles into custody as proof of my win.'

Tianjan stood up and drunkenly drew his sword. I thrust the tiles for QUIXOTIC into my pocket and got to my feet, ready to run from the room if he advanced. At that moment, a most devious turn came over the king's face. In a dreadful ham performance worthy of the worst hack butchering Hamlet, he pretended to pass out. He rolled his eyes, tottered this way and that, upset several pieces of furniture, and finally ended up sprawled on the carpet, limbs all askew yet by some miracle still clutching his sword. I made no attempt to go to his aid. No, let him stay there. He'd sober up by morning.

'Goodnight, majesty. I'll be back on the morrow to say goodbye.'
Silence.

'Are you sure you won't be more comfortable in bed if you're going to have a lie down? Shall I call one of your wives to undress you?'

Still nothing.

'Well, so long, majesty. It's been a most quixotic evening.'

The king's knuckles tightened on the sword handle but he still didn't move. I smiled and left the room.

The reason for the fainting fit became clear the next morning when I went upstairs to confirm my departure. The king pretended to have been so drunk the night before that he had no memory of any Scrabble game, let alone our wager on the outcome. He simply denied any knowledge of the whole episode, claiming that the last thing he recalled was the reading of my new book. No matter how much I pressed him, he would not be moved. So much for his supposed sense of honour and fair play. It was clear I'd not be granted any kind of exit visa from Lombala.

Now that Tianjin had dishonoured his promise, my one hope of escape lay with Iolango's simplistic 'boat on the beach' plan. Yet contacting my mentor proved harder than expected. While the king avoided me for a few days after the Scrabble game, the surveillance of my movements became worse than ever - particularly from my wife.

I was not allowed outside the palace at all. Even the private beach was off limits. Lalitha was beginning to get on my nerves to a degree that no amount of Kama Sutra acrobatics could compensate. She may have been under duress from the king, yet I soon tired of the constant shadow dogging my every move. Under her scrutiny, nocturnal meetings in South Garden were no longer possible. The best I could do was visit the tiger during the day and try to communicate via the feverish raising of eyebrows.

In the end, it was Iolango himself who sought me out. I was sitting with my wife in an outdoor tavern off West Garden one day, self medicating, closing my eyes and thinking of England. I went to the bar for a couple more cocktails. I turned my back to the bar and was gazing vacantly out to sea when I heard a polite voice behind me.

'Your drinks are ready, sir. And so is your boat.'

# 36

# Carew

I turned around to see a nondescript Lombalan behind the bar.

'Where have you been?' he said. 'Can you come to the garden?'

'My wife won't let me out of her sight.'

'Is there somewhere else we can talk?'

I paused to think.

'The recording studio's the only place. It's near the corner of South and East Gardens - I'll leave a marker outside, tomorrow morning.'

I collected the cocktails and returned to my table.

The next day I told Lalitha the new album needed a remix. At the studio, I tweaked a few levels until Iolango presented himself and asked for an update. I shook my head.

'You were right. Plan A was a washout. Plan B it is - boat on the beach.'

'It's ready to go.'

'How did you pull that off?'

'It always pays to befriend the natives - but we need to leave inside two days.'

'How can I? I'm forbidden to leave the palace and all the exits are guarded.'

'I know a couple of guards who owe me a favour.'

'Can you trust them?'

'I'll give you a hint. They're orange and they've got stripes.'

'I see.'

'No one will expect you to break out through the tiger enclosure.'

'Fine, but how do I get to South Garden in the first place? My wife is all over me.'

'Can't you sneak out when she's asleep?'

'She's got a sixth sense. If I so much as get up to go the bathroom her eyes are burning a hole in my back. I wouldn't get ten steps out of the room without the king or Zambeko knowing.'

'You've got to come up with something, Jimmy. Doesn't matter what - anything! It's up to you now. By the way - what about your band mates? You're not going to leave them in the lurch, are you?'

'They've gone. Jake, Ollie, Amos - they all made it out. Ivan's the only one left.'

'Better bring him then.'

'Ivan? Really? We're not exactly mates, you know. Though we are back on speaking terms, I suppose.'

'You can't leave him here. Is he under the same scrutiny as yourself?'

'I don't think so. It's only me the king's fixated on.'

'Sound him out, at least. Tell him you're thinking of leaving and he needs to be ready. Be discreet - no details until you gauge his reaction.'

'If I really have to, I'll do it now. His room's not far and I don't doubt he's still in bed. Go to room 24 and hammer on the door awhile. Tell him I'm in the studio turning his vocals down in the mix. That'll rouse him.'

'Right then, Jimmy. Remember, time is short. One of the next two nights, you boys come to South Garden. I'll be waiting.'

Not a quarter of an hour later, Ivan entered.

'What's up with the mix? Sounds fine to me. Leave it alone.'

'Forget the mix, Ive, we need to talk. Answer me this: how long do you reckon we've been in Lombala?'

Ivan's face took on a blank expression, as if he were searching his own memory. Eventually, he replied.

'No idea. What do you think?'

'Same as you - no idea - but whatever it is, it's long enough. I'm itching to get back to the world. Trouble is the king won't stamp our exit visas. We're captives here. Did you know that? The other boys got out in time, but you and me, mate, we're here at his majesty's pleasure.'

'Why would he do that?'

'Old Super-fan's taken a shine to us. Trouble is he's got the power to do what most of the other crazies can only dream of. We're grounded.'

'Can't Hoffman do something?'

'Hoffman! He's the bastard trapped us here in the first place. Why not call him by his real name? You know it as well as I, don't you? Elijinx has managed us into a fine mess this time - and just so you know, me and him have parted company. You might think about doing the same.'

An odd look crossed Ivan's face before he replied.

'That's easy for you to say. He saved me. I'm forever in his debt.'

'Saved you, did he? That's one word for it. He's 'saved' a lot of people I daresay. So your own personal salvation, how did he conjure that? You never told me that yarn.'

'It's a long story.'

'Same as always, when he's got something to do with it. Still, before you tell it, let's get back on topic and decide what to do about the king's bounty. I've had about as much of his benevolence as I can stomach. If he won't give us official leave to pull up anchor, I'm going to do it unofficially - if you catch my meaning.'

'An escape? How are you going to pull that off, Jimbo? Don't tell me you've constructed a light aircraft out of all those cocktail umbrellas.'

'Not likely. Fact is, I've quite lost the knack for industry in this paradise. The only reason we banged out that album so fast is this studio's the only place I can get away from my wife. As for the escape, never mind details. Let's just say it's on the cards, so I'm duty bound to sound you out.'

'It's nice of you to think of me, mate. We've had our ups and downs, but more ups than downs.'

'Right. So with regard to that little episode of blackmail that cropped up a while back, I'll write it off against the world domination we achieved, of which - who knows - there may yet be more to come. Bottom line is we'll let bygones be bygones. What do you say? If you give me your hand on that, I'll keep you in the loop as to imminent exits.'

'This is all very touching Jimbo. I had no idea you gave any kind of a damn.'

'Let's not flatter each other, Ive, there's a selfish agenda to this. There's still the matter of the new album you promised me. That cobbled together collection we fobbed off on the king doesn't count. So what do you say? Have you had as much of a gutful of Lombala as I have - or do you want to stay here drinking fluorescent fizzy drinks 'til doomsday?'

'Leaving's not that easy. I have commitments.'

'What, Nefertiti? Sure, with a wife like that I don't blame you for being travel-shy. I felt the same way about Lalitha until she turned all ball and chain on me.'

'It's not my wife. It's Elijinx. I can't leave without his say so.'

'What's it got to do with him?'

Ivan laughed, in the same way he used to laugh at foolish questions in an interview. For a while he sat silently, staring into time, then began to speak.

'If you pull off your escape this may be the last conversation we ever have, so here's the yarn. You already know about Rookwood, Ed Bentley, and this so called doppelganger of mine, Anton Carew.'

'What's the story? Ed reckons he's your father or grandfather. My money's on cloning. You're the product of some secret new technology. Am I right?'

'None of the above. I was born in Birmingham in 1946. I am Anton Carew.'

'Is that so?'

'The very same.'

'Well, if nothing else, Ive, you're up for a skin care sponsorship. Here I was thinking I was old enough to be your father when it was the other way round all along.'

'I was a post-war baby. Just another who grew up in the rubble, born to be a factory drudge. Tony, they called me. Then I found out I could sing and started calling myself Anton. I was the great white hope for a while there. Plant and Rodgers had nothing on me. There wasn't a pair of shades dark enough to block out the brightness of the future in front of me.'

'Until you lost it all. I know that part. Ed Bentley already told me.'

'Bentley! I curse the day I met that drugged out loon. Him and his crew of witches, if you can call them that. It was a poor excuse for a coven. Hippies, freaks, and opportunists, the lot of them.'

'Why did you get involved?'

'Ask yourself that question. You got sucked into it too, and you a man of mature years. I was just a kid, and Elizabeth even younger. It's all fun and games until someone loses an eye, so they say. We never found one, for all Bentley's spiel. The hell with him and his Moonflight, look where it got me. Sure, we were friendly for a while. Then as soon as Liz went out that window, Bentley couldn't get out of the country quick enough. Left me in the stew without a backwards glance.'

'An injustice I don't wish to repeat, which is why I'm keeping you in the loop as to our departure.'

Ivan seemed not to have heard me, being too tied up in past grievances to divert from his tale.

'So there's me made an example of, served up as a sacrificial lamb on the altar of public decency and left to rot in that dungeon thirteen years. You think we've been in Lombala a while? There are worse eternities than this one.'

'I know that, mate. I've done prison time myself.'

'I don't know about Thailand, but Dartmoor was no holiday camp. Thirteen years of my prime squandered in that hole - and for what? To be made an example of and held up as tabloid fodder. You know my hatred of crowds, Jimmy. Ever wonder where it came from?'

'I thought you were just being a diva.'

'Not for no reason. The public raised me up on that pedestal. Then look who couldn't wait to form an orderly queue and throw rotten eggs first chance they got. The mob rules? We'll see about that. Remember that gig in Barcelona when I made them wait two hours? Rude, you said. Inconsiderate, you said. What's two hours up against thirteen years?'

'I see where you're coming from, Ive, but was that the right way to go about it? It wasn't the Spanish fan base put you away.'

'Come on, you've been around the world now. Deep down, people are the same wherever you go - scum, given the chance. Even here in the great Lombala. What kind of a paradise is it you have to be locked *into*?'

It was strange looking at Ivan as he spoke. If the story was true, the handsome young man in front of me was well into his sixties. His mood seemed to be worsening by the moment. He'd need to stay calm for our escape, so I tried to ease him into more positive territory.

'Did you ever try to make a comeback when you got out of jail? That's what *I* did.'

'How long were *you* inside - a few months? Try thirteen years. That takes a toll, body and soul. I was pushing forty by then and for rock music in those days, forty was considered geriatric. My ship had sailed. So there I am homeless, bound for the grave via the gutter, no doubt about it. Along comes our friend. It wasn't Hoffman he called himself in those days, but what's in a name when it comes to him? He offered me salvation, rejuvenation, and retribution in a package deal, and all I had to do was bide my time. Eventually, along comes you, looking for a singer and here's old Anton Carew back from the dead, ready to claim what should have been his all those years ago. Call yourself the Black Phoenix? You've nothing on me, Jimmy. And once I was back on top, I swore to exact my dues from that faceless mass for what they did to me.'

'What did you do all those years since then? Elijinx came to you in - what was it - the late eighties?'

'It was 1992, twenty years after my incarceration. What did I do since then? Worked for him, one way and another, in ways you don't even want to know about. Let's just say that young guy in Berlin weren't the first I took down a notch. So there I was, rejuvenated by the dark powers and every time the calendar ticked past my birthday, I grew another year younger, not older, until I reached the same age I was when I met that dog Bentley. Then our paths crossed, Jimmy, and here we are.'

'Well, shipmate, what a story! I'm just glad I could play a part in your hate-fuelled resurrection.'

'Don't think I'm not grateful. Thanks to you, I lived the life I should've had all those years ago, and at the same time quenched my thirst for payback. You took me to task for womanising, Jimbo. Sure, I did try to fornicate my way through as many as I could, all the while telling myself they were the daughters and granddaughters of those who tormented me forty years ago. And while I'm defiling and defacing their pretty progeny I'm saying to them all - what do you think of Anton Carew now? Why do you think I've never let you drop 'Waves Upon Waves' from the setlist?'

'Hmm, some people say I'm twisted, Ive, but I reckon you've topped me. Still, can we get back to the here and now? What say we let go of the past and get off this island while we can?'

'I'd like to, but if I understand it, Elijinx isn't backing you. This is none of his doing, right?'

'No, he wants me to stay in Lombala 'til doomsday. So not a word to him, alright? A moment ago you were saying you owe me. Don't sell me out now. Can I trust you?'

'I'd say we're all square. I won't betray you, Jimmy. As for escaping, count me out. I'm twenty-five going on seventy. It's only the power of the Maelstrom sustaining the illusion of this body, and that's via Elijinx. What happens if I cross him? I don't know but it's not a pretty speculation. That's a road I won't go down. Anyhow, what does a man get in this world? Three score years and ten, wasn't it? I reckon I've had mine, close enough. Anton Carew 1946 – 2014, or whatever year it is now. Lay a tombstone for me when you get back.'

'I'd lay one at Rookwood, if I could - but are you sure you want to stay in Lombala?'

'I've no choice. Sure, there's something not right about this place. But whatever it is, I'm stuck here for the foreseeable eternity, or whenever Elijinx sees fit to release me. Not so bad, is it? There's worse things than to be twenty-five and stuck in a tropical paradise with young Nefertiti. There's nothing in the real world for me to go back to. So off you go, Jimbo, let's shake hands and say goodbye.'

'As you wish. I had a hunch you'd pass on the escape, anyway. So, I've one last favour to ask you.'

'Name it.'

'It's Lalitha. She's clinging to me like a barnacle. I need something to distract her for a while so I can make a move. Damned if I could figure out what - until I thought of you.'

'What about me?'

'Use your womanising for good instead of evil for once.'

'I don't follow you.'

'That's the idea - you follow me so she doesn't. Goddammit, you can have her. Get her out of my hair for a spell - do your worst. I've seen the way she looks at you. Well, take her! She's all yours.'

'Oh I see. Normally when a mate asks for a favour it's a drag, but to make free with the lovely Lalitha? I'd be honoured to give one for the team.'

'Fine. Just do me that favour and don't be thrifty with the foreplay. We'll have none of your wham-bam-thankyou-ma'am air hostess rubbish, alright?'

'You've got no worries there, mate.'

'Right, here's how we do it. I'll tell Lal that you, me and Nef have agreed to a change of dance partners. She'll put up a token protest but it won't last long. Then I'll head over to your room. Never mind, I won't have time to return the favour with Nefertiti, I'll be over the wall first chance. Just make sure you keep Lal occupied as long as you can.'

'This better not get back to Nef.'

'She won't know a thing. Now, I'll spring it on Lal all of a sudden, don't give her time to talk herself out of it. It'll be one of the next two nights after dinner - be ready. Make sure you're both in your room and I'll come knocking. Got it?'

'Done. One question though. Much as I'm happy to help you out, why don't you just tell your wife you're going to the studio and get away from her like that?'

'The escape is at night and she knows I never go to the studio after dark. If I start doing it all of a sudden, it'll tip her off for sure. No, it's got to be you, Ive. That's the best plan I can muster at short notice.'

'Glad to be of service.'

'I trust you.'

We stood up and shook hands. With the practical details out of the way, I felt moved to make a more formal goodbye.

'Thank you Ivan. Anton. Our temporary kingdom has come to an end, as all kingdoms must. Though extinction claims us, we are triumphant. Our existence will soon be forgotten and it will be as if we never lived. Yet we did exist and no force in Heaven or

Earth - not gravity, entropy, or the Maelstrom itself - can change that. When I am an old man on my deathbed, I will think of you, perhaps long gone yourself, or still here in Lombala frolicking on the beach with Nefertiti and Lalitha. Rest in peace.'

And thus did the former mortal enemies Jimmy Brandt and Ivan de Vangelus smile, shake hands, and depart as colleagues in redemption and retribution and peace of mind.

# 37

# The Abyss

With the agreement reached, I resolved to spend one last day preparing, then make my escape the next night. Yet barely had Ivan departed than three loud knocks sounded on the studio door. I frowned, suspecting my wife was checking up on me again. Instead, it was the king's messenger with an immediate summons to the throne room.

I'd hoped to avoid any further contact with Tianjan. There was nothing for it now but to get the visit over as soon as possible. As I ascended the spiral stairways, I steeled myself for the unexpected. If Tianjan was planning another of his surprises, I'd be ready. For all that, I was stymied again, for I had not expected to see Elijinx seated at the king's right. I ignored him and bowed to the king.

'Majesty.'

'Jimmy. How delightful.'

'What pleases you?'

'A game of chess is what pleases me. A farewell game before you leave.'

I felt the muscles in my face tense up, and hoped it didn't show. I took a slow breath before answering.

'Leave, majesty?'

'I think you know what I'm talking about.'

Tianjan's face wore the same smug expression it had during most of our scrabble game. From the corner of my eye, I detected a similar look from Elijinx. So they knew? If the escape plans were rumbled, that was that. Still, I'd brazen it out for a while. What else could I do?

'You're letting me go back to England? Oh thank you, highness. Truly you are a noble sovereign.'

'England? Don't be absurd. I've been talking to your manager and we both agree it's time for the next step.'

I glanced at Elijinx then turned back to the king.

'If you mean him, forget it. He's no longer my manager. Why don't you ask him how well he managed Rookwood?'

At Tianjan's quizzical look, Elijinx smiled and offered a smooth reply.

'It's his house outside London, sire. I ask you, have you ever known such a one for truculence? What's Rookwood up against his dukedom? No more than a hovel!'

'Quite right, I'm sure,' said Tianjan. He turned back to me. 'You'll find out soon enough where you're going. The renovations are complete.'

'I don't follow you,' I said.

'You've been enjoying the king's benevolence far too long, Jimmy,' said Elijinx. 'It's high time you started earning your keep.'

I continued looking blank, until Tianjan lost patience with me.

'Don't play the fool, Jimmy! It's your dukedom, of course. You're moving there tomorrow to take office.'

'Really? I thought I was confined to the palace.'

'Well, you kept banging on about wanting to leave. I was worried you might make some foolish attempt to escape.'

The king looked at me pointedly. I didn't reply.

'Your manager's quite right,' he continued. 'It's time to take on your governmental duties. I'm tired of armchair critics, most of all those who work in the entertainment industry! It's easy to sit on the sidelines, moaning and complaining. Let's see you step into the job and do better. At first light, you're off to your dukedom.'

'It won't all be hard work, ' said Elijinx. 'I've seen your new estate. You'll soon forget Rookwood.'

'Is Lalitha coming?' I asked the king.

'Of course. Along with a bodyguard of armed men to ensure your success and longevity in the role.'

'All hail the Duke of the Black Phoenix!' said Elijinx, with a sardonic salute.

'Yes, all hail indeed,' Tianjan echoed. 'Now, how about that game of chess? It'll be the last one for a while. I don't expect you back at the palace for at least a month.'

I let him win, then took my leave. So there it was - my hand was forced. The escape would have to be brought forward to tonight. Was there any other way? While a move to my dukedom would get me out of the palace, I'd be thrust into a new and unknown set of circumstances. If I was assigned a personal bodyguard, my movements would be more closely watched than ever. There was no guarantee I'd be able to escape my own dukedom, let alone find my way back to the palace and Iolango. No, the escape must be tonight. It was my last chance. I returned to my quarters with a sense of urgency.

Absence makes the heart grow fonder. In Lalitha's case, our separation of four hours had made her amorous. Perhaps she sensed I might soon be gone. With an unexpected pang, I realised she would not be the only one to suffer, for whatever this woman was, I had once had the illusion of loving her.

I fended off Lal's advances for the moment, claiming fatigue from the morning's work but hinting that after dinner might be a more propitious time. Instead, we lay down for an afternoon nap and held each other close, each alone with our own thoughts. My wife's arms were tight enough around me that she could safely doze. Meanwhile, I was running through the details of the escape.

In theory, it should be simple enough. As long as Ivan could keep Lal busy, all I had to do was make it to South Garden, climb in unobserved, then follow Iolango to the beach by whatever means he had in mind. Then it would be off to sea on a wing and a prayer.

The afternoon passed with glacial slowness. When it had eventually inched towards nightfall, I took a last tour of the palace, with Lalitha my inevitable shadow. In my mind, I said goodbye to the enchanting castle where I had whiled away so many hours. I made a last circuit of the walkways above the Royal Gardens of Lombala with their four fearsome guardians. It was farewell to the leopards in the west, the lions to the north, panthers to the east, and tigers to the south. There, Iolango was waiting in his tiger form, staring at me through the observation glass at ground level. I raised my eyebrows to signal that the moment was at hand. On the way back, I called upon Ivan to silently convey the same message - tonight's the night.

Back in my room, I copied the files for the new book onto a portable device, slipped it into a waterproof seal and then my pocket, before erasing the laptop's hard drive. Thank God I'd had the sense to send my Gibson Explorer guitar home with Amos. If not, I could never have got it off the island.

Lalitha and I dined at our favourite restaurant over West Garden. Considering my state of mind I could barely swallow, but with the prospect of days at sea ahead, I had to force myself. My wife gazed at me during the meal with a sense of loving possessiveness that induced in me sorrow more than anything, for I was about to abandon her. It was strangely reminiscent of the night I left Finzi for the first European tour. All creatures love in their own way. Whatever their lacks and imperfections, it's an awful thing to betray a tender and innocent heart. At that moment, it occurred to me I could yet change my mind and stay here. There were worse ways to live. I could surrender to Lalitha and Tianjan and Lombala itself. I would be the Duke of the Black Phoenix and live a life of dominion. But no, the cascade of recent events - the movie, the execution, the discovery of Iolango, and Elijinx's betrayal - left me little choice.

In our bedroom after dinner, my wife entwined herself around me and nuzzled my neck lovingly - and the moment of truth had arrived.

'Lal, we need to talk.'

'Do we, Jimmy?' she pealed. 'I think that would be quite superfluous.'

'I mean it.'

'Oh do be quiet,' said my wife as she continued her nuzzling seduction. For a ghastly moment I thought I'd fallen into an American rom-com of the very type I'd decried with regard to the *Vortex Winder* film. Still, I figured that might not last long given the suggestion about to be made.

'You see, Lal,' I said, disentangling myself. 'There's something bothering me and I want to have it out with you before it ruins our marriage.'

'What on earth are you talking about, Jimmy Brandt? Oh very well, speak up if you must, so we can get back to the main agenda.'

'It's like this. The other night we were in exactly this position, only with less clothes on, and at the crucial moment I thought I heard you say Ivan's name.'

Lalitha pealed that Bollywood laugh.

'What nonsense! Wherever do you get such an idea?'

'I don't think it *is* nonsense. I've seen the way you look at him across the table. I don't blame you. Ivan's a very attractive man. Why not admit it?'

'Of course he is - and looking is for free! But you're my husband. You're the only man for me.'

'It's very touching to hear that, Lal. Still, if we can be honest and get everything out on the table, we'll all be better off. Of course you're attracted to Ivan, why shouldn't you be? In the same way, I don't mind admitting I've directed the odd lingering glance

at young Nefertiti. In fact I told Ivan as much just this morning -
and you'll never believe what the young scamp replied.'

'Go on.'

'I can't quote him verbatim and I'm not sure it would be fit
for your dainty ears either, but there's no doubt as to the gist of it.
What I mean to say, more or less, is he told me he didn't mind a bit.
Then he said he's got a hard-on the size of his mike stand for you
and what would I say to a change of dance partners for one night?'

'Oh, Jimmy!'

'Don't blame me. It was Ivan said it. Don't shoot the messenger.'

'The cheeky young devil! I hope you put him in his place.'

'I meant to, Lal, but in point of fact I told him I'd run it by you
and see what you said.'

'What! You're serious? You want to invite Ivan and Nefertiti
around here for an open house?'

'Oh hell, why not? We're all friends here and it's what we all
want. Goddammit, it's win-win in my book. Even for you - I can
hear by the pitch of your voice the idea's got you all aquiver.'

'That's as maybe, but do you seriously mean it wouldn't bother
you to let Ivan ravish me right in front of your eyes?'

'That's just it, Lal, you've hit on the crucial snag in the whole
idea. It's all very well in theory. Oh yes, in theory it's all systems
go, and let there be comings and goings of all sorts. In practice, I'm
not sure I'm ready for the sight of young Ivan in action when it
pertains to you. We might have to build up to that. So how's this
for a Plan B? Ivan's already given this same spiel to Nef and she's
all for it. So what say, Lal, I slip over to Nef's room for a spell and
send Ivan over here?'

'What if the king finds out?'

'Why would he? It's hardly the first time I've visited Ivan's room. If anyone asks, we'll say I had a couple of stiff drinks and passed out, then he came over to fetch you to help take me home.'

'Oh Jimmy, are you sure?'

'No, but what the hell, let's do it.'

'Quick then, before I change my mind.'

'Then this is it.'

I took my wife in my arms and looked tenderly into her eyes.

'Lalitha, no matter what happens, I'll always love you. Never forget that.'

My wife kissed me, but rather distractedly as her mind was already running ahead to anticipate Ivan. I only hoped he would take care of her once I was gone - now and forever.

I left my room for the last time and skirted round the corridors towards Ivan and Nefertiti's room near the border between West and South Garden. I tapped on the door and Ivan came out. We shook hands and went our separate ways.

I reached South Garden and, for the first time, was not able to climb down unobserved. Some ridiculous courting couple was sitting on a bench canoodling. In the garden, Iolango's tiger was looking up at them, growling softly but there was nothing he could do. I paced back and forth along the terrace in front of the pair. They seemed quite oblivious to me, so that I wondered if I might slip down discreetly after all. Rejecting this as too risky, finally and in desperation, I sat down close enough to the young lady to make the couple uncomfortable. The sense of agitation must have been coming off me in waves. It came from my urgent wish to make the escape, but they may have taken it for something else. No sooner had they gone than I was tying the sheets together and climbing into South Garden for the last time.

I'd not thought to ask Iolango how we were to get across the garden's outer wall. Still, when my mentor urged me into a rough hewn tunnel under the wall, my priority was to scramble through rather than launch an academic inquiry into methods. Iolango, now in his human form, followed me in. Then we were under and through and out the other side, running full pelt from south to west towards the beach.

I felt something fall upon my face, familiar but strange. What on earth was it? Rain, by the powers! The wind picked up and the breakers thundered. Lombala had sensed its captive breaking free and was mustering forces to prevent it.

A pair of headlights appeared on the road ahead. Iolango and I darted into the jungle, hiding behind trees and vines. As soon as the car passed, I tried to move forward but the vines had entangled me. Hearing my shout, Iolango turned back and pulled away enough vine strands to allow me to burst into the open once more.

The beach loomed up ahead. Away out to sea the moon was full, illuminating the scene before us - the wrathful crash of the breakers, the palm trees thrashing in the wind, and the rain slanting down at forty-five degrees like a hail of arrows. Our feet sank into the wet sand but through sheer force of will, Iolango led me to the boat and together we heaved it out from its cover and into the sea. This was no rowboat, thank God. Iolango fired up the engine, then we were away, up and over the waves and heading out to waters unknown.

We'd made it - we had escaped Lombala! Or had we? Even as I dared hope, I realised we were stuck in the classic running away nightmare where escape is close but never attained. As the lights of the island nation began to fade in the distance, Lombala conjured a localised storm in a last effort to destroy us. The waves rose and fell in great swells, the boat riding them rollercoaster style, up one mountain of water then down the other side, and moments later doing it all again. At the same time, the driving rain assaulted us from above. And all the while, the wind howled its otherworld fury.

Away in the distance towards the shore, three black tornadoes came swirling out from Lombala toward us. Three separate funnels in angry alliance, approaching with lethal intent. Swirling this way and that, separating and coming together, circling in widening arcs like an outflung lasso. The tornadoes gained on us rapidly, then attained a violent orbit around the boat. As the three towered over us, a face formed at the head of each one. Tianjan. Lalitha. Zambeko.

I stared in appalled fascination at the unholy triumvirate. Zambeko, haughty and domineering, peering down with overlord disdain. Lalitha, the scorned woman whom hell had no fury to match. And Tianjan, the outraged toddler whose favourite toy had fallen from the cot beyond his outstretched hands.

The trio of furies continued their brutal swirl. Their arc around the boat reached such velocity that the three melted into one. A tremendous whirlpool began to form around the boat. Or rather, the Maelstrom itself manifested, a wide and terrible sinkhole in the ocean. Our little boat began to skirt the walls of the pool in ever descending circles, heading for the watery abyss below. Holding tight to the boat all the while, I looked up and saw the walls of the pool rising above us. Yet looking down, I saw that they receded far further underneath. The blue-black oblivion was all-encompassing.

Iolango called out to me but I could not distinguish any words over the storm. He mimed a gesture in the region of his neck to indicate the portion of the Maelstrom round my throat, which I had carried since Berlin. In a last futile gesture, I seized it and cast it down, back to its source in the depths below.

The savagery of the storm seemed to ease a fraction and the boat stabilised. There was still hope. And something else was in my pocket - the portable computer stick with the novel. This book would never be published.

'Majesty!' I cried, gazing up at the tornados. 'Here's the new Book I promised you!'

I dropped the device into the abyss where, like so many of my creative efforts, it vanished into oblivion forevermore. The boat began to rise, ascending from its lowly position up the side walls of the giant whirlpool.

One of the tornadoes separated from the others and Tianjan's face appeared, with a look of fury I had not seen before. His mouth opened as if to swallow the boat whole.

There was something else again in my pocket. The eight tiles from my winning scrabble hand, which I'd kept as evidence of my victory.

'And here's my exit visa, Tianjan. You are honour bound to release me. QUIXOTIC.'

I took the eight tiles from my pocket and hurled them into the tornado's open mouth, where they were swept up and scattered to the four corners. The force of the whirlpool weakened and the boat made a mighty surge to break free of the downward spiral. There was a brief cacophony, a sound like an old vinyl LP being played at high volume and sped up to breaking point...

...then silence and a sudden, enveloping calm. The winds receded, the swell died down, and the three tornadoes vanished into the ghostly hinterlands of Lombala. One ghost isle gave way to another, for there up ahead was the mystical island containing Lighthouse XIII itself, after which the band had been named. The great lighthouse loomed up in the distance, luminous white, the XIII painted neatly at the front.

Iolango brought the boat to a stop and we stepped ashore in deathly silence. As had happened once before, we ascended the steps of that ethereal lighthouse to the summit where we looked down upon the gently lapping oceans of eternity.

'So we return, Jimmy. The dream is over, the story ends - and what a story!'

'What happened in the end? Did I win?'

'You made it out of Lombala, didn't you?'

'What was Lombala anyway?'

'The eternal haunting. The Utopia always in sight and forever out of reach. The king was right about that.'

'It was no Utopia. What of Tianjan himself? And Lalitha and Zambeko? Whatever they were, they weren't human. Humans don't turn into tornadoes.'

'Spectres. Figments of Lombala, which itself exists at the second site of the Maelstrom.'

'I'm not sure I want to visit the third.'

'We'll see.'

'That one was adventure enough. It's time for a quiet life again - and still I'm confused. What am I - good? Evil? Indifferent?'

'A human being, that's all.'

'Then what of you, Iolango? You're not human, and if I'm to take matters at face value, you're good to Elijinx's evil. Still, where were you? Granted, you saved my skin in the end, but that was a long time coming. Evil triumphs when good men do nothing, so they say. And that's exactly what you did. Nothing! For a long enough spell, any rates. Where were *you* when I was dying in that hotel room?'

Iolango smiled.

'Maybe so, Jimmy, but here we are. Perhaps Elijinx and I are not the polar opposites you imagine. You might think of me as a guardian angel but I'm no nanny. I'm not out to stifle your capacity for adventure, if that's what you expect. It's one thing to keep an eye on you from afar but you'd curse me for a spoilsport if I jumped in at the first sign of trouble.'

I shrugged.

'Fair enough - and you certainly came through at the end. As for the Vortex Winder, I'll never mistake it for a staunch ally, that's for sure. Long periods of silence then profligate bursts of powers all in a row. Never there when I need it, and even when I do get the powers it all goes pear-shaped half the time. It's quixotic alright. Hell, the Maelstrom was more reliable. It got results, anyhow.'

'Granted, it's capricious. Still, I told you once that the Vortex Winder was a way to release human potential, to create stories. It's a means to an end, that's all, not an end in itself.'

'So, good, evil...?'

'Take heed of Lighthouse XIII itself. It is transcendent, beyond good and evil and the struggles of the world.'

'Struggles is right - and why should I go back to all that?'

'What if you'd done that last time? Then none of this would have happened and the story never been told. It was worth it, don't you think? This isn't over. You should go back. Return to those stormy waters.'

'If I must.'

'I am not speaking figuratively. You must return to those stormy waters of the Arabian sea we just left.'

'Oh hell, I thought we were done with that. What about Tianjan and the others?'

'They can't reach you now, much as they would like to. You'll be back in the real world now, and just in time. There's an ocean liner up ahead.'

'Do I have to go back like this? There must be an easier way.'

'Hang on to your hat.'

With those words, Iolango's gently smiling face faded and I was back in the boat once more. Of my ghostly pursuers, there was no sign. The ocean's swell had died down and there was the ocean liner not far off. I could see some figures on the bridge waving and before long I was hauled aboard and welcomed back to life. From there it was a short trip to Mumbai and a long flight home to tie up loose ends - and then we would see.

# 38

# The Ephemeral and the Eternal

So here I am back in Australia. A quitter once more? No, I'm just taking a break - a long one. One of these days the band will be back with a new lineup. There's no rush. Impatient ambition has caused enough trouble round here already.

What have I learned from all this? I suppose I should say something pious like 'love conquers all' or 'love is all you need' but that wouldn't be true. Love is far more capricious than that. It played a part in the losing of my soul as well as its salvation.

Sandra and I aren't back together, not this time. She made her choice and it was for the best. Still, there's no reason we can't be friends. I did pay off the rest of her mortgage so in a way I had the last laugh, not that she minded.

I'm single at the moment. Both Sandra and Lalitha take some getting over, one way and another. For now I'm looking back, looking ahead. Some days I spend in sober reflection working on this memoir. Other days I'm practicing the five food groups like a man, just like I taught Ollie. He's doing very well, by the way. Newly married and on the rise with his own band - and me here alone and band-less. Oh Ollie, to think as you've done me!

I haven't heard from the other lads, least of all Ivan. He's probably still sipping cocktails on the beach with Nefertiti. Mind you, I laid a tombstone for Anton Carew before I left England. Edward helped me put it in the gardens at Rookwood. Ed was mighty relieved to lay that ghost after all these years.

Between us, we sorted out the whole business about Rookwood. As usual, it was Elijinx to blame for the shambles. Edward was very civilized about it and he's not exactly poor. Between the settlement and some of the band's earnings that not even Elijinx could steal, I made enough to be able to look to the future with optimism.

As for good and evil, it would be easy to make some sanctimonious speech about rejecting the dark side and turning back to the light. As usual, it's a lot more complicated than that. I could pretend to have become a monk - meditating, rejecting earthly pleasures, and generally boring everyone to death - but stow that. I'm no monk, just a man navigating each day between the stairway to heaven and the highway to hell.

I do not regret my reign as the Black Phoenix. Some parts of my Maelstrom allegiance I'm not proud of, other parts I am. For better or worse, it was an adventure. The real evil would have been not to have lived it, to have passed up the whole escapade for a safe life in front of the TV. Elijinx was right about that, give the devil his due.

I know that such a life is not for everyone and we all have our own paths to follow. Still, whatever we do, there's no escaping moral questions. I do believe the destruction of the world, and its salvation, begins with each individual. Anyone who thinks their private actions do not have wider consequences will learn otherwise.

Sometimes I think the human heart is too complicated for me and maybe I prefer cats. Sandra's got a new one from the rescue shelter and he's a charmer through and through. Minzi, she named him. I'd get one too but it's not really fair if I'm going to be off again on tour. A time will come when I'll put all this lunacy behind me and settle down for good. Maybe find the right girl at long last and we'll get a cat of our own. Or a tiger.

Love may not be the answer to everything but without it, I would by now be absorbed into the dream world of Lombala. It is to Iolango that I owe the debt. Iolango and Finzi - and if Sandra had not been so kind as to rescue Finzi from the shelter in the first place, I would never have met that cat. Maybe it is kindness that rules above all.

Any cynicism about love, then, must be written off as so much bravado, for without it perhaps none of us would be here at all. It may come and go in particular forms and faces, and be cursed by the forsaken, for such is the transient nature of this world. Yet nothing is ever really lost. The particular forms rise like waves on the sea, building up and passing away again to return to the great ocean which is their source and destination. Such is the illusion of death amid the great adventure of life. The ephemeral, the eternal, and their endless exchange.

# Afterword

If you liked this book, help spread the word. Tell a friend... or five friends. Your support is appreciated.

The music album that goes with this book is called *The Maelstrom Ascendant*, by Lighthouse XIII. It is available on iTunes, Amazon, Spotify, and YouTube. A second album associated with this book is *Waves Upon Waves* and is also available.

The first book in this series is called *The Vortex Winder*.

Website – www.vortexwinder.com

Contact - Alfadex Books can be emailed at matthew.alfadex@gmail.com.

# Song Lyrics

## Black Phoenix

Now this fall from grace
My spiral descent, from go to woe
A steady slow decline
A heartless coming of age

From the summit to the basement
A graceless arc
The downward spiral, slow decay
Burning idols flashing sparks in the dark to light the way

Let it all burn
Turn to the dark side
To the dark side
The dark side
Of my mind

There's no use incriminations
Fall on deaf ears
Tell someone who cares
My heart is cold as the grave
As the torrent below

And I find a latent talent
Comes to the fore
From the caverns of my soul
Doppelganger rising up from the ashes of love

So gaze in wonder, this mute Pompeii
Petrified values, a fantasy tableau
This godless world is foul
You can't swim against the flow
Take my hand
When evil rules this world
Give yourself to hate,
Embrace the Maelstrom,
Ascendant to the end
Take on your new name,
Let the past go up in flames
Let it burn


## High and Mighty


Choose your vice
Don't let it choose you
Know the price
One day accounts are due

Until then ride on high
High and mighty
Even the pure will die
Sooner or later
Ride on high

Life is short
So make it shorter
Drink, smoke or snort
What you ain't oughta

Then we ride on high
High and mighty
Even the pure will die
Sooner or later
Ride on high

## The Price of Dominion

I saw the mountain on far horizon
That was my destiny
No second thought, I left without question
There was no stopping me

But what is left when the sun goes down?
The dying of the day
And what of those you leave behind?
The price you pay

Lying on this bed of nails
Dominion
Lord of all that I survey
Total control

I killed my cat to become a king
Collateral debris
My wife grew old while I was rising
Exiled in Purgatory

What good is it to rule the world?
This hollow victory
What good if you must lose your soul?
Set me free

I lie surrounded by the spoils of war
My famous victory
I'd trade it all for what I had before
The prize was treachery

What good is it to rule the world?
This hollow victory
What good if you must lose your soul?
Set me free


## Moonlight Tiger


White tiger, born again prince tonight
Come dance now
Dance in the pale moonlight

Two steps forward, one to the side
Head up, eyes open wide
Regal, reborn, mesmerising
Rip it up, rip it up

Tiger, tiger in the moonlight
Spell breaker, a luminous sight
Prince of beasts in the garden tonight

Come tiger, mesmerise with your dance
Awaken
The black phoenix from his trance

Two steps forward, one to the side
Head up, eyes open wide
Regal, reborn, mesmerising
Rip it up, rip it up

Tiger, tiger in the moonlight
Spell breaker, a luminous sight
Prince of beasts in the garden tonight

## I For an Eye

Sublimation
Dive into the oceanic mind
Supplication
Through the gates
Gnosis here to find
Give me an

I for an Eye for an I
I for an Eye for an I
Third sight, Moonflight
I, Eye, I, I for an Eye

Transformation
Lose yourself, leave the world behind
Illumination
No turning back to the ways of the blind
Give me an

I for an Eye for an I
I for an Eye for an I
Third sight, Moonflight
I, Eye, I, I for an Eye

## Haunted

Dozing in a chair
I woke to a chill in the air
Felt I wasn't there anymore

The garden was overgrown
I'd never felt so alone
I was haunting my own home forever more

This moment slips through your fingers
Nothing lasts, nothing lasts for long
This moment will not linger long

The house had been stripped bare
There was no footfall on the stair
I was just a ghost and all was lost

When I woke again
Knew it was a lucid dream
A warning I must heed at any cost

This moment slips through your fingers
Nothing lasts, nothing lasts for long
This moment will not linger long

## Death Bed Regrets

Black cloud shading us from birth
Life is lived best in reverse

Searching for your own right way
Haunted by your final day

Spectral voices lead us on
Live to the full, the urge is strong

When life's chances go astray
Haunted by your dying day

Searching for your own true way
Haunted by your final day
When life's chances go astray
Haunted by your dying day


## Extinction.net

No more books to burn
Vinyl laughs, its slayer joins them
In oblivion
Live by the sword, die by the sword

I will eat the past
Consume all in my path
Let the old ways pass
Let them die
I don't care

Retail on its knees
Publishing dies, I shed not one tear
Music industry
One more victim
Extinction.net

I will eat the past
Consume all in my path
Let the old world pass
Let it die
I don't care

Future rushes on
Black mouth swallows all that's gone before
In time consumer will be consumed
In the world of flux only extinction is sure

## Quitter

I wrote a book, made a whole album
Took me years but that's cool
The tree fell in the forest, no one was there to hear it
Looks like apathy rules

Throw in the towel, lay on the couch
Give me the gold watch and the card
I'm staying home to watch TV
If you can't beat 'em join 'em
I'm a quitter now

You would not pay a few lousy dollars
You tight arse son of a bitch

This grass roots support, it ain't quite what it should be
Gives me a hell of an itch

Throw in the towel, lay on the couch
Give me the gold watch and the card
I'm staying home to drink more beer
If you can't beat 'em join 'em
I'm a quitter now

I'm a quitter, yeah I'm a quitter
I'm a quitter, that gold watch really glitters
I'm a quitter, yeah I'm a quitter
I'm a quitter, hell no I ain't bitter

If I ever fluke it, make it to the big time
Tour the world in my private jet
Don't even think about trying to shake my hand then
There are some things just too hard to forget

## The Maelstrom Ascendant

Talent for cruelty... check
Ingenious folly... no limit yet
Endless  inequity... hell yeah
Goodbye humanity... who really cares?

To the end of the Earth, pray lead us on
To the end of the race, the prize is won

The meritocracy, a fantasy
Suck, stab or steal - the harsh reality
To those who have, shall be given more

And those with nothing, end up with less
Than they had before

To the end of the Earth, pray lead us on
To the end of the race, the prize is won

Why oh why?
Backs will break and hearts will rend
In its thrall to the bitter end

Why oh why?
Backs will break and hearts will rend
In its thrall since the Maelstrom did ascend

One soul at a time, Maelstrom pulls the strings
Willing puppets, collusion from within
Evil empire, racing to extinction
Nihilistic feast, to lose is to win

To the end of the Earth, pray lead us on
To the end of the race, the prize is won

## The Ephemeral and the Eternal

The rise and the fall
The thrill of it all
The dynasties, empires, and kings
The language, the laws
The effects and the cause
The earthly eternal dreaming

435

Far beyond the trade winds
Oceanus is still
Chronos himself does sleep
As the hour strikes thirteen

This too will pass
This too will pass

The fall and the rise
The victor's demise
The soap opera under the sun
The splendour, the farce
The face and the mask
The past that is yet to become

Far beyond the trade winds
Oceanus is still
Chronos himself does sleep
As the hour strikes thirteen

This too will pass
This too will pass

# Waves Upon Waves album

## Mountain Gods

Rock, ice, cold majesty
Tempting your vanity
This test is not for free

To speak of conquest is a dangerous sin
The mountain gods laugh and the cavity grins
Voices die down when the oxygen thins
The mountain gods laugh when the gravity wins

Austere, inhuman power
Brief lives are devoured
Flesh makes mountain flowers

To speak of conquest is a dangerous sin
The mountain gods laugh and the cavity grins
Voices die down when the oxygen thins
The mountain gods laugh when the gravity wins

## SMS: Save my Sanity

Everywhere I go, there's dickheads on the phone
Someone's always blabbering, won't leave my ears alone
I'm riding on the bus, or waiting at the bank
Someone's always yabbering and nobody's talking back

Shut up, turn it off
Turn it down, send a text
SMS, I don't want
I don't need, to hear your call

Why do I have to hear about your boring social life?
Don't care about your business deal
Your husband or your wife
You're talking really loud, do you think you are alone?
There's twenty other people here just trying to get home.

Shut up, turn it off
Turn it down, send a text
SMS, I don't want
I don't need, to hear your call

When I'm out in public, I don't smoke or swear
Or talk out loud by myself to someone who's not there
There's too much noise pollution, and it's jamming up the air,
I'm moving to Japan, 'cause they've still got manners there

Shut up, turn it off
Turn it down, send a text
SMS, I don't want
I don't need, to hear your call

## Between the Stairway and the Highway

Ascetics seem like lunatics,
For the world I love, they shun.
But the physical and the spiritual,
For the pantheist they're one.

There are two ways,
The gift of life can go astray.
The monk's cave, or the early grave,
The stairway and the highway.

I have supped from the witch's cup
Until all my doubts were gone.
Still I hold back, won't burn or fade to black,
It's too soon to drink with Bon.

There are two ways,
The gift of life can go astray.
The monk's cave, or the early grave,
The stairway and the highway.

## Reaper Bones

Nothing lasts forever
Soon ends my life
Bones of the Reaper
Thorns in my side

Mortality
The price of birth
Reality
Of life on Earth.

Bounty hunters seek me
All for my life
Bones of the Reaper
Compete for the prize

Mortality
The price of birth
Reality
Of life on Earth.

Cancer, heart attack
Poverty, war, AIDS
Fire, tsunami, fight it out
For my life
Plane crash, car accident
Murder, suicide, Love, hate, insanity,
Old age!

## Leuchtturm

Ten thousand miles, four thousand hours
You're worth it
One simple boat, engines I hope
They're working.

If the stars are aligned and fortunes are kind
They'll guide us
But if storms are too rough and dreams aren't enough
I'll wake up.

Let me sleep, far beneath
This lighthouse, my home, my tomb
Rust in peace, in the deep
This lighthouse, my headstone.

Now we're drifting off course, west of Cape Remorse
Hope sinking,
When the last race is run, is it champagne or rum
We'll be drinking?

All the spells that were cast, they don't seem to last
These love potions
I sail back to myself, a solitary point
In this ocean.

Let me sleep, far beneath
This lighthouse, my home, my tomb
Rust in peace, in the deep
This lighthouse, my headstone.

## LH XIII

Turn the power on
Send out a siren song
On the right frequency
Thought waves on channel thirteen

Beaming out through the atmosphere
Search the ground, scan the skies
In  the darkness a light is clear
Feel the power, see it rise

Send the signal out
Mobile without a doubt
On the right frequency
Thought waves on channel thirteen

Beaming out through the atmosphere
Sending  waves upon waves
In  the darkness a light is clear
Calling out to the brave

## Temporary Kingdom

Now is the time to judge the judge
To examine the examiners
Your rank and hierarchy is meaningless now
The tables have all been reversed
This is the fate for which tyrants awaits
When the trappings of power melt away
Brought to account in your own private judgment day

With each tick of the clock and each passing breath
The moment of justice drew near
The walls that protect you are turning to smoke
The illusion of power is now clear
Your temporary kingdom has come to an end
Your own Nuremburg is at hand
Enter a new world, the crowded serfdom  of the damned

Now for the faceless underlings
Who murder anonymously
Blinded by rank and prestige and the rules
In their witless complicity

Peddling paper and regulations
Your smothering weapons of choice
Scissors and rock are no match for the paper you wield

Following orders, obeying the rules
The same old excuse once again
Bewitched by a voice and a uniform
Refusing to use your own brains
Bully and sycophant symbiosis
Such pitiful banality
Into the pit with the evil halfwits
Let them burn

Well Dr Jones, we finally meet
Your identity now is revealed
Your scandalous act of arbitration
Can no longer be concealed
An impartial voice, an objective choice
The brief with which you were entrusted
What a sad travesty did you give unto me
Time for justice

Shamelessly backing your brothers in war
Whitewashing all their mistakes
Refusing to see to the slightest degree
Any merit at all in my case
A vile parody of true philosophy
Yellow stain upon your vocation
Now the real judge is here, tremble in fear
Judgment Day

## Retro Stereo

A stereo is so retro
All my music's on my iPod or my computer
It works for me, to get it for free
You won't get one cent out of me

Your album's just a free ad for your live show.
The modern guru said
Well go to hell, I'm not going on tour
For you magpies I would not even get out of bed

A stereo is so retro
And a CD, that is so nineties
Download this song, it won't take long
I want my music for free

Download and pay, that's all ok
You can screw the record company and I still get paid
But steal from me, when you get it for free
And you're just another thieving corporate bastard to me

Your album's just a free ad for your live show.
Generation Download said
Well go to hell, I'm not going on tour
For you magpies I would not even get out of bed

A stereo is so retro
And a CD, that is so nineties,
Download this song, it won't take long
I want my music for free

## Waves Upon Waves

They put him in the grave and thought it was the end
The murderers forgot him but they'll have to try again
He's back now from the dead
Seeking vengeance for the crime
So fire up your arsenal and get it right this time

They conscripted an army all made up of hacks and drones
Their guns were obsolete against the reaper bones
They fired a thousand arrows dipped in poison from on high
Well fire ten thousand more because the undead cannot die

Here I am, born again, like a zombie from the grave
Try to slay me again, I will never be a slave
Flying free, black thirteen
Murdered ghosts rise up once more
Karma wins, meet your sins, we are sailing to your shore
In waves upon waves. Waves upon waves upon waves.
Waves. Waves. Waves.

Threw him in the ocean but they couldn't sink the head
Then they tried to drown him in bureaucracy instead
A Stalinist show trial from an academic gang
Tried to string him up but the bastard wouldn't hang

They sent a thousand mercenaries
Their black hearts so depraved
He laughed and watched the dogs dig their own mass grave
The arsenal's depleted, nowhere else for you to go
No earthly power can save you, better seek help from below

Here I am, born again, like a zombie from the grave
Try to slay me again, I will never be a slave
Flying free, black thirteen
Murdered ghosts rise up once more
Karma wins, meet your sins, we are sailing to your shore
In waves upon waves. Waves upon waves upon waves.
Waves. Waves. Waves.

## New World Alchemy

Now for new world alchemy
All your dreams are mine to steal
Worlds are made from sacrifice
Souls in my cauldron tonight

I will take your lives, your dreams
Make a new world with my alchemy

My will can carve a new regime
From this day we all dream the same dream
I'll stir your souls within the pot
And forge an empire with this sweet broth

I will take your lives, your dreams
Make a new world with my alchemy

Driven by an iron will
Your hopes and fears grist to my mill
Foundries of boiling metal
I'll grind your bones beneath my pestle
Lead transforms itself to gold
When the bullets erase the days of old

I'll carve an empire for all to see
And so find immortality

Transformation, worlds to seed
Wedding whites to widows' weeds
Orphans have no cause to grieve
I'm the only father you'll ever need

## Also Available

## Books By Duncan Smith

The Vortex Winder
The Maelstrom Ascendant
Conquest By Concept
Cultown
The Vast and the Spurious
The Tightarse Tuesday Book Club

## Albums By Lighthouse XIII

Waves Upon Waves
Vortex Winder
The Maelstrom Ascendant
Cultown

## Contact

Alfadex Books - matthew.alfadex@gmail.com.

**Also available by this author**

**The Vortex Winder**

When fading rocker, Jimmy Brandt, saves the life of an insect, his own life is forever changed. The insect turns out to be an advanced being who gives him the 'Vortex Winder,' a device which grants a different special power each week. Each power leads to unexpected results.

Jimmy makes a comeback to rock music and records his album. Yet his comeback is a quest within a quest. Driven by the Vortex Winder, Jimmy makes an amazing journey. From a simple job interview, to a love affair in Germany, or a harrowing stint in a foreign prison, the adventures of Jimmy Brandt are always a surprise. Trailed by his mentor, Iolango, and his tormentor, Elijinx, Jimmy follows the events of his life to a stunning conclusion.

**Conquest By Concept**

A novel about the culture war.

John Gilbert loves Angie, his far-left Antifa girlfriend. Then he meets Edward Hall, a charismatic right wing figure. Hall makes John question Angie's political beliefs. Soon, John can no longer tell which side is good or evil.

John begins a journey through the culture war. Along the way, he has to navigate a 'whiteness' workshop, a Me-Too allegation, and the PC school system in his job as a trainee teacher. Caught in a political 'love triangle' between the far-left and right, John has to make a choice. Will he stay true to Angie's passionate progressive values, or can the seductive Edward Hall turn him to the dark side.

Wars are fought in the mind, not just on the battlefield. It's conquest by concept - but which side is telling the truth?

Reviews of *Conquest by Concept*

"Smith goes where more timid writers fear to tread... serious themes brought to life through brilliant characters and dialogue. Edward Hall is one of the best anti-heroes of our time." PW

"I'm halfway through *Conquest by Concept* and I can hardly put it down. It's brill! A breath of fresh air ramped up to a gale force wind." MG

## Cultown

Thomas Swan forms the Milinish, a cult with an odd mix of scientific and religious beliefs.

From humble beginnings in Sydney, the Milinish moves overseas to become the fastest growing cult in America. Yet Swan's mad reign spirals out of control. Finally, on the brink of disaster, he decides to tell all.

Here, in the ultimate inside story, Thomas Swan reveals the secrets and scandals inside the Milinish, the greatest cult of the 21st century.

'Exposes not just the cultishness of religion, but of science too. This is the best novel yet written on the trouble between science and religion.'

J. Williams, Fuse.

## The Tightarse Tuesday Book Club

This new set of stories has some of Duncan Smith's best work. 'Hook Up Hell' is a comical Tinder farce, 'Badminton Boy' a superhero send-up, and 'Ghost Squad' a wry look at celebrities who pretend to write books. But it is 'Marla Okadigbo,' that is the most timely for its look at the hot topic of racism in modern America.

This is the story of a literary scam that takes America by storm. White male author, Winkler Jones, pens an online review of *The Handmaid's Tale*, Margaret Atwood's book about a world where women have no rights and exist only to serve men. Jones calls it a work of 'oppression porn' and says it's only a matter of time before a black American writes a novel where slavery is restored.

Jones' crooked agent tells him to delete the review and write the slavery book himself. Jones does so, publishing it under the pen name, 'Marla Okadigbo,' supposedly a black American woman. The book is a hit until the author's true identity is revealed. It then becomes a scandal, and perception of the book changes from a story of the struggle for black liberation to one of oppression by white supremacists.

Meanwhile, Jones is haunted by the spirit of the real Marla, a black slave from the early 1800s, and feuds with his girlfriend, Sonia, a white English teacher struggling to help school students in the poor neighbourhood where she works.

## The Vast and the Spurious : 25 Problems For Feminism

Non-fiction

We live in the age of the gender wars, and there is probably more anger between men and women than ever before. Is there any hope for a harmonious future, or will these wars rage until doomsday?

A clear and incisive look at some of the main gender war issues of our time, with some surprising solutions.


"Whether for the uninitiated, the curious, or the indoctrinated, this book offers a witty rebuttal to popular claims and exaggerations. Grounded in common sense and empathy, it makes the rational case, too rarely heard, for harmony between the sexes and respect for men's contributions."

Janice Fiamengo, Professor of English, University of Ottawa, Canada, and editor of Sons of Feminism: Men Have Their Say.

# Lighthouse XIII Albums

## Waves Upon Waves

Songs: Mountain Gods, SMS: Save My Sanity, Between the Stairway and the Highway, Reaper Bones, Leuchtturm, LHXIII, Temporary Kingdom, Retro Stereo, Waves Upon Waves, New World Alchemy.

## Vortex Winder

Vortex Winder, Road Rage, Trade Winds, Black Art, Life Line, Spark, Z Club, Epitaph, Elijinx, Oceanus.

## The Maelstrom Ascendant

Black Phoenix, High and Mighty, The Price of Dominion, Moonlight Tiger, I for an Eye, Haunted, Death Bed Regrets, Extinction.Net, Quitter, The Maelstrom Ascendant, The Ephemeral and the Eternal.

## Cultown

Amnesia, Skeptic Eclectic, Evil But Not Vile, In Nihilum, Cultown, Helix Eternal, Doom Pipers, Fallen to a Higher Place, The Scythe and the Scalpel, Triangle of Fire, Transcendence, The Cultimate Culminates.

www.ingramcontent.com/pod-product-compliance
Lightning Source LLC
Chambersburg PA
CBHW020242120726
47904CB00001B/60